The Judas Scar

The Judas Scar

Amanda Jennings

Cutting
Edge
Press

A Cutting Edge Press Paperback Original

Published in 2014 by Cutting Edge Press

www.cuttingedgepress.co.uk

Printed and bound by CPI Group (UK) Ltd, Croydon, CR0 4YY

ISBN: 978-1-908122-71-1
E-PUB ISBN: 978-1-908122-72-8

For Sian, who brightens life.

Betrayal is the only truth that sticks.

Arthur Miller

PROLOGUE

'Do you remember what else you said to me that day?'

There was an eerie calm to the man's voice that chilled the dead, stale air around them. He looked up at him, those eyes burning with hatred, mouth twisted into a bitter snarl. A fresh hit of adrenalin coursed through his veins as he fought against the cords that bound him, tugging and twisting like a snared rabbit desperate to free itself.

The man leant forward and whispered close to his ear. His breath was hot, his words creamy with intent. 'You said: *And by the way, this is going to hurt you a lot more than it's going to hurt me.*' Then he gave a soft rumble of laughter as he dangled the penknife in front of his face like a hypnotist's watch.

Later. How long had it been? An hour? Maybe two. He lay on the floor alone and bleeding. He craned his neck to see where the man was, if he was near, but there was no sign of him, no sound. The concrete beneath his cheek was cool and uneven, its musty dampness filling his nose with each breath. It was a smell he'd always liked. In his top three, in fact, coming in just behind petrol fumes off a garage forecourt and hot bitumen. His wife thought him mad to like smells like these, but what did she know? She liked vanilla, freshly baked bread and cake; smells that made her fat.

He listened to the hum of traffic outside, cars and vans passing, fewer now than earlier, their drivers unaware of him, unable to help. The gaffer tape wrapped around his head and covering his mouth pinched at his skin, and when he coughed there was a strange rattling inside his lungs that pushed phlegm and Christ-knew-what against his sealed lips, making him gag.

Fuck this, he thought. Fuck lying on the floor in some godforsaken shithole, tied up and bleeding.

He made another futile attempt to pull his hands free, but the ropes dug into his wrists and a sharp pain shot up his arm through his shoulder and into his neck.

A broken collarbone, he thought. The bastard's broken your bloody collarbone.

One of his eyes had swollen closed; through the other he saw a pool of blood that bloomed on the concrete. What the hell was he doing here, lying on the floor, beaten, kicked and cut, watching blood quietly seep from his body? Things like this, deaths like this – was he really going to die? – should happen to other people, two-dimensional characters in ten-a-penny thrillers and crappy television dramas. But here he was dying a fictional death, lying in his own blood and piss, cold and broken. He wondered how long they'd take to find his body. Would the police work it out? Or would he be just another unsolved crime, the murder of a nobody cluttering up their files?

He heard footsteps and his body tensed. A surge of fresh panic jump-started him. His heart pounded as he turned his head towards the approaching noise. The man stopped walking. He was there, not far away, but he didn't move closer. There was a glint of the penknife. He held his breath and waited for whatever was going to happen next. Every cell in his body screamed with pain. He kept as still as possible and played dead, hoping it would be enough to send the man away. Sure enough, when the footsteps started up, they moved in the opposite direction, echoing slightly on the floor.

He lay there some time, aware of his body growing colder. He vaguely remembered reading somewhere that as an injured body lost blood its temperature dropped. His mind drifted in and out of consciousness like a listing ship on a gentle swell. He tried to listen for the cars again, perhaps catch the sound of an ambulance siren, but all he could hear was a faint ringing in his ears. White noise. Just static. His vision had blurred to a hazy mirage and the effort of keeping his one eye open was too much so he allowed it to close. His breathing was steady now and at last the pain began to subside. Perhaps he'd make it after all. All he needed to do was rest, to regain his strength, sleep a bit. When he woke he'd work out how to get help.

His last thought before he finally gave in was of the weather, of how it could be this bloody cold in July.

CHAPTER ONE

Harmony lay on the grass and searched the cornflower sky for clouds. There were none, not even the breath of one. The only thing that broke the blue was a fading streak of white from a long-passed plane. The sun warmed her face as she listened to the sound of Londoners all around them enjoying the hot June Sunday on Wandsworth Common.

'He's so good with the boys,' said Sophie.

Harmony sat halfway up and propped herself on her forearms to watch Will and her nephews. Her husband in knee-length khaki shorts with bare feet, his pink and crumpled shirt rolled to the elbows, and the boys – Cal, Matt and George, aged fifteen, twelve and nine respectively – bare chested, their skin glistening with sweat, playing football on a pitch marked out with T-shirts and trainers. Cal went in for a sliding tackle and knocked his youngest brother's feet from beneath him. George scrambled up, indignant, appealing for a foul while glaring at his brother as he geared up for a fight. Will ran over to George and lifted him high before turning him upside down and diverting his attention from the injustice.

'He likes them. They're lovely boys.' Harmony smiled as Will put George back on the ground and ruffled his hair then hooked an arm around his neck and pulled him close. He whispered something conspiratorial and George's face broke into a smile and he nodded, then the two of them jogged back to rejoin the game, the fight with Cal forgotten.

Sophie looked over at Roger who sat a little away from them in the shade of a sycamore tree, Blackberry in hand, his eyes fixed on the screen as his thumb scrolled. 'Why don't you join them?' she called over to him.

'Got an email that needs to go before noon.' He glanced up at

Will and the boys. 'They're fine anyway. If I join them they'll be uneven.'

Sophie groaned and rolled her eyes at Harmony. 'He's literally never off that thing,' she said. 'He carries his office around in his pocket twenty-four-seven.'

'You're lucky he's so dedicated. Christ knows, Will could do with a bit of the same drive.'

'Will's fine.' Sophie reached into the cool box for the bottle of wine and then poured some into her plastic cup. She held the bottle out towards Harmony. 'Want some? It's a bit warm.'

Harmony shook her head then turned back to watch Will with her nephews. Sophie was right, he was great with them, and she felt a sharp stab of longing in the pit of her stomach.

'He'd make a great dad, you know,' Sophie said.

Harmony nodded. 'Yes, he would.'

'How are you feeling about things?'

'I'm fine.' She smiled at her older sister. 'It's taken its time though. I'd no idea I'd be such a wreck for so long.'

Sophie reached for her hand and gave it a rub.

'And Will?'

'Same old story. I mean, I know he's thinking about it. Sometimes he seems distant and stuck in his thoughts, but you know what he's like, he buries his feelings, makes stupid jokes at the wrong times. He doesn't seem to get it. It's like he's scared of owning up to any emotion. As if it's somehow admitting a weakness.' She sighed and shook her head. 'But what can I do? That's Will for you.'

'That's men for you,' her sister said, directing a pointed look towards Roger who was still glued to his Blackberry. 'I sometimes wonder if my husband would know my smile from my frown from two feet away.'

Roger glanced up briefly. 'You're always happy, aren't you, my angel?'

'See what I mean?' she said to Harmony, raising her eyebrows in mock despair. 'Yes, dearest, always happy,' she called over. He smiled and went back to his phone.

Sophie looked back at the game of football and burst out

laughing as Will faked a fall and all three boys piled on top of him. Harmony watched as her husband fought to get out from beneath them, finally emerging with his blond hair sticking up in all directions and his cheeks red from running. Will stood and began to walk towards her, shoving George away as he flung himself against him in an attempt to bring him down.

'Enough now, big man,' she heard him say. 'You've killed me. I need a stint on the bench.'

He jogged over to Harmony and Sophie and collapsed on the picnic rug. 'They're exhausting, Soph,' he said, panting heavily. 'How on earth do you guys do that every day?'

'We don't do it every day. In fact, we try never to do it. That's why we had three of them, so they can wear each other out without any help from us.'

Harmony reached over and smoothed Will's hair. His brow was clammy with sweat. 'It would be good for you to do this every day, anyway,' she said. 'Look how out of shape you're getting.'

He turned his head and raised his eyebrows. 'Out of shape? What are you talking about? This stomach has plenty of shape.' He patted his thickened middle and laughed, then closed his eyes and tilted his face towards the sun.

Harmony heard a small child yell out. She turned to see a little girl in a denim dress with dimpled knees and dark hair in bunches, tied with bright pink ribbon. She was crying, red-faced and angry, as her steely-faced mother tried to strap her into her pushchair. There was a baby lying on a rug beside them, happily kicking its legs, oblivious to the battle of wills going on between its mother and sibling. The woman finally succeeded in strapping her daughter in and sat back with a weary sigh and a silent mouthed uttering. Then she scooped up her baby and kissed its cheek before standing to truss it into a sling on her front.

Harmony leant down to kiss Will. He opened his eyes sleepily and smiled at her.

'What was that for?' he asked.

'Just because.'

He turned on his side, shifting himself near enough to lay his head on her stomach. 'This is nice,' he murmured as he draped his arm over her.

Harmony combed her fingers through his hair and nodded. 'It is,' she said.

She glanced up, conscious of being watched, and caught Sophie looking at them with a smile on her face. Harmony smiled too then lay down beside Will, linking her fingers through his. She looked up and saw a single cloud, a wispy white smudge, drifting silently through the wide expanse of blue. She watched it as it moved overhead, morphing imperceptibly from one nondescript shape to the next, and when it had passed she closed her eyes and listened once again to the noises of the people all around them.

CHAPTER TWO

'Are you alright?' he asked, as they pulled up on the grass beside the long row of cars parked beneath the oak trees. 'You seem quiet.'

'Do I? I'm fine,' she said. 'A bit distracted perhaps.'

'But you're happy?' There was a hopefulness in his voice that stung her.

'I am.'

'I'm glad; it suits you.'

She furrowed her brow. 'I'm not sure being sad suits many people, does it?'

'I didn't mean that. I just meant it's good to see your smile. Your smile suits you.'

Like a shirt or a new shade of lipstick, she thought. She looked out of the window across the fields that rolled away from the smart estate fencing. The evening was beginning to thicken with dusk and two horses stood beside each other grazing in the last few hours of light, their tails flicking at the midges that hung suspended around them. An ungenerous part of her wanted to tell Will not to be so grateful she was happy, not to be so relieved, but she bit her tongue.

'I'm certainly feeling more like myself,' she said. She reached into the back seat for her bag. 'Come on, we should go, we're late enough as it is. Emma will never forgive me.'

They got out of the car and Will went to the boot to get his camera bag. Their eleven-year-old Clio looked small and scruffy parked next to the shining army of Range Rovers, Porsche Cayennes and BMWs, and Harmony thought of all those glamorous women inside with their designer dresses and judging sneers.

'Do I look okay?' she asked, as she straightened her dress and arranged the pale pink pashmina loosely over her shoulders.

'You look beautiful,' he said. 'I should have told you earlier.'

'You look good too, like a blond 007. Except for your tie, it's on the wonk.' She gestured for him to come to her.

He stepped closer and tipped back his head so she could reach up and straighten his bow tie.

'There,' she said, as she brushed her fingers through his hair in a futile attempt to neaten him. His unruly hairstyle had remained unchanged forever, a foppish mess that in spite of the wrinkles which had folded themselves into his forehead and around his eyes managed to keep him looking young for his years. 'That's a bit better.' She brushed a few loose hairs off his shoulders. 'You might have shaved, though.'

He grinned and rubbed his chin which was covered in light blond stubble. 'I thought you liked me rough and ready.'

'I don't have a choice, do I?'

He leant forward and grazed his scratchy skin lightly against her cheek. 'No, I'm sorry Mrs English, you're well and truly stuck with the scarecrow chic.'

They walked hand in hand up the driveway. The gravel crunched beneath their feet and the still summer air was filled with the delicate smell of burning oil from the flares that lined the way. As they neared the house the noise of the party – the exuberant music and a rumble of chatter and laughing – grew, and Harmony's stomach pitched with nerves. She glanced at Will with a hint of envy; so at ease, his eyes glistening with excitement, his devil-may-care attitude driving him forward without a second thought for all those strangers within.

'I can't believe they've re-gravelled the drive,' he said. 'Christ, can you imagine having so much money you'd redo the bloody drive for a party?' He laughed. 'And when Ian asked me to supply the champagne and told me his budget I nearly choked.'

Harmony wasn't surprised; if you had as much money as Ian said he had, re-gravelling the driveway was nothing. 'From what Emma's let slip over the past few months, the drive is just the tip of the iceberg.'

Will rubbed his hands together and grinned. 'Excellent,' he said. 'Can't wait to get in there and start gawping.'

They reached the entrance to Emma and Ian's imposing Georgian rectory. There were three stone steps leading up to the front door on which were scattered a few handfuls of red rose petals. Harmony remembered Emma telling her they were supposed to look like wedding confetti, but seeing them now they reminded her of drops of blood and she was careful not to tread on them as they walked up the steps. The heavy oak door opened before they had time to ring the bell and they were greeted by a man in striped grey trousers and a black evening jacket who balanced a tray of champagne on his out-stretched hand.

He bowed his head in greeting. 'Welcome to Oak Dene Hall,' he said with theatrical formality.

Harmony smiled; she had to admire her friend's attention to detail. Emma hadn't mentioned a butler, almost certainly because she knew what her reaction would have been. They'd been friends since primary school, but sometimes Harmony wondered if they had anything in common other than nostalgia. They were different in almost every respect. Harmony loved to travel and devoured books, was dedicated to her work, never went to the gym and rarely wore make-up. In contrast, the world according to Emma comprised a few square miles of rural Oxfordshire and a couple of shopping streets in central London, and, for her, this party was the culmination of months of meticulous planning. Harmony would also turn forty in a few months and had made Will promise there'd be no surprise party. She didn't even want a card. She'd be perfectly content if the day passed without mention; like a dirty secret it was best kept hidden, not due to vanity but because of everything forty meant. Past her best. The sands of time nearly run through.

Will thanked the man and took two glasses of champagne. 'I know you're driving,' he said, as he handed her a glass. 'But you should try this, it's one of the best we stock, from a tiny vineyard that doesn't usually supply outside of France. It's very easy drinking, you'll like it.'

She took the glass and they walked over to the circular table in the large entrance hall that held a huge vase of flowers and a bowl of tropical fruit that spilled over the shining mahogany like a nineteenth-century still life.

Will lifted his glass and she clinked hers against it. 'Cheers,' he said, and then kissed her.

She took a sip of champagne. 'You're right,' she said. 'It's delicious.'

He grinned. 'I knew you'd like it. I thought that when Ian was choosing and steered him this way. The other bottle he was thinking about was heavy, like a brick in the face. I'm not sure he could tell champagne from bleach, to be honest.'

'Shhh, Will,' she said, smothering a laugh and glancing over her shoulder. 'Someone will hear you.'

He laughed.

'Will?' she said then, with a certain reticence. She fixed her eyes on her glass, watching the stream of tiny bubbles race to break the surface of her drink to leave a thin, fleeting foam, her tummy flooding with nervous energy.

'Yes?'

'I've been thinking about things over the last week or so.' She glanced towards the front door but the butler in the grey striped trousers was busy bowing and didn't seem aware of them.

'What things?'

Her heart skipped a beat. She was surprised how difficult it was to get the words out. She'd been over them again and again, toying with them like worry beads in her mind, but as she spoke she stumbled. 'I think we should try again.'

'Try again?'

'Yes.' She reached for his hand. 'For a baby.'

Then his face fell. She felt his body tense and his fingers released from hers.

'It's been six months,' she said quickly. 'And, like I said in the car, I'm feeling good, back to normal really. And seeing you with the boys in the park the other day … I think we're ready. I know it's taken some time, but I really think we are.' She paused, halted by the look on his face. Her stomach lurched; his expression of confusion, of shock, said it all.

Two women approached them, their full-length dresses brushing the floor, heads together, sharing a joke behind lifted hands like Cinderella's cackling sisters.

'This isn't the right time to discuss this,' Will said, watching them as they passed, his face tense, his ease of earlier gone.

'Does it need a discussion?'

'Yes,' he said in a low voice. 'It does. This has come totally out of the blue; I had no idea you'd been thinking about this.'

'It's all I think about.'

'I'm not—'

'Hello, my darlings!'

Harmony closed her eyes and swore quietly at the sound of Emma's voice. What a stupid time to pick to talk to Will about a baby. They needed time and space and now she had to smile and chat and pretend everything was okay. She turned to face her friend who was dressed in black from shoulder to toe, the taut satin fabric sparkling with what looked like ten thousand beads and sequins.

'Thank God you've arrived!' Emma threw her arms around both of them and kissed each of their cheeks in turn. 'I was beginning to worry you weren't coming!'

'As if we'd miss it,' Will said, turning his smile on like a light.

'You look amazing, Em.' Harmony's mind was full of Will's reaction, the way he'd looked at her as if she'd spoken in tongues or pulled out a gun.

Emma beamed. 'You do too!' she said. 'I can't believe you spend all your time in jeans and a sweatshirt. I'd kill for a figure like yours.' Then Emma leant forward and gave Harmony a hard stare. 'Are you okay?'

Harmony nodded. 'Will and I were just having a bit of chat, that's all.' She shook her head. 'It's nothing. We're fine.' She gave Will a tight smile to prove how fine they were.

Will smiled back and put his arm around Emma's shoulders and squeezed. 'Good,' he said. 'And I hope you'll let me have the first dance with you.'

Emma squealed. 'Oh, yes please! Now, enough of the serious talking, let's go and have some fun! Oh,' she said, touching his arm. 'You've got your camera, haven't you?'

Will patted the bag that hung over his shoulder. 'Of course.'

'Good,' she said. 'It would be great to get some photos of people while they still look gorgeous. Will you take one of Harmony and me now?'

Without waiting for him to answer she stood next to Harmony and put her arm around her waist. 'God,' she said. 'You really don't have an ounce of fat on you, do you? My bloody stomach looks like a hot cross bun with all the flab and c-section scars.'

Harmony smiled weakly. She leant in towards Emma and posed for the photograph.

'See you in there,' Emma said, and they watched her walk down the hallway towards the party, lifting a hand and shrieking a welcome to another of her friends as she went.

Neither Will nor Harmony spoke immediately. Harmony rested her hand on her tummy – flat, muscular and barren. Would they ever go away, these flashes of sadness? The desperate grief that had come with her miscarriage had been hard to endure. The only time she'd felt anything like it was when her mother died, but at least then the loss had been tangible, an actual person had physically gone, a person of whom she had memories and photographs. It was far easier to miss her mother's hugs or the way she stroked her forehead at bedtime than it was to miss a baby she'd never met. She was painfully aware she was mourning a concept, an unknown foetus barely the size of her thumb – four point one centimetres, the books had told her – no name, no face, even gender unknown.

'I'm sorry,' she said with a heavy sigh. 'You're right, this isn't the right time to talk about it.' She tried to smile. 'I wasn't thinking. It just came out.'

'You don't have to be sorry. You've done nothing wrong. It took me by surprise, that's all.' Will reached for her hand and she squeezed it. He leant forward and kissed her forehead and she rested her head against his lips for a moment and closed her eyes.

'Come on,' he said, taking a step back from her. 'Let's get on with enjoying the evening.'

Harmony hesitated, wondering briefly if Emma would notice if she slipped away, past the ridiculous butler, over the petals on the steps, out to the quiet safety of the car and then home. But instead she nodded and followed Will.

The party was in a marquee that butted up to the side of the house and was accessed through the French windows in the living room, a high-ceilinged room with two huge sash windows, original plasterwork and a number of sofas carefully arranged with gold-tasselled cushions. She gasped as they entered the marquee. It was enormous, covering the entire rose terrace, the neatly clipped box hedging and flower beds incorporated into the design with garlands of flowers and strings of lights and what appeared to be a thousand candles decorating every surface, every corner, beneath a navy-tented roof that was studded with lights to look like stars. There was a table in front of them that held a cake that was more work of art than pudding with hundreds of perfect choux puffs piled three feet high with hardened glistening caramel flowing down them like lava. Waiters circulated with bottles of champagne and silver trays of geometric canapés. The tent heaved with beautiful people with shining white teeth and loud, confident laughs, all vying to be heard over the music.

'Christ, it's like *Made in Chelsea* does *A Midsummer Night's Dream*. Look,' he said then, gesturing with his glass. 'There's Ian. We should go and say hello to Oxfordshire's answer to the great Mr Gatsby.' He started to walk but she didn't follow. He turned back to face her. 'You coming?'

'You go ahead,' she said, trying to sound relaxed. 'I'm just going to nip to the loo.' She took a step backwards. 'I won't be long.'

'Do you want me to wait for you?'

'No, I'll find you.'

Harmony walked back out of the living room and down the panelled corridor towards the downstairs cloakroom. As she walked she straightened her shoulders and breathed deeply. Will's reaction had unsettled her. They hadn't spoken much about the miscarriage. They both found it hard. Will always seemed to say the wrong thing, upsetting her without intending to, oblivious, as far as she could tell, of the emotions she was trying to cope with. But was it really that surprising she wanted to try again? Maybe, as was often the case with Will, he just needed time to get his head around it.

There was a woman in a short red dress waiting outside the loo.

She smiled at Harmony, but rather than get into conversation, Harmony turned to look at the photographs of the Barratt-Joneses on the console table in the corridor. The photographs were all black and white and displayed in a variety of silver frames. Some of the pictures, the better ones in her opinion, were Will's. There was one he'd taken in his studio when Emma had insisted the whole family dress in blue jeans and white shirts and pose in front of a white background. Will had tried to convince her to go for something less hackneyed, a little edgier, but she was having none of it. So there she now was, preserved in manufactured perfection, sitting beside Ian, Abi on her lap and Josh on the floor, all of them immaculate and smiling. Another photo showed Ian and Josh out shooting, Josh a mini-me beside his father in matching flat cap and leather boots, holding aloft a brace of dead pheasant like a trophy of war. Then Abi in her ballet leotard, leg outstretched at the bar, almost regal in her grace and poise; Emma and Ian arm in arm in front of the Colosseum; Josh scoring a try in an under-nines rugby match. A tinge of envy crept under her skin. Harmony pushed it away. What was it she was jealous of anyway? Certainly not the money or the children. Maybe, Harmony thought, it was the way Emma's life had panned out exactly as she'd intended, with no obstacles to negotiate, no trapdoors or landmines to surprise and derail her.

'I'm not going to be poor when I'm older,' she'd told Harmony when she was fifteen. 'Being poor's shit.'

'You might be. You can't predict the future.'

'You can make choices, though, can't you? And that's my choice. I don't want to be poor. I'm done with it.'

Every decision Emma had made since then was part of a grand plan that led to this very point: the large house, the wealthy husband and beautiful children. Harmony had watched with amused fascination as her friend single-mindedly pursued what she perceived to be happiness. Often she'd been scathing of Emma's undisguised aspiration, but looking at these photos, knowing how much the family loved each other, she had to admit the planning had worked. She was pleased for her friend. Of course she was. What kind of person would she be if she wasn't?

Harmony glanced over her shoulder at the sound of the loo door and saw the lady in red disappear inside and another lady come out, smoothing her dress as she passed. She looked back at the photos. Behind the family shots was one of her and Will with Emma and her brothers. They were on the beach at West Wittering, where they'd been camping for the weekend, drinking cans of lager and eating sausages cooked on a cheap disposable barbecue. She picked it up and smiled, stroking her fingers lightly over the faces in the photograph. They were all so young, so full of optimism and possibility. She stared at her own face. She was plumper back then, not overweight, but fuller, her face less angular, but even so she still looked masculine, she thought. Will's mother had once described her as handsome and it was a good description. Her face was symmetrical with an aquiline nose, high forehead and pronounced cheekbones. That day her hair was brushed back into a ponytail and she remembered Will kissing the nape of her neck as she bent to blow air on the struggling barbecue. When she'd turned to smile at him he'd mouthed: *I love you.* A few hours earlier, holding each other in two sleeping bags zipped together to make one, he'd asked her to marry him. She remembered the thrill she'd felt, lying in his arms in the sun-warmed tent, looking at him with tears in her eyes and nodding.

'But you're so young,' Emma had said as they watched the boys throwing a rugby ball down by the water's edge. 'Why get engaged at twenty-two? I mean, what's the point? How do you know it's right? That he's The One?'

Harmony had laughed. 'There's no such thing as The One! It's a ridiculous notion. Your The One might be in India or Papua New Guinea if that was the case and you'd never, ever meet him. And anyway, I know Will's right for me and it's not like we've just met. We've been together ages and he's funny and unusual and we have amazing sex.' She grinned at Emma and then turned back to watch Will catch a high ball and fall backwards onto the sand in a fit of laughter, his strong forearms browned by the sun, his scruffy blond hair falling over his face. 'And I love him, Em. I really, really love him, so much I feel I might actually explode.'

Then Will's words echoed in her head like a spectral prophesy.

And you're sure you're okay with not having children? Because you know that won't change, Harmony. Promise me you understand.

'Yes,' she'd said, kissing him full on the lips. 'I understand.'

But she hadn't understood, not properly. She only really understood the day she lost her baby.

'Are you waiting?' The voice startled her. She turned to see a man behind her. He was very good looking, medium height and slim build with chiselled, tanned features and thick dark hair swept back off his face. He wore a crisp white shirt that was open at the neck, no tie, no jacket. His eyes were dark, almost black, and he looked at her with such directness she felt herself blush.

'Sorry?' she said, putting the photograph back on the table.

'Are you waiting to use the loo?' He pointed at the cloakroom. She looked and saw the door open, an array of scented candles flickering inside.

'Oh, yes, I am actually, but I'm not desperate so go ahead if you'd like.'

He smiled a broad and generous smile. 'No, after you. I'm not,' he paused, 'desperate, either.'

Harmony blushed again. 'Thanks,' she said. 'I'll be quick.'

He appeared amused. 'Take all the time you need.'

As she walked into the cloakroom she turned and mumbled another thank you before closing the door behind her. Harmony looked at herself in the mirror and shook her head; had she really just told that man she'd be quick? She smiled. It felt good to have the appreciative eye of a handsome stranger. She didn't need to use the loo so instead she rifled through the basket of products that Emma had left beside the basin: a hair brush, hairspray, a choice of lip glosses, perfume, a powder compact, and even a small case of expensive bronzing powder and a big fluffy brush to apply it. Had it been her own party she'd have forgotten to check there was toilet roll let alone provide the contents of a chemist for her guests to use. She dragged the brush through her hair and gave her neck and wrists a spray of perfume.

'All yours,' she said, as she came out. As they passed each other their shoulders lightly brushed.

'Will you wait for me?'

'Sorry?' she said, turning back.

'Will you wait for me?' His eyes drilled into hers and her heartbeat quickened. 'I'd like to talk to you. You're the first interesting person I've met tonight and I've been here for over an hour.'

'Oh,' Harmony said. 'Yes … okay.'

He nodded and went into the cloakroom. She stood for a minute or two then laughed under her breath. What was she doing? Waiting for a stranger to finish in the loo because he asked her to? If he wants to talk to me he can find me again, she thought. She began to head back to the party, but a raucous screech of laughter from the living room stopped her in her tracks beside the console table. She hesitated and glanced back at the cloakroom and as she did so, the door opened.

'You waited.'

Harmony blushed and cast her eyes down at the table, pretending she'd been looking at the photographs. 'No. I was admiring the pictures in the quiet actually. I'm not in the mood for a party.'

'Well, I'm glad you stayed. Everybody else here is very dull.'

'Everybody? That seems a bit of a generalisation and incredibly dismissive.' Harmony glanced back at him and lifted her eyebrows. 'Some of those people are my friends, you know.'

'I'm sure the ones that are your friends are fascinating.'

She smiled, pleased she no longer felt girlish and silly.

They surveyed the pictures, side by side in silence. She was aware of him next to her, it was as if he had a force field around him that crackled the nearer he was to her. After a moment or two he leaned in close to her. 'So what do you think?'

'Of the pictures?'

He nodded.

'I think they're beautiful.'

He shook his head. 'They're not beautiful. They're staged and smug with a hint of narcissism that makes them unbearable. They reek of self-promotion.'

A small laugh escaped Harmony's lips. Immediately, she clapped her hand over her mouth, but it was too late, her disloyalty hung in the air around her and she felt a twinge of guilt. 'You can't say that,' she said. 'They are a lovely family and very good friends of mine.'

'Not dull then,' he said with a glint in his eye.

She smiled.

'The one with you in it is good though. Exactly how a photograph should be. A perfect moment, suspended in time. You look beautiful.'

She wrinkled her nose. 'I'm young in it and youth is beautiful.'

'Yes, perhaps,' he said, though there was an edge to his voice, a reticence, as if he didn't believe her.

She held her hand out. 'I'm Harmony.'

He shook her hand, his grip firm, holding on for a fraction too long. 'An unusual name.'

'My father chose it,' she said. 'I was lucky. According to my mum the choice was between Harmony and Sunrise.' She laughed lightly. 'He was a Bohemian artist type, a bit of a hippie, apparently.'

'Apparently?'

'He left when I was three.' Like a fart in a storm, as her grandmother always grumbled. 'You didn't tell me your name,' Harmony said.

'Would you like a drink?'

'No, I have one thanks.' She lifted her almost empty glass. 'Aren't you going to tell me who you are?' She was intrigued by the way he looked at her; his eyes didn't waver but stayed locked on hers.

'Why do you need to know?'

The mocking in his voice suddenly grated and the hold he had on her was broken long enough for her to consider walking away from him. 'I don't need to know,' she said. 'But it's fairly normal behaviour in our society; I tell you my name, you tell me yours, we talk a bit, we run out of things to say, we move on.'

He laughed. 'And by society you mean the masses? The herd?'

'So damning of society? Let me guess, society exists merely as a concept and in the real world there are only individuals?'

'Oscar Wilde,' he said. 'I'm impressed.'

It was Harmony's turn to laugh. 'Christ, you can't be impressed by an Oscar Wilde quote,' she said with a derisive shake of her head.

'They fall out of Christmas crackers with knock-knock jokes and plastic key rings.'

He stared at her, narrowed eyes flicking back and forth over hers as if trying to read her thoughts, and she felt her cheeks flush again. She drank the warm, flat dregs of her champagne to fill the silence.

'You said you're not enjoying the party,' he said. 'Why not?'

'I didn't say that. I said I wasn't in the mood.' She paused and shrugged. 'I suppose it's just all a bit loud and crowded in there. I'm not great with parties at the best of times. But it's my best friend's fortieth, I'm sure I'll get into it soon.'

'It's not a very good party. Too showy. No intimacy or subtlety. I'm not enjoying it either,' he said, pausing for a beat. 'At least, I wasn't.'

Harmony dropped her eyes. 'As long as Emma has a good time, that's all that matters.'

He placed his glass on the console table and stared at her, silent for a moment or two, until she finally looked up at him. When she did he smiled. 'Harmony, what would you say if I asked you to leave and have dinner with me?'

Harmony laughed abruptly, taken aback by his question. 'Excuse me?'

'Right now, if I asked you to leave the party with me, would you come?'

Her heart began to race as she realised he was being perfectly serious. 'No,' she said quickly. 'Of course I wouldn't.'

'Why not?'

She faltered. The hairs on her forearms stood proud. Her heart hammered. 'I'm married. My husband's here.'

The stranger held her eyes for a moment or two and then gave a deferential nod. 'He's a lucky man.'

As if on cue she heard Will's laugh, unmistakeable in its generous fullness, one of those infectious laughs that set other laughs off like a line of falling dominoes. She turned to look over her shoulder and saw him standing with his back to her at the entrance to the living room. He was talking to a man she didn't recognise. She was filled with a sense of relief as the tension between herself and the stranger disappeared like water through a cupped hand.

'In fact, that's him now,' she said. 'He's probably come looking for me. I should join him before we sit for supper.'

The stranger stared at her, and then gave a curt nod of his head. 'You must. It was nice to meet you, Harmony.'

She held out her hand again. 'It was nice to meet you, too,' she said. 'Whatever your name is.'

He took her hand and as he did he stroked his thumb against her, barely there, like a butterfly's kiss. Her skin tingled. As she walked down the corridor away from him she felt his eyes burning into her back. She went straight up to Will and kissed him on the lips. The man he was with chuckled drunkenly.

'What was that for?' Will asked with amusement.

'No reason.' She glanced over her shoulder but the stranger had gone and she felt a sharp stab of disappointment.

CHAPTER THREE

Though Harmony looked for him she didn't see the man again that night. She had half-hoped she might find herself sitting next to him at supper. He was interesting and she'd enjoyed his company, and when she recalled him asking her to leave with him she got a rush of excitement. There was a self-assuredness, an inner purpose about him that was different to any other person she'd met, and it intrigued her. Instead she found herself between two men she'd met a couple of times, neither of whom she had much in common with, and she spent most of the meal sitting quietly, toying with her water glass and watching other people as they chatted and drank. Will spent no time at the table; instead he leapt about with his camera like a man possessed. Harmony felt a warm glow as she watched him. She liked to see him taking photographs, filled up with enthusiasm, lit from within.

By two o'clock she was shattered. The number of guests had dwindled, but those who remained were opening more wine or tipping shots back or dancing in happy, sweaty groups, and all looked set to see in the dawn. She found Will chatting to a couple she didn't recognise.

'Do you mind if we go soon?' she whispered, leaning close to him. 'I'm tired and we've got to drive back to London.'

'Of course,' he said, excusing himself from the couple who wandered off hand in hand towards the dance floor. 'I'm ready to go too. Have you said goodbye to Emma and Ian?'

'No, Em's having far too much fun dancing. I had a quick look for Ian but can't see him.'

'He's extremely drunk. Last time I saw him he was clutching a bottle of vodka and stumbling off into the undergrowth with only one shoe on.'

'Let's slip away. I'll phone Emma in the morning.'

There were a few people waiting in the hallway for taxis, putting coats on or standing patiently, eyes tired and heavy with drink. Harmony and Will walked out of the door and down the steps. She noticed the rose petals now crushed into the stone in dirty smears. Most of the flares that lined the driveway had burned down, the low blue flames of those that soldiered on licking sporadically at the darkness as they clung to life.

Within moments of being in the car Will fell asleep. His head lolled forward, and every now and then he made soft snoring noises, like a snuffling pig. Despite the time and the soporific hum of the engine, she was wide awake, her mind buzzing, flitting between Will's look of shock when she mentioned a baby and the man she'd met. There had been something about him, a powerful sexuality – not the bravado of a self-styled Casanova, but something rawer, more innate. As she drove along the M4, passing only the occasional car or lorry, once again she recalled him asking her to leave with him. She'd been with Will since she was twenty, and it was the first time since then she'd felt any type of sexual connection with another man. It was a breath of fresh air to have her mind occupied with such frivolity; there'd been too much sadness and soul-searching over the past few months. She put her hand instinctively against her stomach as a phantom ache took over, right in the centre of her, where her baby used to be, as if the scar left when it was torn out of her had opened up and bled again. She glanced at her husband, still asleep, head nodding with the motion of the car.

'I wish you felt it,' she said, her stomach clenching at the sound of her words against the quiet.

'What?' he said, his voice groggy.

'I thought you were asleep.'

'Just resting my eyes.' He reached for her hand on the gear stick and stroked it. 'What did you say?'

She didn't reply.

'It's about the baby, isn't it?' he said, with a slight drunken slur.

'Yes, it's about the baby. Our baby.' As she spoke a lump of emotion caught in her throat. 'We need to talk about it.'

'I'm not sure what you want me to say.'

His feeble words hung in the air.

Yes, said a voice in her head. I want you to say yes. Yes, you were devastated when we lost our child. Yes, you'd love me to be pregnant again. Yes, you want to be a father as much as I want to be a mother.

But again she didn't say anything.

She turned off the Talgarth Road and into their street and parked in a space a little way up from their flat. She stilled the engine then swivelled in her seat to look at him.

'I just …' She faltered. 'It's what I said at the party. I want to try again.'

They sat in the quiet for a minute or two. She willed him to speak but instead he got out of the car and closed his door.

She stared ahead feeling empty, her hands clasped lightly in her lap. There was a group of girls walking down the street. They were underdressed and swaying, passing a bottle of alcohol between them and smoking, the ends of their cigarettes glowing orange in the dark, as they stumbled, arms linked, in a drunken chain. Harmony rubbed her face hard and got out of the car.

Will was sitting on the steps outside the main door of their building. His elbows rested on his knees. 'I'm sorry,' he said as she approached. His eyes dropped to the ground and he scuffed the side of his shoe against the pavement. 'I know we need to talk, but right now I'm tired and drunk and need our bed.'

She walked past him and unlocked the door that opened on to the communal hallway. Three flats shared the building and as usual the man from Number Two had blocked their way with his bike. Harmony squeezed past it and descended the four stairs to their basement flat. She unlocked the door and went straight along the narrow corridor to the kitchen and filled two glasses with water. When Will came in she handed him one and then leant back against the kitchen worktop. He drank his and put the empty glass on the table.

'Emma seemed to enjoy herself tonight,' he said. She knew he was hoping this would be enough to distract her from what she wanted to say.

Harmony tipped the rest of her water into the sink, rinsed her glass and upended it on the draining board. 'She did. I'll see you in bed.'

Will came into the bedroom as she was climbing into bed. She waited for him to use the bathroom and as he was undressing she mustered the energy to try again.

'Losing our child floored me,' she said. 'You don't seem to feel the same and that makes me feel very alone.'

He sat down heavily on the edge of the bed.

'Will?' Harmony asked. 'Did you hear what I said?'

He lifted the duvet and lay down. 'I didn't expect you to want to be pregnant again.'

'Why on earth not?'

He hesitated.

'Please, Will, talk to me.'

'I know how upset you've been and I assumed you wouldn't want to risk putting yourself through it again.' He sighed then reached to turn his bedside light off and the room fell dark, a sliver of city light pushing through a gap in the curtains.

In the silence that held them, Harmony's thoughts drifted back to the day she'd discovered she was pregnant. A missed period. Then two weeks late. That blue line on the pregnancy test. A life inside her. She'd sat on the floor of their bathroom and hugged her knees tightly. As the minutes passed, euphoria and joy took over from shock, and she realised how deeply she must have buried her desire to have children, hidden it from herself, pretended it didn't matter. She'd convinced herself the two of them were enough, that their evenings out, those long Sundays in bed with the papers or making lazy afternoon love, their impromptu trips to the pub, to the cinema, were enough. Then six weeks later she found herself on the same spot on the bathroom floor, the same position even, knees drawn in tight to her chest, white-knuckled hands clasping them to her as she lost her baby. Dark blood stained her underwear. Smeared her inner thighs. Disbelief and panic flooded her. Then piercing grief as she'd curled up on the floor begging her baby to stay with her, just as she'd done with her mother. She thought about her mum then, lying beside her, a skeleton in a pink cotton nightie, so brittle and feather-light Harmony worried she might crush her with the weight of her arm. Those rattling breaths that came from her struggling body as Harmony cried silent tears that soaked into the pillow.

'Please, Mum,' she'd whispered. 'I love you. Don't leave me.'

Don't leave me, baby. Please. Don't leave me.

But neither her mother nor her child had listened; both left.

Harmony turned on her side and tucked the duvet around her. She had to think of some way to make him see how important this was for her.

'Good night,' she said into the darkness.

But Will was already asleep.

CHAPTER FOUR

'I can't wait to see these photos, Will.'

Will smiled and kissed Emma on both cheeks. 'They're good. There's a gorgeous one of you – you look like a film star.'

Emma beamed. 'How exciting! But first,' she said. 'What can I get you to drink? Wine, beer?'

'A beer would be great,' said Will.

'Could I have something soft?' Harmony asked.

'I've some elderflower,' Emma said. 'Ian's mother made it. Though I hate to admit it, it's delicious.' She smiled conspiratorially. 'Don't ever tell her I said that.'

As Emma went back into the kitchen, Will and Harmony walked through the living room and stepped out onto the terrace. The sun was high and bright, but not unbearably hot, and a light breeze carried the smell of freshly cut grass. There was a table laid with a pressed white tablecloth, a vase of yellow roses and a large white parasol shading half of it, as if a slice of Tuscany had been brought to North Oxfordshire. All trace of the party the week before had gone. The York paving, speckled with moss between the slabs, looked as if it had been vacuumed, and the lawn beyond rolled gently between extravagant flowerbeds in even emerald stripes that reached out like fingers to the strip of woodland that marked the garden's boundary. The woods had been thinned so that individual trees stood like sentinels guarding the view of the undulating countryside beyond. There was a swing that hung from a beech tree, a wooden fort with a slide, and further into the trees was a platform high up in the branches with a zip wire that shot deeper into the wood below. Will heard his father's ghost tut-tutting at these expensive, spoiling toys – No good done but to ruin a child, that muck! – and sat at the table facing away from the woods to silence his disapproval.

He was glad to be out of London and in familiar company. The conversation he had to have with Harmony was hovering over them continuously like a low, black rain cloud. But how to tell her? Every time he tried to formulate the words he knotted up.

Will lifted his laptop out of the bag and made space for it on the table. 'I hope she likes them,' he said to Harmony.

'Of course she will. They're great, and it was nice of you to spend the evening taking them.' She tilted her face up towards the sun and closed her eyes in the warmth, like a cat.

Emma came through the French windows and put a tray of drinks, a bowl of crisps and a small plate of swollen green olives on the table. She sat in the chair beside Will and slipped her sunglasses down from the top of her head to shield her eyes.

'So, Em, who's this nightmare colleague of Ian's you're making us eat with?' Harmony asked.

'God, don't tell him I said that, whatever you do.'

Harmony laughed. 'As if I would!'

'It's his lawyer – he worships the bloody man.' Emma poured Harmony a glass of cordial from a jug filled with ice cubes and freshly cut mint. 'He asked to meet you.' Emma grinned at Harmony and lifted her eyebrows.

'He did what? Who is he?'

'You met him at the party. Good looking. Dark hair.'

'And he asked to meet us?'

'Not *us*, you.'

'Sounds like I should be jealous,' Will said, and sipped his beer.

'Did he say why he wanted to meet me?'

Will saw her sit forward, her interest piqued, brow furrowed.

Emma shook her head. 'I asked Ian but he was typically useless and said something along the lines of him having met one or two interesting people at the party and described you. Ian knew he meant you when he said your husband had mad white-blond hair. Ian said we were having lunch with you and Will and invited him.' She reached for an olive.

'That's hardly asking to meet me.'

'He could have said no to the invite.' Emma gestured towards the laptop. 'Come on, Will. Show me these photos before they get here and I have to start dashing in and out of the kitchen like a lunatic.'

Just then there was screaming as the children ran across the lawn towards the fort. Josh had clearly stolen something from his sister and was holding whatever it was above his head as she ran after him shrieking at him to give it back.

'For goodness' sake, Josh!' Emma called. 'We've guests. At least try and pretend you're not a total bloody monster.'

They both ignored her and disappeared into the woods.

'It's a shame they aren't eating with us,' said Harmony, staring after them.

Will's stomach turned over as he caught the desolate look in her eye.

'I had to feed them before you got here. If they don't eat before midday they'll eat each other,' Emma said. 'They're basically gremlins. Don't worry, though, they'll be like wasps on jam when I bring pudding out.' She smiled. 'They're Pavlova addicts. Literally.' She reached for her glass of wine then leant forward to peer at the laptop.

'These are amazing, Will,' Emma said a few moments later as she looked through the photographs.. 'Oh!' she exclaimed a few moments later. 'I look fab in this one!' She grinned and kissed him on the cheek. 'You're such a great photographer. A miracle worker!'

'I've told him that time and time again,' Harmony said, without moving her face away from the sun. 'He needs to make time for it. I can't remember the last time you used your studio.'

'And that's a great one of you, Harmony.'

Will looked at the photo. He didn't agree with Emma; his wife didn't look great. Her silk dress skimmed her body in all the right places, but she looked thin, her collarbone was pronounced and her cheeks too gaunt. She'd lost far too much weight since the miscarriage.

Emma turned the laptop back and continued to scroll through the pictures. 'There,' she said, tapping the screen with her fingernail. 'That's Ian's lawyer.'

Will looked at the screen. The photo showed two people, a couple – Anne and Cliff – whom Will had met a couple of times before. In the background, cast in shadows to the left of the picture, was a figure Will hadn't noticed until then. It was difficult to make him out properly, but he seemed familiar. Will had certainly met him, but for the life of him couldn't work out when or where. There was an intensity about him that cut through the blurry darkness and locked on to Will. Now Emma had pointed him out it was hard to look anywhere else; his presence held the photo like a curse.

'I recognise him,' Will said. 'But not from the party. I must have met him here before.'

'Not here,' said Emma. 'That was the first time I'd met him myself. I thought he was a bit strange, to be honest, but then I was drunk as a tequila worm by nine.'

Will stared at the indistinct face and racked his brain to place him. 'Must have been with Ian then.'

Emma didn't answer but clicked to the next photo. 'Oh my God!' she exclaimed. 'Just look at Pete in this one! What kind of face is he pulling? And there's Katia and Steve.' She glanced at Harmony. 'They're such an odd pair,' she mused. 'Do you know them? The world's least suited couple. I mean, look at them. Could they be any more mismatched?' She laughed. 'She's tiny, barely speaks English and is only interested in handbags, and Steve is a six-foot-five oaf who lives in vile cycle lycra. God knows what they have in common.'

'Sex!' came Ian's voice from behind them. 'They bonk like rabbits on Viagra.'

Will turned and saw Ian stepping through the French windows onto the terrace. Tall and slim with ruddy cheeks and hair that was greying at the sides, he was a man whose looks had improved with age and privilege; unfairly – in Will's opinion – given what a git he was.

'Excuse me?' laughed Emma. 'Is that any way to announce your arrival?'

'Sex and shoes. He told me she goes like a steam train every night in return for a pair of Lablahniks once a month. They're both as happy as pigs in shit.'

'Laboutins,' corrected Emma. 'Or Manolo Blahniks. Not Lablahniks, for God's sake. And don't say that pig thing – I hate it.' She peered behind her husband. 'Where's your golf partner?'

'Nipped to the boys' room,' Ian said, as he bent to kiss Harmony's cheek before reaching over her to shake Will's hand.

'Hello, Ian.' Will had to work hard at liking Ian. He was pompous, too pumped up with that ludicrous alpha machismo he'd seen so much of at school, and as far as Will was concerned he brought the worst out in Emma. When they'd met they were plain old Emma Jones and Ian Barratt. When they married they became Mr and Mrs Ian Barratt-Jones. Will and Harmony had laughed when they'd heard about the hyphen.

'She always wanted a hyphen,' Harmony said, stifling her giggles. 'How do you think they chose Barratt-Jones over Jones-Barratt? I mean, how did they decide who got pole position?'

If it wasn't for the fact that Emma adored him, Will wouldn't have given Ian a second look. But he was fond of Emma, who, despite her occasionally grating aspirational streak, was warm, kind and funny. He'd got on with her from the moment Harmony introduced them, aged twenty-one, the three of them picnicking beside the River Cam, feet trailing in the slow, brown water, laughing until they cried and getting drunk on Jack and Coke.

'How was your game?' Will asked.

'Played like a fucking moron.'

'Ian!' Emma shook her head indulgently.

'Sorry,' he said, taking a couple of olives and shoving them into his mouth. 'Played like a fucking idiot.' He winked at Will who forced a smile back.

Will's attention was caught then by Ian's companion walking through the French windows, his head slightly bowed as he watched the step.

'He hasn't left you on the eighteenth then?' Emma said, as she walked up to greet him.

When the man lifted his head, Will's heart stopped. It was a face he didn't imagine he'd ever see again.

'Oh my God,' he breathed.

Harmony looked across at him. 'Will?'

Will stared at the man who was now kissing Emma on both cheeks, warmly telling her how nice it was to see her again, how much he'd enjoyed the party, thanking her for allowing him to join them for lunch.

'So let me introduce you,' Emma said. 'Harmony, Will this is—'

'Luke.' Will stepped forward.

Harmony looked between the two of them. 'You know each other?'

Will and Luke held each other's stare and then Will watched a wide smile dawn on Luke's face. 'Will English. Well, I never.'

'I don't … ' Will opened and closed his mouth, his voice sticking in his throat. 'Luke Crawford.'

As he spoke his name he felt a thump to his gut like a heavyweight punch. He recalled the photo from Emma's party. The face in the shadows. How had he not recognised him?

'You know each other?' said Emma, looking from Luke to Will.

'Yes,' Luke said, taking his eyes off Will to acknowledge her question properly. 'We were at school together.' He looked back at Will and stepped forward, hand outstretched in greeting. 'A very long time ago. What a surprise!'

Will shook his hand and was startled by his solidity, a matured masculinity that seemed alien; the Luke he knew was slight and small, a wisp of a child with smooth pale skin and a dusting of freckles. How could he be this fully grown man?

'Yes. I'm … it's … God, I'm lost for words.' Will felt his lungs constrict and his thoughts grow foggy as spiking memories bit into him. He'd spent so long trying to erase this boy, this man, from his head, yet here he was, standing right in front of him.

Luke Crawford.

'You were at school together? Really?' said Harmony.

Luke looked at her. 'Yes. At Farringdon Hall.'

Will winced.

'You didn't tell me that at the party,' she said.

'I didn't know who you were married to at the party.' He looked at her quizzically and Will saw her blush.

'What an amazing coincidence!' Emma said, with a surprised laugh.

Luke smiled.

'Well, come on,' she said then. 'Do sit down everybody. Ian, sort the drinks out, please. This is now a proper celebration.'

Ian clapped his hands together and asked what they'd like. Will was vaguely aware of saying yes to another beer. Of Ian disappearing into the house. Emma laughing. Repeating the coincidence. He was aware of Harmony, poised in her chair, waiting with bated breath for more information, details and stories of the past Will had shielded her from.

'This is a bit out of the blue, isn't it?' He finally managed. 'I was just looking at a picture of you and trying to place you. You've changed.'

'It's been a long time,' Luke said.

'How long?' asked Harmony, her eyes glinting. He imagined how quickly her brain must be whirring, cogs blurring with speed as she grappled with questions he had no interest in answering.

'About twenty-five years? Wouldn't you say, Will?' Luke leant across the table for a crisp, and Will noticed his wrist, fine-boned still, but strong, the skin tanned, a smart watch so polished it glinted in the sun like a mirror.

'Yes, it must be,' Will said. Luke's eyes had the very same intensity they'd had all those years before, dark and earnest, hiding a seething tangle of thoughts and emotions. He glanced at Harmony then back at Luke. Sitting between them was unbearable; two separate chapters of his life, as incompatible as oil and water. 'We were fourteen when we last saw each other.'

'Were you good friends?' Emma asked.

'Yes,' said Luke evenly. 'We were best friends.'

Will clenched his fist.

Ian reappeared with drinks. 'Don't sit down,' Emma said, grabbing his arm. 'I need your help in the kitchen.'

'Is there anything I can do?' asked Harmony.

'No, you sit there and have a catch-up. It's all done.' Emma ushered her unwilling husband back towards the French windows.

Left alone, the three of them fell into silence. There was an atmosphere between them which was almost claustrophobic. Will's heart raced. It was hard to breathe, as if he was sitting in a vacuum. Long-buried memories resurfaced: the crisp chill in the dusky October air, the smell of the ground, damp earth with fallen leaves, that rich, mulchy smell as they began to rot down.

'This is amazing. I really can't believe you were best friends,' Harmony said.

'Actually,' Luke replied. 'We were more than that.'

'There's something better than best?' Harmony flashed him a playful smile.

'Yes, we're blood brothers, that's far better than best.' He held his hand up, palm outwards, five fingers splayed. 'You remember, Will?'

Will's stomach knotted as he saw the white scar that ran from the base of Luke's index finger to the heel of his palm.

'Blood brothers?' Harmony laughed. 'That's all a bit Huckleberry Finn, isn't it?'

Will tried to push away the feelings of unease. He breathed out and forced another smile. Made an effort to keep his voice light and relaxed. 'Yes, of course I remember.' Then he raised his own hand and unfurled his fingers to display his matching scar. 'Blood brothers until we die.'

Will watched as Luke's smile faltered and he lowered his hand.

Emma appeared through the French windows with a tray of food. 'I must say this has made lunch so much more interesting. It's like an episode of *This is Your Life*!'

Will smiled tightly.

'I just found out they're blood brothers, Em.' Harmony reached and took hold of Will's hand. Her fingers laced through his. She turned his hand over and traced her fingertip the length of the thin, raised scar. A tingle ran through him. 'After all these years, I've finally discovered the cause of this.'

Will pulled his hand away.

'So how do you become blood brothers?' Emma asked as she sat down.

'Will had this penknife his father gave him. God, we loved that knife, didn't we, Will?'

Will recalled unwrapping the knife on his thirteenth birthday, the thrill he'd felt as he tore off the brown paper and realised what he'd been given. The inscription on the blade was as cold as the metal itself – To W.P.E. from your father – but Will hadn't cared. It was like unwrapping treasure; a real penknife, a Swiss Army one, with its magnificent trademark blood-red handle, the mirror-like blade reflecting the excitement in his eyes in flashes as he opened and closed it, opened and closed it.

'Anyway, one day we went up into the woods, hid ourselves in some bushes, and took turns to cut our palms open,' Luke continued. 'Then we pressed our hands together, said a few words, pledged eternal allegiance to each other, that kind of rubbish.' He laughed.

'Ow!' Emma exclaimed.

'Yes, it hurt like a bitch.' As Luke spoke the smile fell from his face.

Will reached for his glass and downed the last of his beer.

'I can't believe you did something like that,' Harmony said. 'Can you, Em? Didn't we just read copies of the *NME* and lust over David Bowie?'

'It seemed like a good idea at the time,' Will said.

'Boys can be very odd,' said Emma.

Emma took each plate in turn and laid thick slices of ham on them. They passed bowls of green salad and new potatoes around and Ian poured white wine for them all.

'Your garden's looking beautiful, Ian,' said Will, keen to keep conversation away from him and Luke. 'You've been working hard.'

Emma snorted with laughter. 'Will, you should know by now, my husband's idea of a hard morning's gardening is napping in a deckchair under the willow tree.'

'Excuse me?' Ian retorted. 'The lawn was mowed this morning.'

'By the gardener!' She furrowed her brow and leant across the table to get hold of the bread basket. 'You're such a liar.'

Ian's face fell like a stone. 'Liar? I'm not a bloody liar!'

Emma was obviously startled by his sudden eruption. 'I didn't mean to touch a nerve. I—'

'You haven't touched a nerve,' Ian interjected, 'not at all. But liar is a pretty strong word to use.' He looked at Will. 'Don't you agree, Will? I'm not sure it's on for a wife to call her husband a liar in company. Or at all, to be honest.' Will wasn't sure if Ian expected him to agree with him or not. He hesitated, glancing at Harmony for guidance, but she wasn't looking at him. She was looking at Luke. She wasn't going to let this go. She wasn't going to stop until she knew everything. It occurred to him then that he could get up from the table and leave. Just get up and walk away.

'Emma didn't mean anything by it.' It was Luke who spoke.

Emma looked at Luke with visible relief. 'No, I didn't mean anything. It was a joke, because you implied you did the garden but the gardener does the garden.'

'Well, I pay for the bloody gardener,' Ian blustered.

An awkward silence settled over the table.

'This ham is delicious, Em,' Harmony said. 'You're such a good cook.' She turned to Luke. 'I'm appalling in the kitchen. Every time I eat Emma's food I'm reminded just how bad I am.'

As quickly as it had blown up, the exchange with Ian was forgotten as Emma laughed Harmony's compliment off with a casual wave of her hand. 'You're a perfectly good cook when you want to be. You just don't want to be.'

'Shoddy cooking skills is the price you feminist working types have to pay, isn't it?'

As Ian laughed to show he was 'just playing' with Harmony, Will cut into his ham. Luke's composure rattled him. How could he appear so unfazed? How could he conduct himself with such confidence, remain so unaffected by the crippling discomfort that silenced Will? And how suave he was, leaning back in his chair, casually holding his glass of wine, the crook of his arm resting on the back of Emma's chair. He listened intently as she spoke, engaged and interested, so different to the wraith-like boy he'd known, with his darting eyes, coiled like a spring, so thin his bones threatened to pierce his paper-white skin.

Emma finished a story and they all laughed. Ian stood to refill their wine glasses and as he did Luke turned to Will. 'Tell me, Will,' he said. 'What's happened since we last saw each other? Has life been good to you?'

The table fell to a pin-drop silence and they all turned their eyes on Will.

He wasn't sure how much Luke meant him to tell. He was a child when he last saw Luke; everything had happened. 'Yes, life's been good,' Will said at last. 'I got married to Harmony soon after college, we live in London, in a nice flat. Things are good.' He smiled at Harmony who smiled back.

Luke nodded. 'You certainly seem happy.' He looked at Harmony who lowered her eyes and reached for the pendant that hung around her neck.

'And you? Are you married, Luke?' Will asked.

Luke seemed to do a double take, his cool facade slipping for a fraction of a second. He reached forward for his glass, then sat back in his chair. 'I was.'

'That's a shame,' said Emma. 'But so many marriages fall by the wayside these days.'

'It wasn't quite like that.'

Will saw Ian glare at his wife, who mouthed a 'What?' at him.

'And you're a lawyer?' Will asked.

'For my sins.'

'Best corporate lawyer in the whole damn City,' Ian said, like a puffed-up father boasting about his favourite son.

Luke shook his head. 'Nothing great about being a lawyer. We're just successful parasites.'

'And that's how you met? Through work?'

'We met playing golf, actually. Luke joined the club last year. Met at the bar and hit it off in an instant. A mutual love of fine watches and fast cars.' Ian laughed loudly.

'And you, Will?' Luke asked, ignoring Ian. 'What do you do?'

'I've a wine shop.'

'Oh, it's a fabulous shop!' exclaimed Emma. 'A real treasure trove.'

'This is one of his.' Ian held his glass up, the liquid inside like watered-down honey, sparkling pale gold in the sunshine. 'From one of those mixed cases I bought from you last year at the opening of the shop.'

'It's very good indeed,' said Luke.

The table fell silent again and Will listened to the sound of the children playing on the other side of the house, both happy now.

'He's also a wonderful photographer,' Harmony said. 'Really talented.' Her compliment was delivered with too much enthusiasm, and to Will it sounded insincere.

'I enjoy it, nothing more than that.'

'What about you, Harmony?' Luke said, turning his attention on to her. 'What do you do?'

Will watched her fingers fiddling with the gold Tiffany heart at her neck. He'd given it to her on their tenth wedding anniversary and he loved how she played with it gently between her fingers.

'I'm based at Imperial University, well, in offices opposite,' she said. 'I'm involved in business development.'

'What field?' Luke asked.

'I'm a scientist by training. But I work in technology transfer, which is basically securing funding for various university-developed patented compounds.'

'Oh, she's not just a pretty face,' Emma said, standing to clear the plates. 'Harmony is the cleverest person I know.'

'Of course I'm not,' Harmony said.

'You are,' Emma said. 'How many of my other friends have a Ph.D.?'

Ian leant towards Harmony. 'Of course, we've got to remember who her other friends are. Not too many Ph.D.s required to book a spa day.' He sat back in his chair and snorted loudly.

Emma ignored him. 'Pudding?'

Everybody nodded and Emma picked up the pile of stacked plates and cutlery then started towards the French windows.

Harmony stood and reached for the bowl of salad.

'No, you stay there,' said Ian with dramatised weariness. 'I'll go. If I don't I'll get it in the neck for being lazy.' He winked at Will again.

'So, Dr English—' Luke began.

'Dr Hanney,' Harmony corrected, raising her eyebrows and smiling.

'My apologies. Dr Hanney. What was your Ph.D.?'

'Functional genomics.'

Will reached across the table for the bottle of sparkling water and poured himself a glass.

'And what area are you currently involved in?'

She laughed. 'Are you sure you're interested?'

'Yes, I am. Very.'

'Pharmacogenomics, the bit of pharmacology that deals with genetics and drug efficacy.'

Will watched her run her fingers through her hair then lightly touch the corner of her shirt collar. He turned away and looked across the lawn. Luke's presence was impossible to ignore, impossible to laugh away, and with it came a rush of self-loathing and shame, as familiar as old toys found in an attic after decades of gathering dust. It didn't matter how well Luke looked, it didn't matter how in control of his life he seemed, how undamaged, Will couldn't control the sudden twinges of shame and guilt.

'We're looking at the use of gene type to optimise the potency of a drug while minimising its side-effects.'

'Personalised medicine?'

'Exactly.'

A bird screeched above them. Will looked up. It was a circling crow, cawing high in the sky. It wheeled then flew over the house, its wings flapping strongly, with purpose. As it disappeared out of sight he heard his mother's voice warning him about a single black crow flying overhead. She loved her superstitions and had an impressive catalogue of ominous rhymes for almost everything she encountered. He searched his memory for the one about a lone crow but couldn't recall it.

'… what you do sounds incredibly interesting,' Luke was saying to Harmony.

'It is. And, sadly, very poorly paid,' she laughed. 'But you can't have everything, can you?'

'Unless you're Will, it seems,' he said.

Will saw her lower her eyes as a slight smile passed over her lips.

'Yes, I'm very lucky,' Will said.

Luke and Will locked eyes then, like dogs assessing each other, uncertain and wary. Will gently stroked his thumb over the scar that crossed his palm. He had a vivid image of his blood falling unchecked onto the sun-speckled grass, felt again the tingle of exhilaration as Luke dragged the blade across his hand, remembered the pale skin parting, his blood flowing. A tremor shot through him as he recalled them pressing their hands together, blood and pain combining, wide eyes bolted on to each other, their hold tight.

'We're blood brothers now,' Luke had said to Will with a trembling voice. 'That means we're joined. By blood. Like real brothers.'

'You watch my back. I'll watch yours,' Will replied. 'That's what it means. We'll be there for each other, forever.'

And then they smiled and tightened their grip as their mingled blood ran down their wrists and fell like tears on the earth.

CHAPTER FIVE

By five o'clock the terrace had fallen into shade and a chill had descended.

'I think we should head off,' Will said. 'If we leave now we might miss the worst of the traffic.'

'Yes,' said Luke. 'I should also go. You're right, the Sunday traffic into London is dreadful.'

They walked through the living room and into the hallway. Luke picked up his car keys from the circular table in the centre. The spectacular red and orange flowers from the party still held pride of place despite their fading beauty, a handful of petals fallen like the first leaves of autumn.

At the front door Harmony kissed Emma and Ian goodbye and then looked at Luke. She offered her hand. He shook it and she felt herself blush.

Stop it, she thought. You're behaving like a teenage girl. 'It was good to meet you again, Luke,' she said. 'And amazing that you and Will were at school together.'

He smiled. 'Well, I hope now Will and I have made contact we'll be able to stay in touch.'

Harmony nodded. 'That would be nice.'

Ian clapped Luke on the back. 'Thanks for the game. Shame you played so damn well. I'll give you more of a run for your money next time.'

Luke shook Ian's hand then turned to Emma and kissed her on the cheek. 'Lunch was delicious. Your children are charming, and you're right, they certainly have a passion for Pavlova.'

Emma laughed. 'They do.' She paused and smiled at them all. 'Perhaps we should do this again soon.'

Luke looked directly at Harmony. 'I'd like that.'

She reached for Will's hand and took hold of it before nodding. 'We would too.'

The three of them walked out of the house and across the driveway towards the cars, their feet crunching over the silence. They paused beside Luke's dark grey convertible Audi, its alloy wheels shining like polished silver medals. He pointed his key at the car and it flashed its lights in greeting.

Luke and Will faced each other and Harmony felt the tension between them return. Luke held out his hand. Will stared at it and for a moment Harmony worried he might not respond. But at last he reached out and took hold of it, their two scarred palms clasped.

'It's good to see you, Luke.' Will seemed to hesitate, then he reached into his jacket pocket for his wallet. 'Here's my number,' he said, handing him one of the shop's business cards. 'Why don't you give me a call? Maybe we could meet for a beer?'

'Sounds good.' Luke took the card and smiled.

Will reached for Harmony's hand as they turned to walk back to their car. She could feel Luke watching them. She glanced backwards and, sure enough, he was sitting in his car, door closed, hands gripping the steering wheel, eyes locked on them. He didn't move a muscle. There was no embarrassed look away. No smile. No reaction at all. He just sat there, impassive, watching.

Once in the car, Harmony expected Will to say something to her, but he was silent, his eyes distant, driving on autopilot. Every now and then his brow would furrow as if trying to work something out.

'Seeing him again has thrown you, hasn't it?' she said at last, unable to keep quiet any longer.

He glanced at her and then nodded.

'I spoke to him for quite a long time at Emma's party. He's … unusual.' She paused, waiting for Will to reply. When he didn't she pressed on. 'And charismatic. Was he always like that? I mean, when you were friends at school?'

Still Will said nothing.

She turned to look out of her window. It was so frustrating how guarded he was when it came to his past. She loved to discuss things;

she was a scientist, she liked answers. Her mother used to laugh at her when she was a young girl, always asking questions, determined to know why trees grew upwards and how clouds floated and why snowflakes looked like miniature paper doilies. Facts made life easier to understand. She'd asked Will so many questions over the years and had so many non-committal, one-word answers and dismissive shrugs in return. As far as he was concerned his past was irrelevant. It didn't merit discussion; as unimportant, he said, as a lacklustre lover with a forgotten name. All that mattered was the present, was her, their life together. She'd accepted his secrecy because she'd had no choice, but now his past had been revealed like the tip of an ashen finger in the soil and she was desperate to uncover the rest. Especially about Luke. He fascinated her. There was something about him that brought to mind her father. Charismatic. It was a word she'd heard her mother use when describing him. Despite having spent night upon night dredging her memories for any recollection of the man that might be lurking in a corner of her mind, she had none. The image she carried was based entirely on a single photograph she had of him. She'd found it about a month after their mother's death, when she and her sister finally mustered the courage to sort through her personal effects. They'd wedged a chair beneath the door handle of the new shared bedroom at their nan's house. They'd put their mother's beloved Ella Fitzgerald on the tape machine. Then they sat cross-legged on the floor, her sister holding a bottle of vodka and an expression of grim determination, their mother's precious shoebox between them. They stared at it for a while then in one swift movement her sister tipped the bottle up to her lips, winced, and pulled the lid off the box. There were hundreds of letters inside. All written to their mother from their father. Harmony was staggered as she read them. They were beautiful; incredible expressions of love – poetic, ethereal, surreal even. They were written in curling handwriting with intricate doodles and motifs decorating the white space around words that struck Harmony as the most romantic ever written. As she picked up one of the letters a photograph fell from its fold.

Harmony gasped. 'Is that him?'

He was the most handsome man she'd ever seen. He wore a loose white, unbuttoned shirt and stood on a table laden with wine surrounded by a group of people laughing and clapping along as he played a guitar. Her mother was amongst those at the table. She stared up at him with adoring eyes, her face sliced in two by the widest of smiles, love pouring out of every part of her.

'Fuck him,' her sister had spat as she snatched the picture off her. Harmony was about to protest but kept quiet when she saw the tears coursing down her sister's cheeks. 'I fucking hate him. I *hate* him.' She grabbed the vodka and drank some more then scrabbled to collect the letters and shoved them back into the box with the photo. 'We're burning them all, the whole box of crappy, lying rubbish. He's nothing, a ne'er-do-well and a wastrel, and I hate him.'

Harmony didn't know what a ne'er-do-well or a wastrel was and wasn't sure her sister did either. They were the words their nan used if she ever referred to him, but as the woman spent her spare time dressing Boris, her snappy pug, in miniature human clothes, Harmony had sense enough to know that not everything she said was necessarily the truth. While her sister swigged at the vodka again, Harmony inched her fingers towards the box, removed the photograph of her father and surreptitiously slipped it into her jeans pocket.

'And I'm changing my name. I'm not having that stupid, hippy name he bloody chose a moment longer. I'm Sophie from now on, okay?'

Sophie was her sister's middle name, the name their mother wanted to call her. The piercing look of anger in her sister's eyes made her wonder if she was expected to change her name as well. The thing was she liked Harmony and wasn't keen on Patricia – her own middle name – at all.

As she followed her sister downstairs, Harmony tried to work out why it was all her father's fault anyway. Cancer was to blame for taking their mother away from them, not their absent father. He hadn't been around for years and years. Why was her sister freaking out about him now? It didn't make sense.

They found their nan sitting on the sofa reading the listings from the *Radio Times* aloud to the pug, who wore a hand-knitted pink cardigan with big blue buttons.

'We'd like to burn this and everything in it,' her sister announced. Her attempt to mask her vodka- slur made it sound as if she was pretending to be the Queen.

'What's in the box that you want to burn exactly, Starla?' their nan asked sternly.

'Letters from the wastrel.'

Their nan gestured sharply at the fire. 'Good riddance to bad rubbish.'

'And I'm not called Starla,' her sister said, lifting her chin high. 'I'm Sophie now.'

Their nan nodded and then the three of them watched in silence as the box went up in a rainbow of flames on the log fire.

Harmony pushed the recollection away and looked back at her husband. 'Will,' she tried again. 'Is everything okay?'

'I'm fine. I wasn't expecting to see him, that's all.'

'Talk to me. Please?'

'There's nothing much to say. I knew the guy at school. We lost touch. It was a surprise to see him.'

'It looked like more than that to me.'

They drove in silence for a while and then Harmony heard him take a deep breath. 'It's thrown me,' he said. 'I suppose I'd sort of blanked him out of my head, and seeing him like that was … ' he paused, hesitating, searching for the right words, 'like seeing a ghost.'

His words rang around them like the echo of a church bell. His brow furrowed and his mouth twitched, as if he was trying to decode his thoughts.

They didn't speak for the rest of the journey. The car was hot, the early evening sunshine warming the air inside until it was too stuffy to bear. She opened her window and leant her head against the door so the stream of cool air ran over her face. Her mind drifted to Luke, the way he'd looked at her during lunch, that peculiar directness she found so fascinating. She heard his voice, steady and calm, asking her to leave Emma's party with him. What would have happened if she'd said yes? She closed her eyes and saw herself take his hand. She followed him down the corridor. Into the hallway, past the butler and out of the house. She saw herself climbing into his car. Heard the sound of the car door closing. Saw his hand reach over to rest on her thigh. Harmony opened her eyes and shifted herself in her seat, then glanced at Will, who stared intently at the road ahead.

When they got back to the flat Harmony went to her small study and grabbed a pen and her reading glasses and the pile of papers from her desk. In the living room she sat down on the sofa and put on her glasses.

'I'll put the kettle on, would you like a cup of tea?'

'I'm fine,' she said, keeping her eyes on the notes on her lap.

'Hey,' said Will gently. 'Don't be like that.' He sat on the sofa beside her and took her hand. 'Don't be cross.'

'I'm not cross,' she said, putting her work on the coffee table and looking at him. 'I just wish you'd talk to me about this, that's all. I've never heard you mention Luke before.'

'Look, I'm not keeping it from you for any reason. It's just not important.' He tucked some of her hair behind her ear and then pulled her into him. 'I've told you before, those years at school, none of it matters now. I've put it behind me.'

'Put what behind you? What happened?'

He didn't answer immediately. She could tell he was thinking about telling her, weighing it up, but then he shook his head. 'I really don't want to talk about it. Stuff happened. Stuff that's too hard to talk about. It's best forgotten. And I'm over it. Really, I am.'

'But today—'

'It was a surprise,' he said, interrupting her. 'Christ, you know better than anyone how little time I spend thinking about school. Seeing Luke like that threw me. Last time I saw him he was a kid. I was expecting a nice lunch in the sun with Emma and Ian and then this blast from the past showed up.' He sighed heavily. 'I probably need to work on my acting skills a bit. Perfect the art of hiding shock. That's the second time in a week I've failed with that.'

She shook her head and made a face at him.

'I'm going to grab a beer,' he said. 'You want anything?'

'No, thanks.'

As he left the living room she leant back against the arm of the sofa, turning her head to breathe in its smell; safe and familiar, it wrapped around her like a warm blanket. She and Will had got it in the sales on the Tottenham Court Road the weekend they moved in together. It was the first piece of furniture they'd bought, and as they left the shop he'd squeezed her hand and whispered, 'This is it, Harmony. Our start. It all begins here.'

The sofa was delivered two weeks later, and sat in the middle of their living room in their first flat in Vauxhall in front of an upturned packing box that for five months they used as a coffee table. They sat on it all evening, drinking wine and eating Chinese. Later they made love on it, their wine glasses and empty takeaway cartons discarded on the floor beside them, the ancient television, as deep as it was wide, flickering silently in the corner of the darkened room.

Harmony worked for the next few hours. When the words began to swim, her eyes heavy with tiredness, she put the papers down and stood up. She gasped a little at the stiff pain in her lower back and cursed herself for not working at her desk. She saw her mother wagging a finger at her, telling her off for working slouched on the sofa or propped up in bed: *Sofas for sitting, beds for sleeping, desks for working.*

Will appeared at the living room door. 'I'm going to go to bed,' he said.

'Yes,' she said. 'I'm shattered. I'll get a drink and then follow you.'

Harmony filled a glass of water and as she drank it she checked Will had locked the back door. She peered through the glazed panel in the door at the garden which was bathed in the last of the fading light. They should have done some work in the garden this weekend; they'd neglected it and it was looking untidy. The garden was the reason they'd stayed in the flat, which was too small for them really, with just the one bedroom, the box room she used as a study, and a living room they squeezed a dining table into. The garden was beautiful, though, large by London standards, about forty feet by thirty, with a magical feel. It had grey stone walls that were covered in dark unruly ivy and an area of aged paving, some of the slabs cracked with moss growing between. There were two overgrown flower beds that ran along each of the walls, and at the end of the garden was a stone bench with carved legs, gradually being suffocated by weeds. It was a hidden gem in the slice of urban grey between Baron's Court and West Kensington tube stations. When Harmony found out she was pregnant she knew they would have to move. She'd had to persuade Will, which had been hard, but she explained that they needed somewhere more suitable for a family, somewhere with a proper bedroom for the baby and a utility room, maybe a playroom too. Her resolve to sell it had weakened when she showed the valuing estate agent the garden.

'Oh, this is very special,' he'd said, purring with excitement. 'Yes. Lots of potential here. It'll fly off our books.'

But when the baby died there was no reason to move, no need to justify the expense – the conveyancing fees alone were enough to make their eyes water – but rather than feel relieved that she could stay in her home, she found herself trapped, resentful of the flat that was now inextricably linked to her miscarriage, symbolic of her childless life.

Will was reading in bed. She went to shut the curtains.

'Can you leave them open?' he asked, closing his book and laying it on the bedside table. She hesitated, her hand resting on the edge of the curtain. She didn't like sleeping with them open; she felt exposed, worried about people being able to see in.

She let her hand drop from the curtain and climbed into bed beside him. He reached out and turned his bedside light off.

She curled up close to him, resting her head on his shoulder.

'Are you sure you're okay?' she asked him. 'Everybody around the table today could tell there was something wrong, you know. Did you and Luke fall out at school? Was he the reason you didn't enjoy it there?'

'No, we didn't fall out, we were great friends. I met him towards the end of the first term when we were thirteen. He left though, was expelled actually, and I didn't hear from him again.'

'Why was he expelled?'

Will turned his head to look out of the window into the moonlit darkness. 'I don't know why.' His voice was edged with sadness. 'He shouldn't have been.'

'Was it dreadful there?'

'Yes,' he said, after a moment or two. 'Not all of it. But some of it was awful.'

She kissed his chest. 'I can't believe your parents sent you away.' She was unable to keep the blame out of her voice. 'I don't know how people do it. I mean, what age were you? Eight? It's barbaric. Why have children if you're going to send them away?'

'Mum didn't want me to go, though I remember her saying something about it being good to get away from her apron strings,' he said. 'It was my father. He thought it was the right thing to do. He saw it as some sort of rite of passage, spouted all that nonsense about boarding school turning boys into men.' He paused briefly. 'I suppose it was what people did back then.'

'Not the people I knew,' she said. She thought of her father-in-law, his holier-than-thou attitude to life, his favouring of etiquette over emotion, the malice in his voice when he talked about immigrants, the way he buttoned his coat before leaving for church and tutted at Harmony as she sat at the breakfast table reading the Sunday papers, his sneering and sniping at Will, his inability to show any signs of affection towards his only child.

Will once told her he only saw his parents on the last Sunday of each month during term time. They'd drive to a pub on the A131, order three portions of scampi and chips, then he and his father would eat their food as his mother chattered mindlessly to fill the stony silence. It was from the odd anecdote such as this that Harmony began to understand Will's loathing of his school. They'd driven past the place once, years earlier, after a wedding in Newmarket. Harmony was studying the map as Will drove.

'I thought Clacton-on-Sea was up north,' she said, vaguely. 'My geography really is shocking.'

'Want to go?' Will said, casting her a glance.

'To Clacton-on-Sea?'

He grinned and nodded.

'But it's in the opposite direction.'

'So? Come on, let's go. We can book into a crappy B & B with a grumpy landlady. Walk on the beach and eat greasy fish and chips.'

'What about work?'

'We'll call in sick.'

She hesitated but then nodded. 'Go on, then, let's. It'd be lovely to be by the sea.'

They'd been talking and laughing, thrilled by their decision, but then Will fell quiet. He pulled over and stopped the car, his knuckles white as he gripped the wheel.

'What's wrong?' Harmony asked.

'Farringdon Hall.'

'What?'

'My old school,' he said. 'Back there. We just passed it.'

Harmony turned to look and saw a long red brick wall, too high to see anything behind it. 'Can I see it?' she asked then. 'Will you show me?'

'Why?'

'I don't know. I suppose I'd like to see if it's anything like I imagine. It'll help me picture you then.'

'I can guarantee that place won't give you any picture of me.'

'Please?'

For a moment he didn't move, then suddenly, in one quick movement, he threw the car into gear and reversed at speed back past the entrance where two aged stone lions sat bored on brick piers either side. They turned up the driveway, long and straight and lined by tall, evenly spaced trees like the bars of a prison, and drove towards the huge, gothic manor.

'It's deserted,' she whispered. A shiver passed through her as she looked up at the windows that punctured the brick like dead, glazed eyes.

'School holidays.'

They pulled up in front of the pillared entrance and Will turned the engine off. 'This is where my father handed me over to that cock of a headmaster,' Will said grimly. 'I can still remember his fingers digging into my shoulders and him saying to Drysdale, "Well, all I can say is he's a little bugger. Do what you must." You should have seen the bastard's eyes light up. Parental permission to make my life misery.' He drew a laboured breath and exhaled heavily. 'Come on, it's a fucking shithole. Let's get out of here.'

That was the last time he'd talked about school.

'You know,' Harmony whispered, turning her head on the pillow to look at him, the moonlight from the window bathing his face. 'If you'd been my child I'd have kept you with me as long as I possibly could. I'd never have sent you away.'

'You mustn't worry about me. It wasn't great but I'm fine. It was just school. Children adapt to everything and we all found our ways to cope. It's in the past now and that's where it belongs.'

CHAPTER SIX

Will couldn't sleep. He lay still as Harmony mumbled quietly beside him, every now and then letting out a torrent of mutterings. This was something she did – talking in her sleep – yelling out as if in surprise then murmuring unintelligibly, her head moving back and forth emphatically, arguing perhaps in her dreams before she finally settled. He listened to the noises outside the flat, the occasional car, a police siren not far away, the faint footsteps and muffled talking of a group of people as they passed the living room window. His mind whirred; he was never going to get to sleep. He eased himself out of bed, careful not to wake Harmony, lifted his clothes off the chair in the corner of the room and crept out of the bedroom. He dressed in the hallway, then took his keys off the hook by the door and slipped outside.

Night-rambling, he called it. Walking at night. It was a habit that started when he was about ten or eleven, when one night, unable to sleep for worrying about going back to school, he called for his mother. She'd sat on the edge of his bed, patted his hand, and told him to count sheep. His heart sank as she left the room, closing the door behind her so that he was plunged back into darkness; he suspected counting sheep would do little to ease his fear. He was right. By the time he'd counted a flock of four hundred he was no more sleepy than when he began. It was then, on a whim, that he climbed out of bed, let himself quietly out of the house, and set off on his very first night-ramble. In the years that followed he often found himself creeping downstairs, holding his breath as he stepped over the creakiest floorboards, pausing every now and then to listen for the telltale sounds of adults on the prowl. Back then these night-time treks would set his pulse racing, send adrenalin pumping into his blood, push his worries into the background. As he got older the night-rambles became calmer, those first deep breaths of fresh night air like Valium, his tensions easing with each step he took.

It was a ramble, or at least the repercussions of one, that first brought him and Luke together. One night in the third week of his first term at Farringdon Hall, Will was caught sneaking out by Mr Fielder, a reedy history master with a sparse moustache who smelt of coffee and cigarettes. Will had opened the door to the building and walked straight into him. The man sent him back up to the first years' dormitory, his thin voice laced with what might have been regret as he told him he'd have to see the headmaster the following day. Will's stomach had churned with dread for the whole night and following day until, finally, in the evening after prep, Drysdale summoned him.

'Tell me, English – I'd love to know – exactly why you want to run away from school? Why you'd want to cause us bother? Worry your parents? Hm?'

Will's stuttered mix of ums and ers failed to convince this terrifying man, and the caning that followed was brutal. Will limped back to the dormitory bruised and biting back tears, and climbed straight into bed. Later, after Matron had turned the lights out, a boy on the other side of the room – a quiet, small boy who Will hadn't taken much notice of – crept across the room. The boy stood motionless by Will's bed for a moment or two. Then he glanced over his shoulder and thrust out a closed fist. Will didn't move. Nor did the boy – he just stood there, unmoving, his arm held out towards Will. Will furrowed his brow and shrugged, unsure what he was mean to do. The boy sighed theatrically and leant closer.

'Take it,' he whispered. 'It'll stop the bum-sting.' He grabbed Will's hand and pushed something hard into it then closed Will's fingers around whatever it was before silently slipping back to his bed.

When Will opened his hand and saw what he'd been given his heart missed a beat. Two foil-wrapped toffees lay on his palm like gold coins. Will closed his hand and thrust it beneath his blanket. Sweets weren't allowed. Sweets would get confiscated by the prefects, stolen and eaten, your things ransacked if there was even the smallest suspicion there was more. How had the boy got this contraband? Where had he hidden it?

Will sat up in his bed and looked over at Luke who also sat up. His pale, thin face was lit in a shaft of fluorescent light from the corridor. He stared at Will, solemn and intense, nodded once then lay back down. Will pulled his grey, regulation blanket over his head and waited with bated breath, heart hammering, until the duty prefect had done his final rounds. When Will was sure it was safe, he undid the golden wrappers, coughing to mask any rustling, then popped both toffees in at once, almost too much for his mouth to hold. He sucked slowly, closing his eyes as the creamy sweetness ran down his throat. Luke was right; for a few glorious minutes his throbbing backside, the desperate homesickness, the injustice and loneliness – all of it was forgotten.

In the morning, as they walked down the stairs on their way to breakfast, Will caught up with Luke.

'Thanks,' he said.

Luke smiled, then neither of them said anything more.

Will walked along the deserted back streets of Fulham. His stride was full and his rhythmic footsteps rang on the pavement. The houses were dark, their curtains drawn. He imagined the people who lived in them tucked up in their beds, quietly snoring, deeply asleep. He heard the startled screech of a cat or maybe a fox. He picked up his pace as his thoughts settled on the last time he'd seen Luke, the day he was expelled, both of them perched on hard wooden chairs in Drysdale's office, which reeked of old leather, wood polish and mothballs. He remembered the look in Luke's eyes, the way they'd welled with tears that spilled down his cheeks, and a thick nausea pooled in the pit of his stomach as he strode on.

In the morning Will left their flat and headed up towards the North End Road, weaving in and out of the people on the busy pavements as he walked to the shop.

'Morning, Frank,' he said, as he pushed through the door, sounding the old-fashioned bell that hung on the back.

'Morning, William,' Frank said brightly.

Will was fond of Frank. He'd worked for Will since he opened the shop a year earlier, using the small lump sum his father had left him when he died. Will had met him in the wine merchant's he worked at after college, and as soon as he thought about opening his own shop, he knew he wanted Frank with him. He was great company, eccentric in a very British way, with a great sense of humour and an easy-going nature. He was a short man, and a little rotund, and always dressed in well-fitting suits with his grey hair slicked back with old-fashioned hair cream that he ordered from a specialist gentleman's shop in Bristol. He lived in Chiswick with two Persian cats called Pie and Pinwheel and his elderly boyfriend, a writer of moderately successful science fiction, who was as wiry as Frank was portly. Frank loved wine with a passion, and was a walking encyclopedia when it came to claret and burgundy. North End Wines was nestled in a tired row of shops between the Co-op and a bookmaker's. From the outside it didn't look like much, with its chipped maroon paintwork, dirty white walls and security bars on the windows – a legacy from its days as a sex shop – but the rent was cheap. Inside, however, was an Aladdin's cave of beautiful wine. Bottles were shelved from floor to ceiling and wall to wall, all of them carefully selected by Will from a variety of vineyards, large and small, and already, even after only a year of trading, they had a small but loyal customer base who travelled from various corners of London, battling gridlock to buy their wine.

'So how are you today?'

'Good thanks, Frank.'

'Kettle's just boiled, dear.'

'Lovely. Would you like a coffee?'

'Gracious, no. I've had three already.'

'Three?' Will said, raising his eyebrows. 'It's not even ten. You'll be bouncing off the ceiling.'

Frank smiled and playfully batted the air. 'I've been up since five. I'm surprised I haven't needed more than the three, to be honest.'

Will pushed through the plastic strip curtain, reminiscent of a

Seventies corner shop, and in the tiny cupboard that passed as a kitchen he made himself an instant and dumped two spoonfuls of sugar in it. 'How are the boys?' he called through.

'Fluffy,' Frank said. 'And as lazy as ever. Poor Pinwheel was a bit off-colour on Saturday but the vet wasn't worried; she said it was probably something he ate. A past its sell-by mouse, I suspect. He's such a greedy toad.'

Will smiled to himself and took his coffee back into the shop. The shop settled him; he felt comfortable here, knowledgeable and well respected, with no pressure to be anything out of the ordinary. He didn't have to be talented or skilful, or, if truth be told, to stretch himself. He knew about wine. He'd worked in the business since his early twenties, and being able to work close to home, with no commute and no pressure, suited him. Frank was independently wealthy and worked for Will for the love of it; if the business had to fold, Frank would be unaffected financially. It was easy and pleasant, which is just how Will liked it. He didn't make much money but it was steady, and though there were undoubtedly days when he wished he was out with his camera searching for beauty in the obscure and mundane, they weren't frequent.

'Would you like a custard cream?' Frank asked. 'I've a packet in my satchel.'

'I'm okay, thanks.' Will opened the large desk dairy by the till. There was a delivery that afternoon and he was meeting a new restaurant owner on Wednesday, but other than that, it was a quiet week. 'Did you have a good weekend, Frank?' he asked.

'Oh, well, you know, this and that.' Frank opened his old, battered bag, so stuffed it bulged in the middle, cracking the dry tan leather. He retrieved the packet of custard creams and carefully unwrapped them, took one, then wrapped the packet up and slid it back into his bag. 'I do like a custard cream,' he said to the biscuit. Then he seemed to remember something and waved the biscuit frantically at Will. 'Ooh, something did happen,' he said triumphantly. 'Eric had a death threat through the post. That was rather thrilling.'

'A death threat? A real one?'

'Yes, some poor woman, distraught he'd killed off Princess

63

Aisha in *Far Reaches of Sylion.*'

'Blimey,' Will said.

'To be honest, we're used to it. Some of the diehards were terribly upset. Saw it as a total betrayal that their gorgeous heroine got the chop.' He shrugged. 'I think that was it as far as weekend excitement goes.' Frank put the last of his custard cream into his mouth then brushed the crumbs off his suit. 'And now to work. I was thinking it was all getting a bit untidy in here. How about I give it a dust and a straighten?'

Will smiled; the shop was immaculate as always, but Frank was cursed with a compulsive disorder he wasn't aware of and every Monday and Thursday he dusted and straightened the clean and straight bottles.

'Good idea,' Will said. 'I'll get on with sorting out the cellar to make room for the delivery.'

'How's your mother, by the way?'

'She's fine, I think. I spoke to her last week. Though she wasn't herself. She's been cross with me for months. God knows what I've done.'

'That's grief for you. It makes everything terribly cloudy. When I lost dear old Mum I couldn't talk to anyone. Not even Eric. The only ones who understood were Pinwheel and Pie. They were such a support. She'll come around. Time's the perfect healer. You should visit her, she'd like that.' Frank took a breath and clapped his hands together. 'I must get on, this shop isn't going to clean itself, you know.'

He disappeared through the strip curtain to get his duster and polish. Will perched on the edge of the stool behind the counter and looked at his iPhone. He had an email and clicked open his inbox. Luke's name hit him so hard he felt winded.

From: Luke Crawford
Subject: Following up

Will,

It was good to see you yesterday and lovely to meet your wife. Though wasn't it strange bumping into each other? A small world, as they say. I was thinking on the way home how close we'd been at school. It would be great to catch up properly. I'm away on business next week and pretty busy towards the end of this week, but I'm free tonight or tomorrow evening. Would you and Harmony like to come for a drink or something to eat? Or at yours if that suits you better.

How does this sound?

Luke

'Frank, I'm nipping out for a minute or two,' Will said.

'Everything okay?' asked Frank. 'You look a little pale.'

'Just need some air.'

Will's head was all over the place. This wasn't going to go away. He rested against the wall of the Co-op and covered his face with his hands. Christ, he thought. Why on earth did you give him your card? He had to work out what he should do, but his head felt foggy, his thoughts blurred.

He called Harmony.

'Hey,' he said when she answered. 'It's me.'

'You okay?'

'I'm good. You?'

'In the middle of something.'

He tried to speak but the words stuck in his throat.

'Is it important?' she said, her voice tight with impatience.

'Luke emailed me.'

'Really?' He heard her voice soften. 'That's good, isn't it? What did he say?'

'He wants to meet up. Either tonight or tomorrow at ours or his.'

'Do you want to?'

'I'm not sure. He's keen to see me. Refusing seems rude, I think.'

'Then you should. Do you want me there too?'

'Yes. If that suits you, of course.'

'Tonight would be better for me. At ours. I've got a lot of work to do. At least if the evening runs on, I can get back to it if I have to.'

'So you think I should say yes to him?'

'It's up to you, Will. But if he's coming you need to sort the food out. I'm up against a deadline at work. Jacob needs to see my interim draft by the end of the week.'

Will waited after the phone call ended for a moment or two, then took a deep breath and hesitantly typed a reply.

Hey Luke, yes it would be great to catch up. Why don't you come to ours for 7ish tonight? I'll cook something. Our address is 146a Hanniker Rd, W14.

Will wasn't sure how to sign off. Yours sincerely? Kind regards? Best? He scrolled down to see how Luke had done it and saw a simple 'Luke'. Will added his name and pressed send. Then he stared at his phone in his quivering hand.

'I'm glad you're back,' said a worried looking Frank as Will pushed back through the door. 'A young woman came in asking for a bottle of pudding wine suitable to go with a chocolate roulade. I panicked.'

'What did you go with?'

'A bottle of the Estrella Moscatel de Valencia.'

'Perfect,' Will lied. 'I'd have given her the same myself.'

Frank's face relaxed. 'That's a relief,' he said. 'It was a bit of a punt, to be honest.' Then he picked up his duster and Pledge from the top of the stepladder and went back to his spraying and polishing.

At five o'clock Will told Frank he had to leave to meet a client. Frank didn't seem to mind; he said he needed some peace to tidy the cupboard in the kitchenette. Will walked down to the Sainsbury's Local at Fulham Broadway. As he wandered up and down the aisles, memories of Luke bombarded him; things he'd forgotten came back to him as if it were yesterday, like the time they tore pages from their hymn books in assembly and made tiny paper aeroplanes. Then later they'd bunked off cadet training and scrambled up the wooded hillock behind the science block that was steep and overgrown and where nobody else ever went. They'd spent an hour launching their hymn-book planes in fits of giggles as the flimsy things looped and plopped at their feet or flew off in odd directions, both of them as close to happy as either of them could be in their school that felt more like a prison.

Will pushed through the front door of the flat laden with shopping bags and kicked it shut behind him. Harmony's bag hung on the hook in the hallway.

'Hello,' he called, as he walked down to the kitchen. 'Harmony?'

There was no answer. He put the bags on the worktop and then went back down the corridor to her study. The door was shut. He knocked as he opened it and saw her at the computer, the glasses she wore for close work perched on her nose and her hair tied up in a loose ponytail, revealing the soft, smooth skin of her neck.

'Good day?' he said, putting his hand on her shoulder and bending to kiss her.

She tilted her cheek towards his kiss but didn't look away from the screen. 'Fine.'

'I didn't know you were working from home,' he said.

'I came back at lunchtime. I left some notes here and needed them.' She glanced at him. 'My head's all over the place, to be honest.'

'Luke will be here about seven,' he said. He paused, waiting for her to say something but she didn't. 'I'll leave you to it and make a start on the supper. I bought steak.'

'Lovely,' she said, squinting at the screen. 'Let me finish what I'm doing, then I'll have a quick shower and be with you.'

'No hurry.' Will turned to head out of the study.

'Will?' she said, turning in her chair.

'Yes?'

'We really do need to talk soon. About trying for another baby.' She smiled at him and his stomach turned over.

Before he began to unpack the shopping, he opened the bottle of Italian red he'd brought back from the shop. He always took a bottle home when the occasion deserved it, and this was one of his favourites. He poured himself a large glass, which he drank as he set about making French dressing and a salad, laid the table, put out salt, pepper, mustard, both English and French. A heaviness, a solemn resolution, had settled over him and he felt as if he were preparing a wake. When he'd finished, he topped up his wine and went outside. He sat at the wrought iron bistro table they'd found at a salvage yard a few years back. They'd planned to revamp it, rub the rust back, repaint it in a vibrant colour, something unusual, but it had never been done. Truth be told, Will liked the rust and chipped paint, it suited the garden – the rampant weeds that ate up the terrace, the overgrown shrubs that threatened to suffocate the small patchy lawn area.

Will sat for a while, nursing his glass of wine, his thoughts drifting to the conversation he'd had with Frank about his mother. However distant he'd been from his father, he forced himself to remember how lost she must feel without him. He tried to recall the last time he'd seen her. It was months ago.

The sound of the doorbell startled him.

Just be pleasant, he thought. Be pleasant and get it over with.

'He's here,' he called in to Harmony as he passed their bedroom. He paused to draw a breath then opened the door.

Luke held a bunch of flowers and a bottle of wine.

'Hello, Will,' he said, holding out the bottle.

Will took the bottle and glanced at the label. It was a Saint Emilion, a good year; he'd spent some money on it. 'That's a very generous gift,' he said. 'Thank you.'

'It's hard to buy wine for an expert,' Luke replied. 'The flowers are for your wife.'

'That's kind of you.'

They stood either side of the threshold. Neither moved or spoke. There was a palpable tension between them, thick with conflicting emotions. They held each other's stare until it became uncomfortable and Will was forced to step to one side and welcome Luke in.

'You have a nice place,' Luke said, as he followed Will into the flat.

'We're happy here.' Will cast his eye over the living room, filled with the assorted bits and pieces they'd collected over the years. It was like a shop of curiosities, cluttered and eclectic. There was a lot of kitsch Americana they'd bought while living in the States when Harmony had taught at Stanford for two years; Coca-Cola cool she called it: a battered bubblegum dispenser, an imitation Route 66 road sign, vintage baseball cards pinned along the mantelpiece like cardboard bunting. There were things they'd picked up while travelling in their early twenties: the statue of the elephant-like Hindu goddess, the name of which Will could never remember, some Indian and Balinese throws, a wooden frog from Thailand. Then Will's photographs, which patchworked the walls with arty landscapes, cityscapes, and portraits of Harmony. Luke walked over to one of the pictures of her at the foot of a looming Mayan temple. She wore a turquoise vest top and a pair of safari shorts, her hair held off her face with a red and white bandana, a water bottle resting on her thigh, her skin tanned and smooth as caramel. As Luke looked at it Will recalled making love to her later that evening, how they'd talked about the approaching end of the world, the Mayans' prophesy, how he'd kissed her from head to toe, and how she'd tasted sweet with coconut oil and bitter with citronella.

Luke finally drew away from the photo and smiled at Will.

'Can I get you a drink?' Will said.

'Yes, please. A beer if you've got one.'

Will fetched a glass from the cupboard in the kitchen and grabbed a bottle of Becks from the fridge. Back in the living room he found Luke studying a photo of them on their wedding day as if trying to memorise it.

Will poured the beer and handed it to Luke who thanked him and sat in the armchair by the window.

'So,' Will said, sitting on the sofa opposite, trying to think of conversation as far away from Farringdon Hall as possible. 'You were saying at Ian and Emma's that you work with Ian?'

Luke nodded.

'His lawyer? What sort of thing do you do for him?'

'I shouldn't really talk about it.' Luke fixed his eyes on Will. 'I'm sure Ian will tell you if he feels the need.'

Will looked down at his drink. His hand was trembling and the dark red wine wavered gently in the glass, the reflections from the light overhead dancing on the surface. The living room felt hot and stuffy suddenly. Will stood and went to open the sash window.

'Did you take the photographs?' asked Luke.

Will nodded and sat down again.

'They're very good.' He turned and looked at the picture of Harmony on the steps of the temple again. 'Especially those of your wife.'

'She's very photogenic. An easy subject for anyone to photograph.'

'Yes, the camera seems to love her, but the way you've framed them is impressive, your sense of space and balance.'

Will cast his eye over the photographs, which were as familiar as his own reflection; each one he remembered taking with crystal clarity. 'It's my passion.'

'You're lucky to have a passion,' Luke said.

He stared at Will so intently that Will had to look away.

'You did it professionally, didn't you?'

Will furrowed his brow, taken aback by the question, wondering how Luke knew. He shifted in his seat. 'For a while. It was a few years ago now. I did a couple of weddings and some portfolio shoots. But there's a lot of people doing the same and when the recession hit the work dried up. When things pick up, I might try again.' He smiled and lifted his glass to his lips. 'That's the plan anyway.'

'I remember that Polaroid camera you had at school,' said Luke, leaning forward to put his glass on the coffee table. 'You were always snapping something.'

Will's heart missed a beat as a recollection of that afternoon caught him unawares.

Luke laughed, the noise incongruous and unsettling. 'Always slung around your neck, that camera.'

Will thought about the camera gathering dust in a box above the wardrobe. He hadn't used it since school, but Luke was right, when he was young he rarely went anywhere without it. He'd been given it by a little-known uncle, his mother's bachelor stepbrother, who lived a reclusive life with three boisterous chocolate Labradors in a cottage on the edge of a Scottish loch. They had visited him once when holidaying near Inverness. Will had found the camera on a shelf and been fascinated by it. The uncle apparently never used it and sent it home with Will. From the very first photo he'd taken – a picture of his mother at the sink filling the kettle with water – he was hooked. Watching those images develop, turning from ghostly white to brilliant colour before his eyes, was like watching magic. There was something about preserving a fleeting moment for eternity that bewitched him. His mother had encouraged him, and on those days when his father was in one of his black moods, ready to fly off the handle at anything Will might do or say, she'd pack him a bag with some lunch – a cheese sandwich, an apple and, if there was some in the battered royal wedding biscuit tin, a piece of fruit cake – and send him off to take photos. On one of these trips, not far from the stream that ran through a wooded glade about half a mile from their house, he found a dead shrew. It was half covered with leaves and had been dead some time. Its eyes had rotted away or been eaten by insects and were just empty hollows, with its brown velveteen fur frayed around the socket edges like ragged fabric. Its tiny body was stiff and dry. Its feet were curled into tight balls, its mouth open a fraction to show sharp yellowed teeth. Will had taken a photo of it then sat cross-legged in the long grass and watched the picture emerge like a mirage from the whiteness. When it did he smiled; it was a brilliant photo. Everything was captured. There was even a mini-insect crawling across the shrew's shoulder that he hadn't noticed when he'd taken it. He sat beside the animal and stared at its death portrait, the sun warming him in dappled patches as it shone through the trees. Eventually, when the rumbling in his tummy became too loud to ignore, he said a solemn goodbye to the tiny corpse and walked home. He couldn't wait to show his mother the photo, but when she saw it she'd recoiled in shock.

'I hope you didn't touch it! Good God, child, you'll catch rabies or bubonic plague or something! Go and wash your hands and make sure you scrub under your nails with the soap and brush.'

His father had come up behind him and grabbed the photo before Will had a chance to hide it. Given the mood he'd been in at breakfast, Will had half-expected an impromptu hiding, but instead he rested a heavy hand on his son's shoulder. 'That's a good find,' he said. Will still remembered the astonishment he'd felt at the note of pride in his father's clipped words. 'Did you bring the thing back with you?'

'No, sir.'

'Well, run back and find it,' he barked. 'We'll leave it in a box in the shed to rot down and then I'll show you how to bleach its skull.' Then he patted his shoulder and gave it a slight squeeze. It was one of the only times he'd touched him with any sort of affection.

'Oh, Phillip!' his mother cried. 'That's revolting. I don't want him doing any such thing.'

And then his father had looked at him with a brief flash of collusion and Will had felt as if he might burst with pleasure. He dumped his rucksack and camera on the kitchen table and charged out of the house like a greyhound out of the traps. His heart hammered in his chest as he ran. He scrambled over the fence at the bottom of their garden, ignoring the sting of brambles as they tore at his legs. When he reached the glade, out of breath and lungs burning, he dropped to his knees to look for the shrew. But there was no sign of it. Will frantically searched the ground, snatching at the grass and leaves in desperation.

'Where are you?' he wailed, tears stinging his eyes.

After half an hour of searching he fell back on his haunches, sweat streaking his dusty face, and looked at the darkening sky through the trees. He would have to go home empty-handed. He pulled the Polaroid out of his pocket and stared at the picture of the shrew for a few minutes before ripping it into tiny pieces and throwing them like useless confetti into the undergrowth.

'How are your parents?' Luke asked, breaking into Will's thoughts. He picked up a frame from the small table beside him. It was another picture of Harmony, taken about ten years before. Her hair was kissed golden by the sun, fine grains of sand lay in her eyelashes and dusted her cheek, and her eyes matched the sky behind her perfectly. She smiled back at the camera, back at Will, and he recalled the sound of her laugh just before he had taken the shot. He'd told her a joke. A bad one.

'You fool,' she'd said through her giggling.

Then snap, snap, snap: three photos, one of them the best he'd ever taken. Will wished Luke would put it down; the way he looked at it unnerved him.

'My mother's well. My father died last year.'

'I'm sorry,' he said, finally taking his eyes off the photo.

'Well, we weren't close.'

'I know,' he said. 'I remember. I remember it all.'

Luke stared at him with unfaltering eyes and Will wondered if the discomfort he felt was from Luke's implied judgement or his own overwhelming shame.

CHAPTER SEVEN

Harmony stood in her towel, damp and warm from the shower, and looked in the mirror. Her heart sank a little. Age had crept up on her, sallowed her skin, folded fine wrinkles and creases around her tired-looking eyes, and dotted her hairline with grey. She sighed and rubbed some tinted moisturiser over her face, dabbed Vaseline on her lips, then applied some mascara. She went back into the bedroom and opened the wardrobe. She had no idea what she should wear.

Why do you even care? she thought.

She was surprised how nervous she felt knowing Luke was in their flat. She reached to open her top draw and then paused, hesitating, her fingers resting lightly on the drawer handle. She glanced at the bedroom door and listened. She could hear the men talking in the living room, their voices low, words indistinct. She reached into the back of the drawer and felt for the cardigan. When her fingers found the soft wool her stomach knotted. She pulled it out and held it up, brushing her thumb over the little brown teddy bear stitched to its front. She brought it up to her face and breathed in its smell, closing her eyes as she did so, pretending for a few moments her baby was back, that it was still growing inside her. She pushed it against her lips. This cardigan was the only thing she'd bought for her unborn child. She didn't believe in superstition. She was a scientist and knew better. She walked beneath ladders and thought nothing of black cats crossing her path, but even so, something had stopped her buying things for her baby. Emma had turned up a few days after Harmony told her the news, her car jam-packed with baby paraphernalia, tears of joy in her eyes. But Harmony insisted she take everything back with her; she didn't want anything to do with the baby in the house. Just in case.

'I'm sorry,' she said, trying to ease Emma's disappointment. 'It just feels wrong to jump the gun until the baby's here.'

Emma rested a hand on Harmony's arm, her head tipped forwards with concern. 'It's not jumping the gun, it's being prepared. You've got to channel the inner Girl Guide when it comes to babies. What if it comes early? Take the Moses basket and sling at least.'

But Harmony stood her ground and a disgruntled Emma had driven everything back to Oxfordshire.

Then one day she weakened. It was a crisp winter morning with a royal blue sky and brilliant sunshine that glinted off the shop windows and lit the clouds of vapour as they formed on her breath. She was happy, the type of happy that fills a person up and spills over the edges, and as she walked, stroking her hands lightly over her tummy, she couldn't keep her smile from beaming. Before she knew what she was doing she'd turned into a Baby Gap. The tiny cardigan caught her eye immediately. The wool was soft and warm and she clearly saw her baby buttoned into it and lying in her arms. It had seemed such an innocuous thing to do, to buy the cardigan that day; so easy, so inconsequential. But after her miscarriage this piece of clothing seemed to possess an almost mystical hold over her. It represented so much that should have been and, though she'd tried on numerous occasions, she couldn't bring herself to throw it away.

She breathed its smell in one last time then carefully folded it and put it back in the drawer. Just as she closed the drawer, the bedroom door opened.

'Harmony?' Will said, poking his head around the door. 'Are you nearly ready?'

'Yes, sorry, I'll be two minutes.'

He nodded and disappeared back to join Luke.

They had to talk soon. She'd make him, later, after Luke had left perhaps. It wasn't fair of him to keep avoiding the subject.

When she walked into the living room Luke stood up and placed his empty glass on the coffee table and smiled at her. His presence overpowered the room. There was a luminosity about him she imagined famous actors possessed. He seemed so out of place in her living room and she felt strangely uncomfortable.

'Would you like a glass of wine?' Will asked her.

'I'll have one with supper,' she said. 'Maybe some orange juice if we have any?'

'We do,' he said. 'Luke? Another beer? Or some wine now?'

'Yes, wine would be great,' he said.

Will left the room and Harmony and Luke stood in an awkward silence until he cleared his throat and gestured at the mantelpiece. 'I've been admiring these beautiful pictures of you.'

Harmony felt herself blush again. 'My husband's a great photographer. He can make anyone look good.'

Luke laughed. 'He said they were only good because you were a great subject.'

'He's too modest,' she said, sitting on the sofa as Luke sat down in the armchair. 'It's impossible to compliment him. A bit more self-belief would do him no harm at all.'

Will came back into the room and handed Harmony her juice and put a glass of wine on the coffee table in front of Luke. 'Do who no harm at all?'

'You,' she said. 'I'm talking about your photography.'

She saw him bristling uncomfortably.

'I was saying it would be good if you believed in yourself a bit more.'

'Right, well, I am who I am, I suppose. Anyway, Luke bought you some lovely flowers,' he said, changing the subject. 'I wasn't sure which vase to use so I put them in some water in the sink.'

'Thank you,' Harmony said to Luke. 'I love cut flowers.' He was looking at her in that way again, like he was studying her, taking in every detail, every eyelash, every mole.

'So,' said Will, as another silence took hold of them. 'How about I go and get the steaks on? I mean, if you're both hungry.' Will looked at Luke. 'How do you like your steak?'

'Let me guess,' said Harmony with a smile. 'You like your steak rare.'

'Yes. Always rare.' He leant forward and took hold of his glass of wine, his eyes locked on to hers. 'With the heart still beating if possible.'

She wrinkled her nose and shook her head.

'I presume from your face you like yours burnt to a crisp with all the guilt and flavour cooked out of it.'

'Nothing wrong with having a conscience.'

'Nothing wrong with liking your food to taste good.'

'Well, we'll beg to differ on this.' Harmony smiled. 'I was a vegetarian for years and still can't get my head around the idea of eating bleeding food.'

'And you marched against the war and you believe immigration is the basis for economic growth and cultural advancement?'

'Of course I marched,' she said, the smile falling from her face as she saw the challenge in his eyes. 'Everybody should have marched. It was an illegal war based on fabricated motive. It was an utter disgrace and yet another blot on our country to add to the catalogue of blots that litter the history books.'

Will, who was standing behind the sofa, rested his hands on her shoulders and gave her a steadying squeeze. 'Harmony has an impressive moral compass,' he said to Luke.

'Don't patronise me, Will.' She shrugged his hands off her and turned to glare at him.

'I didn't mean—' Will didn't finish his sentence. 'I wasn't patronising you.'

'There is no shame in standing up for what you believe in, in making yourself heard and sticking to your principles.'

Will drew in a sharp breath as if she'd stabbed him. 'I need to get the steaks on,' he mumbled as he backed out of the room, unable, it seemed, to get away quickly enough.

'He seems on edge,' Luke said after he'd gone. 'Do you think it's something to do with me?'

'No, of course not. At least I don't think so.' She hesitated. 'Will hasn't mentioned you before, he never talks about school. Actually, he doesn't talk about anything from his childhood. I suppose seeing you again is bringing stuff back that he doesn't want to think about.' She sighed. 'I can see he's finding it strange, unsettling even. I shouldn't have snapped at him.'

'I shouldn't be here.'

Harmony shook her head. 'No, you should. It's great that you and Will have met up again. I think it's a good thing for him. Maybe it will help; it can't be healthy to have so much bottled up inside him.' She stood. 'Are you all right for a minute or two? I might see if he needs a hand in the kitchen.'

'Of course, take your time.'

'Hey,' she said to Will as she entered the kitchen.

He was blotting the fat-marbled steaks with some kitchen roll. He was a great cook and she loved to watch him doing it. He made it seem so effortless. When she cooked it was stressful; she was far too concerned about measurements and timings, and had no natural affinity with flavours or seasoning. Will was flamboyant and experimental, loved unusual spices, and always sloshed an extra glass of wine in. But as she watched him drying the meat she noticed none of his usual enthusiasm. He was being deliberate, methodical, his face set in concentration as he pushed his fingers against the steaks. He glanced over his shoulder and tried to smile at her but didn't quite manage it. His skin had paled and he blinked at her slowly.

'I wasn't patronising you,' he said. 'I'm sorry if it came across that way.'

'I overreacted,' she said. 'I don't know why. Work's been difficult today.'

'I shouldn't have said that thing about your moral compass.' He wiped his hands on a tea towel draped over one shoulder and then reached for the pepper mill. 'I'm always saying stupid things. You should just ignore me.'

'Don't be daft. Are you okay?'

'Just need to get these steaks on.'

'No, I meant—'

'I'm fine.' He threw a couple of pinches of salt onto the steaks. 'Do you mind going back and keeping Luke company? I'm nearly done.'

She glanced back towards the living room and hesitated.

'I won't be long.'

'Everything all right?' Luke asked as she rejoined him.

'Yes, all under control.'

'I was looking at your wedding photo. You both look so young.

Did you meet at university?'

'We were at different places but met while we were both students. He was studying photography and media studies at East Anglia and I did natural sciences at Cambridge.'

She thought back to the day she met Will. He was so very different to the boys she'd been out with before; he drank wine, not beer, had longish scruffy blond hair, wore faded blue jeans and a crumpled pink shirt, and his well-bred accent was softened with a laid-back confidence. She'd have written him off as a vacuous posh boy if it hadn't been for his smile – wide and open and honest, it sucked her in from that very first moment.

'We bumped into each other. Literally. He was listening to music, not looking where he was going, of course, and I was late for a lecture and we collided.' Harmony smiled. 'My stuff went everywhere and he helped to pick it up then insisted I go to the pub with him. He was easy to talk to and I felt very relaxed with him.' Luke nodded in agreement, as if this was also his experience of Will. 'I kept wishing my mother was alive to meet him.' She smiled.

'She died when you were young?'

'I was twelve.'

'Losing someone close is incredibly hard.'

'Have you lost someone close?'

He nodded, visibly wincing with remembered grief. 'My wife. Eighteen months ago.'

'I'm so sorry. What happened?'

'She was killed in a car crash. She swerved into oncoming traffic and hit a lorry. He said she came from nowhere.'

'Oh my God,' breathed Harmony. 'How awful.'

He smiled briefly and then looked back down at his glass. His face seemed to set, his lips became tight and she could see him turning thoughts over in his head, submerged in memories. Death did that, crept up, brought unwanted recollections at the slightest trigger: a turn of phrase, a song, a smell even. Sitting there watching him quietly process his grief, she found herself thinking of her mother's death. She remembered climbing the stairs that lunchtime, carefully carrying a bowl of tomato soup, which was all her mother could eat by then, trying not to let the bright orange liquid spill. She set the bowl on the bedside table and rested a hand on her mother's bony shoulder.

'Mum?' she said softly. 'I've got your lunch.'

There'd been no movement, and as Harmony looked at her mother, lips parted as if about to speak, she realised something was different. A calm had settled over her like a fine silk cloth. Her face was relaxed, lacking its usual pained tautness. Harmony had taken hold of her hand and turned it over, traced her finger along the crease that crossed her palm, her lifeline, strong and pronounced, no breaks at all, no warning her life would end at thirty-six, a dishonest line. Then she laid her cheek on her mother's upturned hand.

'Is she dead?'

Harmony lifted her head to see her sister in the open doorway with her arms crossed. 'Yes,' Harmony said. 'I think so.'

Her sister nodded and walked over to the bed. She bent and kissed their mother's forehead, pausing for a moment, her eyes tightly closed, then she reached for the bowl of soup and without saying a word she took it back downstairs.

Harmony looked up at Luke. 'Death is hard however it comes. We were expecting my mother's for a very long time. She was in so much pain and had been for such a long time that in a way it seemed kinder for her to pass away. I still miss her, every day, even after all these years.'

Just then, Will came into the living room carrying three plates like a silver-service waiter. 'Supper,' he announced with exaggerated brightness. 'Burnt, bloody and somewhere in between.'

Harmony pushed her mother's death from her mind and stood. 'That looks delicious, Will,' she said, as she approached the table. She took a plate from him.

'This is very kind of you,' Luke said, as he came to the table and placed his wine down. 'And what a treat – steak is one of my favourites.'

Will wiped his hands on the tea towel, still slung over his shoulder, then pulled his chair out to sit down. 'I hope it tastes okay.'

Harmony looked at her husband and saw how hard he was

working to appear relaxed, how rehearsed his words were, as if he'd been in the kitchen practicing until he could talk without tripping up.

'So how did you two meet?' Harmony said as she cut into her steak. It was just how she liked it, cooked through with the slightest blush of pink in the middle.

'You know how.' Will furrowed his brow. 'At school.'

'Yes, but I wondered how you actually became friends. You seem quite different. It would be interesting to know what drew you to each other, I suppose.'

'We just met,' Will said. 'We shared a dormitory with thirty other boys. No special story.'

'But the thing that pulled us together ... you know, cemented our friendship, was pretty special, wasn't it, Will? Let's be honest now.' Luke finished his mouthful then sat back in his chair. He smiled broadly and reached for his wine.

Harmony saw her husband swallow. 'It was a long time ago. I'm not sure we need to talk about it. It wasn't the happiest of times for either of us.'

Luke laughed. 'It certainly wasn't. But what do they say? What doesn't kill you makes you stronger?'

Harmony felt Will tense. She watched him as he cut vigorously at his meat. 'The steak's a bit tough,' he said. 'I'm sorry about that. I should have let it rest a while longer.'

'Mine's perfect,' said Luke.

Will raised his head. His face was stony, his eyes hooded, and Harmony was shocked to see how angry he looked. He put his knife and fork together then pushed his plate away. 'I can't do this anymore,' he said.

'Will?'

'It's a charade, Harmony.' Then he turned on Luke. 'Don't you remember what it was like? How can you just sit there like the steak is your only care in the world, like you're interested in my photographs or how I met my wife, laughing it all off like it didn't matter?'

Harmony looked between the two men, Will's face reddening, his breathing heavy, hands clutching the table with white knuckles. And then Luke, impassive, his body relaxed, registering no surprise.

'You want me to tell you the story he's laughing about?' Will said to her suddenly.

'No, I don't—'

'You want me to go over it in all its unpleasant glory?' But then Will stopped speaking. He shook his head, pinched his nose between two fingers, and closed his eyes.

Luke leant forward and rested a hand lightly on hers. 'We knew each other, of course, from the dormitory, from lessons, but hadn't really spoken much. Then one day, Will found me tied to a homemade cross,' he said. 'Two scaffolding planks stolen from a building site.' He placed his knife and fork on his plate so they were perfectly straight beside each other. 'A group of boys made it using rope and bungees, then grabbed me after supper. They tied me to it and left me on the lawn outside the headmaster's house.' He spoke with no emotion, his face blank, intonation flat; he could just as easily have been discussing the weather forecast.

'That's appalling,' breathed Harmony. She looked at Will who shook his head slightly, his eyes closed.

Luke ran a hand through his hair. 'The headmaster came out and found me and told me to stop mucking around and get back up to the dormitory, and when my housemaster asked why I was late I was to tell him I'd been playing silly buggers and would need a caning.' Luke then stretched his arms out as if on a cross and started to laugh. The noise was disconcerting against the uneasy silence in the room. 'So there I was, hands and feet tied to this thing, lying on my back with this man shouting at me to get up.' Tears of laughter began to form in the corners of his eyes.

Harmony shifted in her seat. She glanced at Will and saw his face set in a grimace as he pushed a piece of steak fat towards the edge of his plate with the tip of his knife.

'Then Will appears,' Luke continued, his laughter fading, 'and untied me. He asked my first name. I remember that so clearly.' He looked at Will. 'We all called each other by our surnames so him wanting to know my real name felt special.' Luke smiled and looked back at Harmony. 'Will was my hero. From that moment onwards I'd have done anything for him.'

Will looked up at the ceiling and she noticed a hint of exasperation or perhaps impatience in his expression. 'A hero?' he said. 'For Christ's sake, I was just a boy who thought another boy tied to a couple of planks of wood could do with some help. I didn't do anything. I just untied the sodding ropes!'

'Will, I think—'

'For crying out loud, Harmony. Please stop it will you? Just leave it alone.'

CHAPTER EIGHT

The steak sat like concrete in the pit of Will's stomach. He remembered the panic that had coursed through him as he'd fought with the ropes and bungee cords, knots so tight he worried he'd never get into them. All the time his heart pummelled his chest, all the time ready to run if the boys or the headmaster showed up. How could Luke talk about it now with such casual disregard? Will flinched as he recalled Luke's pale skin marked with bruises from where the older boys had held him down, his trousers stained dark with urine, the tear tracks that cut through the dirt on his pinched cheeks, and how, as Will battled with those hellish knots, Luke had gazed up at him as if he was the loveliest thing he'd ever seen.

'All I was going to say is I can't believe those boys would do something like that,' Harmony said with lilting sympathy that stung Will.

'Alastair Farrow's an accountant now,' Luke said, matter-of-factly.

'Alastair Farrow?' Harmony asked.

'One of the boys who tied me to the cross.'

Will's gut twisted as anxiety flooded him and a hatred he tried to keep at bay sprung up in him.

'I found him on Facebook,' Luke went on. 'He has a wife and two children.'

Will closed his eyes and swallowed. Then he shook his head and looked at Luke. 'Why are you here?' he said. 'What do you want? I don't understand. Do I owe you an apology? Because if that's what you're here for, you can have it.'

'I don't want that.'

'Then what?' he shouted suddenly, banging his hand against the table. 'What is it you *want*?'

'Will, don't,' said Harmony.

'I should go,' Luke said, wiping his hands on his napkin and standing.

'Yes, I think you should.' Will pushed back from the table and strode out of the room.

He went into the garden and breathed deeply. He had to be stronger. He couldn't let this get to him. He sat on the edge of the terrace, elbows resting on his knees, his chin in his hands. He shouldn't have confronted him like that. He shouldn't have lost control. He shuddered at the memory of Luke tied to the cross, as he remembered the look of adoration in his desperate eyes, as he remembered what followed.

A few minutes later Harmony appeared beside him and sat down, her body pressed up against his. At first neither spoke. Then she put her hand on his leg and stroked him.

'He's gone,' she said.

He looked down and nodded slightly.

Harmony leant forward and picked a daisy from between the blades of unkempt grass and began to pull off each petal one by one. He imagined her chanting a childish rhyme: *Will he talk? Won't he? Will he talk? Won't he … ?*

Will pushed the heels of his palms into his eyes. When he'd collected himself he took a deep breath and blew sharply out as he tried to find the words he needed to tell her what he was feeling. It was so hard. It had all happened so long ago, but right now it felt like yesterday and the emotions were incredibly raw.

'The bullying was pretty bad,' Will said. The sound of his voice surprised him, as if his words had barged out of his subconscious without his consent.

Harmony moved to face him and rested her hands on his knee.

'Luke was one of those boys who should have stayed quiet, kept his head below the parapet, but he had this temper on him. Christ,' Will shook his head, 'he went mental sometimes, you know, if people teased him. And they found it hilarious so they teased him about everything – about his dad being a vicar, about his clothes, being small, his name, anything and everything – and each time he'd fly off the handle. It was like some vicious circle, the more he reacted, the more they went for him.'

Will was quiet for a moment or two remembering the speed with which Luke's anger would ignite. Sometimes the slightest jibe would set him off – screeching, stamping his feet, slamming his fists into walls.

'I was with him when he broke a window once. A boy in the year above sniggered as we walked past, about nothing much as far as I could tell, and before I knew what was going on Luke grabbed this boy's text book, tore it in half and threw it through a window, breaking the glass. Two prefects had to hold him down until he finally calmed.' Will had watched, first in horror as Luke raged and then with relief as the anger left him like an exorcised spirit, his balled fists relaxing, his breathing slowing to normal, eyes refocusing.

'I should have kept away from him. Being a friend of Luke was social suicide, but I was there, I saw them, those bastards tying him to that fucking cross, all of them laughing and jeering, like a pack of dogs on a rabbit. When … ' Will paused to draw a steadying breath. 'When they left I was about to go to him but then the headmaster turned up. He started shouting at him to stop mucking about, told him to get back to prep, didn't untie him. It was the unfairest thing I'd ever seen.' Will remembered his horror when he saw the look of spite on Drysdale's face, leering down at the child on the manicured lawn, half-naked, piss-soaked, defenceless. 'When I got over to him he was so scared he could barely breathe.'

'I can't believe it,' she whispered.

Will kicked at the ground with the heel of his shoe. 'Word got out it was me who helped him and then I became fair game.'

'What you did was the right thing to do.'

Will didn't reply. Yes, of course, she was right; at the time it was the right thing to do, the only thing to do, but if he could go back in time he knew he wouldn't do it again. He'd have left him tied to that cross so that they never became friends, never pushed their bleeding palms together, never went up to the old oak tree on that crisp October afternoon.

'It sounds like you took quite a risk helping him. And being his friend.'

'Yes,' said Will. Then he sighed. 'But, you know, he was great. He made that first year more fun. We clicked. He was incredibly bright, which didn't help, of course. Even the masters seemed to hate him for that, hated how he mucked around in class then got full marks in everything. You could see it drove them mad. And he was funny. Really funny.' Will gave an involuntary smile as he allowed himself to remember the fun he and Luke had. 'We had a laugh together. He was different to everyone else; there was something unpredictable about him. I envied him in many ways, liked how he didn't follow the crowd and how he didn't believe rules applied to him. He was ballsy.' Will looked at Harmony. 'He did amazing impersonations of our masters. He used to have me in stitches.'

Will smiled again as he remembered the genius of Luke's impressions. He'd have Will bent double and almost sick from laughing at Drysdale and his Magnificent Exploding Cane sketch or his Prof. Thomas the Chemical Car Crash, pretending to break test tubes and set the lab alight with a Bunsen burner as he bumbled blindly around. He even managed to turn his face puce like Mr Franks, their Glaswegian RE master, about to lose it because of forgotten homework.

'You forgot your PREP?!!' Luke would screech, mimicking Mr Franks perfectly, his skin turning redder and puffing up like a toad. 'If you FORGOT your PREP then we MUST all ASSUUUUME, including sweet Jesus HIMSELF, that you HAVE mushy PEAS for BRRAINNNES. You. Are. An. IMBECEEEELE!!!' And then Luke would fall to the floor writhing and twitching, chanting 'mushy peas, mushy peas, mushy peas' over and over while Will creased up with laughter, tears streaming down his aching cheeks.

'I was pretty good at taking shit, kept my cool, didn't react, and by the end of the year they'd eased up on me.' He glanced at her and kicked at the ground again. 'Bullies try and get under your skin. I found that if I built walls it helped. It's probably why I don't talk about any of it. As far as I was concerned, if I let them get to me I'd let them win. I also made sure I wasn't seen out and about with Luke too much. We'd hang out on our own in the woods behind the school instead. There was this den place we made, hidden away in the woods. We went there. Sometimes in the refectory I sat with other boys to eat.' Will felt a sudden swell of guilt as he heard those words out loud, recalling Luke's downcast eyes, resigned and abandoned, while Will sat with other boys in his year, boys he didn't like, but boys he could be seen with without risk. Luke took it on the chin. He never mentioned it, never asked to join them. It was as if he was just pleased to take whatever companionship Will was willing to give him, as if he deserved no more.

'Will?'

'Yes?'

'Why did you ask if he wanted you to say sorry?' she asked softly.

Will's stomach knotted.

'Maybe talking about it will help,' she said. 'You can tell me. I'm your wife and I want you to trust me. I hate the thought that you have secrets from me.'

'I can trust you. I do. My … ' He paused, searching his head for the right word. '… reticence to talk about it has nothing to do with you.' He heard her sigh and took hold of her hand in an attempt to reassure her.

'He doesn't seem angry or upset with you,' she said. 'He doesn't seem to have any bad feelings towards you at all. He seems fine.'

Will put his arms around her and buried his face in the warm, sweet-smelling curve of her neck, breathing her in as if she were a drug. His skin prickled. He lifted his head and kissed her. He wanted to lie her back, and on the terrace in the dying warmth of the day, make love to her. He wanted to lose himself in her – his desire, their sex, blotting Luke and everything that came with him from his head.

They sat like that for a while until eventually she made a move to stand. 'We should go in; it'll be dark soon.'

Harmony cleared the unfinished supper away and scraped the food into the bin while Will scrambled some eggs, which they ate leaning against the kitchen worktop. In bed, she pushed herself into him, her back to his chest, his arms enfolding her so he felt she was part of him. He kissed her shoulder, gently lingering, parted his lips and brushed the tip of his tongue across her skin, the slightly salty taste arousing him, the desire he'd felt in the garden returned.

'You taste beautiful,' he whispered.

He ran his hand along her arm and over her breast, kissed the sweep of her shoulder. She turned to kiss him back. When she touched him, he moaned quietly. She stroked her hand upwards and over his stomach and chest, then ran her fingers over his lips. He opened his mouth and bit her gently. She pushed a finger into his mouth and he closed his lips around her, running his tongue around the tip. They made love for the first time in a while. It was comforting and safe, each of them knowing their role to perfection, instinctively doing what the other liked, the familiar, satisfying sex of a twenty-year marriage. He adored her body – every curve, each imperfection, scar and mole. The touch of her skin excited him, and the smell of her, the real smell of her beneath the creams and lotions.

Afterwards they lay beside each other with their fingers lightly laced.

'There's something I need to tell you,' he said.

'Yes?'

His stomach churned as nerves gathered. 'Harmony,' he paused, feeling the words begin to knot in his throat. 'It's about this baby thing.'

'Baby thing?' she repeated, with a small laugh. 'Is it a thing?'

He turned his head on the pillow and looked at her in the light coming in from the hallway. 'Nothing's changed, Harmony. I wish I felt differently, but I don't. I ... I still don't want a child.'

'But why? You've never explained why.'

The words of the poem he'd memorised at fifteen echoed in his head, as poignant now as they'd been when he first read them. It was the first time a poem had touched him, the words chiming as if the writer inhabited Will's own headspace, the headspace of a boy with no relationship with his father, who had been taken from his mother, his childhood blighted at home and at school. He'd found the poem while trying to find something by Wilfred Owen for a World War One history essay. It was by a man he hadn't heard of before. A poet called Larkin. Standing alone in the library that smelt of old books and furniture polish, he read the words over and over, angrily swiping at the tears they provoked. The words were simple, accessible, not clothed in the old-fashioned pompousness of the poets he was usually forced to read. Man hands on misery, father to son. It was there in black and white, the truest thing he'd read. Don't have children, Larkin told him. Don't ever have children.

Will reached over and stroked his hand down her cheek, tucking a tress of her hair behind her ear. 'There's something I need to tell you. Something I've kept from you. I should have told you months ago.' He hesitated.

'What is it?'

'I don't know how—'

'Just tell me, Will.'

'I … ' He hesitated again. 'I had a vasectomy.'

'What?' Barely spoken, no more than a breath. 'I don't understand.'

'A vasectomy.' He reached for her hand that clutched at the duvet. 'I had a vasectomy.'

CHAPTER NINE

As his words sank in, she stared at his face, caught the weight of his pained expression, saw how his eyes wouldn't meet hers.

'Harmony?'

She didn't move. He reached over and turned his bedside light on. She closed her eyes against the brightness, against him. His words tumbled around in her mind.

Had she heard him correctly?

Disbelief muddied her thoughts, her vision. She felt lightheaded, and as she forced herself out of bed her knees gave slightly.

'You had a vasectomy,' she said. 'You had yourself sterilised?'

He didn't answer.

She walked into the bathroom and closed the door behind her. She stood in the centre of the room for a moment or two, unsure what to do, her body beginning to shiver. She reached for the towel on the rail. It was damp from her earlier shower, but she wrapped it around herself like a cape, then closed the loo seat and sat down, her head swimming as if she were drunk.

Will opened the door. He'd put some boxer shorts on, which gaped unattractively. She felt nauseous and looked away from him. He crouched beside her. Touched her knee.

'Get off me,' she whispered.

'Harmony, I—'

'Get your hand off me, Will.'

He dropped his hand from her and his head fell forward. She closed her eyes again, waves of sickness passing through her as the ramifications of what he'd done began to settle over her.

'Let me get this straight,' she said, unable to look at him. 'You went to a hospital and had a vasectomy without telling me?'

'Yes.'

She concentrated on her breathing, focused on the air passing in and out of her body. Did he have any idea of the damage he'd done? As she sat there she felt her shock turn to disbelief. She fixed her eyes on him, her brow furrowed, her head shook from side to side as she grappled with what he'd told her.

'Have you any concept of how serious this is?'

He didn't respond, just crouched there, struck dumb.

'I can't believe you'd do that.'

His face showed all the shame, all the guilt, of a scolded child. His lips were pursed and his gaze was fixed on the floor between them.

'Why would you do that?' she asked, forcing the question through gritted teeth.

'You know why,' he said. 'You know I never wanted children.'

'But we were going to have one. I was pregnant. That changed things. It must have done.'

He looked at her, his eyes flicking back and forth across her face, his head shaking almost imperceptibly.

'But you must have felt something.' she pressed. 'When it died you must have felt something. Something in you changed, surely?' She was pleading with him, pleading for him to admit some sort of emotional response, something that would reassure her he wasn't a heartless monster.

He sighed heavily, rubbed his face, then stood up and walked over to the bath. He sat on its edge. 'That's the point, I didn't. I didn't feel what you wanted me to feel, not when I found out about it and not when you lost it. I've tried to be there for you but I don't understand how you can expect me to mourn something I never felt attached to.'

Harmony closed her eyes against the anger that swelled up inside her. 'How can you be so callous?' she whispered.

'You don't understand what I'm saying.' Will paused. She opened her eyes and saw his face, twisted as if in physical pain. 'When it died … ' He hesitated. 'When it died I felt … ' He stopped himself.

'What? What did you feel?'

'Relief.'

The word hung between them, poisoning the air she breathed.

'Harmony, I didn't—'

'Fuck you.'

She dropped her face into her hands, struggling to process everything she was hearing. How could he have felt that? She took her hands from her face and stared at him, picturing his heart, black and shrivelled, in his hollow chest.

'I can't believe you didn't discuss it with me.'

'We've discussed and discussed it until we're blue in the face,' he said. 'When we got married – no, when we met – we discussed it. Christ, Harmony, you knew the score.'

'I knew the *score*?' She spat the words out of her mouth like they were battery acid.

'I never wanted children.' He squared his shoulders, looked her directly in the eyes, faced her, ready to defend himself.

She hated him then. Raw hatred. A hatred born of a wound she never imagined him capable of inflicting.

'What the hell is wrong with you?' she shouted. 'How could you do that? You and I might have made decisions years ago but things changed. We got pregnant.' She was crying now, hot tears running down her cheeks. 'You knew how I felt about our baby. You knew from the start. But then you go … and … and have a vasectomy? Without even telling me?' She paused and shook her head, pressing the edge of the towel against her eyes to blot the tears. 'I mean, shit, is it even legal to do that without my consent?'

'Your consent?' He looked genuinely surprised and she fought the urge to slap him.

'Yes,' she said. 'My consent. As your wife. Given that what you did affects me profoundly.'

'You're missing the point. This goes beyond the vasectomy. It goes far deeper. I'm not capable of being a father. I'm not capable of caring for another human being—'

'Don't be ridiculous,' she interrupted, looking at the ceiling to try and stem her tears.

'I'm not being ridiculous.' Then he got up and walked back into the bedroom. 'I don't want to have a child.'

'But I do!' she shouted after him. 'I did!'

Then she started to shake, shock taking hold of her body. She felt cold suddenly and tightened the towel around her. 'Oh my God,' she said under her breath. 'Will, what have you done to us?'

When she stood, her legs were shaky, her heart racing. She made herself walk when all she wanted to do was collapse on the floor. She took the towel off her shoulders and took her dressing gown off the hook on the back of the door. She put it on, tying the cord tightly, and then stood in the doorway and leant against the frame. He was sitting on the bed, his back facing her, shoulders hunched.

'When did you do it?'

He didn't reply.

'Will? I asked you a question. When did you do it? When I was dealing with the pain of losing our baby?'

'Not then.'

'When?'

'I went to see the doctor not long after you found out you were pregnant. I was all over the place. We had this child on the way and I didn't want to make the same mistake again; I didn't want more children.' He turned on the bed to look at her. 'I didn't want to take any more chances.'

'But you would have been unwell – there's swelling, isn't there?'

He didn't reply.

'Will! For God's sake! Tell me when you did it!'

He shook his head and rubbed his chin with his hand. 'At the beginning of December,' he said wearily. 'I told you I had the flu.'

Her mind whirred, thinking back to the week he spent in bed, tucked up in a darkened room, curtains drawn, an extra pillow. Chicken soup. A hot water bottle. 'But I looked after you,' she said. 'I phoned Frank and told him you were too ill to go into the shop.' She put her hand on her forehead. 'I gave you ibuprofen. I fed you. I … ' Her voice trailed to nothing.

'I didn't know how to tell you. I was going to, at one point, but

I kept putting it off, avoiding it, and then you had the miscarriage and, well, I didn't want to upset you any more than you were.'

She laughed bitterly and fixed her eyes on the wall. 'Well, thank you for not wanting to upset me. Thank you for your care and consideration. For your *thoughtfulness*.' She shook her head again. 'You get the prize for caring fucking husband of the year!'

'Don't shout at me.'

'Why the hell not?' A sense of finality mushroomed inside her. It was like he'd fired a machine gun at their marriage which now lay in bloodied tatters at her feet. As she stared at him she had the strange illusion of him turning into a stranger, his features becoming unfamiliar, the set of his face becoming that of someone she vaguely knew, a man with a resemblance to Will, but a man she couldn't place.

'You know,' he said, with a note of anger. 'This is nuts. You're looking at me like I'm the devil, like I've cut your heart out. You knew if you married me you wouldn't have a family. It was a sacrifice, I know that, but you made it. I was there when you agreed to it, standing beside you in the registry office, holding your hand and slipping that band of gold onto your finger.'

'Don't you throw that at me! This is way beyond will we or won't we have a child. Way beyond our marriage vows. If you want to bring marriage vows into it, how about love, cherish, honour – a marriage built on honesty? You've made a mockery of everything that day stood for, every promise you made me. And yes, you're right, I did love you enough to make that sacrifice, and it was a sacrifice, it was the hardest decision I've ever had to make. But this isn't about that day any more, can't you see that?' Tears sprung in her eyes and fell unchecked down her cheeks. 'What you've done is despicable.'

Will walked over to her then, his hands reaching out for her, but she recoiled, turned away from him so he couldn't touch her.

'When I felt our baby inside me,' she said, 'I … felt … complete. Then, when I … ' Her stomach twinged with the pain of her miscarriage. '… lost it I felt as if my world had ended, and all I wanted for was that mistake, as you call it, to happen again.'

She saw him swallow and his shoulders dip as guilt took hold, or perhaps regret.

'I wanted you to have felt it too,' she said, fighting the lump in her throat. 'I wanted you to have imagined being a father and holding your baby, and I wanted you to feel as bereft, as cheated, as I did.' She searched his face for signs of comprehension, of an empathy she now feared he didn't possess. 'I see how foolish it was now, but I just hoped you'd changed your mind.' She blotted her tears on the back of her hand. 'You *have* cut my heart out, Will. Doing what you've done, making that decision without me, taking away the option of me ever having a baby. You've cut my heart out and trodden it into the dirt.'

He moved towards her again but she pushed him away. 'I want you to leave me alone. You can sleep on the sofa. I don't want you anywhere near me.'

'We need to talk.'

She snorted bitterly. 'Oh, now we need to talk?'

'Harmony—'

'Leave me alone.'

For a moment he didn't move and she worried that he might try and approach her again. She walked past him, careful not to touch him as she did, and got into bed. She stretched across to turn the light off and then lay there, arms either side of her on top of the duvet, willing him to go.

She heard him take a breath to speak. 'Leave. Me. Alone.'

Then he left the room. She listened to his footsteps walking down the corridor. Heard him go into the living room. Heard the door close. Then it was quiet. The silence rang in her head. She felt as if she'd been driven over, stunned and confused, her head pounding at the temples. It scared her to feel this level of hatred towards her husband. She thought of her mum then, of a conversation they'd had when Harmony was about seven. She'd been crying in bed and crept downstairs and sidled into the television room where her mother was watching the news. Her mum had opened her arms and she'd climbed onto her lap and curled herself into her, burying her face in her wool sweater, reaching up to stroke the balding patch that had appeared on the side of her head.

'What the matter, petal?'

'Stupid Frankie Graham says my dad left because he didn't love me.'

Her mother had tightened her arms around her. 'Well, what does Stupid Frankie Graham know about anything anyway?'

Harmony had shrugged.

'Nothing, that's what.' She kissed the top of her head. 'Your dad loved you all the way to the moon and back.'

Harmony turned in her mum's arms and looked up at her. 'Why did he go, then?'

Her mother hadn't answered immediately, but had taken a deep breath and then finally smiled. 'Some people are like birds,' she said. 'You can't keep them caged. He needed to fly, that's all. I'd hoped he wouldn't fly too far, but sadly for us he did.'

'Do you hate him?'

'Hate him?' Her mother laughed softly and then rested her chin on top of Harmony's head. 'No, I don't hate him. I could never hate your dad. I love him and you can't turn love on and off like a tap. There's nothing he could do, even leaving, that would make me stop loving him. Just like he still loves us, whatever he does, wherever he is. You remember that next time Stupid Frankie Graham says anything daft about your dad.'

Harmony's thoughts were interrupted by a sudden wetness between her legs as Will's semen seeped out of her. She cringed as she remembered their lovemaking. Less than an hour ago, when she'd been happy, when she'd felt close to her husband and allowed herself to think about trying for a child. She recalled the way he'd kissed her, so tenderly, so full of love, but all the time he knew what he'd done, how he'd driven a stake through the heart of their marriage. She shifted her body against the discomfort she felt, pulled the sheets between her legs to dry herself. The thought of it turned her stomach; she was revolted by the dead and useless liquid, that ejaculate that tainted her body with its deceitful sterility. It was like venom inside her, and suddenly, violently, she wanted all trace of him out of her.

She got up and went to the bathroom and set the shower to as hot as she could stand, and there in the quiet darkness she stood beneath the scalding water and scrubbed herself clean of him.

When she'd finished, she wrapped herself in a dry towel and walked back into the bedroom. Then she went over to her drawers and opened the top one. She reached in and felt for the cardigan, closed her fingers tightly around its softness, pulled it out. For one last time she buried her face in it, breathing deeply, and allowed herself to cry. When she finally stopped, she walked over to the bin in the corner of the room, the pain in her stomach making each step unbearable, and dropped the tiny cardigan into it, then turned her back on it.

CHAPTER TEN

Will lay on the sofa and stared at the ceiling, picturing the cracks that crept across it, invisible in the darkness. He thought about the moment she'd told him she was pregnant. It was a Thursday morning. She was about to leave for work. He remembered it clearly, even what she was wearing – a dark navy skirt and jacket, a white shirt, her Tiffany heart, trainers on her feet, her smart-heeled 'meeting' shoes that gave her blisters in her bag for when she arrived.

'I'm pregnant.'

She'd said it just like that. Out of the blue. She was packing her briefcase with her notes, her reading glasses, an apple, and then she just stopped, both hands resting on her bag, and said it.

I'm pregnant.

There had been a quiver in her voice and when he looked at her he saw she was trembling, but her eyes gleamed and there was the promise of a smile that lit her face and turned the corners of her mouth up ever so slightly.

'I'm pregnant.'

His heart stopped.

'But how? How can you be?'

'I don't know.'

'Did you forget a pill?'

Her smile fell. 'You think I did it on purpose?'

'What? No.' Will shook his head, confused; he hadn't even considered she might do it on purpose. But then: '*Did* you do it on purpose?'

'Of course not! I wouldn't do that and I didn't miss a pill either. I've not missed a pill in eighteen years.'

'Then how?'

'I've no idea. I suppose the stats say it's only ninety-nine point-eight percent effective. I guess we're the point-two percent.'

And then Will saw the wonderment dawn on her face.

'Oh my God,' she breathed, 'I'm pregnant!'

Lying on the sofa Will rested his palms on his face. He could smell her on him and his loins stirred inappropriately as he remembered moving his body inside her. He heard the shower start in their room. She was awake still. He wondered about trying to talk to her, considered what he would say, how he would convince her he was sorry. He should have been honest from the start. That was where it all went wrong. He should have told her on that Thursday morning. It had been a mistake to let her believe he was okay with it, that he was looking forward to having a baby. He could see his mistakes so clearly now. Why had he lied?

'What are you thinking?' she'd said, as she walked over to him and placed the flat of her hand against his cheek.

Will noticed how her other hand rested on her tummy, a protective barrier between him and it. Protecting it from what? From his reaction? From his coldness? He should have said something right then, as her hand rested lightly on his face and there was under-standing in her voice. But he didn't.

'I know it's a shock,' she said, 'but … ' She broke off without finishing her sentence and her face broke into the widest of smiles. 'It's a good thing, isn't it? Don't you think? This will be good for us. It's what we need. It's fate.'

But you don't believe in fate. You're a scientist. Fate doesn't exist for you.

'I mean, I know we weren't planning it, but you're happy, right?' She rubbed his shoulders and asked him again. 'Please say something, darling. Tell me you're happy.'

Looking down at her face tilted up towards his, her eyes shining, he lied.

'Yes. I think I'm happy. A bit shocked, that's all. But I'll be fine. I just need a day or two to get my head around it.'

And then, as these lies eddied around them, as they filled her eyes with happiness, he smiled and kissed her and held her back when she threw her arms around him.

'That's good enough for now,' she whispered into his ear, before pushing away from him, her face childlike in its excitement. 'Oh, Will! We're having a baby!' Then she jumped back into his arms and kissed him again.

But would telling the truth have helped? She'd never have got rid of the baby. Then he thought about the vasectomy, about the phone call he'd made to the private hospital, the way they'd run through the details, the price, the ease of the operation, the approximate time it would take him to recover. At the time it had seemed rational. Obvious. He'd been annoyed he hadn't done it years earlier. He remembered feeling suffocated, the walls of his world inching in from all sides, the cold sweats, that agonising mistrust of himself. Those damn words, Larkin's words, ringing like a tolling bell in his ears. He'd spent every waking moment of those first few weeks trying to imagine himself with a child. He tried to be positive, told himself how it could be a good thing, how this was an opportunity he should embrace. But he hadn't been able to convince himself and his anxiety had grown until he found it difficult to eat or sleep or breathe. Yet all that time he'd put on this ridiculous mask of happiness. He smiled when she told him how wonderful it was. He pretended to listen when she read aloud from baby magazines, told him how large the foetus was, which bits of its body had developed that week, how her ankles would swell soon, how her stomach would grow until her tummy button turned inside out.

He was a coward. He always had been.

CHAPTER ELEVEN

Harmony woke later than usual, after eight. Her eyes ached from crying and lack of sleep, and she felt cold and shivery. She washed her face and dressed in black work trousers and a thick grey winter sweater. As she walked along the corridor to the kitchen, her heart pounded. She was unsure about seeing Will; remnants of last night's animosity came at her like shooting pains, a rage inside her so strong she could barely draw breath.

He was sitting at their small kitchen table. He was wearing last night's boxers and a sweater he'd taken from the dirty laundry basket. His hair was all over the place and she could tell from his puffy, tired eyes that he'd had no more sleep than she had. She wondered briefly how long he'd been out pacing the pavements. As she approached him he stood. They faced each other like nervous teenagers, both knowing they were supposed to say something, neither having the faintest clue what.

'Would you like some coffee?' he asked at last. 'I've just made a pot.' His eyes searched hers, worry written all over his face.

She nodded and he poured her a cup and added milk from the carton, then handed it to her.

'Harmony, I'm—'

'Don't,' she said, feeling her eyes well with angry tears. 'Not yet.'

Her stomach churned and her throat tightened as the kitchen grew unbearably claustrophobic. She opened the back door to let some air in. The day was duller than the last few days with a slight chill and maybe the promise of rain. She breathed in the freshness and stared out across the garden to the flats beyond their boundary. She saw the shadow of a figure walk past one of the windows.

'Do you ever ask yourself if this is it?' she said, turning to face him. Her voice was calm and level. She looked at his face intently, trying to find signs of the man she was supposed to love.

'What do you mean?'

'I mean this. Us. The flat, the shop, my work?'

'No,' he said. 'I never think that; I have everything I want.'

She narrowed her eyes at him, feeling herself fill up with spite, wanting to hurt him. 'Well, I do. I look at this place and I see a dead end.'

'Our flat?' His brow furrowed. 'But you love it, don't you?'

'No, Will, I hate it. I didn't always hate it. For a long time I thought it was perfect.'

'It still is.'

'It isn't. It's as far from perfect as it can be. We had all these plans. You remember? We were going to redecorate, apply for planning to build over the side return.' She turned and looked back across the garden. 'And then there's the garden. I mean, look at it. It's a mess.'

'I thought you liked it wild and overgrown. You said it's romantic.'

'No, Will, *you* said it's romantic. It's not romantic; it's untidy and uninspiring. I don't want to sit out there in the evenings with a glass of wine and each other for company, and I should, shouldn't I? That's what it's all about, isn't it? Looking forward to simple pleasures like that?'

She heard him draw a breath as if to speak. 'I am trapped here,' she said before he had the chance.

'Because of what I've done?' he said, his voice full of reticence, as if he didn't want to hear her answer.

'Yes. You've taken my options away. It feels like I'm stuck here with no future. Like I'm trapped against my will. Last night I was thinking, wondering why I'd been so excited about the pregnancy and why I was so desperately lost after the miscarriage. Being pregnant lifted me out of some sort of rut I was in and the miscarriage pushed me right back down.'

'You were that unhappy before the pregnancy?'

She let his question tumble around her head. It sounded odd. She'd never thought of herself as unhappy before the baby. Had she been? She trawled her mind, trying to pin down exactly what it was she'd felt. Had she been bored, maybe? Or unfulfilled? Numbed? Were these feelings real or just a reaction to the bombshell he'd dropped on her?

'All I know,' she said, picking at the edge of her thumb nail, 'is that for much of the last six months I've felt alone and uncared for, and at times it was like I've been abandoned in the middle of an ocean. And then hearing what you did, knowing you could do something like that … ' She shook her head and left the sentence unfinished.

Say something, Will, she begged silently. You need to tell me it's going to be okay. That everything is going to be okay because we have each other and because you love me.

But he said nothing.

'I need to leave,' she said. Her stomach turned over at the sound of her words. 'I can't be here.'

'What do you mean?' he asked.

She began to chew on her lip, unsure what was unfurling, unsure if she believed the words that hovered on the tip of her tongue. 'I need to leave,' she repeated. And as the reality of what was happening took root, she felt another stab of pain to her gut. She walked past him, unsteadily, and then out of the kitchen and back to their bedroom. He followed, then watched silently from the doorway as she bent to pull a suitcase from beneath the bed. She gathered clothes and flung them into the case.

'Where are you going?'

'I'm going to work and then I'll stay with Sophie.' She went into the bathroom and filled a wash bag with the things she would need. 'I have to have space to think,' she said, as she came back into the bedroom. 'And I can't do that here.'

'You can't leave. That's crazy.'

'Stop it, Will!' She turned to face him, hands on her hips. 'Did you not listen to a word I just said? It isn't crazy. If our marriage has a chance in hell of surviving I need some time away from you to think clearly.'

He walked up to her, grabbed her upper arms and held her

firmly, almost too hard. 'Don't do this.'

She noticed his eyes prickling with a suggestion of tears and her stomach clenched. Will didn't cry. He'd told her once he'd given up crying when he was a child; he said crying only made things worse, it was a luxury he'd learned to live without.

'Don't do this,' he said again.

'I haven't done this,' she said. 'You have.'

She watched his expression change from distress to panic. His eyes grew wide, darting back and forth over her face, and he bit down on his lip so hard Harmony worried he'd bite through it.

'I need space,' she whispered. 'You do too. Maybe you should go and see your mum.'

'My mum? What's my mum got to do with this?'

Harmony growled with frustration. 'I don't know! I just know that you're not doing the right thing by those of us you're supposed to love.' She sighed heavily and closed the suitcase. 'You need to sort your life out, Will. You need to start behaving like a grown-up.'

Harmony found it impossible to concentrate on work. The words swam on her screen as she read or wrote. Her thoughts kept drifting back to Will, her mind on a roller coaster as she tried to work out what she felt. She lifted the phone and dialled her sister.

'Hello?'

'It's me.'

'What's wrong?' her sister asked, immediately concerned.

'I can't talk now,' she said, glancing up as a couple of colleagues walked past her desk, deep in conversation. 'Can I stay with you tonight?'

'Of course you can. You sound awful. Do you want me to come and get you? Are you at work?'

Harmony's eyes welled. She dried her tears on the back of her sleeve. 'No, I need to try and get some stuff done here.'

When the clock finally hit six o'clock she walked down to South Kensington tube station, battling through the crowds of commuters and camera-toting tourists with her suitcase. The tube was hot and stuffy. Her head pounded. She reached into her bag for her bottle of water. The woman in front of her glared at her suitcase and muttered under her breath. Harmony closed her eyes. She hated the underground, especially in the summer, crammed shoulder to shoulder with sweaty, tired bodies, sticky skin brushing sticky skin.

Harmony wondered if she was making a mistake. Should she be heading home to face him? Was going to Sophie's the equivalent of shoving her head in the sand? She thought of him as she'd left him that morning, standing on the steps of their block, hands in pockets, grim acceptance written on his face as he watched her leave.

When Sophie opened the door of her sprawling Wandsworth home she wrapped Harmony in a tight embrace before leading her through to the kitchen. It was reassuringly chaotic, with school bags and gym kits discarded all over the place, shoes kicked off, piles of homework littering the dining table, a pan bubbling away on the hob and the noise of the boys playing football in the garden.

'It's nice to be here,' Harmony said. 'I've missed you all. I'll only be a few days.'

'Stay as long as you want,' Sophie said, and crossed the room towards the fridge. 'Glass of wine?'

Harmony nodded and her sister opened the fridge and pulled out a bottle half-full of white wine, cork pushed in the top. Harmony got two glasses out of the pine dresser that had belonged to their nan. The sight of it reminded her of happier times, before their mum died, of visits to their nan's house and the four of them eating Sunday tea together, the smell of old wood and furniture polish wafting out of the cupboard when they were asked to lay the table. Sophie sat down, tucking one leg underneath her. She wore tight-fitting jeans that hugged her long lean legs and a smart blue polo neck high against her chin, her mousy-blonde hair tied up in a loose bun, a few wisps loose and falling over her face.

Sophie leant forward and rested her hand on Harmony's. 'So what's happened?'

Ever since Harmony could remember, Sophie had been like a mother to her. She'd tried so hard to ease her grief and, even now, just being near her was comforting. After their mother's funeral, when they moved from their flat on the outskirts of Reading to their nan's terraced house in a small village south of Leeds, Harmony lost everyone and everything she knew almost overnight. Sophie became parent, sister, friend and carer, all rolled into one. It was Sophie who'd borne the brunt of their mother's long drawn-out illness, looking after her while she recovered from her bouts of chemo, and then, in those final long months, when she was unable to do anything for herself, it was Sophie who cooked and cleaned for them, who made sure Harmony did her homework and ate breakfast and left for school in a clean uniform. Their nan had been of little help; she was elderly and irascible, needed care herself, and this, too, fell on Sophie's shoulders – it was Sophie's grit that had held them all together.

'I don't even know where to begin,' Harmony said, as a couple of tears tumbled down her cheeks. She laughed helplessly. 'I'm a total mess.'

'Sweetheart,' Sophie said, squeezing and rubbing her sister's hand. 'You've been through such a traumatic thing. Losing a baby is incredibly hard. It takes time to get over something like that.'

'He had a vasectomy without telling me.'

'He did what?'

Harmony dried her eyes with the edge of her sleeve and nodded.

'And you didn't know about it?'

Harmony shook her head.

'Jesus.'

There was a noise from the hob and they both turned to see the pan boiling over, water sizzling as it hit the gas flames.

'Shit,' cried Sophie. 'The pasta.' She jumped up and ran to the hob, snatching the pan off the heat. She took the colander and drained the boiling water off. Harmony watched her sister open a cupboard above her head and rummage around amongst the chaos within for a jar of pasta sauce. She opened it, spooned some into the saucepan, then tipped the steaming pasta back in. Then she abandoned the pan on the side and came back to the table.

'Why the hell did he do it?

Harmony shrugged. 'He's always said he didn't want to have children.'

'Yes,' Sophie said with forced patience. 'I get he doesn't want kids. You explained that to me when you got together – some dead, half-drunk poet told him not to or something ridiculous – but what I'm struggling with is why on earth he got himself done without discussing it. What was he thinking?'

Harmony had a flare of loyalty for her husband, as she often did when her sister was quick to pass judgement on him. 'I don't think he was thinking rationally. He said he panicked when I got pregnant and didn't want to risk it happening again.'

'But that's insane. And I don't buy his aversion to kids anyway. He's always been amazing with the boys, even when they were babies.'

Harmony nodded. She thought of those times she'd watched him with her nephews, seen how happy and at ease he was, wondering if maybe he'd change his mind. 'He loves them,' she said, tracing her finger around the rim of her glass. 'But you have no idea how many times he's told me that when he sees them with Roger he feels inadequate. He's convinced he'd be a dreadful parent.'

'Well, he can join ninety-nine percent of all other parents then. And he's silly to feel inadequate around Roger. Roger's totally crap most of the time, he just puts on a show when there are people around.'

'Roger's a wonderful dad and you know it.' Harmony drank some wine. 'I hate how Will doubts himself like he does. In everything. It frustrates me so much. I blame his father.' She shook her head. 'That man has a lot to answer for.'

Just then they heard angry shouts from the garden. Harmony looked out of the window and saw two of her nephews rolling around on the grass exchanging hefty punches.

Sophie tutted. 'They need feeding. Let me get the pasta inside them and then we'll talk. Help yourself to more wine.' She went to the back door and called her sons in.

Harmony smiled as they piled in through the door and ran to their mother like starving animals. 'Did you say hello to Harmony?' Sophie said.

The boys looked over at her and all three grinned. Cal came over to hug her.

'Hey, Cal. How's things?' she said, wrapping her arms around her oldest nephew. He was now at least a foot taller than her and had filled out since she last saw him. Harmony patted his bicep. 'Been working out?'

Cal flushed pink and shook his head.

'He has!' screamed George, who leant against Harmony by way of a hello.

His older brother shoved him hard. 'Shut up, dickhead.'

'Language,' warned Sophie.

Harmony kissed the top of George's head. Then smiled at Matt who'd made it over to her at his own laid-back pace. He gave her a hug too and whispered in her ear. 'He has been working out. Every day before breakfast. Doing dumbbells in his room.'

'It's because he's got a girlfriend!' sang George.

Cal lunged for George but missed him, instead sending a pile of books tumbling off the table and causing George to erupt into loud giggles. Cal chased him into the kitchen area and punched him in the arm. George screamed as if he'd been stabbed.

Ignoring them completely, Sophie manoeuvred around them to get plates out of the cupboard and cutlery out of the drawer. 'Do us a favour and take your dinner next door,' she said, stabbing a fork into each mound of pasta. She pulled open a bag of ready-grated cheese and dumped a handful on each.

Harmony watched as Sophie busied about, calm amid the chaos, systematically sorting out the things they needed: ketchup, water, a few slices of cucumber. All three boys jostled and pushed and fought, and finally, loaded up with food, they went through to the playroom. A few seconds later the television switched on and it was quiet again.

'It's like a tornado blowing through,' Harmony said with a laugh. 'Can you imagine what Mum would have said if she saw the chaos here?'

Sophie laughed and grabbed a bag of crisps and a bowl. 'She was lucky. She had two neat and tidy daughters. I have three apes who can't even *spell* tidy.' She put the bowl of crisps on the table between them and sat down.

Harmony rubbed at a felt-tip pen mark on the table. 'I'm so angry with him, Sophie. I'm so bloody angry with him I can't even look at him.'

'That's natural. Anyone would be angry in the same situation. It would be odd if you weren't.'

'Do you think my marriage is over?' Harmony asked quietly, looking up at her older sister.

'Only you and Will can decide that.' Sophie stroked her hand. 'But one thing's for sure – whatever he's done, whatever his failings, he hasn't done any of it because he doesn't love you.'

'Mum loved Dad but that wasn't enough to keep them together.'

'That was different,' Sophie said, removing her hand and stiffening. 'Our father was a bastard.'

Harmony was used to the vitriol Sophie directed at their father. She'd never heard a fond word for him from her sister's lips. 'Are you sure he was such a bastard? I mean, now you're married yourself, do you think there was a side to his story that might explain him leaving like he did?'

Sophie narrowed her eyes. 'Yes, I'm sure he was a bastard. And you know what? Now I'm married and have the boys I hate him even more. It makes him leaving even harder to understand. I can't imagine my life without my children.'

Harmony looked down at the table.

'Oh, God, I'm sorry,' Sophie said. 'That was incredibly insensitive. I didn't mean—'

'It's never going to happen, is it?' Harmony covered her face with her hands. 'I'm never going to know what that feels like. Christ, he has no idea what he's done to me.'

CHAPTER TWELVE

Will couldn't find the picture he was looking for. He searched the living room, behind the chest, under the sofa. He was like a dog who'd lost the scent of its prey – fixated, growing more and more agitated as he searched. It was one of his favourites, taken on their wedding night on one of the small disposable cameras they'd left on the tables for their friends and family. When they'd had the films developed, most of the photos were out of focus, off-centred shots of drunk friends gurning at them with over-exposed ghostly skin and demonic red eyes. And then there was the picture of Harmony. He'd taken it in their hotel room right after they made love. They were laughing about something, he couldn't remember what, and he'd reached for one of the disposables that had come back with a bag of bits and pieces from the reception and pointed it at her. She'd complained, put her hands over her face to hide herself, and just as she lowered them he took the shot. Then he threw the camera back on the floor, laughed and kissed her neck.

'I love you, Mrs English.'

'Mrs English?' She wrinkled her nose. 'God, that makes me sound like your mother!'

Grainy and a little out of focus, the picture was perfection, her eyes vague with wine and tiredness and sex, her hair mussed up, mascara smudged, love and lust for him pouring out of her. There was a decadence about it, a raw sexuality, that stirred him each time he looked at it.

The flat was dark and lonely without her. He sat on the sofa and stared ahead at the mantelpiece, their paraphernalia strewn over it, the postcard bunting inappropriately cheerful. He felt as if he'd been scooped out, emptied, left hollow to his core. He closed his eyes to rest his mind but as soon as he did Luke was there.

Glaring memories of that afternoon invading his mind – the last afternoon they'd spent together, before Luke was sent away – the damp blanket of leaves beneath their feet, the sun's last light breaking through the canopy above them. Then Alastair Farrow's face as he and his friends stumbled upon them. His eyes burning with intent. The sense of dread that grew as Will realised they were in trouble. He saw the boys who stood with Farrow, fists clenched at their sides.

Will opened his eyes and shook his head to banish the memory then walked down to the kitchen. He opened the fridge door, leaning on it as he stared at the contents. There was a large chunk of cheddar that he'd bought from the deli counter in Sainsbury's for the supper with Luke. He cut himself a chunk of it, spooned some wholegrain mustard onto the plate, and poured himself a small glass of wine from the corked bottle on the sideboard. As he watched the wine fill the glass he thought of Farrow again. What was it Luke had said? He'd seen him on Facebook. A wife and two children. An accountant. Will couldn't imagine him grown up, with a life somewhere out there, going about his day-to-day business like a normal human being. Will needed to see his face. Farrow wasn't going to leave him alone. Seeing Luke had brought him back to haunt him. He needed to see him. He took his supper through to the study, waited for the computer to heave itself into life, then brought up Facebook. He logged on, closing his eyes to help him remember his password. He rarely used the account. Frank had set it up for him, horrified he wasn't using social media – a 'dinosaur', he'd called him. Will had seven Facebook friends; one was Frank and another was Harmony, who was no better than Will when it came to using it. Will had three attempts at the password before finally getting it right. He took a deep breath and typed Alastair Farrow into the search box. Eleven faces appeared. Will cast his eyes over the list and halfway down his heart skipped a beat.

There he was. Alastair Farrow.

He'd put on a lot of weight and lost some of his hair, but Will would recognise him anywhere. He clicked on the entry and

Alastair Farrow filled the screen. No privacy settings had been used, and his whole life was on view: photos, comments, personal information. Alastair Farrow. Born 1968. Lives in Surrey. School: Farringdon Hall. Married. Works at Hammerson Frith Accountancy.

Will clicked on a photo album. They were holiday snaps; somewhere in the Mediterranean, Will guessed. He was with his children, or at least Will assumed they were his children. The first photo showed him in a swimming pool, a young girl with dimpled knees on his shoulders, next to him a boy, a few years older, with chocolate ice cream all over his face, and a dumpy wife with a toothy camera smile. The next picture showed Farrow and his wife raising orange cocktails overladen with colourful paper umbrellas and slices of pineapple towards the photographer. They were sunburnt, the light reflecting off their reddened faces to give their tight-looking skin a polished sheen. Will stared at the faint scar that ran from Farrow's cheekbone to his jaw. He felt sick as he heard the blood-curdling scream echo in his head. He wondered what story he'd told his wife to explain the scar. He'd bet all the money in the world he hadn't told her the truth.

Will tore his eyes off the scar and began to read Farrow's timeline, the vacuous everyday status updates of a normal man, with a normal family, a normal life.

Status update: Kids and wife badgering me to get a dog. I don't want a dog. Will they settle for a goldfish instead?

Comment from Diane Farrow: Labrador puppy or we're leaving en masse. ;)

Status update: Rugby with the boys on Sunday. Can't wait. Bring it on!!!

Status update: Son turned five. How did this happen? Party on Saturday with twenty kids and a bouncy castle in the garden. A & E expect a visit!

And so it went on. Will drained his wine then spent the next few hours poring over Alastair Farrow's albums, reading about his wife, opening the pictures of each of his friends, reading their details, piecing together his life. It was all so anodyne, so conventional. Over the years Will had Farrow in mind as this towering figure, a ten-foot nemesis, the epitome of evil, but here he was, a podgy, balding father of two with a jolly wife and a modest home with a neat front garden in suburban Surrey.

Will moved his cursor over the *Add Friend* button and hovered there.

'No,' he said aloud, his voice stark against the stillness of the study. 'Don't.'

But then, as if someone had moved his hand for him, he pressed send.

Friend Request Sent.

'Bloody hell,' said Will, as he sat back and rubbed his face. 'Why did you do that?'

Will sat in the dead silence and closed his eyes. He saw the silhouette of Alastair Farrow's face burnt on to the back of his eyelids, a ghostly retinal scar. He opened his eyes quickly and then leant forward and turned the computer off.

The phone rang, piercing the silence. He snatched at the receiver.

'Harmony?' he said urgently.

'No. No, it's not Harmony, William. It's Frank.'

Will's heart sank. 'Hi, Frank. Is everything okay?'

'Um, well, that's the thing,' said Frank, his voice shaky and faint. 'I don't think it is. You see, Eric's away, being important at a writer's retreat or something, and … ' He broke off and Will heard him take a steadying breath. 'Well, it's Pinwheel. He's had a little accident … ' He didn't finish his sentence.

'Do you need me to come over and help?'

'I don't want to put you to any trouble,' said Frank, so quietly Will could only just hear him. 'But the poor darling is in a bit of a state, and I, well, he needs a vet. It's his leg. Oh dear, I'm not very good at coping with things like this.'

'I'm on my way,' said Will. 'You sit tight. I'll be as quick as I can.'

Will grabbed his keys from the hook by the door and went out to the car. Frank and Eric lived in Chiswick, which was about fifteen minutes away without traffic, in a pretty mews house with lilac-painted woodwork. When Will pulled up outside he saw Frank, hovering anxiously on the doorstep, pale-faced and jittery.

'I think he's going to be fine,' Frank said, as Will got out of the car. 'I hope I haven't got you here under false pretences.'

Will's heart went out to him and he rubbed his shoulder. 'Don't be silly. Harmony's out tonight. I wasn't busy. Let's have a look at him, eh?'

'Yes, yes, thank you. I'd appreciate that,' he said, with a slight hesitation. 'The vet has an out-of-hours surgery. I should probably have called a taxi and gone straight there rather than bother you.' Frank smiled weakly at him.

'It's no bother at all. Now where's the patient?'

Will followed Frank as he walked slowly into the kitchen. 'Eric normally deals with this sort of thing. He's absolutely super in traumatic situations. He knows just what to do and has this amazing sense of calm about him. I get in all of a dither. I hope my boy is going to be all right. He seems terribly quiet.'

Frank led Will to where Pinwheel lay wrapped in a soft blue towel on a cushion on the kitchen table. The cat's eyes were open but he wasn't moving, his tongue lolled from the side of his mouth and Will could hear how laboured his breathing was.

'I found him on the side of the main road,' whispered Frank. 'I was calling and calling for him, but he didn't come in. He usually comes at my first call; he's terribly greedy, you see.' Frank had one hand against his mouth and he nibbled on his thumbnail as he spoke. 'He couldn't get to me, because, well, he's hurt his leg.'

Will lifted the edge of the towel to look at the cat and winced. One of its hind legs was badly broken, blood and dirt matted its fur and the jagged bone pushed through the wound. But it wasn't the leg Will was worried about. Pinwheel's back looked broken too, with an unnatural curve to it. He laid the towel back on the cat and gently ran his fingers over his head. Pinwheel blinked slowly.

'Poor thing,' Will said under his breath. 'Let's get you to a vet, shall we?'

Will carefully picked Pinwheel up. The cat mewed and his

small body tensed. 'It's okay, sweetheart. We're taking you to the vet. You'll feel better in a bit.' Then Will looked at Frank. 'You'll be all right to hold him while I drive?'

Frank nodded.

Frank directed Will to the vet's surgery, but other than that they didn't talk. Will glanced over every now and then to see Frank cradling Pinwheel like a baby, his eyes shining with a film of tears. He parked at the back of the surgery in the small, scruffy car park filled with rubbish and overflowing wheelie bins, and aggressive signs threatening clamping for unauthorised cars.

A young girl answered the door when they rang. 'Is this Pinwheel?' she asked.

Will nodded. 'He looks like he's been hit by a car.'

'Take a seat,' she said, gesturing to some wooden chairs in the window. 'Stephanie will be with you in a minute.'

They sat and waited in the reception area. It was quiet and still and smelt of animals and surgical spirit. The shelves were crammed with sacks of pet food, plastic animal toys, leads, collars, muzzles, and the noticeboard was covered with photographs of past patients who'd made fabulous recoveries and information posters on fleas. Will looked at Pinwheel; his eyes were closed now but he was still breathing, though with more irregularity and an ominous rattle that came every now and then from his chest.

'Would you like to bring Pinwheel though?' said the vet as she came into the waiting room. Will stood but Frank didn't move.

'Come on, Frank,' Will said gently.

As soon as the vet looked at Pinwheel, Will knew she wasn't going to give them good news. There was a look of genuine regret on her face, but either because she had to or because she thought it would be best for Frank, she went through the motions of checking the cat over, listening to his chest, taking his temperature, feeling his stomach. She put a pair of silicone gloves on and then, very gently, investigated the wound. Then she stroked the cat and removed her gloves.

'I'm afraid it isn't good. It sounds to me as if his lung is punctured and obviously his leg is badly damaged, his pelvis is broken in several places, and I'm afraid his back is also broken, though I can't say for sure how badly without x-raying it. There appears to be no reflex in his legs, which indicates damage to the spinal cord. I'm certain there's nothing I can do for him. I'd prefer not to put him through any more discomfort by having an x-ray taken.' Here she paused, looking from Will to Frank. 'It's very much your decision. I will x-ray if you'd like me to, but perhaps you should consider—'

Her sentence was interrupted by a moan from Frank. Will jumped at the noise, loud and strangled, and looked at Frank, whose face was twisted into a pained grimace. Will put his arm around him and stroked him.

'There must be something we can do?'

The pain in Frank's voice cut through Will, who glanced at the vet. 'Is there?' he asked her.

'The damage is extreme,' she said, shaking her head. 'I could amputate the leg and set his pelvis, but he's almost certainly paralysed in his back end. He wouldn't have the strength to move himself around, he wouldn't be able to go to the toilet or walk. His quality of life would be greatly compromised.' She paused and shook her head. 'Then, of course, there's his lung.' She exchanged a look with Will that suggested there was no hope. 'I hate putting animals to sleep and really, we do this as the very last option in all cases, but with Pinwheel … ' She left the sentence hanging.

Will nodded and then turned to Frank. 'He's had an amazing life with you and Eric. The very best an animal could wish for. It's the kindest thing. It really is.'

As Will spoke, Frank leant down and pushed his face into the cat's fur. A few moments later he lifted his head and looked at the vet and nodded.

'It will take me a few minutes to get things ready.' She put a hand on Frank's shoulder. 'Do you want to be here with him while I do it?' she asked gently.

Frank couldn't speak but nodded again.

'We'll both stay,' said Will, reaching for Frank's hand.

On the way home Frank stared out of the window, no doubt

reliving the euthanasia. It had been awful to watch, Frank cradling Pinwheel in his arms, whispering apologies, his tears soaking the cat's soft fur as the vet injected the lethal blue liquid to still his heart. When they arrived back at Frank's house, Will turned the engine off and they sat in the car in silence for a few minutes.

Eventually, Frank spoke, his voice distant and soft. 'Have you ever had a pet, William?'

Will didn't answer straight away. It was something he'd never talked about, not even to Harmony. 'A long time ago,' he said. 'A cat too.'

'Were you sad when he died?'

Will tensed and hesitated. 'It was a she, and yes, I was. Very.'

'But you have good memories of her?'

'Lots.'

'Tell me about her.'

Will stared at his hands on the steering wheel. 'I found her in a disused farm building amongst some rotten straw bales. I was taking photos and heard this faint mewing. I followed the noise and there she was, between two bales, her little feet pressed together and these big blue eyes looking up at me. I picked her up and she started to purr immediately.' Will felt his stomach knot as he remembered the kitten. How she'd batted his fingers and pounced on his shoelace when he'd waggled it on the ground like a snake for her. 'I looked for her mother but there was no sign. I think she'd been abandoned. I couldn't leave her there alone, she looked so helpless, so I tucked her into my jacket and took her home.'

Frank nodded. 'I would have done the same. You couldn't have left her, the foxes would have had her in no time.'

'My father hated animals, especially animals in the house, so I was sure he'd say she couldn't stay, but he happened to have seen a rat that morning and my mother suggested she might be useful in keeping them away. Anyway, he said yes. I couldn't believe it. I'd wanted a pet for years, I was an only child and was mostly very lonely.' Will looked at Frank. 'She wasn't allowed in the house though. I had to promise she would stay in the shed. Mum and I found a cardboard box and we cut a bit of one side out so she could get in and out, and got some old towels for blankets.'

'What was her name?'

'I called her Socks because of her little white feet. She used to wait for me by the garden gate if I went out and as soon as she saw me, she'd scamper over and wrap herself around my legs, purring like mad.'

'No wonder you were sad when she died.'

'Yes, I was. It was awful.'

Will didn't tell Frank any more. Not about the day she died, that day in early January, so bitterly cold the river had frozen over. He'd gone out to the shed to see Socks and found her curled up in the corner of her box. She was shivering and when he came in she didn't get up as normal, but stayed in a ball, her eyes flicking upwards at him, just a single mew the only noise she made. It was arctic in the shed, with swirls of thick frost on the inside of the window pane, and the air so cold it stung his lungs.

'It's too cold for you out here, isn't it little girl? Don't worry, I'm here now.'

He picked her up, then hesitated – his father would hit the roof if he found her in the house. But then he caught sight of the frozen water in her bowl and without thinking any more he hid her under his jumper and walked back to the house where his parents were watching television.

'I'm not feeling too well,' he said as he walked past the door to the living room. 'I'm going to go up to bed. Good night.' Then he went up the stairs, keeping his eyes to the floor, praying his father wouldn't notice anything unusual, and once inside his bedroom, he closed the door.

'Right, you,' Will said, lifting his jumper up and putting Socks on his bed. 'Not a peep, okay? You can sleep under my duvet tonight. It'll be like a den for you. You'll be toasty warm.'

He stroked her head and she stood up on her hind legs to meet his hand, purring, and rubbing her nose and cheek against him. He undressed, put his pyjamas on, then, needing to use the bathroom, he opened the door to his room. He jumped out of his skin to see his father standing outside it. He pulled the door shut behind him, and keeping his hands on the door knob, looked up at him. His father blinked slowly and stared, his mouth twitching at the sides.

'Is everything all right?' Will asked him, trying to keep his voice light.

'What are you hiding?'

'Nothing.' He dropped his hands from the door handle. 'I'm just going to clean my teeth and then I'm going to bed. I'm not feeling very well.'

'You're hiding something, William. Don't lie to me. You know if you lie it only ever makes things worse.'

Will swallowed. What should he do? Lie or tell the truth? If he lied and then his father found the cat he'd go mental. 'My cat,' he stammered. 'She was so cold. I bought her in to warm her ... '

His father stared at him as if he was speaking a foreign language. Then without a word he opened the door. Will dived in front of him, putting himself between his father and the cat, who was sitting on the bed, licking her paw, cleaning herself. His father glared at him.

'Get out of my way,' he said.

'She was cold!' Will said, opening his arms wide to stop his father's advance on Socks. But his father pushed him aside and grabbed her by the scruff of her neck. He held her up, pushed her towards Will's face. She squirmed in his grasp.

'What is this animal doing in my house?'

Will tried to speak but his voice failed him.

'Answer me, you idiot! I asked you a bloody question!'

Will watched his father's hand squeeze into the cat. The cat screeched.

'Stop it!' Will shouted. 'You're hurting her. She was just cold! You're hurting her!'

His mother came up the stairs. 'Phillip?'

'The boy brought this bag of fleas into my house. He told me there was nothing in his room. He's a bloody liar.' With each word his father shook the cat, who was writhing in his hands, the whites of her eyes showing.

'No, I didn't lie. I—'

'The bloody cat should be out-bloody-side!'

'It's all right,' his mother said calmly. Will looked at her, and she opened her eyes wide at him, trying to communicate, nodding with purpose. 'William's sorry, aren't you, William?' She continued to nod at him slowly. 'He'll take the cat back to the shed.'

Will shook his head. 'But it's too—'

'Won't you, William?' Her voice barked at him with a level of sharpness he seldom heard. She stared at him, willing him to take her lead. 'It's best that cats live outside, and she likes her shed.'

Will glanced at his father who seemed to have relaxed a little. He'd stopped shaking Socks and she had stopped twisting and turning, and hung in his hand like a rag doll instead.

'I'm sorry I bought her inside.'

His father held the cat up to his face and looked at her. 'I saw a rat again a couple of days ago. If this thing doesn't get rid of them it's gone. You hear me?' He gave the cat a final shake, and then, from nowhere, Socks put her ears back and hissed at him, swiping at his face, her claws bared.

His father yelled and before Will could do anything he'd hurled Socks at the wall. The thump of the impact of cat against wall reverberated around them. Will screamed and ran to Socks, but his father clamped his hand on Will's shoulder and yanked him out of the way. He watched in horror as his cat lay on the landing, dazed and struggling to get to her feet. His father lifted his foot. Will screamed.

His mother ran up to his father and rested an arm on his. 'No, Phillip. Don't.' His eyes rounded on his wife and Will noticed three faint scratches streaking his top lip.

'How dare you tell me what to do!'

Then he raised his foot and powered it into Socks, sending her tumbling down the stairs. Will ran to the banister to see her bouncing down the last step. He pushed past his father and leapt down the stairs two at a time and fell to his knees at the bottom. There was a thin trail of blood from the cat's nose and her eyes were open and staring. She was totally still, not breathing, unresponsive when he touched her.

'You've killed her,' he said, as his father came down the stairs. 'You killed my cat.'

His father wiped at the scratches on his lip with a handkerchief. 'I didn't kill it. You did. If you'd kept it in the shed, like you agreed to, it would still be alive.' And then he walked away from them, into the living room and switched the television back on.

Will picked up his cat, her body limp and lifeless in his arms.

'I'll get our coats,' said his mother without emotion. 'We'll bury her.'

But the ground had been too hard for either he or his mother to dig, so they wrapped Socks in newspaper and left her in the shed. The following day a noise woke him in the garden. It was only just light and the world was frozen. He knelt on his bed and stared out of his window, his breath blooming and fading on the icy pane. His mother was standing in her boots and a heavy grey overcoat prodding a fire in the galvanised incinerator. Will watched her bend down and pick up the roll of newspaper with Socks inside. She dropped it into the fire, then put the lid on. When she turned around Will saw she was crying. He'd never seen her cry before.

Will got out of the car and went around to open the door for Frank. 'Do you want me to sleep on the sofa tonight, Frank? I'm not sure you should be alone.'

'Bless you. I'm fine, though. I've got Pie to look after me.'

Will took him inside, and while Frank got ready for bed he made him hot chocolate and then carried it up to his room. He was already in bed with Pie curled up beside him.

'Did I do enough?' Frank asked.

'Yes,' Will answered. He placed the hot mug on the table beside the bed. 'You did everything you could. There was nothing more you could have done.'

Frank nodded and stroked Pie. The cat arched his back and stretched his paws out in front of him. 'He'll miss Pinwheel,' Frank said sadly, stroking him again.

'He's got you,' said Will. 'And Eric. You'll call if you need me, won't you? I don't mind what time.'

'Thank you, William. I couldn't have done that on my own.'

As Will drove home his head was full of his cat and what his father had done to her. It made him sick to think of her, so vulnerable and dependent on him. How could Harmony expect him to have a child? It terrified him. Just the thought of being responsible for a baby made him feel weak. He was incapable of looking after anything, he always had been. That would never change.

CHAPTER THIRTEEN

Harmony watched the clock limp around to six to signal the end of another unproductive day at work. She leant forward and wearily turned off her computer then packed her papers into her bag in the vain hope that she would manage to get some work done at home. Will hadn't called since Tuesday evening. Before then he'd been calling every few hours, and in the end she'd texted to ask him to give her the space she needed. She'd hesitated before sending it; she knew she couldn't hide from him forever, but she was still so angry and hurt, so full of regret. She felt utterly betrayed by him.

'See you tomorrow, Alice,' she said to the department PA, who was cleaning her gold-rimmed glasses on the sleeve of her cardigan.

'Will do. You make sure you try and get an early night tonight.' She smiled kindly. 'You look exhausted.'

No wonder I look exhausted, Harmony thought. Trying to sleep in George's narrow bed, surrounded by Lego constructions and *Star Wars* figures with her mind racing was near impossible. She walked down the stairwell and into the building's reception area. In the main entrance lobby she saw a man sitting on the sofa, reading a newspaper. As she neared him, he lowered the paper and looked up at her and smiled. Her heart skipped a beat.

It was Luke.

'Oh my God, hello,' she said, unable to mask her surprise.

She walked over to him and he stood up, still smiling broadly. There was an awkward hesitation during which she wondered if they were supposed to kiss or shake hands. In the end she did neither.

'What are you doing here?'

'I had a meeting in Knightsbridge that finished early and it's too late to go back to the office now, so I thought I'd pop in and say hello.' He paused then smiled again. 'It's nice to see you.'

She blushed and glanced at the man behind the reception desk who was casually flicking through a car magazine. 'It's nice to see you too,' she said looking back at him. 'How did you know I was here? I mean, how did you know where I worked?'

'You said. At lunch.'

'Yes. I suppose I did. But sometimes I work from home, or have meetings off-site.'

'Well, I asked this gentleman if you were in today and he rang up to your office,' he said with wry amusement. 'Nothing more sinister than that; you don't have to look so worried. I passed Imperial in the cab on my way to the meeting and then remembered that you worked opposite and thought it might be nice to go for a drink.'

She tried to smile.

'So have you got an hour or do you have to race home?'

'No, I can't stay. I should get back.'

He leant closer to her. 'I'd like you to come.' She caught the smell of him, fresh with a hint of aftershave over a natural mustiness that quickened her pulse. 'And it's Friday tomorrow. It's nearly the weekend. An after-work drink to celebrate?'

'I'm staying at my sister's. She's expecting me back.'

'Your sister's?'

Harmony didn't say anything.

'Look, I'm here now – just a quick drink.'

She hesitated and looked at her watch. It was ten past six; it would be chaos at Sophie's when she got there, the boys would be midway through eating, they'd be fighting, the television would be blaring, then Sophie would be trying to get them to do their homework, shouting as all three did their best to avoid doing it.

Luke saw her indecision and seemed to take that as a yes. 'Good,' he said. 'There's a great restaurant a few minutes' walk away. It's smart but very laid back. You'll like it.'

'I can't stay for dinner.'

Luke laughed. 'Don't panic. Just a drink.' He smiled and gestured for her to walk in front of him.

What are you doing? a voice in her head demanded as they

walked down the steps and turned left onto Exhibition Road. Go back to Sophie's, ring Will, sort your life out. Oh, ignore her, said another voice. It's fine. It's a drink. God knows, you could do with one.

As they walked she was conscious of him glancing at her every now and then. She wondered if people assumed he was her husband as he guided her through the crowds, close beside her, every now and then touching her shoulder. She turned to give him a casual, friendly smile to reassure herself she was doing nothing illicit. He nodded and smiled back – a simple, easy smile. Nothing untoward at all. You're being silly, she told herself. What's wrong with you around this man?

'Here we are,' said Luke. The restaurant was on a side street, with a few tables set out on the pavement, menus, glass jars of golden olive oil and small white bowls of sea salt on each one.

Luke held open the door and allowed her to walk into the restaurant first. She knew of the place, but she had never been before. It was expensive, the haunt of minor celebrities, MPs and glamorous, designer-clad twenty-somethings. A waiter with jet-black hair and doleful eyes welcomed them, nodding his head in exaggerated hospitality, his greeting almost unintelligible beneath a thick Spanish accent. The main restaurant was dark and cosy but steps at the far end led down to an airy conservatory-style area. There were murals on the walls of curling vegetation and oversized flowers. Harmony felt like a screw in a box of nails beside the sophisticated men and women talking and laughing animatedly, dressed in expensive clothes with glistening hair, a world away from her knee-length black skirt and ponytail secured neatly at the nape of her neck. The opulence unsettled her, made her feel insignificant, insecure. Until her mum died they'd lived in the cramped second-floor flat on the Park Green estate in Reading. Her abiding memory of the place was the threadbare carpet with its garish Seventies pattern of black flowers on a red background. When their mother became too weak to get out of bed, she'd ask them every now and then to 'tidy the carpet', and the two girls would get down on their hands and knees and colour in any new patches of wear with black felt-tip pens.

'I don't see why we have to do this,' Harmony would grumble as she lay flat on her tummy, legs kicked up behind her, searching for hessian strands to blacken. 'I mean, it's not as if anyone ever comes to visit. You'd think the Queen or Princess What's-her-name was coming for tea.'

'Anne,' her sister said, as she busily coloured.

'Yes, her, Princess Anne, the one with the hair. She's not coming though, nobody comes, only the nurse, and I doubt she can even see the floor, her stomach's so massive.'

'Mum's dying, Harmony. She wants lots of different things, like soup instead of beans on toast, and three sugars in her tea, and if she wants the carpet coloured in then that's what we'll do.' She pointed at the floor beneath Harmony's elbow. 'You missed a bit.'

'Table for two?' the waiter asked Luke in his Spanish lilt.

'We're not eating,' Luke said. 'We've just come for a drink.'

'Certainly, sir. Would you like to sit at the bar?' He gestured to the other side of the room where there was a dark wood bar with mirrors behind and a row of empty leather stools.

Harmony asked the barman what white wines he had by the glass. He recommended a white Rioja with enthusiasm. She thought of Will, who wasn't fond of Spanish whites.

'That sounds lovely,' she said. 'A large glass of the Rioja.'

'And I'll have a beer,' Luke said.

They were quiet as the barman prepared their drinks. Harmony shifted in her seat, glancing up at Luke to give an embarrassed smile as she tried to think of something to talk about. The barman put their drinks and a dish of almonds on the bar in front of them.

'Thank you,' Luke said. Then he lifted his drink to her. 'Cheers.'

Harmony clinked her glass against his. She noticed how long and slim his fingers were, his nails cut short and clean. They reminded her of her father's fingers, or at least how her mother had described her father's fingers – long and graceful like a concert pianist's.

'Your dad had the most beautiful hands,' she heard her mother saying.

Luke smiled at her, his eyes burning through her to the point

127

where she had to look away. As she did, she noticed the woman on a table nearby staring at Luke while the man she was with stared at his newspaper. When she realised Harmony was looking she glanced away, the skin on the back of her neck reddening as she stirred her drink.

'So are you and Will okay?' he said, taking a small handful of almonds.

'Will and I?'

He nodded and put an almond in his mouth.

'Yes,' she said, trying to keep her voice light. 'Yes, of course. Why?'

'Things were … ' he hesitated, 'strained the other night, and you said you're staying at your sister's. And there's also something about you today. You seem … ' he paused. 'Sad.'

Harmony was aware of her body tensing. She lifted her chin and shifted her weight on the stool. 'That doesn't mean there's anything wrong. I'm staying with my sister for a few days; we're close and I haven't seen her for ages.'

'I see. I've drawn the wrong conclusions. Forgive me.'

She was about to agree but something stopped her. She sighed. 'No, you're right.' She picked at the edge of the scallop-edged drinks mat that sat beneath her wine glass. 'We're having a few problems. It's been a difficult six months.' She hesitated and glanced up at him. 'I lost a baby and it's making life hard to deal with for both of us for different reasons.'

'I'm sorry,' he said. 'Losing a child is devastating, I know what it feels like.'

'You do?' she said.

'Yes.' His brow furrowed and he swallowed. 'You and Will must be going through all sorts of emotions.'

A lump rose in her throat. 'I am. I'm not sure he is.' She tried to banish the memory of Will telling her he was relieved when the baby died. 'Actually, do you mind if we don't talk about it?'

He nodded and touched her knee lightly. 'Of course not. I'm not interested in talking about Will.' He paused. 'It's you I'm interested in.'

'Me?'

'Do you ever get the feeling you're supposed to be with someone? That it's an imperative?' He leant forward, his face only a few inches from hers. 'Because that's how I feel about you, Harmony. I want to be with you. I want to fuck you. Very much.'

Harmony reeled at his words. She drew back from him, unsure if he was joking, but the look on his face was deadly serious and any comfort she'd felt in his company evaporated. Her stomach lurched. 'Don't say that,' she said. 'You can't say that. I'm married.' She felt as if people were watching them and glanced at the woman who'd been staring at Luke, but she was now occupied with her iPhone, while the man she was with was still absorbed by his paper. Harmony reached down for her bag. 'You told me you just wanted a drink.' Her voice was shaky. She pulled her jacket tighter around her.

'I wasn't entirely truthful.'

'I'm married, Luke.'

'But not happily.'

'I have to go.' Harmony stood, angry at his presumption, angry that she couldn't snap back and tell him how wildly happy she and Will were. 'It was wrong of me to come.'

Luke grabbed hold of her above the elbow.

Her heart pounded. 'Let go of me.'

'I know you feel it. You felt it that night at the party. I know it from the way you look at me, the way you act around me. I can read you like a book.'

Harmony didn't know what to say. Her cheeks felt hot and her mouth dry. She was embarrassed, mortified she'd been that obvious, annoyed she hadn't done more to hide her attraction, her fascination.

He brought his face close to hers, his mouth near her ear, his breath hot against the side of her face. 'You're inside my head.'

He eased his grip on her. She felt faint. Her head pounded with a mix of emotions, the nerves and vulnerability vying with excitement and a sudden feeling of empowerment. The bar, the other people enjoying themselves, the waiters shouting orders, the clatter of plates, all of it faded into the background. Heat pulsed through her. All she needed to do was move her face a fraction closer, lift her chin, and press her lips against his.

Will's face flashed into her mind.

'I have to go,' she whispered.

'Don't go.'

She turned her face to look at him. His eyes locked on hers. She felt herself weaken for a fraction of a second. No! a voice in her head screamed. For God's sake what are you doing? She closed her eyes and lifted her hand, placed it flat against Luke, briefly felt the hardness of his chest, the heat of him beneath his cotton shirt, then pushed him away from her.

'I have to go,' she repeated.

'Because of Will?'

'Yes,' she said. 'Because of Will. I'm married to him. I shouldn't be here.'

'Desiring something shows you're alive, Harmony. You don't have to feel guilt. Without desire we might as well be dead. Desire is our fuel. To live without desiring, without wanting, is to deny your humanity, and God knows how fleeting life is. Never deny yourself pleasure. There's so much shit in the world, these moments of pleasure are like gold dust.'

Harmony felt her chest tightening as if a vice was slowly squeezing the air from her lungs.

'Look at them,' he whispered. He turned her head gently in the direction of the couple at the table near them. She looked at them, the woman on her iPhone, the man with his newspaper. 'They're not old,' Luke said. 'They're married, yet they've run out of things to say to each other. They are in this beautiful restaurant and she's looking at other men, bored and disappointed, wondering why she's there, while he reads *The Times* vacancy pages, idly flitting over everything. He's wearing a grey suit, has grey skin, grey hair, sitting with a wife he's not interested in, dreaming of a job he hasn't the guts to go out and get. Is that what you want? To be too scared to make changes that would make you happier? I want you, Harmony. I want to fuck you, to taste you. I want to be with you in a way that other people can't be with you.'

Harmony breathed heavily, intoxicated by his words, feeling herself weaken with every syllable. Will's face came into her head again. She closed her thumb on her wedding ring, felt its hardness against her skin. 'Christ, what am I doing?' she whispered.

She grabbed her bag and ran through the restaurant away from him, pushing out through the door and onto the pavement. She walked quickly down towards the Cromwell Road, shaking her head, cursing herself for accepting his invitation, for putting herself in that position.

She heard footsteps behind her and looked over her shoulder to see him striding after her.

'Don't follow me,' she said, picking up her pace. 'You've got to leave me alone.'

He drew up beside her and took hold of her arm to turn her to face him. 'Harmony—'

'No, Luke. I'm married.'

Luke looked up at the sky. He seemed annoyed, frustrated even. When he fixed his eyes on her again, they narrowed. 'But you want me.' He stared at her. 'I'm right, aren't I?'

'No, you're not *right*. Who the hell do you think you are to draw all these conclusions?' She was cross with herself. Cross for opening herself up to him, for indulging such juvenile feelings of lust and attraction, for falling for his playboy looks like a teenage girl. She'd met him three times and there she was, tempted to do something stupid, something that would seal the fate of a marriage that already hung in the balance.

She turned away from him and started to walk back down to the main road. When she reached it she looked left and right for a taxi. There were none and she swore. 'I need a cab,' she whispered. 'For God's sake, I need a cab.'

'Don't go.'

He was beside her. She turned and they faced each other. 'I know you're not telling me the truth,' he said. 'I know you feel it too.' She noticed a fragility about him, an innocence even, that belied his boldness.

'Luke,' she said, hesitating. She threw her head back and sighed.

'I feel it, okay? I feel it.' She paused and shook her head. 'But it can't happen.'

He didn't reply.

'Do you understand? We can't be anything more than friends.'

They stood on the street, people walking past them, unaware of them.

'That's not enough. I don't want to be friends. Being your friend doesn't interest me.'

Harmony didn't know what to say. Like a chameleon he'd changed again. The vulnerability she'd noticed had vanished, replaced with a rawness, that pulsing sexuality that both scared and excited her. She'd only ever desired Will before now, her desire inextricably linked to love, to one man, a man she knew, who made her laugh and lifted her spirits, whose happy-go-lucky attitude brought her out of her diffident self. But this man standing in front of her looked at her in a way she didn't think possible. His demeanour was calm and measured, but there was a searing passion in his restraint.

'We have one life,' he said. 'Fate brought us together – fate and circumstance – and I'm not going to apologise for feeling this way. Tell me one more time to leave you alone and I will. We don't know each other. You can walk away. We don't need to see each other again. It's easy.'

Everything inside her screamed at her to kiss him. She stepped backwards. 'I can't.'

She saw a taxi coming towards her with its light on and relief swept over her. 'Taxi!' she shouted and stepped off the edge of the pavement, into its path, desperately waving her hand in the air.

'50 Greenslades Road, Wandsworth, please,' she said to the cab driver through the window.

Luke was right behind her. 'You're making a mistake.'

'No,' she replied. 'I'd be making a mistake if I stayed.'

She got into the taxi and closed the door without looking at him again, and as they pulled away she laid her head back on the seat. She thought of how close she'd come to kissing him, then thought of her husband. She had to sort this out; hiding at Sophie's, nearly kissing Luke, avoiding the issues she had to face, wasn't going to help.

She had to talk to Will.

She leant forward to tap on the glass screen between her and the driver. 'I'm sorry,' she said. 'I gave you the wrong address. Can we go to Baron's Court instead?'

CHAPTER FOURTEEN

In the wine shop, Will was trying to focus on the website of a little-known producer from the southern tip of Italy who had just won a prestigious award at a regional wine festival in Naples. He was keen to begin importing from some different vineyards as his stock was becoming predictable and this one looked promising. It was impossible to concentrate, though. His thoughts constantly drifted back to Harmony, as they had done ever since she walked away from him, her gait uncertain, her small suitcase bumping along behind her. He was desperate to speak to her but every time he telephoned she either left the call unanswered or spoke in flat, single-word utterances that left him bereft. At night it was worse, her side of the bed cold, the bedroom quiet without her restlessness, his stomach like a roiling sea. He'd walked each night, pacing the pavements, anxiety consuming him.

He forced himself back to the Castella de Valde webpage, trying to read words that blurred on the screen. The bell on the door jangled and he looked up.

'Harmony!' he exclaimed, jumping off his stool and coming out from behind the counter.

She stood in the doorway, the evening sun behind her casting her face in shadow. He combed his fingers through his hair, aware of his dishevelled appearance, cursing himself for grabbing yesterday's shirt off the floor that morning.

'Are you back? Are you coming home?'

She tucked a few stray strands of hair behind her ear. 'I'm not sure what I'm doing.'

'I've missed you,' he said, as he approached her, carefully, as if she were a wild horse, likely to bolt.

She didn't move. Her eyes flicked over his face, her hurt as raw as it had been when she walked away from him.

'Shall we go home?' he said. 'We can't talk here.'

She didn't answer.

'Harmony?'

'No, I don't want to be in the flat. Let's walk. I'll go back and change my shoes and put some jeans on. Meet me there in ten minutes.'

He watched her walk out of the shop. He stood for a moment, unsure whether she was back to tell him she was coming home or leaving for good. He would have sold his soul to turn back the clock to before the vasectomy, before the miscarriage and the pregnancy, back to when their lives weren't on this emotional roller coaster.

He'd sent Frank home earlier that day. He was still devastated about his cat, and Will couldn't cope with seeing him so fragile, so grief-stricken, not with the way he was feeling himself. Two of them moping about the place was too much. Will emptied the till, locked the money in the safe, switched the lights off, then turned the sign on the door from *Open* to *Closed*.

As he turned into their street he saw her coming out of the front door, wearing jeans and a sweater, her hair pulled free of its ponytail. He started to jog and reached her as she stepped onto the pavement. They stood in front of each other, apprehensive and uncomfortable.

'Where do you want to walk?' he asked.

'Is doesn't matter.'

'Shall we go down to the river?'

They walked in strained silence for most of the way, passing groups of people enjoying the warm evening, standing outside pubs, spilling onto the pavement, laughing and joking, others rushing to get home or heading to the park for an evening kick-about.

Without warning she stopped in her tracks. 'You know,' she said, her voice tempered with anger. 'I never once questioned you. I never once asked you to tell me why. I just accepted it because I loved you.' She glanced over his shoulder and placed her hands on her hips, looked at him again. 'You need to tell me why. You need to explain it to me. Right now.'

He thrust his hands deep in his pockets and thought for a

moment or two, trying to formulate his mush of reasons into a coherent answer. He knew there was nothing he could say that was going to help. The argument they were going to have was unavoidable. 'I have no idea how to be a father.'

'That's not good enough! Nobody knows how to be a parent until they become one.' She shook her head. 'You can't have that.'

'It's true. The thought of it scares the shit out of me. I learned nothing from my father. Nothing at all. How on earth can I think of becoming a father if I've nothing to fall back on?'

He saw his family then, the three of them standing in the car park outside the halls of residence, his mother fussing around him, reminding him to do his laundry, kissing him, trying not to cry, his father in the background, hands clasped behind his back, face devoid of emotion. For Will this was a new start. Moving out of home with no intention of moving back. His first step into adulthood. He'd looked at his father, given him a moment or two to step forward, but the man didn't make any move towards him.

Be the bigger man, Will told himself. You must be the bigger man.

So Will walked up to him and offered his hand. His father took it and they shook briefly, both grasping the other too firmly. Will straightened his back and smiled awkwardly.

'I guess I'll see you at Christmas, then,' he'd said, unsure what else to say.

'I'm sure we'll see you before then,' his father had replied, his eyes stony. 'You're bound to cock it up. You always do.'

Will looked at his wife, her questioning eyes burning with livid incomprehension. 'I'd get it wrong, Harmony. If I tried to be a father, I know I would. It's not worth the risk. I'm not strong like you.'

'I'm not strong.' She started walking again, her eyes focused on where she was going, her mind working overtime. 'I'm not strong at all.'

'But you are,' he said, catching up with her. 'It was the first thing I noticed when we got talking the day we met. You'd seemed vulnerable and sweet when you were scrabbling around on the floor for your books and then we got talking and I was blown away by how determined you were. How independent, with all this fight inside you. You hadn't had things easy, but you were gutsy and secure, and so optimistic.'

My anchor in a storm, Will had thought, after they'd made love for the first time, squashed together in her narrow bed, basking in the glow of sex. She was his salvation. She was everything he wanted to be: tough, in control, focused on the future, not shackled by the past.

'I'm not like you. The way I've coped, the way I get through life, isn't to fight, it's to leave the things that have happened behind me. Move on. Not let it get to me.'

'But that's just the point!' she yelled, throwing her hands in the air in angry frustration as she marched. 'You aren't moving on, you aren't leaving it behind, you're letting it all govern your whole fucking life! Your past, this very thing you're trying not to dwell on, is making all your decisions for you.'

He shook his head. 'This isn't a nice world. Children are vulnerable. I'd want to be there all the time to make sure nothing could hurt our child but that's not possible, is it? If you have a child you have to accept that at some point they'll get hurt. I mean, look at us. Your dad leaving, your mum dying, my dad being a cunt, crying myself to sleep in a room with twenty other eight-year olds, all of us trying to keep our crying silent so we didn't get the shit kicked out of us. I don't want a child of mine to feel those things.'

Her eyes welled and she snatched angrily at the tears with the back of her hand. 'But our child wouldn't have felt those things,' she said. 'Our child would have been loved and cherished. Our child would have been happy.'

'You can't guarantee that.'

'Of course I can guarantee that!' she screamed. 'We'd have loved him or her with every breath in our bodies and if you couldn't have managed that, I'd have loved it enough for both of us. Christ, I can't believe this conversation!'

'I think you're being naive.'

'Naive?' she repeated.

'Yes, naive,' he pushed on, trying to ignore her outrage. 'Fine, things at home would be good, our family would be content, but what about the bastards out there?' He shook his head and looked up at the sky, blocking an image of Alastair Farrow, eyes glinting with spite.

'You're fear-mongering, Will, and it's pathetic. You've convinced yourself the world is an evil place, but it's not. It's an amazing place with amazing things in it – knowledge, laughter, love – all these things make life worth it.' She shook her head in frustration. 'If every person thought like you the human race would cease to exist. And why? Because of fear. How is that good? Yes, you and I have experienced pain, we've cried as children, but we found happiness, and not just superficial happiness – bona fide, gratifying happiness. You don't think that makes up for the bad stuff?' She didn't pause long enough for him to answer. 'I do. I think it makes it all worthwhile. What you're saying, this crap you're spouting, belittles everything we have together.'

She stormed ahead then, her feet slamming into the pavement, her hands balled into tight fists at her sides. He followed her, turning over her words, knowing there was truth in them, wondering if she were right. She made so much sense when she argued and he found his thoughts were muddled.

She stopped at the railings that overlooked the Thames and he came up beside her. The tide was low, and the pebbles and rubbish revealed on the shoreline were covered in thick, dirty silt. Will waited for Harmony to say something, but she stayed quiet, leaning over the railings, watching the listless, muddy water pass by.

'You know,' he said, gripping hold of the metal railing which was still warm from the day's sun. 'This is going to sound harsh and I know it's going to upset you, but … ' He stopped himself then, wary of the words he wanted to say.

'For fuck's sake, just say it,' she said, looking down the river, the slight breeze brushing her hair across her face.

'I've felt this way since I was eighteen. When most people were struggling with politics or religion or trying to get laid, I was dealing with this. The decision I made, not wanting to be a father, is fundamental to me – rightly or wrongly, it makes me who I am. The man you married. If you don't understand that … then,' he paused.

'Then maybe it's you who doesn't love me as much as you should and not the other way round.'

She lifted her hand and slapped him hard. The noise rang in his ears and his cheek burned.

'You self-absorbed fuck. You think I don't love you?' she said bitterly. 'You really think that? If I didn't love you I wouldn't be here. I wouldn't be bloody standing here trying to work our marriage out.' She shook her head, tears spilling down her cheeks. 'You fuck,' she said, batting her hand feebly against his chest. 'You utter fuck.' And then she turned on her heel and walked away from him.

'Harmony!' he called. But she didn't reply, just kept walking, head down, arms wrapped around her body. He turned and slammed his hands against the railings, swearing under his breath.

When he got back to the flat she was sitting at the kitchen table. As he approached the table she lifted her eyes to look at him. They were red from crying, the skin beneath them puffy.

'I heard what you said,' she said calmly. 'About being a father. I can't change how you feel, I know that, but I can't forgive what you did. What you did goes beyond your reasons for not wanting children. It was dishonest and hurtful and made decisions affecting my life that you didn't have the right to make.'

'I'm sorry.'

'A sorry isn't going to make this better.' She sighed and exhaled slowly. 'You lied to me. When I lost the baby, when I needed you the most, you gave me no support. You didn't care. It's taken you this long to open up about something you describe as fundamental to who you are. You don't tell me anything about your past. I know there's something you're not telling me about Luke. I can see it. Why won't you tell me? I find it terrifying how easily you can keep things from me. And, right now, right this minute, I feel like I've wasted the last twenty years of my life investing in this relationship.'

'Don't say that.'

She didn't reply.

'Look, Harmony, you're wrong,' he said. He pulled out a chair and sat opposite her. 'It's not easy keeping things from you. It's harder than you can imagine, but I do it because that's how I deal with things. I don't want to spend time discussing what happened at school with you. Luke, Alastair Farrow, the caning, the bullying, it's not worth talking about. I don't need your sympathy or pity, and I don't want all of that shit fouling our lives. It's irrelevant to me.'

'Of course it's not irrelevant. Your past, that intricate jigsaw of experiences, makes you the person you are today.'

'No,' he said. 'I put it away so I could become the person I am today. But listening to you I can see I should have let you in more. And when it comes to the vasectomy there's nothing I can say to defend it. I made a huge mistake not discussing it with you. I can see that now.' He paused. 'I don't think straight all the time. I have all this crap in my head. I'm not like you. I don't have the same way with words. When you had the miscarriage, you were so upset I didn't know what to say.' He shook his head. 'You say I didn't care, but that's not true.'

Her eyes filled with tears again and she looked down at her hands.

'I was desperate to help you, but everything I did or said seemed to make it worse. I went onto the internet and read up about it, about losing a baby, and what I should do to help, but nothing I found seemed right, and … ' He paused, finding it difficult to speak. 'And of course I'd had the operation and I was crippled with guilt. I could see how devastated you were, but I didn't want to talk, in case the question of another child came up. The more upset and withdrawn you became, the harder I found it to know what to say. In the end I convinced myself that if I just got on with it, eventually we'd be okay. I told myself these things happen and it was just life, and if I was happy and strong, you'd recover. I got it wrong.' Then he leant forward again and placed his hands on hers. 'Give me another chance, Harmony.'

'A part of me wants to, the part of me that wants us back to how we were,' she said. 'But there's another part of me that's just so bloody angry with you. So angry I can't look at you. And where does that leave us? What do I do about that? Hope it goes away?' She sighed heavily. 'Because the way I'm feeling at the moment, I don't think it's ever going to go away.'

When she left the table, he didn't follow. There was nothing more he could say, so instead he went into the garden. It was peaceful. Dusk had seen off the heat of the day and there was a suggestion of rain in the air. A movement from behind the study window caught his eye. He watched Harmony sit down at her desk, her shadowy figure moving slowly. He saw her put her glasses on and then become still as she stared at the monitor in front of her. He wondered if this was what the rest of their lives might look like, two separate beings tied together in marriage, detached and resentful, circling each other warily. Would it have been different if he'd shared everything with her from the start? If he'd described that first horrendously lonely night at prep school? All those eight-year-old boys curled up in uncomfortable beds, abandoned, the sound of stifled crying intermingling with the creaks and groans of ancient timbers and pipes. If he'd described how he'd lain awake trying to work out what he'd done to upset his parents so much they would send him away? He remembered how his blanket had stunk of disinfectant and how he'd hidden from the smell by pushing his face into the teddy he'd brought, as specified on the uniform list: One soft toy, if required.

It started to spit with rain. Will turned his face upwards and closed his eyes, waiting for the tiny specks of wet to hit him. He thought of Harmony's face when she'd told him about the miscarriage, how her eyes had been puffy from crying then as well, her pale skin blotched deep pink. How he'd found her slumped on the edge of their bed, her fingers clutching a ragged piece of tissue, her chin trembling as she said the words.

'Our baby died.'

And then she looked up at him, tears coursing down her cheeks, her breath coming in short snatches.

'A miscarriage?'

She nodded and her shoulders began to quiver.

He'd sat beside her and pulled her into him, his arms around her, his chin resting on her head. 'I'm sorry,' he whispered, kissing her hair.

His thoughts had been a jumble. He hadn't known what else to say. Everything that came into his head sounded trite and insincere.

His emotions were all over the place. The relief he'd felt shocked and shamed him, the sadness surprised him.

'Do you need me to take you to the doctor?'

She sat back and shook her head, pushing the disintegrating tissue against her red-rimmed eyes. 'I've already been. I went this morning.'

'I should have taken you.'

'There was nothing you could do,' she said in a tearful voice. 'I didn't want to worry you if nothing was wrong.' She sniffed. 'I was hoping they'd tell me it was okay, that the bleeding was normal and my baby was fine. But when they scanned me there was no heartbeat. Nothing there at all.' Then she started to sob again. 'Oh, Will, it was awful.'

The drizzle turned to rain. He sat there for a while, but soon the drops became too heavy and too cold. Inside, he took his wet shirt off and threw it in the direction of the washing machine. He was surprised to see it was nearly ten o'clock. He peered into the bedroom and saw Harmony was already in bed, the covers pulled tightly over her shoulder, her back facing him. He knew if he went to bed now he would only lie staring at the ceiling, battling his thoughts, and it was too wet to walk. He went through to the study and turned the computer on, shivering slightly as his damp skin cooled. He pulled Facebook up, wondering if Alastair had accepted his friend request.

God knows why he would, Will thought. He probably just laughed.

But when the page loaded a small red number one stared at him from his notifications. He clicked on it and his stomach turned over.

Alastair Farrow hadn't just accepted his request, he'd sent him a message.

Will English? My God, you haven't changed a bit! What a blast from the past. It's been a long time. Are you still in touch with any of the lads from school? I was glad to hear from you – surprised too – I was a bit of a cock at school! I notice you're in London. I'm not far away, near Camberley in Surrey. Married to Diane. Two ankle-biters, a boy and a girl, Charlie and Bea. We should go for a drink. It would be good to meet up again and hear your news. In fact, another friend from school (Toddy – not sure if you remember him) mentioned hooking up for a drink soon. I'll let you know if we do. If you can join us that would be great. Cheers and no hard feelings, Al

Will's first response was a burst of spontaneous laughter. He leant closer to the screen, his hand rubbing at his chin, head shaking slowly in disbelief. He reread the message a couple of times. Had Alastair really written that? Had he really dismissed his behaviour in that offhand way? Called himself a 'bit of a cock', introduced his children, then signed off with 'no hard feelings'? It was unbelievable. Will sat back in his chair and stared at the small picture of Farrow to the left-hand side of the message.

Alastair Farrow.

The seventeen-year old who recurred in Will's nightmares wanted to meet up to laugh about all the cock-things he'd done, slap Will on the back and buy him a drink for old times' sake, let bygones be bygones, catch up on all the news. Will stared incredulously at the message until Farrow's unfathomable words blurred and his back stiffened.

Harmony was asleep, or perhaps pretending to be, when he finally crept into bed. He lay beside her, drumming his fingers against the duvet, his mind whirring. He should ignore Alastair's message. He should unfriend him. He had enough to worry about with his marriage without wasting time on Alastair bloody Farrow. He should just forget all about him. Erase him. But the more Will thought about the flippant, dismissive tone of the message, the more outraged he became. How could he pass off what he did with some glib, throwaway comment? Did he seriously expect Will to have 'no hard feelings'? Was that how the mind of a bully worked?

He thought back to that afternoon.

You're pathetic, English. Get the fuck out of here.

Will got out of bed and went into the bathroom. He leant over the basin and turned the tap on with one hand. With the other he splashed water on his face. He lifted his head slowly and stared at himself in the mirror, his face lit only by the moonlight, his skin in shades of blue, shadowed. It was hard to decipher his features – he seemed indistinct, fading into nothingness. A nothing man.

He bent and splashed his face again, drinking from his cupped hand, then rubbing the back of his neck with it.

You're pathetic.

CHAPTER FIFTEEN

She was so angry she could barely see straight. Talking to Will hadn't helped. If anything it had made it worse. She knew now there was nothing he could have said that would have made his actions easier to comprehend; hearing him apologise was as bad as hearing him try to justify it. How could he have even let the thought enter his head and not dismiss it immediately? She thought about how he'd booked the procedure, travelled to the hospital, signed the operation papers, all without a thought for her. How dare he betray her trust like that?

The phone on her desk rang – an internal call. She pressed the button to divert it to voicemail; she didn't want to speak to anyone. Instead, she pulled up her email and began to type a new message out, her fingers frantically punching the keys. When she finished typing, she hesitated, but only for a moment, then she pressed send.

From: Dr Harmony Hanney
Subject: Re

Hi Luke,
I'd like to see you. I'd like to talk about you and Will. Would you be able to find time for a quick coffee?
Kind regards
Harmony

She stared at the screen. Her heart thumped against her ribcage. She looked over her shoulder, imagining people watching her, but nobody was anywhere near. They moved about their business as normal, oblivious to the email she'd been on the verge of sending for the last few hours. She had no idea if she was lying to him, or to herself, when she used Will as the excuse to see him. Maybe he *could* help? Maybe he *did* know things about her husband that would help explain his actions? But then she had yet another flash of Luke leaning close to her, whispering in her ear, telling her he wanted her.

She shook her head and glanced down the bullet-pointed list Jacob had emailed her following his read-through of her draft report. As she tried to concentrate on the points he'd raised she found her attention drifting again. She squinted at the screen in front of her in an attempt to focus. His email didn't seem to make sense. He seemed to contradict himself. Maybe she'd misread. She started from the beginning again, allowing herself to digest each word in turn to try to make sense of them.

... document needs more detailed/relevant definition of gene expression and your section on drug toxicity contains a number of inaccuracies that weaken the overall argument. Please remember, this is for use by people without scientific background and therefore needs to be easily understood. I know you are aware of this – it is your job after all. Here is a specific list of issues and queries I have with this document. I'm afraid, this report isn't up to your usual standards. I think we need to meet to discuss. Around 2 p.m. would suit ...

Harmony muttered under her breath, while flipping to the pages in her report that dealt with toxicity. Out of the corner of her eye she saw an email appear in her inbox. She put the pages down and opened the email.

I'd like to see you too.

That was all he'd written. She glanced around her again, then stared at the email, imagining him saying those words to her, his eyes boring into her. She remembered the feel of his hand on her knee and his breath warming her cheek. A rush of excitement bowled into her. His words rang in her head for the umpteenth time, unbidden, exciting: *Because that's how I feel about you, Harmony. I want to fuck you. Very much.*

She thought of Will and felt a surge of bitterness. When she'd left Luke yesterday evening her thoughts had only been of Will, of needing to be with him, of needing to talk to him in the hope they could make things better. After they'd talked she had felt worse, as if they really had come to a dead end, that there was no way forward. She'd been consumed by a maelstrom of emotions, anger-hurt-confusion, and then, somewhere in the mix, there was Luke: clever, suave, articulate and driven, everything Will was not. She found herself imagining what it might have been like to kiss him outside that Knightsbridge restaurant, saw herself getting into a taxi with him, leaning against him as he held her.

As she read the email again amid an office of people chatting softly, reading, writing papers, preparing for presentations, she remembered his smell as he'd leant close to her, the heat that had come off his body, the way her skin had tingled when he touched her.

She dropped her face into her hands and breathed in the hot, trapped air.

'Are you okay, Harmony?'

She swung around to see Alice standing behind her. She closed the email and gave a strained smile. 'I'm fine.'

Alice furrowed her brow. She'd worked in the department for a long time and was a few years older than Harmony. She had, as the office all agreed, a heart of gold, and took the health and well-being of her colleagues very seriously.

'You look flushed. Do you have a temperature?'

'I'm fine.' Alice looked at her as if she didn't believe her. 'I'm perfectly well,' she said a little more firmly. 'Thank you for asking.'

Alice didn't look convinced. Harmony smiled at her and nodded and at last Alice reluctantly went back to her desk. Harmony glanced at her inbox again and saw a second message from Luke. As she opened the email her hand trembled.

Are you at the office?

She rubbed her throat with her hand, catching Will's Tiffany heart with the edge of her finger. She stared at the message, unsure what she should do.

Though that wasn't true, of course. She knew what she should do. She should delete it. She should ignore her thumping heart. Ignore the part of her that wanted to punish Will. Ignore the part of her that wanted to feel Luke's breath on her neck again. She should write back to him and tell him she'd made a mistake, that she didn't need to see him.

But she didn't delete it.

She glanced over her shoulder and saw Alice deep in conversation with someone.

Yes.

Then she pressed send and held her breath. She imagined him at work, in his office, maybe in a large open-plan area on the top floor of a glass and steel building, or a private room with an antique writing desk and leather chairs like you'd find in a gentleman's club. She saw him typing his reply. His hair falling over his forehead, his long, slim fingers brushing the keys, his lips slightly parted. She imagined those intense eyes locked on his screen.

She sat back from the computer and looked around again. Her breath caught in her throat. She needed to calm herself. She closed her email and turned the computer off, then took her bag off her chair and walked down the corridor towards the ladies. She kept her head low, and hurried past Alice's desk without making eye contact. As soon as she reached the toilets her phone buzzed faintly to tell her an email had arrived. Her stomach turned over. She locked herself in the cubicle, closed the lid of the loo and sat down before retrieving her phone and opening the email.

I'll be with you in twenty minutes.

Her heart started racing again. This time with panic.

I can't leave work now.

Tell them you're feeling unwell. Walk up towards the Albert Memorial and wait for me on the corner of Exhibition Road.

'Shit,' she breathed.

I've got a meeting.

Harmony waited for his reply but none came.

'Shit,' she whispered again. 'I must be losing my mind,'

She looked back at her phone, waiting for another email to appear in her inbox, but still nothing came. Oh my God, she thought. He's on his way here. Her stomach knotted with nerves as she opened the cubicle door and left the toilets.

Alice passed her in the corridor. 'Are you sure you're feeling all right?' She laid a hand on Harmony's arm and rubbed it gently.

Harmony hesitated and then, before she could stop herself, she began her lies.

'You know,' she said, putting the back of her hand to the side of her face. 'I am feeling a bit off-colour.' She rubbed her throat. 'A bit faint.' An image of Luke came into her head, of his touch on the small of her back as he'd walked her through the bar in Knightsbridge. A shiver of heat ran from the base of her spine and radiated outwards, up her back, along her arms, and down to her fingertips. 'A temperature, I think.'

'Maybe you should go home,' Alice said, with a sympathetic smile. 'There's an awful bug going around at the moment.'

Harmony felt as if she was teetering on the edge of a very high precipice, looking down at the world below, feeling nauseous with vertigo.

'Yes,' she said, her throat tightening as the lie gathered weight inside her. 'Maybe I should.'

'In fact,' said Alice, taking hold of her arm. 'You're looking very pale suddenly. You say you're feeling faint? Maybe you should sit down until it passes? I'll get you a glass of water and a sweet biscuit. Sugar's ever so good if you're feeling queasy.'

Harmony couldn't look at her. 'I need some air, that's all,' she whispered. She began to walk away but Alice caught up with her.

'Are you sure you're going to be okay getting home? The tube will be very hot. It's so close out there today.'

'I'll catch a cab.'

'Let me come down and wait for one with you.'

'No, no,' she said too quickly. 'Thank you. No, you don't need to do that.'

But Alice looked unconvinced, walking with Harmony, giving no sign of letting her leave alone. Alice needed a task to distract her.

'Actually,' Harmony said. 'Would you be able to tell Jacob I'm not going to be able to catch up with him this afternoon? Tell him I got his email and it all makes sense. I'll make the changes for him by Tuesday at the latest.'

Alice nodded, satisfied at last that she was able to help. 'Yes, of course. I can sort that out for you. Leave it with me. Now you go home and get yourself into bed. Maybe have a nice bath first.'

'Thank you,' Harmony said with relief. She smiled at Alice and then walked on. The butterflies in her stomach were becoming almost unbearable. What was she doing? Lying to Alice, leaving work early, meeting a man she didn't know for reasons she didn't fully understand? You can still stop this, she thought. But she walked on, pulling her ponytail loose and shaking her hair, an undeniable thrill igniting the emotional tinder box inside her, making her feel more alive with each step she took.

The day was muggy, the sky grey and laden with rain. She waited on the corner of the road as he'd told her to and watched the cars and taxis as they turned into Hyde Park. A man in a suit gave her a lingering look as he passed and she cast her eyes down, feeling seedy, as if there was a neon sign above her head, pointing her out as she waited on a street corner to meet a man who wasn't her husband, a man she barely knew. She hesitated, about to turn away yet again, but then he was there, his car pulling up on the double yellow lines in front of her. She froze. A taxi blared its horn. She caught the driver's angry face as he swerved around the Audi.

Luke leant over the passenger seat and opened the door.

A voice in her head begged her not to get in the car. But seeing him again, just a few feet from her, she felt her legs weaken. Her breath became shallow, her skin prickled. She pictured herself kissing him, right there and then, not saying a word, just leaning into the car and pushing her lips against his.

'Luke. I … ' Her voice caught in her throat. 'I'm … '

'Get in the car.'

There was a note of force in his voice that she wasn't expecting. She glanced back down Exhibition Road towards the university, half hoping Alice might be there to stop her.

'Come on, don't look so worried,' he said more gently. 'I'm not going to do anything to you. I'm parked badly. Just get in.'

She looked around her, wondering if the people passing her knew what she was doing, if they were tutting under their breath. But nobody even seemed to notice her; they weren't interested, she was anonymous to them, just a woman meeting a man – a friend, a husband, colleague, a lover – it didn't matter to them.

She climbed into the car and closed the door. He didn't drive off immediately, but turned in his seat to look at her. A heavy silence held them, wrapped in the heat of the car, its smell – new leather and the scented air freshener that hung off the rear-view mirror – sickly sweet.

'I've never done anything like this before.'

'It doesn't matter to me what you have or haven't done.'

'But I haven't. It's important you know that.'

'Why?'

She didn't know why. She wondered whether it was herself she was talking to. Whether she was trying to excuse her actions, convince herself of her own good character.

She looked at him and laughed nervously. 'I'm not sure I even know what's going on.'

'I'll tell you what's going on,' he said. 'You and I met through a mutual connection. I have a past with Will and you have a present with him. I am as interested – no, fascinated – in his present as you are in his past, and that has drawn us to each other.' He reached out and drew the tips of his fingers down the side of her face and then played with strands of her hair. Her cheek tingled where he'd touched her. She lifted her eyes to meet his and as soon as she did he smiled again – a gentle, unthreatening smile. 'Added to that,' he said, 'unless I'm reading the signs wrongly, we are both attracted to each other and that attraction has become impossible to ignore.'

Harmony tried to speak but no words came out.

'Is that fair?'

His question reverberated in the still air of the car.

Fair? she thought. On who? Not on Will. It wasn't fair on Will in the slightest. To do this, to take her anger out on him like this in a way that would devastate him, how was that fair?

He took her chin between thumb and forefinger and turned her face towards him. He slid his hand down over her jaw and throat. He leant closer to her, his face just centimetres from hers, the smell of him filling her. His eyes were fixed on hers.

'I'm going to kiss you,' he said. 'And then I'm going to drive you to my flat and fuck you.'

He moved closer to her so that his lips brushed hers, sent electric pulses shooting though her body, and at that moment she knew it was too late, she knew she would sleep with him, and her head swam with anticipation. She turned in the seat, the skin of her thighs sticking to the hot leather, and wrapped her hand around his neck. Her fingers knotted into his hair and she pulled him to her. Their lips met and she was overwhelmed with desire. It erupted inside her as if she was taking her first breath of oxygen. He kissed differently to Will, harder, more insistent, his tongue forcing its way into her mouth, exploring her, tasting her.

He drew back from her. His lips glistened with a sheen of saliva. 'I am consumed by you.'

She trembled with adrenalin, her hands quivered, her lips tingled. 'You don't even know me,' she whispered.

The ghost of a smile passed over his face. 'I know all I need to know. I knew it the moment I first saw you.'

Luke turned the engine on and pulled away from the curb.

'You believe in love at first sight?' she asked as he drove.

He shook his head. 'Love at first sight?' he said with derision. 'No. I never talk about love. It's a fatuous, overused word that's impossible to quantify. How long does it take to fall in love?

Minutes? Years? Love means different things to different people. Love is a one-way street; one of the pair always loves more than the other. Love is cruel. What I'm talking about – attraction, desire, chemistry – these are the things that matter. You can love a car or a country or a food, but sexual desire is much more specific. Do I believe in desire at first sight? Yes, of course I do. True chemical desire is instantaneous.'

She knew what he meant. She had felt it too. Outside the cloakroom at Emma's party she'd felt the immediate attraction. Perhaps the future had been written out then. Perhaps it was inevitable she would sleep with him. Perhaps it had nothing to do with her faltering marriage or Will's dishonesty or her lost baby, but everything to do with this man, this stranger.

A sudden thought came into her head. She didn't want to know more about this man. She had no desire to get to know him, to see his weaknesses, to have him anything other than this mysterious ghost from Will's unspoken past. The thought of knowing him scared her.

'Luke,' she said. 'I don't want to go back to your flat.'

'Why not?'

She hesitated. 'I can't explain. I just don't want to.' She didn't want to try and tell him that she didn't want to see his home, she didn't want to know anything more about him, she didn't want to find out what books were on his shelf or which pictures decorated his walls. She needed him to stay a stranger.

'Where, then? A hotel?'

She imagined the judgmental frown of the lady on reception. A person who'd seen them all before, countless clandestine couples with false names grabbing a few hours of sordid sex. 'No,' she said, then glanced into the back seat of the car.

He smiled briefly. 'Don't even think it.' He paused. 'What about the photography studio?'

She did a double take and furrowed her brow. 'How do you know about that?'

'Will told me.'

'Did he?'

'The other night, we were talking about his business. How else would I know?' he laughed. 'Is it far? Do you have a key?'

'There's a padlock, a code. I know it.'

Harmony thought about it. They couldn't. Not in Will's studio. But as she thought about it she wondered if it might be perfect. It was safe and anonymous, not somewhere she felt connected to in any significant way. It would hurt Will if he knew, but then he'd hurt her. He was part of the reason she was here, part of the reason she was doing this. Why should she feel guilty? This was just sex, this was nothing compared to what he'd done. Her anger spiralled and she smarted as his voice repeated in her head.

When it died I felt relief.

'Yes,' she said. 'We can go there. He's at the wine shop today and never goes there after work. To be honest he hardly goes there at all anymore. Head down towards Battersea. It's a few minutes from the power station.'

She glanced at him, his face set, his eyes on the road. She looked down at his hand on the gear stick, saw his long fingers loosely gripping it and imagined them reaching for her. She felt for her wedding ring and began to turn it in precise quarter revolutions as she recalled the moment Will had slid it on to her finger. His eyes had sparkled and he'd laughed, standing there in his light blue seventies-style suit, flowery open-necked shirt, scuffed leather shoes and mismatched socks.

'Who's going to see my socks?' he'd said, as they dressed together, bucking tradition and driving to the registry office in the same car. But his trousers were a couple of inches too short and when he sat down they rode up his legs, revealing the black sock on one foot and the striped one on the other. After they exchanged rings he leant forward and told her he loved her, three whispered words that had made her heart sing.

'I love you too,' she'd replied.

Just meaningless words? Was Luke right? Was love just an immeasurable concept as unstable and ever-changing as a sand dune?

'Take it off.' Luke's voice jolted her from her thoughts.

'Sorry?'

'The ring. If it's bothering you, take it off.'

'It's not the ring that's bothering me,' she said.

'Well, if you're having second thoughts, you need to tell me. I don't want to force you to do something you don't want to do. If this is too much for you, I'll drive you home. Do you want me to do that?'

Harmony thought of the flat, dark and cramped, filled with sadness. She thought about Will and her moving around each other in their separate spheres, her avoiding being in the same room with him, those loaded, bitter silences.

'No. I want to be with you. I want to be here.'

Harmony directed Luke to turn into the small yard where Will's photographic studio was. She told him where to park and then they got out of the car. The small, unevenly cobbled forecourt was full of weeds, patches of earth and potholes. There were four warehouse-like buildings, prefabricated and boxy, that bordered three sides of the yard. One was vacant and dilapidated; another was used as a private storage facility; the third belonged to a motorcycle mechanic; and then there was Will's studio. It was smarter than the others. She and Will had spent a few weekends painting it – the walls in white emulsion, the window frames and door in a navy gloss. They'd painted the inside as well, pulled out the rotten carpets, replaced the broken panes of glass in the window, and cleared away the rubbish. She remembered Will eagerly screwing the stainless steel sign to the door then stepping back and reading it out.

'Will English. Professional photographer,' he'd said, as he'd wrapped his arms around her shoulders and kissed her.

Harmony and Luke walked up to the door and with a shaking hand she turned the number dials on the lock that secured it.

1209.

Will's birthday.

She stalled as another wave of doubt passed through her. Luke bent down and lightly kissed her neck. She shivered and leant her face against his, closing her eyes, breathing him in. She pushed Will from her mind and slid the handle back to open the door. It was dark inside and they were hit by a wall of stale, cool air, heavy with the smell of the damp concrete floor. Harmony reached to the side to turn on the lights, and a moment or two later the fluorescent strip lights flickered into life. She stared at the large empty room, the sofa to her left, the white wall in front of her, lighting stands and spotlights to the right. Will's space. She saw him then, tinkering with his camera, glancing up at her, smiling as he focused the lens on her.

Luke opened his mouth to speak.

'Don't say anything,' she said. 'Just kiss me.'

His eyes searched hers, flicking almost imperceptibly back and forth, then in one movement he grabbed hold of her shoulders and pushed his open mouth onto hers. One hand went to the back of her neck and the other moved over her breast, pushing hard against her. All hesitation vanished and she was filled with an all-consuming need for him. Everything she felt, all the confusion, the hurt, the betrayal and anger, was suddenly directed on this one thing. Every part of her ached for him. She moved her hand to the front of his trousers, took an intake of breath when she felt him hard. She grabbed at the waistband and fumbled with the button and zip. His fingers dug into her, his tongue forced its way into her mouth. He pushed her backwards against the painted brickwork of the studio as his hand went to the hem of her skirt and he pulled it up, over her hips. His fingers felt for her underwear. She broke away from kissing him to pull them down and step out of them. He dropped his head and buried his face in her chest, she pitched her head backwards, raking her fingers across his back as he lifted her against the wall and she wrapped her legs around him. He kissed her neck and chest, ran the flats of his hand up her sides and the insides of her arms, pushing them above her head and clenching her wrists against the wall. There was a roughness about him, a mounting aggression. She opened her eyes and was taken aback by the look on his face. Not lust or tenderness, but a reflected anger, his eyes glazed over, mouth twisted into a grimace. His fingers tightened their hold on her wrists as if she were trapped in a vice.

'Be careful,' she whispered. 'You're hurting me.'

His fingers loosened immediately and he breathed into her neck. 'I'm sorry,' he said. 'I didn't mean to.' His breath came in short, grasping bursts.

She put her hand against his cheek to calm him. When she felt him relax she whispered into his ear: 'Fuck me, Luke. I want you to fuck me now.'

When he pushed himself inside her he cried out, then bit down on her lip and she winced, tasting the metallic tang of blood.

'I've wanted this so much,' he said hoarsely.

As he drove into her he seemed to disappear into himself, become distant from her, as if he was somewhere else. It was over quickly and his head collapsed into the crook of her neck as her body slid down the wall. She loosely draped her arms around him and they both breathed heavily. She turned her head, her open mouth resting against his hair, soft and thick.

It's done now, she thought. It's done.

She pushed her skirt down and Luke pulled up his trousers, then ran his hands through his hair.

'What do we do now?' she asked.

He smiled. 'We do it again.'

He took hold of her hand and led her to a side room off the main area. It was small and contained a tattered chaise longue that Harmony had fallen in love with at the Portobello Market, a coffee table, and an old chest filled with unusual items – a bowler hat, a silver-topped cane, beads, a plastic pot plant, a large Chinese fan and the like – that Will used as props in portrait shoots. His old camera and camera case and a long lens lay on the table. The camera was plugged into the socket in the wall, the green light showing it was fully charged.

'He never puts anything away,' she muttered. 'It drives me mad—'

'Don't think about him.'

She held her tongue, resisting the urge to tell Luke that it was impossible not to think about Will. He was there with her. This was as much about Will as it was about her.

'Why were you angry just then?' she said.

'What do you mean?'

'When we had sex.'

'I wasn't angry. It's you who's angry.'

'Yes,' she said after a hesitation. 'I am angry.'

'Why?'

She contemplated telling him, but in the end she just shrugged. 'It's complicated.'

'For me too.'

She nodded.

'I want to look at you.'

She smiled. 'You are looking at me.'

'No, properly.'

He reached out and began to undress her. His face was blank. He undid each button on her shirt methodically. Ran his hands down her shoulders to slide it off her. Undid her bra. Gently lowered the straps down her arms then leant forward and kissed each of her breasts. He bent to undo the zip of her skirt. He eased it down over her hips. He kissed her between her legs. She moaned softly.

Luke stepped back and stared at her. His dark eyes took her in. Unease settled over her. Having him study her like this, naked and in full light, made her feel vulnerable, as if he was inspecting goods, looking for imperfections. She became aware of her body, of those bits of herself she didn't like. Her bony hips, the appendix scar on her stomach, the large, dark mole on her hip, the broken veins on her thighs. For the first time since they'd kissed in the car she felt dirty, as if she was worthless and cheap, a husk of herself, her morals and self-worth sucked out of her. She lifted her arms to cover herself.

'Don't.' His voice was firm; the sound of it made her heart skip a beat.

'I don't like how this makes me feel.'

'How what makes you feel?'

'The way you're looking at me.' Harmony was conscious of how quickly she was breathing, how shallow and hurried each breath was. 'Being naked like this in front of you, with you dressed. I feel exposed.'

He touched his fingers to her mouth to quieten her. Then he reached for his shirt buttons and started to take his own clothes off. They made love on a rug on the floor. This time there was no rushing or desperate snatching of each other's bodies. He was gentle and soft. She should have enjoyed it but she didn't. Without the rush of anger and passion she was left with the very real feeling that this wasn't her husband. It was as if a curse had lifted off her. With every touch, with every moan of pleasure he made, she wanted him less. At one point she put her hand to her mouth to stop herself crying out. Guilt and shame overwhelmed her. As he kissed every part of her, as if he had all the time in the world, all she could think of was Will. Everything about this other man felt wrong now, alien. His smell, the feel of his skin, his hard, muscular body, and his unrelenting insistence, pushing himself against her in a way her husband never did. Luke whispered words she couldn't hear into the curve of her neck. He kissed her breasts and her stomach, ran the tip of his tongue along the line of her throat, picked up each of her hands in turn and kissed the skin on the inside of her wrists. Afterwards she lay beside him, not quite touching. He turned on his side and lifted a hand to smooth her hair. As he did, she caught sight of the thin white scar that cut his palm in two.

Blood brothers.

'Are you thinking about him?'

'No,' she lied.

'Good. You can't think about him when you're with me.'

'It doesn't work like that.'

'It does. When you're with me, I don't want him anywhere near you.' He sat up and his eyes burned into her.

'I think we should go,' she said.

'Not yet. I want to stay with you like this for a while.'

'I have to get back, Luke.' She sat up, covering her chest with crossed arms. 'I need to get back to Will.'

He sat up too and grabbed his trousers angrily. Harmony knew she should say something, apologise maybe, but instead she watched him dress without speaking. She studied his body – not an inch of fat, toned, with clear muscle definition. She imagined he spent hours in the gym or maybe played football twice a week or ran every lunchtime. She was reminded how little she knew about him.

Harmony was careful to leave the studio as they'd found it. Luke put the padlock on the door and spun the numbers to lock it. Harmony strapped herself into the car then reached into the back for her bag. She got out her phone and saw Will had texted her earlier that afternoon. She recoiled as a tremendous wave of guilt crashed over her.

What time are you home?

'Can you drop me at Fulham Broadway?' she asked, chewing lightly on her lower lip.

Luke nodded stiffly and turned the engine on as she typed a reply to Will.

Sorry phone been off. Home about six-thirty.

She hesitated then added a kiss.

They were quiet on the drive back through London. At one point he reached for her hand and stroked her. Her body tensed; she wanted to pull away from him. It was all wrong now, his touch, not exciting but duplicitous.

'I'm away on business for a week from tomorrow,' Luke said, as he pulled over to let her out just up from the tube station. 'I'll contact you when I'm back in the country.'

'I don't know,' she said with hesitation.

'That wasn't the response I was hoping for.'

'I'm sorry.'

'I'll call you.'

'Do you have my number? I don't remember giving it to you.'

'It was on the bottom of the email you sent me.'

'Well, please don't call me. And don't text either. Use my work email address, the one you used this morning. It comes through to my phone, so I'll pick it up.' She slipped her bag onto her shoulder and reached for the door handle.

His jaw clenched with displeasure and his eyes flicked away from her.

'Luke,' she said. 'You can't put any pressure on me. This is hard enough as it is.' She opened the door and got out. She looked at him but he stared out of the windscreen as if fixed on something in the distance, his fingers tapping rapidly on the steering wheel. Finally he glanced at her and nodded. Then she closed the door.

He shifted into gear and pulled away. She watched the car weaving through the traffic, and then turned in the direction of the tube station.

She arrived home a little earlier than she'd said. She stood in the entrance hall of their building for a few minutes breathing deeply, trying to gather herself before opening the door. She fumbled with the key in the lock, images of her and Luke bombarding her, each of them sending a small pulse of heat through her body and a simultaneous stab of guilt.

'Hi!' called Will from the kitchen. 'Good day?'

His voice cut into her. Familiar, the most familiar voice in the world. He was excited about something. How could he be? What was there to be excited about?

'One minute,' she called back. 'I'm just going to jump in the shower. It's like the tropics out there, I've been sweating all day.'

'Okay,' he said. He appeared in the doorway. 'I'll be in the garden. Come out and join me when you're ready. I've something to show you.' He turned away but then stopped and looked back at her. 'Oh, and Emma called. She asked if you could ring back when you got in. She sounded a bit stressed.'

'Thanks. I'll shower first,' she said.

She walked into the bathroom, her legs like jelly, and slid the lock shut. She ran the shower, undressed, made sure she pushed her clothes deep into the laundry basket, then stepped under the water and cleaned herself all over. When she was finished she wrapped herself in a towel. She caught sight of herself in the mirror. There were red scratches over her chest and neck, and her lip had a small cut on it. She brought her fingers up and ran them lightly over the cut. She recalled the way he'd cried out as he pushed into her and a wave of sadness swept through her as she realised she was a different person now. Two weeks ago she was one half of a long-term marriage, a loyal wife whose only desire in the world was to conceive a baby with the husband she loved. Now she was a stranger to herself, a person who'd had sex with a man she barely knew, she was a liar, a cheat. She walked through to the bedroom and sat on the edge of the bed. She felt unwelcome suddenly, as if the room was telling her she had no right to be there, that she didn't belong anymore.

'Oh God,' she whispered. 'What on earth have you done?'

CHAPTER SIXTEEN

First year dormitory,
Farringdon Hall,
October 1986

Dear Mother and Father,

I hope this letter finds you well. School is fine. I've been doing my best and if you saw how hard I was trying you would be proud of me. The only thing I can't do at all is rugby. I know this will disappoint you, Father. I'm just a lot smaller than everyone else and also not very fast at running. I will keep trying though! I quite like swimming, but it's very cold and the water is quite green. If you are in the swimming team, you get to wear swimming trunks, but if you're not then you have to swim naked, nothing on at all. When I said that I didn't think that was fair to the PE teacher, he sent me to the headmaster for a caning. I'm learning the hard way that it really is best to keep your complaints quiet. Though I find it very hard! I've been saying my prayers every night and asking God to help you do your work. I hope the new church is built now and the villagers are happy they have love in their hearts at last. It's sometimes quite hard here. Lots of the boys are still unkind to me. There is this one boy, a prefect if you can imagine, who is awful. Mother, you'd say he has the Devil in his eye. I never knew what you meant by that until I saw him. Now I know just what you mean. I'm teased every day but I do try to do what you said and ignore it, though it does get annoying and makes me very cross sometimes. Things are better now because ... wait for this ... I have found a friend!!! His name is William (Will) and he's great. We like all the same things like adventure stories and the Beano, and we play this game where we pretend we are marooned on a desert island with cannibals who'll eat us alive if they catch us. I know you will think this is a very foolish game but it's really fun! Will is tall and quite strong for his age (our age, I mean!) and he thinks I'm very funny. It's great! When I hear him laugh it makes me feel so happy I could burst. I feel like he is the only person in this whole place who understands me and likes me for being me and it is very comforting. As you know I have found it very lonely here but now I have Will things are looking up! We talk about everything and I can tell him what I'm thinking and even what I'm feeling deep inside. He has a camera so I'll ask him to take a picture of us together and send it to you. I've grown a lot! You'll see what good friends we are (you'll just be able to tell).

The food here isn't great apart from the puddings. Mother, you would love the jam sponge! They serve it with custard which is as yellow as the African sun and thick like glue but they must put a sack of sugar in it because it's so sweet it makes my teeth hurt! The showers are stone cold and take your breath away but I'm used to those now. One bad thing here (there are a few but I won't tell you them all!) is the morning runs we have to do on Tuesdays and Fridays. They make us get up at five-thirty in the morning and run up and down this hill four times. The hill is nicknamed The Killer and at the top you have to touch this tree and a prefect gives you a tick on a piece of paper when you do. It's very steep and there's another prefect who stands at the bottom and basically has the job of shouting. I am always one of the last to finish however hard I try and run. The masters are quite scary but they seem to know their jobs and I am certain I am getting a very good education, which I know is what you want for me. I miss the heat of Africa. I wonder if I will see you at Christmas or if I will be going to Aunt Grace's? It would be nice to come home if you will let me. I'm not sure Aunt Grace likes having me under her feet all the time …

I am doing well in Latin and with my oboe. I'll take Grade Six in January and Mr Granger thinks I should get a merit at least and a distinction if I'm lucky. I must sign off now as the bell is ringing for supper. (It's right outside the study and is so loud it deafens you!) If I did have one wish it would be that you came and got me but I know this isn't possible so I will not think about that anymore.

Please send my love to Nairobi. I miss it. I will try not to get cross or do anything that will make you embarrassed and I will keep trying at rugby, Father. Maybe God will help me with that one!

I know God loves you and the important work you do and I hope He loves me too.

Your loving son,
Luke Matthew John Crawford

CHAPTER SEVENTEEN

Will's stomach buzzed with nerves as he waited for her. He began to pace, his eyes fixed on the back door. When he saw her coming into the kitchen he ran up to the back door and watched her face as she came into the garden. She stopped on the back door step, her hair wet from her shower, her skin flushed and glowing, and took it all in. The surprise on her face dawned gradually, her eyes jerking from one thing to another, her head slightly shaking in disbelief. He wanted her to love it and he crossed the fingers on one hand behind his back.

'I did the garden.'

'I can see,' she said, giving him a brief smile before returning to survey his work.

'I know it doesn't make things better, I know it's not as simple as that,' he said. 'But, well, I couldn't stop thinking about what you said, about it being neglected and scruffy, and well, once I got started, I couldn't stop.'

She stepped out onto the terrace, which he'd cleared of weeds and swept. He watched her slowly absorbing the changes.

'Do you remember how excited we were when we walked out here when we were buying the place? That estate agent droning on about how close the flat was to the tube station and the patisserie that sold the best custard tarts in West London and all we could do was grin at the garden?'

'Did you have any help?' she asked. She glanced at him before walking over to look at one of the flower beds.

'No, but I started first thing this morning. I called Frank and told him I wouldn't be in and then as soon as you left I got going.'

He'd made himself a sweet, milky coffee, then dressed in a pair of jeans and an old T-shirt and set to work. He dug out an assortment of garden tools from the narrow lean-to shed, including an electric mower which hadn't been used since the year before. He got a load of rubbish bags from the kitchen, some matches, and a big blue tarpaulin that he could collect leaves and weeds on. The more he worked the more driven he felt, moving in some sort of frenzy, digging, cutting, weeding, dragging, burning. Sweat poured off him as the June heat beat down. This was his way of showing her the future. He didn't stop to wonder if this was what she'd meant when she talked about the garden being a mess, he just knew he needed to tidy it up, that whatever the outcome, whether it helped or made no difference, it was symbolic in some way.

At just past one o'clock he took a break and went inside. He made himself a tall glass of orange squash which he drank in one beside the sink, then he opened the fridge, cut a chunk of cheese and rolled up a slice of ham, which he ate as he went back outside to assess his morning's work. The place resembled a war zone, with rubbish, piles of weeds, clods of earth and clippings littering the whole area. He heard his mother's reassuring voice in his head telling him things always looked worse before they got better and for the first time in months he missed her. If she lived closer then he'd have called her to come and help. She was a fantastic gardener, one of those sleeves-up kind of people who got jobs done quickly with no complaining. He wiped the back of his hand across his sweaty forehead and went back indoors to send a text to Harmony to ask what time she'd be back. She was usually home anywhere between five and seven, and today, the later the better. He wanted to have it perfect. He tidied up what he had done then spent an hour and half turning the soil to reveal moist, deep brown earth, which made a world of difference.

'Flowers,' he said to himself.

He checked the phone for a reply from Harmony, but there was nothing. It was three o'clock. He'd take a chance and drive to Homebase, the nearest place he knew that stocked plants. There he filled two large trollies with a variety of herbs, flowers and shrubs. He also picked up a couple of terracotta planters he thought would look great holding the herbs, a huge shiny blue urn, a fully developed specimen rose bush with flowers of such a deep red they could have been stained with blood, an Indian-style parasol with tassels and embroidery in a rainbow of threads, a small cast-iron barbecue, and some citronella candles to keep the midges away.

He checked his watch. He'd be home by half past four. He had wanted to cook her supper as well but if he was going to plant he wouldn't have time. When he got home he put a good bottle of Pouilly-Fuissé in the fridge and checked there was enough ham left. There were some olives as well, and right at the back of the cupboard, he found a jar of roasted peppers. Enough for supper. He went outside and began to plant. At half past five he finally got a text from Harmony to say she'd be home at six-thirty. He had quite a few plants left in pots and raced to get as many in the ground as possible, but as the clock reached six he knew he wouldn't have time to finish, so he placed the rest on the beds in their pots. It wasn't ideal but it gave an impression of what it would look like. Then he laid a rug on the freshly cut lawn, leant the parasol at an angle over it, lit the citronella candles and placed them around the rug, and then went inside to rinse the dirt, sweat, and grass clippings from his sunburnt skin. His heart began to pound with excitement; he couldn't wait to see her, he couldn't wait to show her, to start trying to make her love him again.

He called out to her from the kitchen as she came in but she disappeared straight to the bathroom for a shower. His heart sank a little. When she appeared ten minutes later he looked at her face; she looked different, less angry, but perhaps that was merely wishful thinking.

She glanced at him but looked away, as her eyes filled with tears.

'Hey,' he said. 'It's not supposed to make you cry.'

'It looks great.' She walked across the small area of mowed grass to the other bed. 'You've done so much. The plants are lovely,' she said. 'Do you know what they all are?'

'I've kept the labels. I thought I'd try and learn their names.' He smiled and walked over to her, then took her hand and gently pulled her up to the top end of the garden where he'd put the rose in the large blue pot. He touched its leaves. 'This one's called *Danse du Feu*.

Isn't that lovely?' He turned to her. 'It reminds me of the time you and I went to Anglesey, and we lit the fire on the beach.' He stared at her, waiting for her to nod, but instead she avoided his eyes, transfixed by the brilliant red petals of the rose. 'We danced in the sand beside the fire. Do you remember? When I saw the name I thought of that evening. I had to have it in our garden then every time I look at it I'll remember that night. We were so completely happy then, weren't we?'

She looked at him and nodded. 'That seems a long time ago.' Her arms were crossed, hands clasping her elbows tightly. He could see the whites of her knuckles. He tried to fight his disappointment. He had no idea what he'd been expecting from her but this passive sadness was heartbreaking.

'Harmony,' he said with a deep breath. 'I don't expect you to forgive me. I just listened to what you said, that's all. The garden needed doing and I wanted to do it for you. For us.'

She didn't say anything, just looked at the ground, hugged herself more tightly.

'You look around. I'm just nipping into the kitchen. Back in a sec.'

He went to the fridge and took out the wine, which he sank into the clay wine cooler she'd given him the day North End Wines opened for trade. He put it under his arm and then picked up the tray he'd already filled with the food, two glasses, a corkscrew and some paper napkins.

Harmony was sitting on the seat at the far end of the garden, her hands loosely clasped and resting on her knees. He put the tray on the rug on the grass, then knelt down, smarting a little at the pain in his lower back. He thought of his mother again, of all the times he'd seen her out in their garden, pausing to stretch her back as she weeded on her knees for hours at a time.

Harmony came to join him and he handed her a glass of wine then leant over to put the bottle back in the cooler. He thought she looked pale suddenly. 'Are you feeling unwell?'

'No.' She sat on the rug, knees pulled tightly in to her chest. 'I'm tired, that's all.' She glanced at him again. 'I love the garden, though.'

She gave a thin, watery smile that didn't hold.

'Well, you were right,' he said. 'When you said that the garden was neglected. There was no reason for it and it's my fault.'

She shook her head. 'It's both our faults. You've transformed it.'

'This isn't about the garden,' he said. 'I don't give a shit about the garden. It's you I care about.'

Still she wouldn't meet his eyes.

'Did you hear me?'

She picked up a small leaf and turned it over in her fingers.

'Harmony?' He paused, wishing she didn't look so pained. 'Do you want this to work or not?' He regretted the question as soon as he'd asked it, worried in case she said no.

Finally, she looked at him. She was chewing on her lip and he noticed a small red graze on it. 'I'm confused.' She looked like a child, her eyes large and wet with tears, vulnerable, exposed.

'I wish we could turn back the clock and do things differently.'

'Yes, I wish that too.'

'Do you want to eat? Are you hungry?'

'Yes,' she said softly. 'I am a bit.'

He was filled with a sense of relief, as if her accepting supper in the garden was a step in the right direction, but though they talked as they ate, they avoided anything of importance and their conversation was stilted, as if they were on an unsuccessful blind date, unsure of comfortable ground, preferring instead to keep to neutral subjects. She asked him about the garden, about how much he had needed to burn and how hard the earth had been to dig. He told her about the stag beetle larvae he'd found, two fat white grubs that looked like a pair of albino slugs. He had reburied them because he remembered reading somewhere they were endangered. She nodded and told him they were. Like bats.

The sky eventually grew dusky and with it came a chill in the air. Harmony rubbed her arms.

'Are you cold?' Will asked. 'Can I get you a sweater?'

'I'm going to go in,' she said. 'I might take some work to bed; I've some notes to read through.'

He stood too and they faced each other.

'We'll be okay,' he said.

His sentence hovered in the still air as if unfinished. She folded her arms across her stomach and looked at the ground. He reached for her with a sudden feeling she was floating away from him, that if a heavy gust of wind blew she'd be carried away with it.

'You still love me, don't you?'

She lifted her trembling hand and placed it flat against his cheek.

'Because if you do, that's enough.'

'Is it?' she asked, dropping her hand from his face. 'I'm not sure it is.'

'Yes, of course it is. Nothing is more important than that. If we love each other that's all that matters. We can work through this, Harmony.'

She bent to pick up the tray and plates and took them back into the kitchen.

Will blew out the sickly-sweet citronella candles and folded the rug. He closed the parasol and threw the last olive into the bushes, then picked up the glasses and gathered the rug and took them inside. He suspected his marriage was over. It was there in her eyes. She was distant from him; she had been since the miscarriage, but there was something else between them now, something he couldn't pin down. She hadn't been able to look at him, the only touch she'd given him was when she'd placed her hand on his cheek, and that gesture held more regret and sadness than he'd thought possible. It was as if she were saying goodbye. Helplessness gave way to anger, which billowed like a mistral wind, bringing with it images of Alastair Farrow, leering at him with malignant eyes.

Will sat up until late, staring mindlessly at the television, desperate to keep Alastair Farrow at bay. He watched the news, then a poorly written sitcom with jerky camera work, then the shopping channel, a man in a shiny suit desperate to flog steam cleaners to his zombified post-midnight audience. But as much as he tried to keep Farrow from his head, all he could think about was the message he'd sent him. Glib, fatuous, facetious, sitting on the wall of his Facebook account, laughing at him.

I was a bit of a cock at school! No hard feelings.

He walked through to the study and turned the computer on, logged onto Facebook. He reread the message, Farrow's pudgy, balding head beside it, and felt a swell of bile hit his throat.

'You shit,' he said aloud. 'You absolute piece of shit. This is all your fault.'

Hi Alastair, Good to hear from you. A drink sounds great. It's been a long time. I happen to be coming over your way for work next week. Are you able to meet up for a quick one, maybe Tuesday or Wednesday? Thursday would work at a push. Let me know. Will.

He jammed his finger on the return key and his message etched itself into the computer screen.

CHAPTER EIGHTEEN

Emma Barratt-Jones walked into the kitchen and dumped her shopping bags on the black granite worktop that shone like a mirror. She sighed. It was quiet. Too quiet. She didn't like it when the house was this empty, just her rattling around between school drop-off and pick-up. Nearly all her friends moaned about the school holidays, about having their children under their feet, about the mess and the I'm-bored-mummy cries. Emma loved the holidays. Loved having Josh and Abi around. The house lit up when they were in it. To hear them playing, running around, to cook for them, chat to them, laugh with them, it all gave meaning to her life. While they were at school the house was dormant, like a museum, and all she could hear over the silence was her own breathing and the ticking of the clock in the hall.

As she turned to unload the shopping bags, she caught sight of the worktop around the sink and oven. The sunlight streamed in through the windows, highlighting a fine layer of otherwise invisible dust. She left the shopping and took the J-cloth from where it hung, folded and damp, over the rise of the expensive designer tap. She wiped the surfaces, making sure every speck of dust was lifted. Then she rinsed the cloth and refolded it over the tap. She unpacked the shopping and thought about Ian. She'd tried to call him that morning but he'd been too busy to talk to her. His secretary had been vague, as if she was hiding something, as if she was lying when she said Ian was in a meeting. Nothing was right with him at the moment. It worried her. Usually, she was able to work out what was wrong with him, soothe him. She was a good wife. She knew that. She kept an immaculate house. She listened to him. She didn't even shop as much as Ian would have their friends believe. In fact, she prided herself on being frugal by nature, something that came from her upbringing. Watching her mother racked with stress as she tried to feed her family of six on next to nothing had stayed with her. Emma never wasted food and always shopped in the sales and took advantage of offers. She'd managed to kick her coupon habit; coupons made her feel poor rather than thrifty. But for the last month he'd drawn further and further away from her, and nothing she did seemed to bring him any closer, or provide him any relief or comfort.

She felt lost and helpless. After putting the last of the shopping away, she folded the canvas bags neatly and put them in the drawer then turned the kettle on. She waited while it boiled noisily. When it clicked off, and the rumbling boil ceased, the kitchen was plunged into dreary quiet again. She didn't want tea. She wanted to talk to someone; the god-awful quiet was eating away at her. She leant back against the worktop and reached for the phone.

'Hello?' said Harmony.

'Hi, it's me.' she said. 'Am I disturbing you?'

'A little,' Harmony said. 'But don't worry. I'm sorry I didn't call you back yesterday.'

Emma could hear the tightness in her voice and knew Harmony was working. 'It's okay, I know how busy you are. Are you sure you're not in a meeting or something?' she asked.

'No. I'm working from home today, but I'm trying to concentrate on something.' Harmony sighed heavily. 'My boss sent me a pretty blunt email last night asking for this piece of work. I'm finding it hard to focus, though.'

'Anything wrong?' Emma leant on the worktop on her elbows, chin resting on her hand. Harmony seemed to hesitate. Emma ran her finger back and forth over the granite and waited for her to speak. She thought she heard Harmony sigh again.

'No, not really.'

'Have you got time for a chat?'

'Yes,' Harmony replied. 'I could do with a break.'

They chatted about this and that but Emma could tell there was something wrong. Harmony wasn't herself, she was uptight and withdrawn, and she wondered if she'd done something to upset her, though for the life of her she couldn't imagine what.

'Are you sure you're all right?' she asked.

'Not really. Will and I are having a bit of a tricky time.'

'You and Will?' Emma exclaimed. 'I don't believe it. What's happened?'

'Do you think I'm too hard on him, Em?'

Emma furrowed her brow. 'Hard on him? No. I don't think you are at all. Why do you say that?'

'I don't know. I just wonder whether I'm understanding enough. Whether I've been sympathetic enough. I mean, like when he gave up his photography. He was so disappointed, had the wind knocked out of him and … oh … I don't know … I just can't remember if I was kind to him.'

'You certainly weren't unkind. Not as far as I was aware anyway. I've never known you be unkind to anyone or anything in your life. Least of all Will. To be honest, I'm not sure I ever heard you talking about it at all.'

'Maybe that's what I mean. Maybe I was so focused on him having a *sensible* career that I didn't give him enough credit for following his dream. I suppose I always thought he should do something with wine. After all, he's been working in it for long enough. I didn't support him enough with the photography, I didn't appreciate how difficult it was for him when it didn't take off. I just told him to stop being silly and get on with finding another job.'

'You're being very hard on yourself,' Emma said. 'You were having to think about bringing the money in and all that. He seemed to realise, certainly when Ian and I spoke to him, that businesses go under all the time. And he's done brilliantly with the wine shop and it's not as if he hates it.'

'I know,' she sighed. 'I just wonder if we all take other people's dreams for granted.'

'Listen, I've known you a very long time and I don't think you've ever assumed anything to be unimportant. You take everything very seriously. It was a few years ago anyway and he always appears very content and relaxed. I … ' She was stopped in her tracks by a sudden wave of emotion. 'Sorry,' she managed. 'Give me a sec.'

'Are you crying?'

Emma took the phone away from her face and pressed her sleeve into her eyes to stop herself from crying. 'No,' she said, bringing the phone back. 'Not really.'

'Gosh, what a pair we are,' Harmony said gently. 'What's wrong?'

'Probably nothing.' She paused. 'I've just had one of those weeks, ignore me.'

'Go on, tell me, I can hear you're upset.'

'I am a bit.' She paused again. 'Are you sure you have time? You should be working, shouldn't you?'

'Don't be silly, of course I've got time.'

Emma dried more tears with her sleeve. Then she rubbed at an invisible mark on the worktop. 'There's something going on with Ian.'

'What type of something?'

Emma hesitated, shaking her head again, grimacing at the sound of the words out loud. 'I don't know,' she said, her voice unsteady. 'He's not himself. He's back late, drinking all the time. I know there's something wrong but he won't tell me. He keeps saying he's fine. I know he's not. He gets cross with me and the children so easily.' She paused. 'I'm worried,' she said. 'Really worried.'

'Do you have any idea what it might be?'

'I'm not sure. It could be all sorts of things. He's just so tense.' She gave a frustrated groan. 'I keep catching him on the phone talking quietly or taking a call then shutting himself away in his office to talk. I asked him about it last night but he got so angry and shouted at me. He said I had to leave him alone and that there was no problem. But … ' She hesitated again. 'Oh, Harmony, I think he's got another woman.'

Harmony was silent.

Emma waited for her to say something.

'Harmony?' she said. 'Did you hear me?'

'Yes, I heard you,' she said. 'I … ' She struggled to speak, images of her with Luke coming at her, then Will's face, his eyes downcast, his defeated demeanour, his desperation to please her in the newly planted garden. 'I'm sure you've got it wrong.'

'Are you? I'm not sure I've got it wrong at all. In fact, I'm convinced. I can't think of anything else. He worked late twice last week but when I called his direct line there was no answer. He's secretive, he can't look me in the eye.' She sighed. 'He hasn't wanted sex for a over a month and you know what he's like, I mean, it's Ian, he's the original sex pest, usually all over me like a rash.'

'That doesn't necessarily mean he's having an affair.'

Emma wanted to protest, tell Harmony all the other things that pointed to Ian playing away, but she'd run out of energy. She was exhausted with all the worrying she'd been doing. And it didn't seem as if Harmony was that interested, certainly not in offering the support Emma needed. She had hoped Harmony would laugh and tell her not to be so ridiculous, reassure her that Ian wasn't capable of such a thing. But she seemed subdued, almost as if she suspected Ian herself.

'I always imagined I'd be one of those wives who wouldn't get her knickers in a twist over this sort of thing. You know, husband gets a mistress, one less job on the to-do list, but, well, truth is I do mind. I mind terribly. I was just this minute thinking about it and felt myself about to cry. That's why I called. I mean, when do I ever cry?'

'Never.'

'Exactly. But last night I cried proper buckets. I had to hide in the larder, sobbing my eyes out. The children thought I was in there stealing chocolate biscuits.' She breathed out heavily. 'I don't want to lose him, Harmony. We've been together too long. He's my husband and I know he's no angel – he's a bloody pain most of the time – but I love him.'

Harmony was quiet again.

'And the children? If he … leaves us … '

'He's not going anywhere, Emma.'

Emma sniffed. 'Well, for the last week or so he's barely been able to look at me.'

'Have you asked him about it?'

'No!' she exclaimed. 'I don't want him to tell me he's fallen in love with someone else. I don't want to know. I just want him to get it out of his system and come back to me.' Emma stopped speaking then, overwhelmed by tears. 'I'm sorry,' she managed through sobs.

'Do you need me to drive down?'

Emma knew from her voice that she didn't really want to. Not that she'd expect her to – she had work to do, after all. 'That's so sweet of you to offer, but it's far too far,' she said. 'I'll be fine. I just needed to share it with you. And you're probably right, it's bound to be nothing, just me overreacting as usual. I know he's got lots going on at work. He's probably just exhausted.' Emma laughed through the end of her tears. 'I'll cook him a steak and kidney pie tonight. Remind him why he loves me.'

Emma nodded and then took a couple of breaths to steady herself. 'I'm absolutely fine. Everything is absolutely fine. I'm sure there's a simple explanation.'

CHAPTER NINETEEN

Will waited in his car outside the pub. Rain hammered at the windscreen, and despite it still being early the black clouds that hung low overhead darkened the sky. He'd answered Alastair's chirpy message which suggested Tuesday in a similarly enthusiastic style. He'd ended with a cheery *looking forward to it* and had a quickly returned a reply saying *likewise*.

At each point Will questioned his motives: with each message sent, as he'd grabbed his car keys, walked out of the flat, drove through Hanworth and crossed the M25, followed the signs to Lightwater, then Camberley. Yet despite all the doubt, there he was, in the car park of The Dog and Duck, waiting to meet up with Alastair Farrow.

He took a breath and patted his hands against the driver's wheel and unclipped his seat belt.

The pub was low-ceilinged, with a brash tartan carpet and horse brasses that hung on black-painted beams, and cheap dark tables with wooden chairs with green PVC seat pads. It smelt of old beer, last Sunday's roast, and the faint tang of bleach. Will walked up to the bar and smiled at the heavy-set barman who was wiping a cloth over one of the beer taps.

'Yes, mate,' he said, balling the cloth and dropping it onto the bar top.

'I'll have a glass of red wine.'

'Large or small?'

'Large, please' Will replied. 'Is there a wine list?'

The man shook his head. 'No, we do a choice of two. Merlot or a cheeky Cabernet Sauv.'

'The Cabernet Sauvignon and a bag of ready salted, please.'

Will kept his eyes on the bar and focused on the voices around him, trying to pick out any that might be familiar. He didn't like how anxious he was feeling. It was ridiculous; years had passed. He forced himself to turn around to check the pub properly. As soon as he did he saw Alastair. It had to be him. Same balding head from the Facebook photos, same reddened skin. He was sitting at a table with his back to Will. He was reading a newspaper, sitting bolt upright, holding the paper in front of him at arm's length. He wore a green sweater with a pink shirt, a gold watch on his right wrist. Will craned his head around a group of men obscuring his view and saw Alastair was wearing brown cord trousers and tan leather shoes with a stripe of a red sock just visible. As he studied him he felt his knees give way. He reached for the bar to steady himself, breathed slowly and evenly as he allowed the memories of that afternoon to play out, not fighting to block them as he usually would. He felt the thump of fists into his sides and back. He remembered Farrow's smell, cigarettes, school soap, alcohol. He felt his full weight on him as Farrow held him down and pushed his face into the dirt, struggling and panicking as he felt the air squeeze out of his lungs.

'That'll be six-fifty, mate.'

Will took his eyes off Alastair and took his credit card out of his wallet. 'I'm meeting someone for a few drinks,' he said. 'Can I set up a tab?'

The barman nodded and took Will's credit card, dropping it into a beer glass on the back of the bar with the till receipt. Will thanked him and picked up his crisps and wine and began to walk to the table.

'Alastair?' he said as he drew level with him.

The man looked up in mild surprise and then hurriedly closed his paper and stood. He held out his hand.

'Will English!'

Will shook his hand. A shiver ran up his arm as their skin touched. 'Alastair Farrow.'

'Call me Al. Nobody calls me Alastair these days, except for my mother, but only when she's cross with me, of course.' He guffawed with laughter. He was plumper than he'd been in the photos, his hair cut close to his head to make light of the baldness. His eyes were surrounded by deep laughter lines and his lips were so dark in colour they appeared almost purple.

Will gestured at Alastair's pint glass which was three quarters full. 'Do you want another before I sit down? I've left a card behind the bar.'

'I'm good for the moment, thanks,' he said. He sat down and moved the paper off the table onto the seat beside him. 'Don't want to get into trouble with the wife.' He winked at Will, who managed a tight smile and sat down opposite him. This was even harder than he'd imagined it would be.

'So what's it been?' asked Alastair brightly, showing no nerves at all. 'Twenty years? Must be. At least.'

Will plastered his face with a smile. 'Yes,' he said. 'At least.'

'And what do you do?'

'I have a wine shop,' he said. He stared at Alastair's face, eyes drawn to the scar that ran down his cheek.

'Ah, wine. Nice. I'm a bit of claret man myself. Do you sell much claret?'

'Yes,' said Will, dragging his eyes away from the screaming scar. 'Quite a bit. How about you? What do you do?'

'Accountant, I'm afraid.' He smiled at Will. 'Bit of a conversation killer.' He lifted his beer and drank. 'You married?' he asked as he placed the glass down.

'Yes, I am.'

'She's all right, is she?'

'All right?'

'You know, a bit of a harridan or good and quiet?'

Will stared at him for a moment or two and then Alastair laughed loudly. 'Mine's a bit of a harridan. I'm sure yours is lovely. Lucky bugger.'

Will moved his wine glass to the side and leant forward. 'I need to talk to you about what happened.'

Alastair looked confused.

'At school,' Will said. 'You see, when I read your message the other night, I thought it odd you weren't more apologetic.'

'For what?'

Will laughed in astonishment. Indignant anger flared inside him.

'For what?' Will repeated. 'For being a fucking cunt, that's what.'

Alastair's smile fell from his face like a stone through water. He stared at Will as if he was pointing a gun in his face then glanced nervously over his shoulder. 'Steady on,' he said, laughing tightly. 'That's a bit much.'

'A bit much?' Will needled his eyes into Alastair's puffy face. 'You're joking, right?'

'And this is about school?'

'Of course it's about school!' Will shook his head and stared at the man with incomprehension. He sat back in his chair. 'You remember what you did, don't you?'

Alastair's face broke into a smile. 'Will, come on. We were at public school, that's just what happened. A bit of banter. Mucking around.' His smile broadened. 'You know that. That's just what went on. There isn't a boarding school in the country that doesn't have the same. There's no need to get worked up about it. Like I said in my message, I was a bit of a cock, I know that. But, that's the way it was.' He reached for his beer and drank. 'Just banter.'

Will felt his blood boil with rage. He wanted to punch him. That would wipe that stupid smile off his fat, ugly face, wouldn't it?

'Banter?' He said instead. 'No, banter is joking around, playing, it doesn't hurt anyone. What you did, beating up young boys, scaring the shit out of them, and doing … ' He hesitated. '… doing God only knows what – that isn't banter, that's bullying. Bullying at best and abuse at worst.'

Alastair's features hardened and Will saw a flash of the boy who had hurt him, who had beaten him, pushed his face into the ground until he thought he might suffocate, and an old fear materialised, a fear he hadn't felt in a very long time.

'Yes,' Alastair said. 'That's what I call it because that's what it was.'

They stared at each other. Then Alastair ran his hand over his head, rubbed the back of it a couple of times. He leant forward, turned his face so his scarred cheek faced Will and jabbed his finger hard against it a couple of times. 'You see this? You see it?' he said through gritted teeth, his voice low. 'Am I moaning about that? Am I going on about needing an apology? No, no I'm not. Because it was just mucking around.' He sat back and gave a dismissive shake of his head. 'Jesus Christ, English, grow some bloody balls. School should have taught you to be a man rather than the wimp you are. That is what went on. At Eton, at Harrow, at Gordonstoun and at bloody Farringdon Hall. Men who had it a lot worse than you have managed to get over it. Bloody hell, some of this country's greatest leaders would have seen the back of an older boy's hand. Do they sit there like you, licking their wounds, feeling sorry for themselves, and asking for bloody apologies?'

Will couldn't believe what he was hearing. It was like listening to his father all over again. All that repellent claptrap about how boarding school bred real men, men who ran the world, men who built the sodding Empire, men for whom this type of thing was character-building and expected.

'It happened to all of us,' Alastair continued. 'It happened to me when I was in the bottom years, and the boys who had their fun with me had the same done to them. Yes, some got it worse than others, but that's survival of the fittest. You might not like it. It might not stand up against all that namby-pamby, politically correct rubbish we're forced to suck on today, but that's the way it was. There were those of us on top of the pile and those of you at the bottom and, like it or not, the system worked.' He reached for his drink, sniffing loudly, and rolled his shoulders a couple of times as if he was limbering up for a boxing bout. 'Have you got children? A son, maybe?'

Will stayed silent and didn't move a muscle. It was like being stuck in a parallel universe, surreal and nightmarish. He thought of Harmony, of how lovely it would be if he was sitting with her, sharing the packet of crisps that sat unopened on the table, chatting about everything and nothing. He thought of her smile, of the way she played with her necklace, the look in her eyes before she kissed him.

'I've got a son, and you know what? He pulls the legs off beetles and the wings off flies. He punches his friends and they punch him back. For fun. For exercise. Because that's what boys do to amuse themselves. And it's not just Charlie. They all do it. We got sent away to school. What age were you?' Will didn't answer. 'Well, I was six. All of us in it together, no parents anywhere near us. It was *Lord of the bloody Flies* and you know it. Most of the masters were wankers. They knew what was going on and it amused them. Those that didn't like it turned a blind eye.'

Will pictured Drysdale then, that sick look of pleasure that settled over his face as he lifted his cane and bent it a couple of times to *loosen her up*.

'So what did we have? No parents. All boys. Masters who didn't step in. And you're sitting there like a saggy-titted feminist wanting to … ' He bent his voice into whiney sing-song. '… talk about what happened.' He leant forward, his mouth turned down, his eyes narrowed, cold as ice. 'You want to know what happened?' he spat. 'I'll tell you what happened,' he continued, not allowing time for Will to answer his question. 'Nothing. Nothing bloody happened.'

Will stared at him, his round face shining beneath a thin sheen of sweat. 'No, Alastair, something did happen.' He kept his voice low and calm. 'You know what you did and so do I.'

Will saw Alastair Farrow's face darken like an approaching storm. Will's heart began to race as the fear he'd felt on that late afternoon began to creep up on him again. The noise of his panting breath loud in his ears as he'd turned to run, Luke's screams echoing in the trees around them.

'You don't know anything.' Alastair crossed his arms and stared hard at Will. 'I was there, when you said nothing happened. Don't go making stories up now.' He unfolded his arms and shook his head, reached for his glass and finished the remainder of his beer. Then he picked up his paper and made to leave. 'I don't know why I agreed to meet up with you,' he said with poisonous contempt. 'Why I had to sit here and listen to you whining. You know full well how it was. It was kick or be kicked, and keep your mouth shut.' He looked at Will then like he was shit on the bottom of his shoe and gave a derisive laugh. 'No wonder wankers like you got the crap belted out of them.' Alastair shook his head again as he looked down his nose at Will. 'Moaning and complaining, feeling sorry for yourself. I bet you blame your shitty existence on your dreadful schooldays, don't you? Wondering what might have been if only you'd skipped through childhood in a rosy haze getting cuddles and love. You know, English, if you'd just played the game, showed some bloody backbone, maybe you and those other wastes-of-space would have been left to get on with your sad little lives.'

'Played the game?'

Alastair smirked and stood. 'It was good to catch up,' he said. 'Don't bother trying to contact me again.'

Everything inside Will erupted then, every part of his body filled with anger and loathing. His hand shot out and grabbed Alastair round the neck, his body slammed against the table and knocked both glasses over. There was a loud shout from the barman. Two men nearby jumped to attention; one of them rested a hand on Will's arm, the other told them to calm down, 'Easy now, take it outside.' Will watched Alastair's eyes widen as he closed his hand tighter around his neck. Alastair's hands lifted to grasp Will's arm.

'I could fucking kill you. You're the waste of space. You, Alastair, not us. You don't deserve to live.'

'Hey, come on gents,' said the man beside them. 'Let go of him now. We're all having a nice quiet drink here. Nobody wants this.'

Will glanced at the man, and caught sight of the barman walking over with an angry grimace. What was he doing? What was this accomplishing? Nothing. People like Alastair Farrow would never be made to see sense by talking. Their morality was set. He'd never admit what he'd done was wrong because he didn't see it as wrong. Talking was futile.

Will let go of Alastair with a final push and he fell back onto the chair, rubbing his neck and swearing under his breath. The barman and one of the men nearby grabbed hold of Will.

'Are you okay, Al?' the barman said, his fingers digging into Will's arm.

Alastair nodded. 'I'm fine. Just a misunderstanding. My friend's leaving now.'

'People like you make me sick,' Will growled, shrugging the two men off him.

'Just piss off.'

Will stared at him. It was he who was pathetic, sitting there, denying what he'd done. Will saw what he was then, a foul bully with an over-inflated sense of self-worth. He glanced at the two men either side of him who were poised and ready to grab hold of him if they had to. He turned back to Alastair and shook his head.

'You know something? You're not worth it,' he said through gritted teeth, the taste of bile pinching the back of his throat.

Will turned his back on him and walked out of the pub. He jogged through the rain and climbed into his car. He closed the door and rested his head against the steering wheel. He shook as he thought of Alastair's smug face, his lack of remorse that so baffled Will. He wished he'd been more eloquent, wished he'd been able to argue against Farrow with conviction, make him see how abhorrent his behaviour had been.

'Fuck!' he shouted then, lifting his head and banging it twice against the steering wheel. 'Don't do this to yourself, Will.'

He saw himself, back in his study, desperately trying to concentrate on his English essay, when his housemaster, Mr Fraser, came to find him. Mr Fraser was a short man with tufts of grey hair that fringed a shiny bald pate. He was decent, firm but fair, popular with the boys.

'English,' he said. His voice was quiet, almost apologetic, and his eyes seemed unable to meet Will's directly. 'Mr Drysdale needs to see you.'

Will's stomach had turned over. 'Why, sir?'

The housemaster seemed reticent. 'Best get to his office,' he said.

'Am I in trouble, sir?' Will asked as he closed his exercise book and put the lid on his fountain pen.

Mr Fraser had rested a hand on his shoulder. 'Just tell the truth and you'll be fine.'

All he had wanted was to lay the ghost of Alastair Farrow to rest, but he knew now it would never happen. He sat up, turned the engine on and threw the car into reverse, then drove out of the car park without a backward glance. Will sped along the roads, his mind full of Farrow's barefaced denial. The man's unshakeable belief that he was blameless. Had he heard right? Had Alastair said that what had happened was his – Will's – fault? When he got to the main road he pushed his foot to the floor, feeling the engine strain, feeling like he wanted to drive faster and faster. The windscreen wipers worked overtime against the heavy rain. As he gained speed, his anger and frustrations boiled over and he began to shout, loud and guttural, banging the steering wheel with one hand as hard as he could. When, finally, he couldn't shout any longer and his pent-up rage had begun to dissipate, he eased off the accelerator and breathed heavily, emotionally spent and desperate to be home.

He walked into the flat and closed the door and found Harmony on the sofa, feet up, hugging a cushion and watching the news. She was wearing a pair of leggings and an old baggy T-shirt, her hair loose, a little straggly. She glanced up at him and gave him an unconvincing smile.

He sank heavily into the armchair opposite her. He wanted her to pat the sofa beside her like she usually did, ask him to sit with her, but she didn't move. He closed his eyes, resting his head against the back of the armchair. He was exhausted; his limbs felt cast in concrete, as if he'd never be able to move them again.

Just then her phone rang. He opened his eyes and watched her pick it up. She turned it off without answering it and put it back on the coffee table. Her mouth twitched like it did sometimes when she was angry. He felt as if he was about erupt; his emotions, the pressure of keeping it all inside him, dealing with it all alone, suddenly became too much.

'I saw that guy earlier today. The one Luke mentioned. Alastair Farrow.'

'The one from school?'

Will nodded. She turned the television off with the remote and looked at him and he noticed there was a softness about her that he hadn't seen since the night Luke had come to supper.

He pushed the heels of his palms against his eyes. 'I lost my temper. I shouted in the middle of a crowded pub. Christ, I grabbed him by the bloody neck.' He sighed heavily and looked at her. 'I thought he might show some sort of remorse, might at least seem embarrassed, but he just laughed. He couldn't have cared less.'

'What did he do to you?' she asked then. 'This man. At school, I mean. Why did you think he would show some remorse?'

'He made people's lives hell for fun, that's what he did. A bully, a vile one at that.' He broke off and looked at her. He knew he had to talk to her. It was out now, everything he'd worked so hard to keep hidden had re-emerged. He took a deep breath and braced himself. 'There was this one afternoon,' he said, starting slowly. 'The day before Luke was expelled. He and I were in the woods. There was this den thing we went to, a small clearing with some logs to sit on. We used to play there. It was late October, we'd had supper and were supposed to be in prep, you know, doing homework. But we'd crept out, bunked off. I had my Polaroid camera and was taking photos of stuff and Luke was trying to make a harpoon with the Swiss Army knife my dad gave me, but these guys, proper nasty bastards in the sixth form, found us. Farrow was one of them.'

The incident he described had been buried for twenty-five years, he'd never discussed it with anyone, but as he recounted the skeleton of the story to Harmony, every single detail played out in his mind as if it were happening there and then.

'They asked what we were doing in their smoking room, said this part of the wood was for sixth form only. They said we were trespassing.'

Will recalled the malice in Alastair Farrow's voice. He was much older than them, a senior prefect and captain of cricket. He was popular and respected in his peer group and the staff room. He had brown hair that flopped over his eyes and that air of confidence that came from a combination of good looks and sporting prowess. But there was a look in his eyes, the Devil's look, Luke called it. He had a way of staring at the younger boys, his nose flared, lip curled, as if he wanted to draw and quarter them. When the group had found them, cigarettes clamped to their mouths, beers clutched in their hands, Farrow's eyes had lit up in a way that turned Will's stomach, in a way that told him he and Luke were in big trouble.

Farrow and the others had laughed and jeered as they drew on their cigarettes and drank from their bottles.

Look at him! Thinks he's David fucking Bailey with that stupid camera. What a wanker!

'How many of them were there?' Harmony asked.

Her voice broke his reverie. 'Five,' he said.

Will had looped his camera over his neck and looked desperately around for an escape route, then glanced at Farrow who smiled and shook his head slowly. Will felt sick. He turned to look at Luke. His eyes were set like stone, staring at the boys like he wanted to kill them, his lips twitching, fists clenching and unclenching at his sides like beating hearts.

'Don't do anything,' Will had pleaded silently. 'Please don't do anything.'

He kept telling himself they were okay, it was just Farrow and his friends having a laugh, messing about, that soon they'd get bored and leave them alone. He willed Luke to keep calm, willed him to keep his temper in check, but he could see him seething.

'Alastair asked me to give him my camera,' he said to Harmony.

Will closed his eyes as a vivid image of Farrow flew into his head. The older boy putting his arm around his shoulders, drawing him close.

So, we have David Bailey and Puke Crawford – Bible Boy – hiding out in the woods like a couple of homo-hobbits.

Will recalled the smell of his warm, sour breath laced with cigarettes and beer.

'He said if I didn't give him the camera they'd beat the living daylights out of us.' He glanced at Harmony. 'Those were his words. The living daylights.'

Harmony shook her head, lips parted, eyes reflecting her horror.

'I didn't want him to have my camera so I took it off my neck and threw it as far as I could into the bushes. I don't know what I was thinking about, looking back on it. It was only a stupid camera, but it was my favourite thing in the whole world and the thought of him breaking it or stealing it was unbearable.' Will sniffed and clasped his hands in front of him. 'Anyway, Alastair Farrow didn't like that too much.'

The older boy had angered like a wasp.

Go and get it.

But Will had stood his ground.

Farrow shoved him so hard he went down on his knees. Then a kick to the stomach. Luke began to scream.

Don't hurt him! Get off him! Get off him!

Will tried to tell him to be quiet but was too winded to speak.

'Alastair was … ' Will hesitated, '… he was hurting me. The others were laughing. Luke was screeching at them to leave me alone and all I could think was: shut up, Luke. Shut up. Stop screaming at them, you idiot, you're making it worse.' Will paused and laid his head back against the chair. 'The next thing I knew Farrow was on top of me, had my face pressed into the ground. I had all these leaves and dirt in my mouth, and he was punching my head and body again and again.' An unwelcome memory of the earth and grit in his mouth passed over Will and made him want to spit.

'My God,' whispered Harmony. Her voice stuck in her throat. Will didn't look at her. He didn't want her pity. His skin crawled with guilt.

'Luke began to make this awful sound, like some weird war cry, and he ran at Farrow and the next thing I knew he'd pushed him off me. Then I heard Alastair scream. When I looked up I saw his face was covered in blood. Luke had sliced his face open with my penknife.'

Dread filled Will as he watched Luke standing there, panting, his eyes crazed, hand lightly clasping Will's knife. The silence that fell around them was terrifying, all he could hear was the slight rustle of the wind in the leaves of the great oak tree that towered over them. Farrow's eyes glinted. A sheen of bloodied saliva coated his lips , there was more blood on his teeth. One side of his face was scarlet, blood flowing from a cut that ran from his eye to his chin.

You little bastards.

Will closed his eyes as he recalled Alastair's words. He'd stared, horrified at the blood on the older boy's face, the fury that blazed in his eyes, his lips curled back to show gritted, bloodied teeth.

I didn't do it! Don't hurt me. It was him, not me. It was Luke!

Will remembered the look on Luke's gaunt face, one of bewilderment and shock. Will's hand flew up to his mouth, but it was too late, the words were out.

You're pathetic, English. Get the fuck out of here.

No, Will. Don't leave me.

Luke and Will had locked eyes.

You watch my back, I'll watch yours. Remember, Will? You remember what we promised?

Then he lifted his right hand like a Red Indian to show Will the scar that crossed his palm.

Farrow began to laugh and he shoved Will backwards.

You're pathetic.

Will remembered Luke screaming for him to help him as Farrow set upon him like a ravenous lion on a deer.

Harmony stood up and went over to Will. She sat on the side of the armchair and stroked his head. He leant against her, his eyes squeezed closed trying to block out the memory of Luke's screaming. The sense of relief at having shared the memory with his wife, of feeling her sympathy and support, was overwhelming.

Her phone buzzed, the ringer on silent, the vibrations making it dance on the table top.

'For God's sake,' she breathed.

She got up and turned the phone off and then went back to Will.

'Take the call if you want to,' Will said.

'It doesn't matter. Just work. This is more important.'

'I'm fine. Honestly. Thank you for listening. I should have told you years ago. Alastair is a bastard, but I promise you, I'm fine. He did what he did, he's a nasty piece of work, but there's nothing we can do about it. Some people are just arseholes.'

She nodded and then wrapped her arms around him, resting her chin on the top of his head. 'I'm so sorry that happened to you.'

'Are you going to leave me?

She didn't answer immediately. 'I don't want to. I know deep down that I belong with you. But things have changed, haven't they?'

'I want to make it better.'

'I know you do.'

Will woke in the middle of the night and felt for her. She wasn't in bed and the duvet was neatly pulled up on her side, the pillow untouched. He heard her cough from her study. He lay still and listened. She was talking to someone. Though he couldn't hear her words there seemed to be a level of urgency, as if there was some sort of problem. He got out of bed and walked down the corridor and opened the door to her study. She wasn't on the phone, but was working at her desk. Her computer was on, and she sat at her desk in her dressing gown and slippers, her glasses perched on her nose. She jumped when he came in.

'You scared me,' she said with a nervous laugh. 'Have you been there long?'

'No, but I heard you on the phone. Is everything all right?'

'It was Emma. What she's doing calling at this time, I don't know,' she said. 'She said she couldn't sleep. She's pretty upset but I told her I'd call in the morning.'

'Anything serious?'

'Problems with Ian. Sorry if I woke you.'

'I don't think you did. Can't you sleep either?'

She shook her head and looked at the desk. 'It's bloody work, that's all. I can't stop thinking about it.' She glanced back at him. 'Annoying. I'll be glad when it's dealt with.' She put the tip of her thumb to her mouth and chewed on it gently. 'I need to sort it out.'

'Can I get you anything?' he asked.

'No, thank you,' she said, turning back to her computer screen. 'I won't be long. I've just got this one thing I want to deal with tonight.'

'But then you'll come back to bed?'

'Yes,' she said. 'When I've dealt with it, I'll come back.'

CHAPTER TWENTY

Harmony walked into the restaurant and scanned the place for Luke. It was a huge, airy room with modern furnishings. It bustled with noise as conversation fought to be heard above the sounds of the open kitchen where a dozen sweating chefs could be seen cooking and yelling orders. She watched a flame leap a foot out of a pan, the chef turning his head and leaning back to avoid it then heaving the pan upwards a couple of times, tossing the food into the air and catching it. He swept his arm across his brow and called out in rapid Italian to someone behind him. It was reassuringly busy, every table filled, and nobody noticed her as they talked avidly, laughed and ate.

Her stomach buzzed with nerves. Luke had called three times yesterday and sent a handful of texts, each of them incriminating should Will happen to see them. He said he was desperate to see her, that he hadn't been able to get her out of his head, that he was going insane with desire. She'd been an idiot to think that having sex with Luke would do anything to ease her anger at Will. All it had done was complicate a situation that didn't need complicating. She couldn't continue it. She didn't want to. She had no idea whether her marriage was over or not, but this guilt-ridden limbo was unbearable.

She'd spent the morning at the British Library rather than in the office. Libraries calmed her. Row upon row of stacked shelves, insulating her, holding her safely. She'd always felt at home with books. While Sophie had spent any rare free time attempting to cook up half-decent dishes from the meagre supply of store-cupboard ingredients her grandmother kept in stock, Harmony would curl up on the sofa and read. She read anything from Ray Bradbury to Stephen King, Jane Austen to Jilly Cooper. There was always a dictionary beside her. If she came across a word she didn't know she'd stop and look up the word. Sophie teased her for being a geek, but Harmony didn't care. Stories were an escape from her fatherless, motherless world, a security blanket for whenever she felt vulnerable.

'Can I help you, madam?' asked a man dressed in a spotless black polo shirt, the name of the restaurant stitched across his left breast.

'I'm meeting someone,' she said. 'I'm not sure if he's here already.'

'And the name of the reservation?'

'Crawford,' she said. 'I think it was for one o'clock. I'm a bit early.'

The man looked down his list and then smiled at her. 'Mr Crawford hasn't arrived yet. Shall I show you to your table?'

The table was near the back of the room and as she sat down she felt immediately less conspicuous and her body relaxed.

'Would you like something to drink?'

She nodded. 'Iced water, please. Tap is fine.'

He smiled at her and placed two leather menus on the table. 'I'll send someone over with your water. Can I get you anything else?'

'No, thank you, I'll wait until my friend arrives.' Friend sounded too intimate, too telling, and she wished she'd said colleague instead.

When Harmony saw Luke come through the double glass doors into the restaurant she froze for a moment or two. She felt her skin flush and she took hold of her glass of water and had a sip, lifting her eyes over the rim of the glass to watch him talk to the waiter in the polo shirt. She saw the waiter point. Luke smiled and nodded in her direction. She cast her eyes downwards so as not to catch his gaze.

As he approached the table she looked up. 'Hello, Luke,' she said, her voice shaking.

He leant in and kissed her cheek. 'I've missed you,' he said. He sat down and immediately waved over a nearby waiter.

'Yes, sir?' said the waiter as he hurried over.

'We'd like to order some wine and some sparkling water.' He looked at Harmony. 'Would you like red or white?'

'Not for me, thank you,' she said, her voice catching in her throat. 'And I'm on tap water.'

'No wine. Just the sparkling water.'

She resisted the urge to thank the waiter, who didn't seem to mind Luke's brusqueness.

'I've been thinking about you constantly,' he said. 'God, even the way you blush makes me want you.'

'Shhh,' she said.

'Why?'

'I don't want anyone to hear.'

He laughed loudly. 'Who's going to care?'

'Me,' she said. She picked up the menu and fixed her eyes on it. 'And I gave you specific instructions not to call or text me.'

'Specific instructions?' he repeated with amusement.

'Yes.'

'I was desperate to speak to you.' He leant forward and laid his hand on her lower arm. 'I can't think about anything else.'

'I told you to email me.' She laid the menu on the table and looked at him. 'I specifically told you not to call me. Will was with me when you did. I can't believe you did that.'

Luke fell silent, his disappointment plain. 'I see,' he said. 'Please accept my apologies.'

She lifted the menu. 'So what's good?' she said, not wanting to acknowledge the hurt in his eyes.

'It's all good. I don't do mediocre.'

'Christ, you're an arrogant so and so, aren't you?'

'It's been said before.'

She glanced over the top of the menu at him and saw him smiling, and despite herself she smiled back.

'If you like seafood, the salt and pepper squid is fantastic. If you don't, the carpaccio is delicious. And the pasta here is always good.'

'I dislike carpaccio,' she said. 'Remember? The well-cooked steak and the liberal's conscience?'

'Ah yes, of course, all the guilt cooked out of it.'

The smile slipped off her face as she was reminded about the two of them together. 'Luke, I came here to—' She was cut short by the waiter who arrived with their bottle of water. He opened it and poured each of them a glass, then retrieved a notepad. Harmony ordered the salt cod soup and a fennel risotto, Luke the carpaccio and a seafood linguini.

'So you ignored my recommendations?'

'I did.'

Luke leant forward, his forearms in front of him. Harmony stared at his hand on the white tablecloth, those long fingers and perfect nails, gentle moons of white at the base of each one. She recalled his fingers on her skin, grasping her hair, inside her. He moved his hand so the tip of his middle finger rested against hers. She drew her hand away from him. 'How was your business trip?' she asked, her eyes fixed on the table in front of her.

'All I could think about was you, so it was both a waste of time and frustrating. Did you think about me?'

'Yes. I thought about a lot of things.' She paused, took deep breath and lifted her eyes to look at him. 'What we did was wrong.'

'Wrong?' he said, his brow furrowing in confusion. 'It was anything but wrong.'

'I can't do this.'

'Can't do what?' He sat back in his chair and folded his arms.

'Have an affair.'

'Don't call it that,' he said darkly.

'But that's what it is.'

His features became set, his eyes narrowed, burning with the same intensity as they has done when they'd first had sex, when he'd been filled with angry desire.

'I'm married, and having sex with another man is an affair.'

'But your marriage isn't working.'

'My marriage is fine.'

'You're lying. If your marriage was fine you wouldn't have come looking for me.'

'I didn't look for you,' she said, making an effort to keep her voice level. 'We met at the party and then you … ' She paused as the waiter appeared with a basket of bread, continuing only when he left. 'And then you pursued me.'

He lifted his eyebrows. 'Pursued you? Is that what you think?'

She reached for her glass and drank some water. She didn't want to rush, didn't want to say the wrong thing, something that would lead him on. She needed to keep her head straight. 'You made your feelings pretty clear at the party. Then you came to my work and took me for a drink and then asked me, in no uncertain terms, to sleep with you.'

'And you said no and then I left you alone.' He paused and reached for some bread, then tore a small piece off it. 'Then you emailed me. You told me you wanted to meet me and you took me to your husband's photography studio and we fucked. Twice.' He put the bread in his mouth.

'Stop it,' she whispered.

'Is it easier to believe I chased you? That you had no option but to fall into my arms?'

'Yes,' she retorted. 'Of course it is. If I think too hard about what I've done, about what I'm doing, I feel sick.' She drew another deep breath. 'But there were reasons. Things have happened in the last six months that left a chasm between Will and me.' She paused. 'Neither of us dealt very well with losing our baby. He wasn't able to support me and I felt very alone. I was angry at him.' She paused. 'And there was this numbness around me, like all my anger and resentment was building up in a bubble around me. Then being with you, like that, seemed to release the pressure, like a vent and ... ' She stopped talking, aware she was being too candid, aware she was being side-tracked, that she should focus on ending the relationship, not on justifying it.

'And what?' he said. 'I want to know.'

'Whatever Will's done, I love him. I won't betray him like this. What we did should never have happened.'

'But it did happen,' he said, reaching beneath the table and laying his hand on her knee, slowly moving up her thigh, stroking her gently. His touch sent tingles down her spine.

'No.' She pushed his hand away. She reached for her water again and found she was shaking. 'I want to be with Will.'

'Do you?' He sounded accusatory rather than concerned.

'Just because a marriage has rough patches or people make mistakes, doesn't mean you stop loving each other.'

He let out a contemptuous sigh. 'That word again. Love. What does it even mean?'

'Don't do that. Don't dismiss what I'm saying. You know what it means. Or maybe you don't. But I do. I love him. And,' she paused, 'he needs me right now.' She glanced at Luke. 'Lots of things he's tried to forget have resurfaced since he saw you. Yesterday he met one of the men who bullied him.' She watched his face for a reaction, but there was nothing.

'Which one?' he asked.

'Alastair Farrow?'

'Farrow,' he repeated. 'Why did he see him?'

'I don't know. I think they contacted each other through Facebook. I didn't ask. Anyway, Will was in a state when he got home. I think he wanted some sort of closure but ended up getting angry with him, made a scene. Christ, he grabbed the guy by the throat in the middle of a pub.'

Luke was silent.

'He needs me.'

'So you won't leave him because he has problems? Surely the fact he has problems is exactly why you should leave him.'

'That's a very simplistic way of looking at it, Luke. It's not just because he has problems. I've been with him for over twenty years, lived with him and his problems for all that time. But his issues clearly have roots in a difficult childhood. He's internalised what went on. All this time he's told me his past doesn't affect him, but it does.'

Luke blinked slowly and sat back in his chair. 'It's difficult to articulate what damage can be caused by people like Alastair Farrow. We all deal with bad experiences in our own ways, whatever ways we think will work best, but for all of us there will be times when we can't control our emotions. But you can't stay with Will because of something that happened to him twenty-five years ago. You have to stay with him because you want to stay with him.'

'I want to stay with him.'

'That's not what it looks like to me.'

'I was angry with him. So angry it clouded my judgement, but he's my husband. You were married,' she said, glancing at him, unsure if mentioning his wife might upset him. 'You must understand what I'm saying. There are times you are close and times you drift apart. It's not as simple as falling in and out of love, something starting and something finishing.'

'This isn't about my marriage. Or yours. It's about us.'

'You're not listening to me … ' She stopped speaking then as she saw a group of men come into the restaurant. 'Jesus Christ!' she hissed sharply and dropped her head, lifting a hand to shield her face from them. 'It's Ian!'

'Really?' Luke glanced over his shoulder. 'I know he likes this place.'

She turned on him angrily. 'You brought me to a place that you know my best friend's husband goes to?'

'I didn't know he'd be here.' Luke seemed unconcerned.

'Hide your face!' she said, as she began to panic. 'He's going to see me.' Her eyes darted around as she looked for the nearest escape from the restaurant. 'He'll think there's something going on between us.'

'Then he'll be right.'

'You did this on purpose, didn't you? You knew he was coming here. Oh my God, you want Will to find out.'

He didn't say anything.

'Jesus,' said Harmony, glancing over at Ian's group.

'Calm down. We're just having lunch,' he said. 'We bumped into each other. It's perfectly innocent.'

'What will Emma think?'

'He won't tell her.'

'Of course he will,' she said through gritted teeth. She glanced up again and saw Ian and his companions about to sit at a table on the other side of the restaurant.

'He won't because I'll tell him not to. I'll tell him not to tell either of them.'

'And you think he'll do what you say?' she asked, shaking her head in disbelief.

'Yes, he'll do what I say. I'm his lawyer.'

She shielded her face, while keeping her eyes bolted on Ian who was sitting with his back towards her. 'I'm not staying here and letting Ian know we … ' She stopped herself from finishing the sentence. 'I don't want him to know we're having lunch together. Will can't ever know about this.'

She tried to stand but he grabbed hold of her wrist.

'Will doesn't deserve you,' he said then. 'He has no idea what he has. He takes things for granted, Harmony.'

Luke's fingers dug into her skin as a raw anger seemed to be taking hold of him.

'Let go of me, Luke,' she said firmly. They locked eyes for a moment or two and then she felt his fingers release. She stood and picked up her bag. 'It's over.'

'It isn't.'

She leant in close to him. 'Yes, it is. Leave me alone. You and I are finished.'

'We haven't even started.'

'Then there's nothing to finish, is there?' she hissed.

She stood up straight and glanced over towards Ian again. He was deep in conversation with one of his companions. She took a deep breath and then started to walk towards the door, her head angled away from his table, eyes on the floor. Her heart thumped as if it might break through her chest. Any moment he was going to spot her. Any moment he'd call her name across the restaurant.

When she reached the door, she pushed out into the sunshine and walked as quickly as she could past the window. As soon as she was clear of the restaurant, safe from Ian's view, relief washed over her. She glanced back towards the door, but thankfully there was no sign of Luke and she broke into a jog to put as much distance between them as possible.

CHAPTER TWENTY-ONE

His aunt sat in the driver's seat and clipped her seat belt in. He sat in the back seat and stared at the back of her head.

'Your father,' she said, as she turned the Morris Minor's engine on, 'is speechless.'

Luke studied her hair, the way it clumped together in greasy, grey whorls. The rosy pink skin on the back of her neck was patched with some kind of flaky skin condition that left dandruff on the shoulders of her heavy black coat.

'Did you hear me?' She shook her greasy head and and then turned to look at him for a moment, her lips pursed together as if she'd tasted something nasty. 'I asked him: "Simeon, do you have a message for your boy?" He said: "I do, Grace, tell him he has let us down. Tell the boy he has let us all down."' She shook her head again and he saw flakes of dandruff falling on her coat like snowflakes on a coal face. 'Expelled!' she shrieked so suddenly he jumped out of his skin. 'Expelled from school. And I had to look that headmaster in the eye. I've never been so humiliated in all my days! I feel quite faint. I won't be surprised if I have one of my turns. Oh, the shame … '

As she droned on, Luke rested his forehead against the cool of the window and watched the world pass as they drove down the long driveway, through the dappled shade of the lime trees, past the stupid lions on their stupid pillars, leaving Farringdon Hall behind. The injustice of what had happened overwhelmed him. He imagined his father in the stark whitewashed room he called Meeting Room, the African sun squeezing its way through the small high-set windows. He could see him sitting in his straight-backed mahogany chair, the cushionless seat curved with a polished dip where three generations of Crawfords, all of them men of the cloth, had sat and passed judgement on the sins of others. He imagined him shaking his head, his grey eyes ashamed and disappointed, his hands clasped and lying heavily on the Bible that rested on the empty desk in front of him. He heard him preaching on love – on God's love, on human love. His father, the expert on love. But he knew nothing. The closest he and his mother got to love was taking hold of each other's hands as they walked into the hut they called Church every Sunday morning to preach at the 'black-skinned heathens'. His father knew nothing of true love, nothing of opening your heart so wide to another that you'd weep if you thought about it too carefully. He knew nothing of the impact that love could have. Or of betrayal. The antithesis of love.

Luke stared at the scar on his palm, still red and angry even after so many months. But it was healing. It didn't hurt or itch anymore. The skin was repairing, knitting itself together. He clenched his fist closed, his fingernails raking against the scar. He wouldn't let them win. None of them. Not his father, not Drysdale, Aunt Grace, Will, Alastair Farrow, or any of them. They knew nothing. They were idiots. They knew nothing about anything. But he knew. He knew about love. Love was out there. Somewhere in this putrid, unjust world, love flourished.

CHAPTER TWENTY-TWO

'Mum, it's me,' Will said, as she answered the phone.

'William? Gosh, I wasn't expecting a call from you.'

'I'm sorry I haven't called for a while.'

There was a silence from the other end of the line.

'We haven't seen you in ages, as well,' he said then.

'No,' she said.

'I was hoping we might come down today? Are you around?'

'Oh, well, there's a few things I was supposed to be doing, but I suppose I could cancel them. Are you sure you want to make the journey? It's such a long way.'

'It's not that far, and I … ' Will hesitated. 'I'd really like to see you.'

'Then that would be lovely. If you want to you could always stay the night? I could cook supper.'

'Yes, okay, let me talk to Harmony first. I haven't asked her yet. I'll call and confirm when I have.'

Harmony was dressing when he went back into their room.

'I've just spoken to Mum,'.

'How is she?' Harmony said, as she sat on the edge of the bed and pulled her jeans on.

'She sounds okay. We didn't talk for long. I thought we might drive to Cambridge to see her? She suggested we stay the night. What do you think? The forecast is for hot weather. We could take her for lunch at The Horseshoes.'

'I can't. I'm sorry, there's some work I need to finish. I'm behind already. I have to get it done.'

'Really? But it's the weekend. You've been working so hard recently. You could do with some time off.'

'I've got Jacob on my back – he's still not happy with my report.

I'll stay here and work today, then catch the train down.'

Will tried to hide his disappointment. He'd hoped they'd be able to travel down together. The way she'd hugged him when he spoke to her about school had given him hope. He was convinced their marriage was salvageable. Though Harmony seemed a thousand miles away, lost in another world and unable to meet his eye, he was desperate to keep her near him. The thought of them spending the night apart made him nervous, as if he needed to keep her in sight at all times in case she disappeared into thin air like a magician's dove.

'Jacob should give you a break, you know.' He paused to let her speak, but she said nothing. 'Look, I'll take the train today and leave you the car, save you mucking about with tubes and taxis.'

He walked through the kitchen and unlocked the back door and breathed in the fresh, early morning air. There was a dewy dampness to it that made everything smell more vibrant. He went out into the garden and turned the hosepipe on and began to water the plants, transfixed by the rainbow sheen in the sunlit spray.

'You're enjoying the garden, aren't you?' said Harmony, from behind him. He looked back towards the house and saw her leaning against the doorframe, barefoot in her dressing gown.

He smiled at her. 'Yes, I am. Who'd've thought it, eh?' She smiled back at him and his heart leapt. He put the hosepipe down so the water ran into the flower bed and walked over to her.

'Harmony, I know there's lots wrong and I—'

'I'm not sure I'm able to talk now,' she said, drawing her dressing gown tighter across her body.

'I don't want to talk. I've said it all. You know where I stand. Everything I've said, how sorry I am, how determined I am to change, it's all still true. But I can see you're unhappy.'

'I'm—'

'No, let me finish. I don't want you here just in body, us living in the same space but not really together. It won't work like that. If we're going to stay together I want you back properly – body, mind and soul. I'm terrified of life without you, but stepping around each other on eggshells is unbearable.' His voice began to crack as he spoke. 'Being with you but suspecting you don't want to be here isn't how I want to live my life.'

Harmony nodded. 'I want to be here. I want to be with you.' She stopped there, but Will could see there was so much more she wasn't able or willing to say.

He ended up spending longer in the garden than he'd intended. He found gardening restful, a chance to let his mind drift, and before he knew it, it was nearly lunchtime. He went inside and packed his bag, then opened the door to her study to tell her he was going. She was staring at her phone. She looked up at him, her face pale and pinched, and turned her phone face down on her desk.

'You okay?' he asked.

She pursed her lips and nodded. 'Are you off?'

'Yes, I've just phoned Mum and said I'd be there by three.'

Harmony chewed on her lip and he saw her eyes had filled with tears.

'Do you want me to stay?' he asked.

'No. You must see Gill. It's been far too long. You need to spend some time with her.' She gave him a weak smile. 'I'll see you tomorrow.'

Her phone began to vibrate on her desk. He saw her tense. She glanced at it but didn't pick up.

'Are you going to answer it?'

'No,' she said. 'I'll call whoever it is back when you've gone.'

As he left the flat he wondered if she would make it down to Cambridge the following day, and if she didn't, whether she'd be there at the flat when he got home.

At Kings Cross Will bought his ticket, then went to the newsagent to buy a can of Coke and a newspaper. He waited on the platform for the train and realised how long it had been since his father's funeral, which was the last time he'd been to their house. That was back in May of the previous year. He'd last seen his mother when she came to stay with them at Christmas. Six months was a long time not to see her and he felt a rush of guilt. When she'd stayed with them at Christmas, she'd still been lost without his father, wandering from room to room, unsure where to put herself, offering to help but not knowing what to do. Harmony had been kind to her, given her jobs to try and occupy her. She'd asked her to peel the potatoes then quietly removed any bits of skin she'd missed without comment. She'd made her cups of tea and talked to her, sat and stroked her hand when she cried. Will had observed his mother's grief with mild irritation. He couldn't understand, Christmas or not, how she could still be so upset seven months after the man's death. He'd bitten his tongue on numerous occasions to stop himself telling her she was better off without him, that after years of living with his overbearing, authoritarian nonsense, she was finally free to enjoy her twilight years. But he was good and said nothing. He watched her cry, watched her stare silently into the middle distance, watched her trudge about the place. It hadn't been a good Christmas. Sophie and Roger were in Scotland with his family, so it was just the three of them in their flat for four days. It had rained and sleeted continuously, and his mother hadn't wanted to do anything or go anywhere, so they'd sat in the living room, watching television in numb silence. On Christmas Day, Harmony's morning sickness had meant she'd barely eaten anything, and when he lit the brandy on the pudding and the blue flames had leapt up to dance their graceful dance around it she fled the table with her hand over her mouth, leaving him and his mother waiting at the table listening to the sounds of her throwing up in the bathroom. She returned to the table, her skin tinged green, and as she sat down he passed her a portion of pudding.

'Half that size,' she said weakly.

So there they were, three silent people with paper hats gamely balanced on their heads, sitting in front of untouched Christmas pudding with foetus-friendly brandy-free butter slowly melting its sugary innocence over their best china plates. Harmony had tried to smile as he stood to clear the plates.

'It will be a lot noisier next year, won't it?' she said to him and his mother. 'I mean, with this little one.' She patted her tummy. 'And we'll be with Soph's lot too.' She looked at him, her face falling for a second. 'Maybe we should stay here if we've got the baby. We might prefer to be at home rather than at Sophie's. God, how on earth will we all fit in?'

Will had walked away from the table with a disparaging snort.

'For God's sake, Harmony, the child isn't born yet. Can't we just enjoy this joyous Christmas without worrying about the next one?'

No wonder she couldn't look at him.

The train pulled into Cambridge and he stood and took his holdall off the luggage rack. He loved Cambridge; it was full of glorious memories of him and Harmony in their youth. His mother and father had moved from their rectory outside Ely to the terraced house on the outskirts of town as soon as his father was diagnosed with colon cancer. His mother was heartbroken leaving the house and garden but his father showed no emotion whatsoever, though in fairness he had more pressing things on his mind. He had lived another two years, battling his illness with a stoic bravery that Will had begrudgingly admired. He'd been in and out of the oncology unit at Addenbrooke's on what seemed to be a weekly basis. Chemo, radiotherapy, surgery – he'd had it all. Each time his mother would call to say it looked like the latest treatment had worked and the cancer was beaten, and each time Will had to muster the enthusiasm she needed to hear. It wasn't that he'd wanted his father to die, more that he had an indifference to the inevitable.

Will got out of the taxi, paid, then walked up to his mother's front door and rang the bell.

'Hello, Will,' she said, when she opened the door. She kissed both his cheeks and then peered behind him. 'No Harmony?'

'She's up to her eyes with work at the moment, I'm hoping she'll make it tomorrow. You look well.'

'Thank you,' she said. 'I feel well.' She lifted a hand to her greyed hair, cut as it always was in a neat bob with a blunt fringe. She seemed to have put some weight on, which suited her, he thought, and her face was less taut, less racked. She was dressed in a shirt, a pair of black trousers and a dusky pink sweater. 'You look tired, though,' she said.

He smiled at her honesty. As long as he could remember there'd never been any unnecessary bolstering; a spade was a spade and if you didn't like spades then tough.

He followed her through to the kitchen and they sat at her small, cheap table with its white plastic top. Their old oak one had been too big to fit anywhere and been sold to a neighbour for £50 and four bottles of homemade quince wine. She passed Will a cup of tea in a commemorative mug that celebrated the wedding of Prince Charles and Lady Diana, their young, hopeful faces worn with time. He played his fingers over the smooth surface, fighting the urge to let go of the mug and watch it smash on the floor.

'How have you been?' he asked.

'Busy.'

'That's good. What have you been up to?'

'I've got a job.'

'Really?' he said. 'That's surprising.'

'Why?'

He shrugged. 'I suppose because you've never worked before and most people your age are retiring, not starting a career.'

She gave him a fleeting smile. 'It's hardly a career. I help out at a local café, tend their window boxes and a small patio garden they have at the back. You know, pick up leaves and weed, dead-head the roses. They give me a couple of pounds every Monday, Wednesday and Friday and I potter about for three or four hours.' She took a sip of her tea. 'It's better than sitting around the house.'

'If you enjoy it, that's great,' he said.

'I do. One thing I've learned is that life is what you make of it. If you're happy then you'll make those around you happy. Too many people sit in the dark waiting for life to find them when they ought to be out finding life.'

'That's very wise,' he said. 'You've turned into a philosopher too.'

'I'm old. It's easy to see sense when you're old. Harder when you're young.'

'I need a bit of wisdom. I'm making so many mistakes.' He paused then reached for her hand. 'I'm sorry I haven't called you much.'

'It's not just you,' she said, matter-of-factly, withdrawing her hand and patting him. 'I haven't called either. I should have done. Especially since you and Harmony lost the baby.' She paused. 'How is she coping?'

'We're not having an easy time at the moment.'

'Most marriages go through a rough patch or two at some stage. You just have to work through them. If you love each other most problems have solutions. Do you want to talk about it? Not that my advice would help. Advice is one of those gifts that should be given in moderation and generally ignored.'

He smiled ruefully. 'Unless given in retrospect, when it always seems sensible.'

She nodded. 'Indeed.'

'Are you still missing Dad?' He avoided her eyes as he asked the question.

'Yes, very much. It's miserable living alone and some days I wonder why the bloody hell I have to. But I try to fill my days so I'm not thinking about it too much. I've got this job, and I've started playing bridge again on Monday and Tuesday evenings. Then there's the WI on Thursdays. They're a very peculiar group of ladies but kind, and it keeps me off the streets, so to speak. There's a horticultural society I've joined which meets once a month, and I've even been to a few of the lectures that the university runs, some of which have been extremely interesting.'

'I'm impressed.'

'Like I said, life won't find you. I spent months sitting alone in this house, which I don't really like, in one room, staring at the television and moping, then one day I just thought: how ridiculous to be wasting my time. That's another thing you start to value as you get older, the time you have left.' She smiled. 'So in answer to your question, I'm feeling better about losing your father's companionship, though I will always miss him.'

Will nodded. 'Can I ask you something?'

'Of course.'

'Do you wish you had a grandchild?'

'Goodness, I can't answer that. I wouldn't presume to have an opinion on something like that. That's between you and Harmony and has nothing to do with me.'

He nodded and looked down at the table. 'Do you ever wish you hadn't had me?'

'Why on earth do you ask that?' she said, shock in her voice.

'I suppose I know I made things hard for you. I know my father fought with you about me and you had to intervene all the time.' He sighed and rubbed his face. 'I suppose looking back on it, having me must have been exhausting and difficult for you. I don't remember making your life any fun.'

She leant forward and and patted his hand. He looked down at it – liver spotted, veiny, her thin gold wedding band dull with the years. 'You were my life, William. You're my child, the most important thing that has ever happened to me, the most wonderful gift. Life without you would have been unthinkable. And do you know what? Having said all I've just said about grasping opportunities and experiences, I would swap the rest of my life for just twenty-four hours with you as a baby in my arms, to smell you and kiss you and have you look up at me as if I was the most beautiful person in the world. That was quite simply the most magical time of my life.'

Will nodded. 'I'm sorry I was such a shit to you.'

She laughed, a gentle peal of laughter that he realised he missed. 'Gosh, you were at times. I'd look forward to you coming home from school so much, and then you'd shut yourself away in your room, your music so loud the walls shook. That ridiculous long hair of yours, too, that I know you only grew because it annoyed your father. And all those damn cigarette ends you threw into the guttering which I had to scoop out. But, you know, most of the time you were lovely. You were such a joyful child when you weren't so full of angst. You made me laugh and I missed you so much when you were away at school.'

'Why did you send me?' he asked then. It sounded more like an accusation than he'd intended. 'I mean, if you missed me, why did you send me away?'

'It was hard with … ' His mother stopped before finishing her sentence.

'Go on.'

She hesitated as she tried to formulate her words. 'It was hard with your father sometimes.'

'He wasn't a good man.'

'You're wrong.'

'I'm not.'

She sighed and looked at the ceiling as if trying to find the right words to use. 'Your father,' she began, then she hesitated. 'Your father found it hard to show his emotions. He had a difficult time growing up. His father—'

'I don't care, Mum,' Will said, interrupting her, as a wave of anger washed over him. 'I don't care what happened to him when he was a child. I don't want to hear it. Lots of people have crap upbringings or have things happen to them as children and they don't all turn out bad. You can't make excuses for him.'

'I can and I will,' she said, her voice hardening. 'He was my husband and I loved him.' She got up and took their cups to the sink. She turned the tap on and started to wash them. Then she turned the tap off and stared out of the window over the garden. 'You broke his heart, you know.'

Will shook his head. That bastard didn't have a heart to break, he thought.

'You did. His heart and mine.'

'How did I break your heart?'

She turned and looked at him. The fingers of one hand pulled at the sleeve of her sweater. She fixed her eyes on him, a diluted shade of blue, rheumy with age. 'You should have made your peace with him before he died.'

'What do you mean my peace with him?'

'I mean exactly that.'

'Is this why you've been angry with me?'

She didn't answer him. Her face was steely, her eyes bore into his.

'I just don't understand,' he said. 'It was he who had the issues. Why on earth was it up to me to try and make peace?'

'Because he was dying. Because you needed to repair your relationship. Because it would have meant the world to him.'

Will laughed then, bitter laughter born from years of wishing that might be true, trying to get his father's approval, desperate for his love. 'That man never gave any signs that he cared about me in the slightest. He was cold and detached and went out of his way to crush any self-respect or confidence I might have had. You can't mend that damage with a death-bed heart-to-heart or a meaningless final embrace. It doesn't work that way. We had no relationship; there was nothing to repair.'

Will recalled the one or two trips that he and Harmony had made towards the end. His father lying in bed, frail with yellowed skin, the clinical paraphernalia that surrounded his bed making him even more remote than usual. Will had never told anyone, not even Harmony, how little he'd felt when he took the phone call from his mother saying he'd died. There wasn't even an emotional release. Just nothingness.

The night of the funeral, a few hours after the last person had left the stuffy wake and the food and drink had been cleared away, the three of them sat in front of the fire, staring silently at the flames licking the pile of logs in the grate, eating beans on toast on their laps.

'Why didn't you tell him you loved him?' his mother had said in a flat, monotone voice, the light of the flames dancing in the shadows on her face and reflecting in her grief-stricken eyes.

'Because I didn't.'

Will closed his eyes as he recalled the way she'd crumpled, the plate of beans on toast falling to the floor. Harmony had leapt to her side, her hand rubbing her back, his mother collapsed in frightening sobs that Will didn't comprehend.

Will pushed thoughts of that night from his head and opened his eyes. 'I don't want to talk about this,' he said. 'It was nearly a year ago and there isn't anything we can say to change what happened. He's dead. I didn't make my peace with him because whether you like it or not there was no peace to be made.'

'He was your father.'

'In blood maybe,' Will said, doggedly clinging to the argument, ignoring the voice in his head that told him to tell her what she wanted to hear: that he regretted it, that he would have to live with his decision for the rest of his days, that he'd never forgive himself. Instead he ploughed on. 'But in my book you have to earn the right to be a father. You need to earn respect, not demand it. You have to *be* a father.'

His mother crossed her arms and stared at him, her eyes prickling with angry tears. 'You are a selfish, selfish boy,' she said then.

Will opened his mouth to speak but she interrupted him.

'Did you ever stop to think about how much it would have meant to me? I know how difficult he was – good God, I put up with enough of his rubbish myself. But he was dying.' She reached for a roll of kitchen paper from the window ledge behind the sink and tore a piece off then pressed it against her eyes. 'Did you ever think how I might be feeling? I wanted him to pass away having had some sort of reconciliation with my son. With you.' She paused. 'You're right, it was difficult being in between you both, listening to your constant fighting, seeing so much hatred for him grow in your eyes. I hated it. It was exhausting. We don't get to choose our parents. But we don't get to choose our children either.' She paused and balled the piece of kitchen roll and closed her fist around it. 'Do you know what I used to wish for?'

Will looked at the floor and stayed silent.

'I used to wish the three of us could just sit down in front of the fire and play a game of gin rummy like a normal family. That was it. Not much to ask, was it?' She shook her head. 'But you're right. He's dead and gone now. It's done.'

His mother straightened her shoulders and took a deep breath. Will saw her battling with the regret and sadness that haunted her, trying desperately to conceal it. He stood and went over to her and then he put his arms around her and held her. 'I'm sorry, Mum. You're right. I didn't think of you. I didn't think of you at all.'

When they separated she looked up at him and nodded. 'You know, it's good to see you,' she said. 'I've missed you. I let my disappointment get in the way of what matters.'

'No,' he said. 'It did matter to you. I'm sorry I didn't work that out on my own.' She smiled at him and at that moment he'd never felt closer to her. A rush of warmth spread through him that made him feel short of breath.

'Hey,' he said, jumping away from her and moving back towards the hallway. 'I've got something to show you.'

'Oh yes?' she said, pressing the balled kitchen roll against each eye for a final time then putting it in the bin beneath the sink.

Will picked his bag up off the hall floor and then came back into the kitchen and got his camera out. 'You might need your specs.'

'What is it, then?' she said, as she reached for her glasses from the kitchen work top.

Will found the pictures he'd taken of the garden. He stood close to her so he could scroll through them. 'I've started gardening,' he said.

She looked up at him and smiled, then put her glasses on and looked back at the camera screen. 'Well, I never,' she said. 'Doesn't it look beautiful? I knew it would.' She touched her finger to the small screen. 'That right-hand wall looks so much better now the ghastly hawthorn's gone.' She handed him back the camera. 'It looks lovely.'

'I should have done it ages ago.'

'Well, better late than never.'

As he put the camera on the table something caught his eye at the door. He turned to look and saw a grey tabby cat slinking its way into the room.

'There's a cat in the house,' he said unnecessarily, as his mother bent to stroke the animal's back. The cat jumped up on the table and began to purr.

'She's called Penny,' his mother said, as she tickled the cat beneath its chin. 'When she came to me she was called Sylvia, but I didn't think it suited her, so I call her Penny. You like that better, don't you, poppet?' The cat lifted herself off her front feet and pushed her cheek against his mother's hand. 'She was abandoned by some awful person.' She shook her head. 'He'd just disappeared on holiday and left six cats locked in a top-floor flat in Ipswich. The RSPCA officer who found them told me the place was full of faeces and stank to high heaven.' She looked at Will and raised her eyebrows. 'The poor creatures had been left for ten days and only survived by drinking water out of the loo.'

Will reached out to stroke the cat. 'When did you get her?'

'A couple of months after your father passed,' she said. 'I was terribly lonely and needed something to look after. She's been a godsend. Haven't you, darling?'

Will had a flash of his father kicking his kitten against the wall and closed his eyes as as he felt a familiar surge of hostility. 'How did you live with him?'

She took her hand away from the cat and gently pushed her off the table. The cat started to curl herself around his mother's ankles. 'He was my husband and I loved him and, whatever you think, we were happy. Nobody knows what makes a good marriage. People have these ideas of marrying the ideal person, the love of their life, but in reality it rarely happens. Marriage requires care and attention and hard work, like anything worthwhile. There's no such thing as the perfect marriage but if you love someone enough to marry them then the very least that's expected is your loyalty and your support.'

That night he slept in what his mother called the spare room, which was essentially a small storage room, stacked high with boxes of things she and his father couldn't bear to throw away when they moved to the smaller house. He closed the door and sat on the edge of the bed. There were piles of his father's clothes, laid carefully on their hangers over the boxes. There was a tweed jacket on the top that his father had worn for as long as Will could remember. He placed his hand on it and pictured his father standing in their old living room, one hand on the mantelpiece, the other on his hip, as if posing for a Victorian photograph.

He reached across and turned the light off. The room was lit by the street lamps outside. He thought of his mother next door. She'd taken Penny upstairs with her and Will had smiled as he caught sight of them when he passed her door, the animal curled up on his father's side of the bed, nestled beside her, contentedly cleaning itself. He imagined how angry his father would be if he was able to see it, and how happy his mum was, lying in her button-up nightie, covers neatly tucked in around her, her fingers idly stroking the cat's soft fur as she read.

Will was woken from a heavy, dreamless sleep by his phone

buzzing the arrival of a text. He grabbed for it sleepily and glanced at the clock. It was twelve-thirty, earlier than it felt. He blinked in the light of his phone and saw the message was from Harmony.

I'm parked outside. Are you awake?

CHAPTER TWENTY-THREE

As soon as she heard Will leave the flat, Harmony came out of her study and went into the kitchen to get a drink. She felt weak with worry. What had she got herself into? Luke hadn't stopped calling or texting since she'd walked out of the restaurant. She didn't answer any of the calls any more. He didn't listen to her when she did – he just kept telling her life was too short, that they had to be together, that he could make her happier than Will ever could.

The night before, she'd sat on the floor of her study, knees pulled into her chest, back against the door in case Will tried to come in, and stared at her phone as it buzzed calls and texts throughout the night, hoping that each one she ignored would be the last, that eventually he'd get the message. Then, at around four in the morning, as dawn crept up on the dark and her mind had become bleary with exhaustion and panic, she answered.

'Why are you doing this?'

'You know why.'

'Please, Luke. Don't do this to me.'

'I need to see you,' he said. 'I'll leave now and be with you in half an hour.'

'Christ, don't come here,' she whispered desperately. She took the phone away from her face and looked up at the ceiling. Then exhaled slowly, before returning to the phone. 'Please, don't come here.'

'I have to see you. I need to make you understand. You're not thinking straight.'

This had to stop. Harmony squeezed her eyes shut as she thought about what she should do.

'Harmony? Are you there?'

'Fine,' she said, keeping her voice steady. 'We'll meet. But not now. I'm tired and need some sleep. I'll text you when I wake and we can arrange it.'

In the morning, as Will watered the plants, she sat at the kitchen table, nursing a cup of tea she was too nervous to drink, and picked up her phone.

What time shall we meet and where?

Within a moment her phone beeped his reply.

I'm free all afternoon. We could meet in a pub and then get some supper?

No, she thought. I don't want to be seen out with you.

Let's meet at 3 p.m. But not in a pub.

Come to mine.

She hesitated, her chest tightening. She remembered how she'd panicked when she saw Ian in the restaurant, how not being seen had taken precedence over making sure Luke knew it was over. She needed to focus on finishing this cleanly, on making him promise not to call, on convincing him to leave her alone so she could give her marriage a fighting chance.

Fine. I have to leave by four.

She decided to get off the tube two stops early at Westminster so she could calm herself with a walk along the river. She crossed Westminster Bridge and turned onto the South Bank, which heaved with weekend crowds. People poured in and out of the Aquarium and the galleries, and hung around on the Embankment eating chips and taking photographs. Harmony weaved through the crowds. Ordinarily, she'd have walked with a spring in her step; she loved this part of London. It was unique, with historic buildings and famous landmarks nestling comfortably beside utilitarian pieces of modernist architecture. It was even more beautiful at night. She and Will used to come here to eat fish and chips and look at the lights strung like pearls beside the river, their reflections rippling silently in the oily night-time blackness of the water. Those were happy times, she thought. When nothing mattered but the two of them. When love was straightforward.

His flat was in a huge concrete and glass building beside Blackfriars Bridge that loomed over the river. When she walked into the reception area the dark grey of the exterior was replaced with a shiny chequerboard floor and wall-to-wall mirrors. There were two lifts, and she pressed the button and waited, tapping her foot as she did so in an attempt to ease her nerves. His flat was on the top floor, and by the time the lift got there she worried she might throw up. She wondered if she'd made an error agreeing to meet at his place, and that perhaps thay should have arranged to meet in a pub or cafe after all.

'Don't be silly,' she whispered aloud. 'He's a lawyer, a friend of Ian's, not a bloody axe-murderer.'

When he answered the door he smiled at her as if nothing was untoward. He leant forward to kiss her mouth but she turned her head, deflecting his kiss so it landed on her cheek. His smell filled her and she had a sudden flashback to the afternoon they'd spent together, the clash of their bodies, the frenzy and desire, the way he'd clung to her, buried his face in her neck. But any attraction she'd felt had vanished and the recollection made her shudder.

She walked past him and into the flat. 'I can't stay long,' she said.

He closed the door and she heard the click of the Yale lock.

She pushed her shoulders back and lifted her chin.

'You look lovely. I've not seen you without make-up before.'

'There are lots of things about me you haven't seen.'

He laughed. 'Yes, I suppose there must be.'

She followed him into the main room, which was twice the size of her and Will's flat alone. There were two full-height windows that overlooked London as far as the eye could see and glazed double doors that opened onto an empty concrete roof terrace. Harmony walked up to the central window and took in the panorama: the Houses of Parliament, the London Eye to the left, the glinting towers at the hub of the City, the majesty of St Paul's. 'That's an incredible view,' she said.

'It's at its best at dawn.'

'How long have you lived here?'

'I bought it after my wife died. I couldn't sleep in our house without her so I sold it and bought this.' He smiled at her. 'Can I get you a drink?'

'No, thank you.'

She turned around and looked at the room itself. The walls were brilliant white with abstract paintings in muted black and greys. The floor was polished concrete with a high sheen in a swirl of charcoal greys. There were no rugs to soften the effect and the furniture was sparse: a large white corner sofa, a glass coffee table and a couple of Sixties-style chrome-and-black leather seats. There was a stainless steel kitchen area with an ornate faceted metal ceiling light that hung over the island unit and a solid steel-and-glass dining table to one side. The whole place was spotless – no clutter or books, no ornaments, nothing on the kitchen surfaces apart from an expensive-looking coffee machine. She tried to keep herself relaxed, but as she looked around the sterile, soulless room, she felt her skin begin to prickle with unease.

He told her to sit down so she did, perched on the edge of the sofa, knees pressed tightly together, hands in her lap. She watched him open the fridge and get out a bottle of champagne.

'I don't want a drink, thank you.'

'Just a small glass?'

'No.'

He popped the cork on the champagne anyway and the noise echoed. He poured himself a glass then put some music on. Her mouth and throat felt dry as she began to worry how vulnerable she was. She was painfully aware now that nobody knew where she was, and as she looked out of the huge window in front of her and the far-reaching views over London her head started to spin as if she had vertigo.

'I thought I made it clear this was over. That anything we had was finished,' she said as he sat down beside her. Too close. His knee touching hers. She pulled herself away. 'You can't call me, or text or email.'

'I don't have a choice.' Suddenly there was a dark desperation about him; his eyes flicked back and forth over her face as if searching for something.

'Of course you do.' She was aware that her breathing had

become quick and shallow. She tried to take a fuller breath to calm herself. 'Luke, listen to me. I made a mistake. I was in a bad place and I should have been stronger.'

'There are no such things as mistakes. There are things you do and things you don't do. You need to recognise that what you and I have is important.'

'You and I have nothing, Luke.'

'No, we have a connection.'

'We don't have a connection, for God's sake!' she said with exasperation. 'We had sex against a wall and on a grubby floor in a damp lock-up.'

Luke reached out and took hold of her arm below her elbow. 'Leave him.'

'Christ,' she said, shaking her head. 'You really mean that, don't you?'

'Yes.'

'But you don't even know me!'

He stared at her, his face blank, his mind turning over. 'Come with me,' he said, leaning forward to put his glass on the coffee table then standing.

He walked away from her and disappeared into another room.

'Luke?' she called after him. He didn't answer her. She swore quietly and then followed him to the doorway. 'I don't understa–'

She stopped speaking and stared, trying to process what she saw. It was another large white-walled room with a neatly made bed and a bedside table with nothing on it but a stainless steel lamp and a photo frame. But above the bed, hanging on the wall, was a large canvas, a photograph. A photograph of her.

'Where did you get that?' she breathed, her eyes fixed on the picture.

The canvas was at least a metre in width and half a metre high; it was the photo Will had taken on their wedding night on one of the disposable cameras they'd put out for their friends. It was one of Will's favourites. He'd taken it just after they'd made love. She stared at it, mesmerised, fear mounting with every breath she took.

As she stepped closer she saw the photo frame by the bed also had a picture of her. She walked over and picked it up. It was her profile picture from Facebook.

Luke leant against the wall. His arms were crossed, his eyes dead, mouth set. She noticed to the left of him there was a chest of drawers and on it were a dozen or so more photographs.

All of them were of her or Will.

A cold sweat crept over her body. One of the pictures showed her walking down the steps at work. It was winter, and there was a thin layer of snow on the ground. She wore a woollen hat and gloves and her long navy trench coat. The quality of the picture was grainy, as if it had been enlarged.

'You photographed me?' she whispered.

She looked back at the canvas above his bed, the face of a young woman so besotted with her new husband, the scent of their love fresh on her skin, her eyes full of him. She heard his voice telling her to smile, laughing as he stroked his hand down the inside of her thigh, telling her he loved her, that he would always love her.

Oh, Will, she thought. I've been so stupid.

She picked up the smaller version of it, the one in a silver frame on the chest of drawers. 'You took this from our flat.'

'Yes, when I came for dinner and you went to talk to him in the kitchen.' There was an eerie flatness to his voice that startled her.

'But ... but why ... ' she stuttered. 'Why have you got these?'

'He'll hurt you, Harmony. I've come to save you from him.'

She pushed her fingers against her temples and moved them in small circles, trying to relieve the pressure that was building. She looked back at the photographs. Looked at the ones of Will. Will walking into the wine shop. Will laughing in a café, the picture taken from outside on the street. Will opening their car door. Then she noticed a yellowed Polaroid tucked into the frame of another photo. Two boys, about thirteen or fourteen, both in short-sleeved shirts and grey shorts, school ties loosened at the neck, arms looped around each other's shoulders, matching grins on their faces from ear to ear. One of the boys she recognised immediately – her husband, his crop of white-blonde unruly hair catching the sunlight, his ruddy cheeks smeared with dirt, that smile of his luminescent even then. The other boy was skinny with clear, pale skin, shorter than Will, his good looks feminine, with high chiselled cheekbones and delicate pink lips. They were outside on a games field, rugby posts in the background, other boys sitting about on the grass behind them, talking, watching sport, picking at blades of grass. She put the Polaroid back and then cast her eyes over the pictures of her husband. She heard Will's voice, the desperate anguish as he'd stood up from the dinner table and asked why Luke had come, the look on his face at that lunch when Luke had walked through the French windows, a mix of alarm and distress. It was as if a blindfold was removed from her eyes.

'This isn't about me, is it?' she said then. 'It's about Will.'

'It was. At the beginning. But then I fell in love with you. I didn't expect to but I did. You gave me hope.'

'I don't understand … ' Her words drifted to nothing as she tried to untangle her thoughts, went back over everything that had happened, every conversation, every look, trying to work out how she hadn't seen any of this.

'We argued the night she died.' He leant his head back against the wall, closed his eyes. Harmony noticed his fists were clenched. 'She told me I was impossible to live with, that my head was too messed up. She wanted to leave me.' He turned his head to look at Harmony. 'She was pregnant,' he said. 'Eight months pregnant with our daughter when she died. I lost them both. I lost everything.'

Harmony felt her stomach turn over. She tried to swallow. 'But none of it is Will's fault,' she managed to whisper.

'It's all his fault. Will lives a life he doesn't deserve.' Luke pushed himself off the wall and walked towards her. 'He doesn't deserve you. He doesn't deserve your love.' He smiled at her then, a smile that made her flinch, it was so out of place. 'I lied when I said I didn't believe in love,' he said. 'Love is all we have.' He lifted his hand to stroke the side of her face and she recoiled from his touch. 'I can give you the love you need, Harmony. I'll be there for you in a way he never can be. Love will be our salvation.'

'You need help, Luke,' she said. 'There is no *us*. I don't love you. It was never even close to love. I don't even know you.' She shook her head with incredulity. 'It was sex. Just sex, for God's sake.'

She turned on her heel and walked out of the bedroom, back into the living room.

'So, that's what you are?' he suddenly shouted, following her. He grabbed her arm, his fingers digging into her. He yanked her around to face him and she saw his eyes had turned cold and hard. 'That's what you are? Some cheap dirty whore who has sex with men she doesn't know?' His lips curled into a sneer and his eyes grew wide. 'You're a fucking whore?'

His venomous words, piercing and angry, cut into her like a blade. She stared at him, trying to speak, but she couldn't form any words. She felt her eyes begin to well with tears. Don't cry, she told herself. Stay strong. Don't cry.

'Is that what you do? You go around flirting with men, seducing them, leading them on?' His rage grew with every syllable.

'Let go of me, Luke—'

'Is this a game to you?' He dragged her towards the coffee table and bent to pick up the bottle of champagne. 'The drinks? The flirtatious glances? The fiddling with your fucking necklace while you flutter your eyelashes?' He lifted the bottle close to her face, pushed the icy glass, wet with condensation, against her cheek.

Adrenalin pumped around her, she flicked her eyes towards the door, wondered if anyone would hear her if she called out.

'You think this is a game?' he repeated.

'Of course it's not a game,' Harmony said in a whisper. She swallowed and leant backwards away from him. Everything in her body screamed at her to run. 'You're scaring me. Please put the bottle down. It's not a game. I don't think that. I—'

'Be quiet!' he shouted.

He drew his arm back and for a moment she thought he might bring the bottle down against her, but instead he hurled it hard against the wall. It smashed loudly, broken bottle and champagne spilling down the wall and onto the polished concrete floor where it made a pool of fizzing liquid and shattered glass.

Harmony watched, terrified, as his hands flew to his face, his fingers clawing his scalp, again and again. He cried out as if he'd been wounded then dropped to the floor, crouching, bouncing on the balls of his feet. Then his rage began to fade and he folded his arms over his head as if sheltering from falling debris. She stood frozen to the spot and stared at Luke who was shaking, cowering on the floor in front of her, battling the demons that fought inside him.

'I'm sorry,' she managed to whisper, her heart hammering with fear, knees feeling like they might buckle at any moment. 'It's not Will's fault, it's mine. Whatever happened back then, he was just a child. But I'm not and I shouldn't have let this happen. Luke, he was just a child.'

Luke lifted his head, his face drained of colour, drained of fight. 'We were all just children.'

Then he turned his face away from her, stared out of the window, his eyes glassy, unblinking. 'Please leave me alone now,' he said.

For the briefest of moments, she wondered about leaving him in this state, but then she glanced at the mess of glass and champagne on the floor.

'I'm sorry,' she said, as she turned and fled.

A few hours later, with an overnight bag in the boot of the car, she drove along the Talgarth Road, heading out towards the M4. She couldn't stop thinking about the look in Luke's eyes, that eerie mix of hatred and hurt. She relived the crash of the champagne bottle as it hit the wall. She tried not to think of him following them, of the pictures he had of her and Will in his empty, cold bedroom, but it was difficult to think about anything else. She knew she should tell someone but she didn't dare. She would have to confess her infidelity and if Will found out about her and Luke she was convinced it would be the final straw, that her marriage would collapse, and she was determined to do what she could to try and save it. There were issues they'd have to work through – those hadn't gone away – but the episode with Luke had focused her mind; she and Will had too much to lose.

When she joined the M25 she found it gridlocked. The traffic was solid and unmoving. Harmony swore and craned her neck to see how far the line of stationary cars stretched. It seemed to go on for miles.

'Must be an accident,' she said to herself, wiping her brow and lying back against the headrest. 'Of all the nights.'

An hour passed and she'd only moved two miles. She kept glancing at her phone, imagining she heard it ring, imagining it was him, calling or texting. She would have to get a new number, a new email address too, maybe even change their landline number. She wondered how she would explain that to Will.

Up ahead, some way away, she saw the blink of flashing blue lights and heard the distant sound of sirens. 'Come on,' she whispered. 'Hurry up and clear the traffic.'

She eventually crawled past the accident, a multi-car pile-up with a couple of cars so badly crushed they no longer looked like cars. Three serious-faced policemen waved the queue through a single lane. Fire engines and ambulances lined the hard shoulder. She wondered how many people had been hurt, and how many families would have just received the horrific news that a loved one had died. She thought of Luke then, of his pregnant wife dying, imagined the look on his face when they told him, the news shattering him. Tears sprung in her eyes as she imagined how she would feel if she received a similar phone call about Will.

The journey, which should have taken a little over an hour and a half, ended up taking over four. By the time she pulled up outside Gill's house it was well past midnight. Just being near the house, seeing it, knowing Will was inside, reassured her. She was glad she hadn't told him she was on her way. Surprises weren't in her character but Will was romantic about things like that. She unclipped her seatbelt then got her phone out of her bag to text Will. When she turned it on, she braced herself for missed calls and texts from Luke, but there were none and she breathed a sigh of relief.

I'm parked outside. Are you awake?

She pressed send and waited. Out of the corner of her eye she saw a movement in the window upstairs. The curtain moved to one side and the shadowy outline of her husband looked down at her.

'Oh Will,' she breathed. 'Thank God.'

CHAPTER TWENTY-FOUR

He opened the door and there she was, lit by the soft light of the porch, wearing jeans and a navy T-shirt. She'd never looked more beautiful. Her Tiffany heart rested on her chest, her hair was tied up loosely, her face bare of make-up.

She shook her head, seemed unsure of herself, but then smiled at him and opened her arms. He held her tightly, kissed her on the top of her head, the side of her neck, her shoulder. A weight lifted off him and he breathed in deeply and exhaled as if he'd been holding it in forever. She was back. He could feel it in the way she held him, in the way her hand stroked his back, the way she pushed her cheek against his chest. He pulled back from her and looked down into her face as she gazed up at him. He tucked a few strands of escaped hair behind her ear, brushing his fingers down her cheek as he did.

'Wait there,' he whispered. 'Don't move, okay?'

She nodded, her eyes alight. The last time he had seen them alive like that was when she'd told him about the pregnancy, the glorious accident he'd turned his back on. He felt a sharp stab of regret as he realised his mother was right. He was a selfish man, only able to see things from his own viewpoint, blinkered. He turned away from her, reminding her not to move. She laughed. It was the sweetest noise he'd ever heard. He ran through to the kitchen and grabbed his camera from the table, pulling the lens cap off as he returned.

'No photographs now. I've been in the car for four hours. Let's go in,' she protested gently, as he lifted the camera and began to fiddle with the focus.

He smiled at her. 'All these years I've photographed you in the moments that matter. Let me take a photo of you now.' He pressed the button, moved around to capture her from different angles. She laughed, and he pressed, praying that would be the one, a record of an unfettered laugh that would remind him for years to come of this moment when she gave him a second chance to be the husband she needed.

He lowered the camera. 'I didn't take any photos of you when you were pregnant.'

He saw her smile fade.

He took her in his arms again. 'I didn't see how important that was to you, to us, but I do now.' He pressed his lips against her hair. 'I want to have a baby, Harmony.'

He felt her tense. He leant back from her so he could see her face. He smiled at her and he knew then he meant it, that it wasn't some empty platitude. What had changed? Perhaps talking to his mother, perhaps nearly losing Harmony. Perhaps he finally knew that he wasn't his father, that he wasn't that young scared boy who couldn't stand up for himself, for those he cared about. But he could now. He had to. All these years he thought he'd put his past in a box, forgotten it, moved on, but he never really had. He'd been carrying it around with him like a concrete weight dragging behind him, holding him back. It was time to free himself, to be his own man, not to live in the shadow of his younger self.

'No,' she said. 'Don't say that. You wouldn't have done what you did if that were true.'

'I didn't know what I was doing. I panicked.' He shook his head. 'I'd convinced myself I wasn't able to look after anything. Even you. You're always the one looking after me but when you lost the baby you became so vulnerable – the way you looked at me changed, like you needed me to do something, and I had no idea what it was I should do and that scared me. I was scared I was going to fuck it up.' He kissed her again. 'And then I did.' He tightened his arms around her. 'I mean it about the baby.'

Harmony stepped back so their arms fell away from each other. 'Really?' she said.

He nodded. 'Yes. I want to give you a baby and want to raise that baby with you. I want a father-child relationship I can be proud of. I want to get it right, where my own father got it so wrong.'

'But what about the vasectomy?'

'I spoke to the hospital this afternoon. They said a reversal is straightforward enough and because it's such a short time since it was done it's almost certain sperm production will come back. Something to do with a low chance of epidermis blockage.'

Harmony smiled. 'You mean epididymal.'

'Do I?' He furrowed his brow. 'What did I say?'

'It doesn't matter.' She shook her head and took hold of his hand. 'I'll just get my bag from the car.'

'I'll do it,' he said. 'Did it really take four hours to get here?'

She walked to the car with him, opened the boot and let him take her bag for her.

'Yes, it was a dreadful journey,' she said. 'There was an accident. And it was hot too.'

'Shall I run you a bath? I could jump in with you.'

They walked up the stairs quietly so as not to wake his mother, and then Will went into the bathroom. He poured some bubble bath in and pushed his sleeves up to swish the water. Harmony came in and Will slid the lock closed on the door. Then he turned the light off, leaving the room gently lit by the glow of the street lamps. They got undressed and climbed into the bath. Will sat behind Harmony, who lay back against his chest. They kept the water running until it was only a few inches below the lip of the bath and then turned off the taps. It was quiet and dark and the warm water enveloped them.

'This is lovely,' she murmured.

He moved his hands back and forth through the water so it made a gentle lapping sound. The feel of her skin against his was magical. He rubbed his hands down her arms from shoulder to fingertip, then pushed his fingers through hers and clasped her hands. He leant forward and reached for the flannel that hung on a hook on the wall and submerged it in the water. He took the soap and rubbed it against the flannel and then began to rub her skin, carefully and softly, the light from outside the window glinting on her wet, smooth shoulders and chest. She turned her head and kissed him, touched the tip of her tongue lightly to his. Then she climbed wordlessly out of the bath and laid a towel on the floor. She took his hand and pulled him gently out and they kissed. He stepped back from her and took in her body, wondering, as he often did, at how beautiful she was. He smiled at her and she returned it, then held his hand and they dropped to the floor.

Afterwards, they lay with their limbs entwined like pieces in a jigsaw, her head resting lightly on his chest.

'I was shopping this afternoon,' he said softly, 'so I could cook Mum some supper, and there was an elderly man in the queue in front of me. He was dressed in a suit with a green waistcoat and a tie, but it was pretty grubby and crumpled. In his basket was a single portion of reduced shepherds' pie, a Battenberg and a can of cider.' He stroked her shoulder lightly. 'It was sad. Really sad.'

'Why?'

'I don't know, I suppose the thought of this old man dressing himself smartly in a suit he doesn't clean, buying out of date food for just himself each day. It was one of the loneliest things I'd ever seen. I convinced myself I was going to end up like that.'

'You won't end up like that.'

'I was terrified you weren't coming back to me.'

She kissed his chest and stroked his hand. 'Well, I did come back. And I'm here, right where I want to be and I'm not going anywhere, so you'll have to share your Battenberg.'

CHAPTER TWENTY-FIVE

Harmony was in the kitchen with Gill having a cup of tea while Will nipped out for some twine to tie back the rambling rose outside the back door. The car was packed and ready for them to head back to London as soon as he reappeared.

'It's lovely to see you both,' Gill said. 'Will seems much happier this morning. I'm so glad.'

'We're both happier,' Harmony said. 'It's been a tough few months.'

She glanced again at her phone which lay face up on the table, but there had been no phone calls or texts from Luke since she left his apartment. The relief was immense, and waking up beside her husband that morning had felt like waking up to a new life.

'You will make sure you eat properly, though, won't you? You're looking a little thin.'

Gill went upstairs and Harmony looked out of the window at the driving rain, the wind blowing the drops against the window, collecting in rivulets that ran down the glass. She went through to the living room and cast her eye over the book shelves. She pulled out a copy of *To Kill a Mockingbird*, a favourite book she'd read countless times, sat on the sofa and opened it at the beginning. There was a chill in the room so she reached for the blanket that lay folded over the arm of the sofa and pulled it over her.

Her phone ringing made her jump. Panic rose in her immediately. She grabbed for it, ready to turn Luke's call off, but saw her sister's name instead. She smiled and shook her head. Silly to be so jumpy, she thought.

'Hey Soph,' she said. 'How are—'

'I don't know what on earth is going on but I've just had some man on the doorstep saying he's having an affair with you.'

Harmony's heart skipped a beat.

'Hello? Did you hear me?'

Harmony cursed Luke silently. How dare he go to her sister's house?

'What did he say?' she asked, tapping her finger rapidly on the arm of the sofa.

'Oh my God, it's true?' Harmony could hear her sister's disapproval beneath the shock. 'He told me Will is so angry about it he's worried for your safety. He asked if I knew where you were.'

'Did you tell him?'

'No, I didn't tell him. I said I had no bloody idea where you were, which, as a matter of fact, I don't. But even if I did, I wouldn't have told him; I didn't like the way he was talking to me.'

'I'm sorry,' Harmony whispered. A cold sweat crept over the back of her neck. She stood up and her head swam as if she were drunk.

Sophie sighed down the phone. 'The man seems unstable, Harmony.' The irritation in her voice had abated. 'How does he even know where I live?'

Harmony was bombarded by flashes of the photos he had of her and Will in his apartment. She wondered how long he'd been following them. Just the thought of it gave her the shivers. 'I have no idea.'

'And who is he?' She paused. 'Do you love him?'

'God, no! It's over. It was nothing. Just an afternoon.' Harmony dropped her head into her hand. Her stomach turned over and over as she realised she'd been naive to think this would just go away. 'Are you cross with me?'

'I'm not cross with you. I'm surprised, that's all. I didn't think you'd ever do something like that.'

Harmony didn't reply. There was nothing she could say.

'If it's over, why did he tell me you're leaving Will?' Sophie asked. 'Is he right? Are you?'

'No, of course not,' Harmony said. 'But I've got myself into a real mess and I'm not sure what to do.'

'Do you want to tell me what's going on?'

Harmony told Sophie what had happened, everything from meeting him at the party through to the afternoon they spent at Will's studio and the attempt she'd made to end it at the restaurant. She told her about the barrage of phone calls and texts, but not about going to his apartment and the rage he'd got into; it would only worry her more.

'You're going to have to tell Will, you know.'

'No,' Harmony said, shaking her head. 'No, I can't. He'll be so upset. I can't do that to him. It's not fair. And what would it achieve? If this situation has shown me one thing it's that I want to make my marriage work.'

'Well, he's going to find out. That man has no intention of letting this lie. He's delusional. He thinks the two of you belong together.'

When Harmony finally put the phone down a wave of nausea swept over her. Gill called through with an offer of a sandwich.

'No, thanks,' she called back, trying to stop her voice from shaking. 'I'm fine.'

She sat on the edge of the sofa. She couldn't risk Luke or anyone else telling Will. It had to come from her. As she tried to think of the best way to tell him, tears began to pour down her cheeks. It wasn't long until she heard the front door open and close. Will was home. She wrapped her arms around herself and waited for him.

'What's happened?' Will said as soon as he saw her face. 'What's wrong?'

She looked up at him, her eyes red from crying, tears soaking the tissue she was clutching. 'Everything. I need ... to tell you ... something,' she said through sobs. 'Can you ... close the door? I don't want ... your ... mum to hear.'

He closed the door and sat beside her on the sofa and took her hand. She looked down at his hand on hers. Large, soft hands, with a light dusting of blonde hairs across the top of them, short nails, the edge of one thumbnail bitten into an irregular shape. She stroked his skin with her other hand and shook her head. Two tears fell onto his jeans. The ache in her chest was unbearable.

'Hey,' he soothed. 'It's okay. Everything's okay. I'm here.'

She felt as if she was part of a firing squad, rifle aimed at a blindfolded innocent, her finger hovering on the trigger.

'I had … ' She sniffed and pushed the kitchen roll against her eyes. 'I got involved with someone.' She took a deep breath and watched as his face fell. 'It lasted one afternoon.' She lifted her hand to the side of his face and rested the flat of her palm against him.

'I don't understand.' His brow furrowed in confusion.

'I shouldn't have let it happen, but it did. I finished it, but … ' She hesitated and tears began to fall again. 'But he won't stop calling me.' This was even harder than she imagined it would be. 'He even went to Sophie's—'

'Who is it?' Will demanded. He stood up and walked over to the fireplace and gripped the mantelpiece with one hand.

She didn't answer.

'Do I know him?'

She closed her eyes, dropped her head and nodded.

'Who is it?'

'Luke,' she whispered.

'What?'

'It's Luke.'

She looked up at him and saw the horror on his face and her heart lurched.

'How? Why?' he whispered. 'Luke?' She could see him concentrating, as if he was trying to translate a foreign language. 'Luke Crawford? Who I was at school with? But you don't know him. I mean, you've only just met.'

'It should never have happened. I was … ' she hesitated, 'I was all over the place. It was a mistake. I felt alone, and … confused. I … was … I was so angry with you, Will. About the vasectomy, the miscarriage, about feeling pushed away by you. And … and … I was flattered by his attention and I wasn't thinking straight. It meant nothing. Do you understand that? It meant absolutely nothing.'

'Of course it meant something. Everything means something.'

He moved back to the sofa and sat down, pushed himself into the corner, keeping distance between them.

'This didn't.' She rubbed her eyes dry and took a few deep breaths.

Will rubbed his face. 'Where?' he said then, turning his head to fix his eyes on her.

'What?'

'Where did you fuck?'

Her stomach turned over. She looked at him in shock, surprised at the tone in his voice, the harshness of his words.

'Tell me where you fucked.'

'Please don't do this.'

'Tell me.'

'How will it help?'

'It won't help. But I want to know. Did you fuck him in our bed?'

'No,' she said. 'Of course not.' She felt wounded by his question, shocked he would think she'd do that. But as she sat there, looking at his emotionally battered face, shoulders hunched, dazed and confused, she realised how ridiculous this was. Why was sleeping with Luke in their bed any more awful than sleeping with him at the studio or in the back of a car or some bed and breakfast off the M25? She was sickened by her own hypocrisy. Her eyes prickled. 'It was at the studio. I'm so sorry,' she said.

Will swore under his breath.

'There's more, though,' she said. 'You were right, he blames you for something. I didn't quite understand, but he said something about you having his life. He says he loves me and ... and he won't leave me alone. I told him I don't want to see him. I told him I love you but he won't listen.' She gave way to more tears. 'He wants me to leave you. He's got it into his head that he and I should be together.'

Will stared straight ahead.

'Will?' she said, his face blurring through her tears.

He stood up, and without a word he walked out of the room. Harmony heard him pick up his keys then walk out of the house, slamming the front door behind him. A moment later she heard the car engine start up and the car pull away with a screech of acceleration.

Will didn't come back. Harmony sat at the kitchen table and watched the clock march slowly around. She held her breath when the phone in the house rang, terrified it was going to be the police saying he'd been in an accident. By six o'clock she began to think about people he might have gone to. She phoned Sophie and Frank, and sent deliberately vague texts to a couple of Will's other friends, asking them to get him to call if he happened to show up. Then she telephoned Emma.

'If he turns up at yours, you'll call me? Even if he tells you not to?'

'Yes, of course. We're in tonight. Ian came back with some dreadful war film he bought for a couple of pounds from Tesco. Anything but talk to me.'

Harmony could tell that Emma wanted to talk about Ian again, but she didn't have the energy. 'I've got a few more calls to make,' she said. 'I'll call you for a chat tomorrow.'

'I'm sure he'll be back soon.'

Harmony closed her eyes. 'I hope so,' she said.

She hesitated before calling Luke. Cold dread filled her at the thought of Will confronting him. Might he have gone to find him? She dialled Luke's number.

'Luke?'

'Yes.'

'Is Will with you?'

'No.'

'I told him what we did and then he left the house in the car. That was hours ago and he's not come back. I thought he might have come to talk to you.' The churning in her stomach was unbearable. 'He was angry. Really angry. I … I don't want you to fight.'

'He's not here. Where are you?'

'Jesus, Luke, I thought I made all this clear yesterday. I'm not telling you where I am and if you go to my sister's house again she'll have you arrested,' she said with a flare of anger. 'How did you even find out where she lived? Did you stalk her too?'

'You told the taxi driver her address the evening we had a drink after work.'

'Just get in touch with me if he turns up.'

There was silence from Luke.

'Please,' Harmony said, trying hard to keep her voice calm.

Still silence.

'Luke, please will you call me if you see him.'

'Yes. And will you call me if he shows up?'

'What?'

'I'm not a monster, Harmony. If something happens to him behind the wheel of a car because he's upset about what happened between us I'd never forgive myself. It's happened before, remember? Not to mention I'd quite like to know he's not about to show up to kick the shit out of me.'

'Sure, I'll let you know.'

Harmony had lied to Gill and told her Will had rushed back to London to check on the wine shop. She said the burglar alarm had gone off and he'd been called in by the systems alert service that the shop employed. That's why he'd left in such a hurry. When he didn't return by suppertime she told her it had been more complicated than it should have been, but that Will assured her he'd be back as soon as possible to pick her up.

'Do you need to get back for work?' Gill asked her. 'I could call a cab to take you to the station.'

Harmony hesitated. She was pretty sure he'd come back to his mother's house and she wanted to be there when he did. 'Do you mind if I stay? I'm a bit tired and I don't have to be at the office tomorrow. I've got things I can be getting on with – if I can use your computer?'

'Of course. It will be nice to have your company.' Gill stood to leave the kitchen but paused at the doorway. 'Are you all right, Harmony? You seem very distracted.'

'I'm actually a bit worried about Will. I'd have thought he'd be back or called at least.' She wondered if she should tell Gill she'd lied about the burglar alarm.

'Good gracious, I've been worrying about that boy for the whole of his life.' Gill smiled. 'He'll be fine. He always is.'

Harmony made them bowls of soup and buttered toast for supper, which they ate while watching a costume drama that Harmony found hard to concentrate on. When they finished she carried the empty bowls back to the kitchen and washed them up, staring out of the window as the night settled over Gill's small, neat garden. It lacked the flare and excitement of the garden at her last house. It was as if the passion had gone, as if she didn't have the time or energy to create anything special. It was easy to think their garden had been the place Gill escaped to on those occasions when her husband's behaviour was too much to bear. On the other hand, perhaps gardening was a hobby they both enjoyed and it was this shared pleasure that revealed itself in the haven they created. There were always several sides to a story. Perhaps that's why she felt safe with science. Options were minimised. There were rules and theories. You worked on a theory until you had a rule. Grey areas unsettled her. She dried the bowls and put them away. Then she called the flat and Will's mobile again. But there was still no answer from either.

'I think I'm going to go to bed,' she said to Gill, poking her head around the living room door. 'Is there anything you need before I go up?'

Gill was stroking the cat, who purred so loudly Harmony could hear it from the doorway. Gill glanced up and gave a brief smile. 'No, thank you, I've got everything I need right here.'

At eleven-thirty her phone beeped a text. She grabbed at it. It was Luke.

Is Will back yet?

No.

She wasn't sure what else to say. She pressed send then stared at her phone until the screensaver gave way to black.

She lay awake for most of the night, as a confusing mix of feelings and emotions jostled in her head. She wanted to know where Will was. She was terrified he was lying dead or dying with the car wrapped around a lamppost somewhere. She hated how he drove when he was angry, and hearing him screech off like that was hideous.

She woke with a start as soon as she heard the front door open. She looked at her clock; it was four-thirty.

'Will,' she breathed. She leapt out of bed and ran to the stairs.

He looked tired, deep grey bags beneath his eyes, his skin pale, clothes rumpled with smudges of dirt over them. She put her arms around him, one hand against his head, held him close to her chest.

He pulled away from her and walked back down the stairs. She followed him and closed the kitchen door behind her so they could talk without waking Gill.

'Where have you been?'

He wasn't able to look her in the eyes. 'I drove a bit. Walked a lot.' He leant heavily against the work surface. 'I had some thinking to do.'

'And?' Harmony sat at the table.

'I love you. I don't think I knew what that really meant until yesterday. All this time I've been coasting through life, hiding stuff from you – from myself, even. There was so much I should have told you, but I just hid it, hoped it wouldn't interfere. It's been like wearing invisible shackles that held me back, that stopped me being truthful to both of us. I've been living a lie. But when I thought about you with another man, when I thought about you leaving me, I saw my world fall apart.'

'I was so angry, but it was wrong of me. Unfair to use my anger as an excuse to betray you like that.'

'My father used to take great joy in telling me how unfair life was. "Life isn't fair, William," he used to say. "Life is ugly." I used to think he was a dick for saying it, but I know what he meant now. Life isn't fair. I wasn't fair to you and you weren't fair to me.'

'Can we get through this?'

He took hold of her hand. 'Yes, I think we can.'

'What if he calls again? He hasn't left me alone, Will. He even went to Sophie's.'

'You don't need to worry about him anymore. I'm here now.'

They went upstairs and Will went into the bathroom. Harmony went into the bedroom and grabbed her phone from the bedside table.

He just got back. Now leave us alone.

CHAPTER TWENTY-SIX

Alastair Farrow settled down on the sofa to watch the television. His wife had got up to take the empty plates through to the kitchen, so he grabbed the remote and started to flick through the channels. There was no way he was watching some reality crap about orange-skinned nobodies he'd never heard of. Christ, her taste in television – no, in all things – was appalling. He trawled through until he found a repeat of *Have I Got News for You* on Dave and then hid the remote beneath a cushion. He swilled his whisky gently, listening to the ice cubes clink against the glass, and began to laugh loudly along with the show.

When the phone rang he checked his watch and muttered under his breath. Who the hell could that be? It was nearly ten o'clock. He heard his wife answer with that irritating sing-song phone voice she put on, and a few moments later she came into the room.

'There's someone on the phone for you,' she said.

'For me? What do they want? If it's someone trying to sell something you can tell them to piss off.'

'He isn't a salesman, he said he wants to talk to you. He said his name is Will English?'

'For crying out loud,' snapped Alastair. He took a heavy breath and shook his head. 'What's wrong with that idiot?' He drank some whisky and turned back to the television. 'You can tell him to piss off anyway. I'm not interested in talking to him.'

'He sounded quite insistent.'

'I don't care!' shouted Alastair, not taking his eyes off the television. 'He's a moron.'

'I'm sure it won't take long.'

'Did he say what he wants?' Alastair asked irritably.

'No, he just said he needed a few moments and that he's sorry

242

to disturb us this late.'

'Is that all?'

She nodded.

Alastair thought for a moment or two, remembering the things Will had said to him in the pub. He didn't want to hear any of that rubbish again. It was a part of his life he didn't need to revisit.

'I don't want to talk to him. It's late. Go and tell him to write me a letter or something. In fact, no, don't say that. Tell him to go fuck himself.' He chuckled quietly at the thought of his wife passing that message on, and then drained his whisky.

'Perhaps you could tell him yourself?' she suggested. 'It might be better coming straight from you. He's got a very nice voice,' she said, as if this might persuade him.

He banged his glass down on the side table. 'Jesus, woman, this is ridiculous! It's ten o'clock on a Sunday night!'

'You talk to him and I'll fill your drink. How about that?'

Alastair Farrow stood up and straightened his clothes. 'I'm not happy about this at all,' he grumbled as he passed her.

'I know you're not, dearest.' She walked over to the side table and picked up his empty glass.

'Farrow speaking,' he said as he picked up the phone.

'Listen very carefully. I need to see you. I didn't say what I wanted to say last time. I lost control and I'm sorry about that. You're going to tell your wife you need to talk to me and then you're going to get into your car and drive to an address I'm going to give you.'

'Ha!' Farrow couldn't help laughing. 'Don't be ridiculous.'

'Don't say another word. If you do I will tell your wife what you did at school. I can show her. I have a photo. Of you that afternoon.'

'You don't have a photograph. You're lying.'

'I had my camera that day. You threw it into the bushes. You remember that? Well, I went into the bushes and found it. I have a photo. And it's a good one. I have no qualms about showing your wife, your kids, your boss, I'll tag it on your bloody Facebook page, do you hear me? All you have to do is give me five minutes of your time then you'll never hear from me again. I need some … ' he paused, 'closure.'

Closure? Who did this guy think he was? Peddling politically correct American therapist claptrap like that. He was even more of an idiot than he thought.

'You owe me that much.'

Farrow looked up to see his wife coming out of the kitchen with a glass of whisky in one hand and a large gin and tonic in the other. She handed it to him as she passed. He waited until she was back in the living room before replying. 'You're blackmailing me,' he hissed.

'I am asking that you talk to me and then we can both forget all about it.'

'Where is this bloody place?' he asked, keeping his voice down.

'Not far. Under an hour.'

Farrow shook his head. 'Address?' he snapped. He tore a piece of paper off the pad by the phone and grabbed the pencil that lay beside it, wrote the address down, then slammed the phone into its cradle and swore. 'You should never have picked up that bloody call!' he shouted. 'It's some idiot I was at school with. He's an utter lunatic and now I've got to go and talk to him.'

She ignored him and laughed at something on the television.

'Did you hear me?' he yelled.

She looked up at him. 'Please don't wake the children.' Then she turned back to the television and drank some of her gin.

'I'm going out. Don't wait up for me.'

She didn't look away from the television.

Alastair Farrow knocked his second whisky back in one and then took his car keys off the table in the hall. It was dark outside; not pitch black, but dark. Farrow noted it was past midsummer's night now so the days would be getting shorter. Great, he thought. Cold, dark commuting to look forward to.

He looked out over the cul-de-sac they lived on. He hated it. Hated the dull tweeness of it. It was a dead-end street populated with dead-end people and nothing like where he imagined he'd be at forty-three. He thought he'd be in a large pile somewhere, with a couple of staff and an indoor swimming pool. His neighbours to the left were clearly out for the evening, no car in their driveway and all the lights off. Stupid idiots, he thought, why not leave a sign on the door telling all and sundry there's nobody home? He made a mental note to speak to them about it in the morning. It wasn't good to encourage attention from burglars in The Close. Burglaries always happened in clusters. Burglars were a lazy bunch.

He climbed into his company car, which was just about the best bit of his excuse for a life, and clipped his seatbelt. It was a four-year-old BMW and he kept it immaculate. The children weren't allowed anywhere near it; they and their sticky fingers were only allowed in the rubbish-strewn Galaxy. Just looking at the crisp crumbs, books, plastic toys and accumulated child detritus turned his stomach.

As he turned on the engine he realised how utterly ludicrous this was. It was a farce. Raking up the past like this was pathetic. Will English was a wimp; he always had been. He'd deal with him quickly, get the photograph, burn it and get on with his life. He pulled the piece of paper out and then tapped the address into his satnav. Fifty-one minutes. If he put his foot down he'd do it in forty. Three minutes with the idiot. Then forty minutes home. He checked the clock on the dash. Nine minutes past ten. He'd be back by half past eleven for a large whisky and bit of internet porn before bed.

The monotone voice of the satnav told him he was nearly there. He put the indicator on and turned into a small business park. It was dark and set back from the road with a large pair of metal gates open against an overgrown hedge. There were a number of garage-type units. One of them, number three, the number Will English had given him, had its door ajar, throwing a stripe of fluorescent light across the forecourt. He pulled up and turned off the engine. Then he pulled down the visor and checked his appearance. He ran his hands over his head and straightened his shirt collar before getting out of the car.

'Hello?' he called, his voice echoing off the walls of the prefab building. A police siren sounded over the noise of the traffic on the road outside. He walked towards unit three. 'Hello?' he called again. 'English?'

'In here.'

As soon as he stepped inside he saw it was some sort of photo-graphic studio, with painted breeze-block walls and lights on stands. The door closed behind him with a thud.

He turned and saw a man with his back to him sliding closed the bolt on the door.

'You're not Will English.'

'No,' said the man, well dressed in an expensive suit and a foppish haircut framing his pretty-boy face. 'I'm not.'

'Who the hell are—'

The man walked over to Farrow and the next thing he knew he'd taken a punch to the stomach. The pain shot around his body. Farrow bent double, too winded to call out. He tried to stand upright, tried to catch his breath, but then there was a blow to his head.

When he came round he was lying on the floor and the left side of his head throbbed. He tried to get up but found his hands were tied behind his back. Both his wrists and his ankles hurt. He looked down and saw his feet were also tied with a couple of brightly coloured bungee ropes. Where the hooks met they pushed into his skin. His mouth ached and he realised with horror that he'd been gagged. Fear took hold and he began to panic. He kicked his legs in an attempt to free himself, wriggled back and forth. The man who'd locked him in, who'd punched him, and who, Alastair assumed, had tied him up like this, came into his sights. He crouched beside him and stared down at him. His eyes were dark and cold, but his clothes, the way he held himself was at odds with his menacing look; he looked more like a management consultant than a mugger.

The man grabbed Alastair by his arm, hooking his hand through the crook of his elbow, and yanked him to his feet. He gestured to a chair a few feet from him.

'Sit down.'

Alastair glared at him and shook his head as he retched at the stench of the rag stuffed in his mouth.

'Sit.' The man held up a Swiss Army knife, the blade open, glinting a little in the light.

Farrow didn't move.

The man lifted his hand and brought the knife down across Farrow's face, over the scar that ran down his cheek. The pain was excruciating and Farrow tried to cry out but the sound was muffled by the gag.

'Did that hurt as much as last time?' hissed the man. 'Does that turn you on?' He stepped closer, until his mouth was next to his ear. 'Does that make you want to fuck me now?'

And then Farrow knew who it was and his legs buckled beneath him.

Luke Crawford grabbed hold of his shoulders and sat him on the chair. His face stung and he was aware he was bleeding profusely. Crawford spent a few moments tying him to the chair with more bungee cords that he got from a large holdall. He closed his eyes and thought back to that day. That little shit, that skinny runt – Bible Boy, Puke Crawford – humiliating him in front of his friends. He'd seen their faces when he'd looked at them, his face sliced open; they hadn't known whether to laugh or scream. One of them – Toddy, was it? – had clamped his hand over his face to cover a smirk. Rage had balled inside him as he'd looked back at that crazy boy with his mad eyes and lunatic temper. Standing tall and strong, telling him to leave his friend alone. They'd all had so much fun with him, pressing his buttons, watching him fly off the handle, sending himself straight to the end of Drysdale's cane. But that cut. The river of blood that had flowed. His face, he knew even then, would be scarred forever, and there he was, that little shit, bony fists clenched at his sides, knife gripped tightly, facing him like David against Goliath. He'd grabbed him, knocked the knife out of his hand and growled words he couldn't remember. A red mist descended over him. Anger like he'd never felt. The boy needed to be taught a lesson. You didn't fuck with Alastair Farrow.

The act itself had been quick. The others watched in a semi-circle around them. Silence had fallen over them like a mantle. The only sound he could hear was a soft whimpering from Crawford. He'd hated himself, sickened but at the same time filled with such rage, a rage he couldn't control. He couldn't explain it. Now it seemed heinous, toxic, but then his instinct overwhelmed him, this need to dominate, to punish. When he pushed himself away from Crawford, blood from his face covering both of them, the boy had slumped on the ground like a beaten puppy. He watched with contempt as Crawford struggled to pull his trousers up to cover his pale skin that looked ghostly white against the deep browns of the woodland floor. Farrow turned away. He still remembered the revulsion he felt. Still remembered how he had used every piece of strength inside him to muster his bravado. He straightened his shoulders. Faced the others. Out of the corner of his eye he saw a figure about a hundred feet away. Will English. They locked eyes just before the boy fled. The look on his stricken face, a picture of disgust, shock and reproach, would stay with him forever.

Crawford finished tying him to the chair and stood up, running his hand through his hair to neaten it.

'I am going to take the gag off your mouth. If you yell or shout, even just one syllable, I will stick this through your throat without a second thought. Do you understand me?'

Alastair stared at the penknife in his hand and nodded. Luke raised the knife and came closer to him. He held his breath, preparing for the pain that might come. He felt a sawing motion as Luke cut through the tape that held the rag in place, tugging his skin where it stuck to him. Luke pulled the rag from his mouth and Alastair flexed his jaw. He considered calling Luke's bluff and shouting for help, but there was a look in his captor's eye that kept him quiet.

'You know,' Luke said, his voice flat and soft. 'People who rape children are the lowest of the low.'

'Rape?' Alastair stuttered. 'Jesus Christ, I did no such thing. I was teaching you a lesson. Teaching you some respect. That's how it was done back then. You know that.'

Luke laughed then, the type of laugh you might hear down the pub with the boys – an unbridled laugh of amusement. He lifted the blade. 'This is the very same knife I cut you with that day. You left me at the foot of that oak tree, bleeding and sore, violated, alone and petrified. And you know what I did after you'd all gone? I searched for this knife. I stayed there, until it was too dark to see, until I found it. It took a long time. It had travelled some way when you smacked it out of my hand. But it was my friend's knife, his most beloved possession. It had a message from his father, who wasn't the nicest of men, but you know how these things are. Will loved that knife and I wanted to find it for him. When I found it, feeling with my hands in the undergrowth, I felt as if I'd won the lottery. In the end, I decided to hang on to it.'

Luke advanced on Alastair.

'Stay away from me!' cried Alastair, fear and anger melding into one indistinguishable rush of emotion. 'Stay away or you'll pay for it.'

'I've already paid for it – every day of my life since that afternoon.'

'You'll go to prison. If you kill me, you'll go to prison. Is that what you want?'

'Like you went to prison?' Luke looked at him and smiled, his eyebrows raised. 'Not everyone gets punished for the crimes they commit. You should know that better than anyone. Not every crime gets the justice it deserves. And anyway, a bit like you, I've got it covered. I'm not going to go to prison. Someone else is going.'

'Enough of this now,' Alastair was panicking. A paralysing fear had begun to creep over him. He wanted this to stop. 'What do you want? You don't have to hurt me. Is it money? Do you want money?'

'Money?' Luke said with a smile. 'No, I don't want your money. I've plenty, but it's kind of you to think of me.'

'Then what?' Farrow thought of Will, of what he'd said in the pub, of wanting to hear remorse. 'You want me to say sorry? Is that it? I'll say it. I'm sorry. Okay? I'm really, really sorry.'

'Your sorry means nothing.'

As he spoke Luke Crawford walked over to him and lifted the blade. Calmly and methodically, he drew it down the other side of his face. Farrow yelled out and as he did so Luke grabbed him by the throat and brought his face close to his. 'Shut the fuck up,' he spat. 'That's what you said to me as you raped me. Do you remember that? You said shut the fuck up.'

Alistair Farrow began to whimper. 'Please don't hurt me. I have a wife and children.'

'I know all about your family. They seem nice. Your wife could do with losing a bit of weight but I can see she used to be pretty and your children seem nice enough.'

'Don't hurt my children,' he whispered. He thought of his family asleep in their beds. Would his wife be wondering where he was? Would Diane have called the police by now? Or would she be happily snoring in bed, blissfully unaware of his plight?

'I'm not going to hurt anybody. Except you.'

Farrow began to scream then. Luke's hand was over his mouth in an instant. Pressing against him, squeezing so hard he thought his jaw might shatter.

'Do you know what happened to me after you defiled me and left me in the woods to limp back to school alone in the dark?' Luke asked him then. He loosened his grip on his face and lowered his hand, lifting a single finger as a warning not to scream. 'I told my housemaster – I know, a bit of a telltale, that kind of behaviour would have got me into serious trouble, but I figured you couldn't do any worse to me – and he sent me straight to the head. Drysdale said I was lying. He said that lying about things like that, spreading muck about respectable members of the school was akin to treason. But I insisted. So I was sent to the nurse and told to sleep in that bed in her office. Nobody sat with me. They turned the lights off and left me alone in the dark. No windows, no moonlight, just pitch black, like lying in a coffin in the ground. I lay awake all night feeling dirty, confused, my whole body throbbing with pain, desperate for someone to tell me I was going to be okay. I was terrified, abandoned and broken, a small child ruined – ruined, as it turns out, forever.'

As he spoke, spitting the words out like bitter poison, he flicked the penknife back and forth.

'I tried everything I could to get on with some sort of life. I was driven. Everything I did I did so I could put what you did behind me. I studied, I kept fit, I worked all the hours I could, searching all the time for someone to love, trying to salvage my life. I thought that would make it better, if I had my own family to love and look after.

Protect from animals like you. Prove to the world that life could be good. But I was wrong. What you did ruined me. You stole my life when I was fourteen years old, you *stole* my life.'

Luke came up behind Farrow, pulled his head back and stroked his fingers gently down his exposed neck. 'My wife died because of me. Because she couldn't deal with me. She tried to help but she couldn't.' He bought himself close to Alastair's ear. 'You know why nobody can help me? Because of you,' he whispered, his breath hot on Alastair's skin. 'Because of you I can't even help myself.'

Alastair tried to shake his head. 'Why are you doing this?' he rasped. 'What have you got to gain from killing me?'

'It's not about what I have to gain, but about having nothing left to lose.'

Alastair Farrow pulled against the bungee cords that held his feet and hands in place as Luke bent to rummage in a holdall at his feet. He came out with some grey gaffer tape, picked up the piece of rag and pushed it back into Farrow's mouth, then wrapped the tape twice around his mouth and head as he pulled back and forth in desperation, panic engulfing him.

Then Luke leant close to his face. 'Do you remember what else you said to me that day?'

Farrow stared up at this man, his crazed eyes locked onto his, and his panic levels surged again. There was an eerie calm to his voice that chilled the dead, stale air around them. He looked up at him, those eyes burning with hatred, that mouth twisted into a bitter snarl. Fresh panic gripped him as he fought against the cords that tied him, tugging and twisting like a snared rabbit desperate to free itself.

Luke leant forward and whispered close to his ear, his breath hot, words creamy with intent. 'You said: *And by the way, this is going to hurt you a lot more than it's going to hurt me.'*

CHAPTER TWENTY-SEVEN

Harmony was tidying the cushions on the sofa when she saw the police car pull up outside their building. She went to the window and watched two men – one in uniform, the other in plain clothes – get out of the car. The one in plain clothes stretched and they exchanged words before walking away from the car. She craned her neck and saw them approach the main door. She jumped when the doorbell rang.

She went to buzz them in, smoothing her hair as she did.

'Hello?' she said, as she opened the door to their flat.

'Good morning, madam,' said the plain clothed officer. His grey suit was crumpled and his white shirt greying on the edges of his collar. He was older than he'd seemed from the window, with deep, craggy lines, a large nose that had been broken on more than one occasion and a small scar through one of his eyebrows.

'Can I help you?' she said.

'Does Mr William English live here?'

'Yes,' she said, looking from one to the other. 'He's my husband.'

'Is he in?' said the other police officer, a younger man with sandy hair and matching eyes and the sallow skin of a heavy smoker.

'He's in the garden.' She turned and gestured unnecessarily to the back of the flat. 'Shall I call him?'

'If you wouldn't mind,' said the older man patiently.

Harmony nodded. 'Would you like to come in?'

The two men came through the front door and she directed them to the living room. They made the room seem small and overcrowded. She went to the back door and called to Will. He was on his hands and knees, wearing shorts and no top, a sheen of sweat coating his sun-reddened back, weeding the bed to the left of the lawn. They'd both been too tired to think about work, so Will had phoned Frank first thing and told him he wouldn't be in, and

Harmony had called in sick. Alice was happy that she was finally looking after herself. They'd ended up leaving Gill's just after midday, with Harmony driving so Will could sleep, though she'd found it hard to keep her own eyes open on the monotonous stretch of motorway. They'd both gone to bed when they got back and had a few hours sleep, and when Will woke he went straight into the garden. He told her he wanted to make the most of the last few hours of sun, but she knew he was still trying to come to terms with the idea of her with Luke. He'd need time; she knew that.

'The police are here,' she said to him in hushed tones. 'They want to talk to you.'

Will looked surprised. He stood up and dragged his arm over his damp, earthy brow. His T-shirt was tucked into his waistband and he pulled it out.

'Do you know why?' he asked as he walked up towards her, putting his T-shirt on as he went.

She shook her head. 'They didn't say. Maybe something to do with Luke?' She began to chew the inside of her lip.

'Why on earth would it be to do with him?' he asked sharply.

She shrugged and dropped her eyes. 'I don't know, all the phone calls and texts, and … ' She hesitated. 'Well … I went to see him to tell him to stop calling me and there were all these photos in his flat.'

'What photos?'

'Photos of us. I should have told you … ' she paused again, wondering why on earth she hadn't told him about the photographs. 'He's not well, Will. He needs to see someone who can help him.'

Will nodded. 'I'm sure it's nothing sinister. Probably some sort of routine check or maybe something to do with the shop. '

Harmony watched him go and then looked up at the sky. It was the blue of a robin's egg, with a few white clouds hanging still as if suspended by invisible threads. She heard some children walk past on the pavement on the other side of the wall. They were laughing and joking with each other. She heard a snippet of their conversation, two boys discussing the football, then she heard a ball bounce, and one of them whooped. Then their happy voices faded as they walked on.

'Would you like a cup of tea?' she said to the three men when she came back into the living room. They stood in a tight triangle and when she spoke they looked at her in unison.

'Is everything all right?' she asked.

Will looked at the floor for a moment or two and then lifted his face again, his brow deeply furrowed, his lips tight.

'They want to ask me a few questions,' said Will.

'Questions about what?' She looked between the policemen for an answer.

'A man's been reported missing,' Will said. 'Apparently, his wife told the police I called him last night and asked to meet him.' He turned to the men. 'Is that right? That's definitely what she said?'

'Yes,' said the older man. 'She said a man called Will English called at around ten o'clock last night and then her husband left the house after telling her he had to go and meet him. He never returned.'

Harmony glanced back and forth between the three men. Fear engulfed her. Oh my God, she thought. What have you done, Will? Where were you last night?

Will was pale as a corpse.

'Will?' She took a step closer to him. 'What's going on? Do you know anything about this?'

'No. No, I don't.' Will looked at her with pure incredulity, his eyes wide, his breath seeming to catch in his throat. She gripped her hands behind her back in the hope the policemen didn't notice how much she was shaking.

'Who is the man? Who's gone missing?' She looked between the three men again in search of an answer, her eyes settling back on Will.

Will opened his mouth to speak but nothing came out. His eyes flicked back and forth. She could see his brain whirring.

'Will?'

He stared at her blankly, as if he wasn't seeing her. 'It's … it's Alastair Farrow,' he said. 'Alastair Farrow's gone missing and his wife said I was the last person to talk to him. That he left the house to meet me.'

'Why would she say that?' Harmony asked.

'We just want to ask you a few questions,' said the detective.

Harmony glanced at the uniformed policeman who stared at Will like a hawk at a mouse.

'Do you need me to come now?'

'Yes, please.'

Will took a breath and nodded. 'Can you give me a few minutes to change? I'm pretty dirty from the garden. I'd appreciate some clean clothes and maybe a chance to wash my face and hands.'

The detective briefly hesitated and then nodded.

Will went out of the living room and into their bedroom.

'Will you excuse me?' Harmony asked the men faintly.

'We'll wait out in the hallway,' the older man said.

Harmony walked them to the hall and opened the front door. She saw the uniformed man check his watch. She was suddenly filled with an urge to flee, to pack a small bag and bundle Will out of the kitchen door and over the wall at the bottom of the garden and run as fast as they could away from there.

Will had changed his shorts for a pair of trousers and taken his T-shirt off, which lay in a heap at his feet. He was bent over the basin, using his hand to wash his armpits and back of his neck. Then he filled his cupped hands and buried his face in the water.

'You need to tell me where were you last night,' Harmony whispered shakily. 'When you left your mum's. You were gone all night. I left messages on people's phones. People know you were missing.'

He turned the tap off and then reached for the towel. He patted his face and neck dry. Then he looked at her. 'I didn't call him. I didn't see Alastair Farrow last night. Do you think I've done something?' Though his question lacked accusation, she could see he was disappointed that he had to ask.

She studied him, his drawn face, lips tight with worry. 'No,' she said. 'I don't think you've done anything.' She stepped towards him. 'But I need to know where you were.'

He rubbed his face hard. 'I went to visit my father's grave,' he said. He furrowed his brow as if hearing those words was a surprise to him.

'What?' She followed him out of the bathroom and into their bedroom.

'I went to his grave and I sat beside it.'

He opened his cupboard and took a shirt off a hanger.

'All night?'

'Most of it.' He began to button his shirt with the sombre air of a man dressing for his own execution. 'Before that I drove to my parents' old house and snuck in over the fence at the bottom of the garden and walked around. Sat in the places I had done as a child – down in the hollow in the copse, on the swing. I was thinking about things. About you and Luke. About how I'd fucked everything up, driven you away. And as I sat there in the dark, thinking about how much of it I blamed on my father, on his choices, I realised it was bullshit. It was like a bolt of lightning hit me. It was only myself I had to blame.' He looked at her as he tucked his shirt into his trousers. 'You can't let the past ruin the present and future. I'd been blaming all sorts of things for my decision to have the vasectomy, for my fear of becoming a father, for keeping things from you – giving myself all these stupid excuses. But you have to take responsibility for your actions, don't you?'

She braced herself against an unbidden memory of Luke kissing her. 'Yes,' she said. 'Blaming everybody else is far too easy.'

'Anyway, that's when I decided to go and see him.' He turned and reached into the cupboard and chose a tie from the shelf.

'His grave?'

'Mum and I talked about him before you arrived on Saturday. She said some things that really stuck. It got me thinking about how much hostility I was carrying around.' He stepped towards her and reached for her hand. 'I drove to the church and sat by his headstone and ended up telling him I was sorry. Not an apology to him, but a sorry to both of us for our relationship. For our missed opportunity. Our wasted years. I told him I was going to have a baby with you,' he said. 'And then I lay down beside the grave and closed my eyes and for the first time in my life I felt close to him. It was as if we shook hands.'

Will turned his collar up and looped the tie around his neck.

Harmony watched as he tried to tie it, his fingers fumbling, trembling too much to allow him to do it. She stepped closer to him and stilled his hands, then smiled gently and tied it for him. When it was done, she folded down his collar and then laid her hands on his shoulders.

'I didn't telephone Alastair Farrow last night,' Will said.

'I know you didn't.'

CHAPTER TWENTY-EIGHT

Will sat in the interview room at the police station and tried not to panic. He was tired from a sleepless night in the police cell. It had been frustrating needing to get out and walk but being stuck in the small, claustrophobic room that smelt of disinfectant. He'd felt like a caged animal, pacing from one side of the room to the other, desperate to calm himself.

He'd answered their questions but then something had happened. A police car had been sent to investigate a business property after a local walker reported finding a body. His dog had pushed through the unlocked door of a warehouse unit and found the bloodied body. The police had found a wallet on the floor beside him containing the credit cards and driver's licence of Alastair Farrow. His car, which had been reported missing, was parked outside. The unit belonged to Will English.

The detective who arrested him explained they would hold him for a period of time until he was either charged or released. They said further questioning would be recorded. And then he read him the police caution.

'You do not have to say anything. However, it may harm your defence … '

The man's monotonous voice faded into nothing and Will found himself thinking about Alastair. About the hatred he'd seen in his eyes that day in the pub, how he'd stared at him coldly, remorselessly, fully believing he'd done nothing wrong. A voice inside Will wanted to tell the police how they needn't worry. That if, as it indeed appeared, Farrow was dead, it didn't matter. He deserved it. He was a nasty piece of work who deserved to be dead. He wondered if his lack of compassion, the unmistakeable smack of pleasure he'd felt, made him a bad person? Surely if he was a good person he would feel horrified by the news of Farrow's death? The seriousness of his predicament hadn't really sunk in. It was only when the policeman raised his voice that he snapped back into the here and now and it began to dawn on him what a mess he was in.

'Mr English?' the policeman barked, leaning forward and staring at Will. 'Did you hear what I said about legal advice?'

'Yes,' mumbled Will. 'Yes, I did. I have someone I can call.'

The detective who was questioning him opened his folder and took hold of his pen. Will noticed he was left-handed and wrote with an awkward, claw-like hold. He pressed record on a tape recorder that sat between them on the table. He said the date then checked his watch and said the time.

They covered the basics: name, address, contacts, work details. The policeman didn't look up, he merely asked the questions and paused, pen suspended, waiting for Will's answers. Will found it difficult to think. His mind was foggy, drifting away from the room, trying to work out how Alastair had ended up in his studio. Who had called him and pretended to be him? Luke? Surely he wasn't a killer? Will began to wonder if perhaps he was actually psychotic and had killed Farrow but had no recollection of it, like a sleepwalker? Maybe the memory of being at his father's grave was an elaborate fantasy created by his subconscious mind. Was that possible? Harmony would know more about that. He wished she were there so he could ask her.

'Mr English?'

Will narrowed his eyes and forced himself to focus on the policeman.

'Can you please answer these questions? Some of them you will have answered already, but if you could be patient, that would be appreciated. Did you know Mr Alastair Farrow?'

Will nodded. 'Yes. Yes, I did. We were at school together. Twenty-five years ago. But we weren't friends.'

'But you met up with him recently?'

Will began to drift again. He saw himself getting into the car to drive to the pub on the outskirts of Camberley. He tried to stop himself turning the engine on. Tried to stop himself going …

'Answer the question,' the policeman asked firmly.

'Yes,' Will said. 'We went for a drink.'

'And this was following contact you'd made with him … ' The man looked back through his notebook, licking the tip of his finger to flip through the pages. '… via Facebook?' He said the word Facebook as if it was something he'd never heard of.

'Yes.'

'And it was you who suggested you meet for this drink?'

'I think so … though … it might have been him.' Will racked his brain to remember which of them had suggested meeting up. Why couldn't he recall? He closed his eyes and thought hard, trying to sift his mind for the answer. 'It's hard to remember … '

'If you weren't friends, why did you contact him?'

'Um, well another boy … a man now … from school … we bumped into each other at a friend's house. I just … ' Will shook his head. 'It's hard to explain. I think it was nostalgia. I was having a few problems with my marriage … ' Will stopped talking as he watched the man scribbling with his hooked hand. What are you writing down? Will wanted to ask. Are you writing down that I was having problems with my wife? Because we're fine now. You don't need to write that down.

'I understand from the landlord of The Dog and Duck—'

'The Dog and Duck?' Will shook his head.

'The public house where you and Alastair Farrow met.'

Will nodded. He turned his right hand over and stared at the scar. He understood now. He was going to prison for a murder he didn't commit, the murder of the only person in the world who he'd ever actually felt like killing. Will almost laughed out loud at the irony. He placed his hand palm down on the table and pressed it hard against the wood.

'There are several witnesses who saw you fighting. We spoke to the landlord this morning. He said you attacked the deceased and he heard you threaten him.'

'No, no,' said Will then, shaking his head vigorously. 'No, I didn't attack him. Or threaten him. We had a row but I didn't threaten him.'

'Did you, or did you not say: "I could fucking kill you?"'

Will closed his eyes and shook his head. 'I can't remember. I might have done. I didn't mean—'

'And you did grab him by the neck?'

Will didn't answer.

'Mr English? Did you grab Alastair Farrow by the neck in The Dog and Duck pub?'

'Yes.'

'What was your argument about?'

Will recalled his feelings towards Alastair in the pub that night, the rage that caused him to jump up and lunge for him, the desire to put him down like a rabid dog.

'He was a bully at school,' he said at last, his head slumped forward. 'Alastair Farrow bullied me and I wanted him to apologise.' He hesitated. 'At least, I think I wanted him to apologise. I'm not sure what I wanted.' Will's mind was hazy. A fresh layer of panic settled over him like thick snow.

'So you wanted him to say sorry for things that he had done to you at school?' asked the man. He looked up and gestured at another man who stood at the door, made some unintelligible sign at him, then the man nodded and left the room.

'Yes.'

'And did he?'

Will looked at the man. He had his pen poised. When Will didn't answer he looked up and they locked eyes. He lowered his hand holding the pen onto the table. 'Did he apologise to you, Mr English?'

Will held his gaze for a moment or two as he was hit by an over-whelming urge to vomit.

'Mr English?'

Will shook his head slowly and then looked down at the table. 'No,' he whispered. 'He didn't. He said he had nothing to apologise for and that him bullying us was nothing more than acceptable boyish mucking about.'

'And you left in such a state you left your credit card behind the bar?'

'Yes. I had to cancel it the next day.'

The man turned to a new page in his notebook. 'The premises where the victim was found. What do you use it for?'

'It was where I ran my photography business from. I don't use it much now.'

'Why not?'

Will shook his head. 'It didn't make money. I couldn't make it work.'

'And who knew the access code to the door?'

'The padlock, you mean?'

The man nodded.

'Just me and my wife,' Will said.

'So only the two of you could have unlocked the padlock using the code?'

'Was it open?'

'Yes, with no signs of forced entry. Whoever went in there with Mr Farrow unlocked the padlock. They knew the code.'

Will's heart pummelled in his chest. Everything pointed to him. But how? he thought, trying to make some sense of the chaos in his head.

Where did you fuck him?

He saw Harmony's face fall, her eyes well with tears and her head shake back and forth.

At the studio. I'm so sorry.

His head began to pound. He squeezed his eyes shut and pressed his knuckles against his temples.

'Why did you call Alastair Farrow's house?'

'I didn't,' Will said, snapping his eyes open. 'I didn't call him.'

'You spoke to his wife and then to Farrow. You called from the phone in your business unit. At … ' The man flicked through his notes. 'At four minutes past ten.'

Will shook his head.

The man stayed quiet.

'I didn't kill him,' Will said, unable to keep the desperation out of his voice. 'I didn't kill Alastair.'

The policeman said nothing. The door opened and the other

man came back in with a cup of tea for the questioning officer. He thanked him with a nod of his head and then reached into his jacket pocket and retrieved a box of sweeteners. He clicked twice over the cup and two tiny white pills dropped into the tea, making circular ripples on its surface. 'Do you know of anyone who might have wanted to kill Alastair Farrow?'

Will's mind whirred. He closed his fist over the scar on his palm. 'Yes.' He dropped his head. 'There's a man. My friend. Luke Crawford. Farrow bullied him too. And then he … ' Will stumbled over his words.

'Then he what?'

'Alastair Farrow sexually assaulted him.' Will hesitated. 'Raped him. I saw it. I saw Alastair rape Luke.'

Will winced as he heard his voice cry out to Farrow.

I didn't do it! Don't hurt me. It was him, not me. It was Luke.

Alastair Farrow had looked at him with scorn, shook his head, blood running from the cut on his face, dripping from his jawline and chin. Will watched Farrow nod at his friends. Watched two of them drag Luke over to Farrow, his feet desperately scrabbling against the ground, his arms flailing in their clutches, trying to wriggle free. Will froze. Transfixed. Watched Farrow advance on Luke, face bloodied, blood on his neck and shirt as if someone had thrown a tin of scarlet paint over him. Will saw Luke's face smeared with terror. He muttered I'm sorry over and over, too scared to move, to get help, to intervene. Farrow held his hand over Luke's mouth to muffle his shouts and tried to force him onto the ground. Luke must have bitten him because Farrow yelled and hit Luke so hard that he spun and fell into the dark, loose earth. Will watched as Farrow pulled him up while yanking his belt open, grasped Luke's hair with his hand, pulled his head back so hard that Will feared his neck would snap.

'You should talk to him. Luke Crawford. He's a lawyer in the City.'

The policeman wrote on a piece of paper and then handed it to the other man at the door. He whispered something to him and the man nodded and left the room. Then he put his pen down.

Will scraped his fingers through his hair. 'I don't want to say any more,' he said. 'Not until I have legal representation present. I can say that, can't I?'

The man nodded. He sat back and closed his file, reached for his tea.

'Can I go home?'

'No,' the man said. He sipped his tea. 'I'm afraid you can't, as it happens.'

Will was taken to a cell and given a glass of water and a limp ham sandwich from a vending machine. He lay on the bed, his hands behind his neck, and stared at the ceiling. He thought about Farrow again, about his plump wife and his red-faced children, about his cord trousers, his balding head, and the smug look he'd given Drysdale in the office, then the colluding smile Drysdale had given in return. Will turned over and hid his face in the crook of his elbow.

At nearly nine o'clock the lock on the cell opened with an ominous clunk. The craggy policeman and a female officer he hadn't seen before stood in the doorway.

'William English,' the policeman said. 'You are being charged with the murder of Alastair Farrow.'

As the policeman read him his rights, Will's thoughts returned to the day after the rape. He remembered waking, sitting bolt upright in bed and looking across the room at his friend's bed. With horror he saw it hadn't been slept in, the grey blanket tucked under the mattress – smooth, without a single wrinkle. Will had pulled his uniform on and then hared along the corridors, down the stairs and across the courtyard to the large refectory. But Luke wasn't there. He sat on the end of one of the long wooden tables and craned his head as each group of boys came in, desperate to see Luke among them. Careful not to be spotted by any masters, he pocketed two slices of white bread and an apple to give him when he found him. All day he looked out for him. At lunchtime he snuck back to the woods, his heart pounding, sweat creeping over his skin, to see if he was still there, too injured to move. After supper, while he was supposed to be concentrating on prep, his housemaster, Mr Fraser, came with that apologetic look on his face and his voice tinged with regret, as he told him that he had to go and see Drysdale. He still recalled the weight of his hand squeezing his shoulder, trying to reassure him.

Just tell the truth and you'll be fine.

When he'd opened the door to Drysdale's office the man had looked terrifying, larger than a giant, his cane laid out on the desk in front of him, his tool of torture.

'Sit down,' he barked.

Will had sat on the chair opposite the desk.

'There's been an incident,' Drysdale had said. 'Involving a boy – a friend of yours, I believe. Luke Crawford.'

Will's heart had started racing. Please be okay, he thought. Please be okay. He'd crossed the fingers on his left hand and slid them under his thigh. Please be okay, Luke.

'He's accusing one of the prefects of a very serious crime.'

Will stared at him.

'Of course,' Drysdale said, 'we know he's lying.'

Will opened his eyes wide and began to shake his head.

'We know he's lying because this type of thing doesn't happen at Farringdon Hall. Farrow is one of the most well-respected members of our school. He's a sterling boy, on track to do great things. His father was at this school and is a valuable benefactor. Alastair Farrow is everything a Farringdon boy should be and he has assured me that he hasn't laid a finger, or anything else, on the boy.'

Will began to protest. Drysdale rose to his feet and leant over his desk, glaring at Will with blazing eyes. He reached for his cane, picked it up, and came round to Will's side of the table.

'Boys like Crawford are easily confused. He's a liar and always has been and I think we all know who's telling the truth and who isn't.' Drysdale walked over to Will and leant close to his face. 'If Crawford is telling the truth the reputation of this school will suffer. Now, you don't want that any more than I do, do you, English? Of course you don't. Crawford says you were there.'

Will stared at him, his tongue tied, unable to speak.

'If you were there you would've seen that nothing untoward happened, wouldn't you? If you do the right thing, if you tell the truth, then I'll spare you the caning for missing prep and playing silly buggers with the Crawford boy. If you lie, I'll make your life a misery. You'll be standing outside my office every day for the rest of the year during afternoon break and I'll suggest to Farrow that he might like your services for a bit of errand running. And you and I both know your father would be most unimpressed to hear that his only son was involved in a scandal so sordid.' Drysdale leant even closer to Will, his breath warm and sour. He laid the cane across Will's lap, tapping his thigh lightly a few times. 'You do know what the right thing to say is, don't you? You know what really happened. Farringdon Hall doesn't need any muckraking. It won't do any of us any good at all. You appreciate this, English?'

Will's eyes stung with tears and he nodded.

'So,' said Drysdale calmly as he turned to lay his cane back on the desk. 'We have an understanding then.' He clasped his hands behind his back and opened the door to his office.

'Farrow! Crawford! In here!'

First Farrow came in, his face bandaged, his exposed eye piercing Will who felt faint with fear. Farrow positioned himself to the right of Drysdale's desk as Luke walked slowly in. When he saw Will his face lit up. Will felt a surge of relief. Luke had been crying, his cheeks were even more sunken than usual, and his arms hung limply, but he was okay, he was alive. Luke smiled at him. Will looked away and glanced back at Farrow and then Drysdale who was sat back in his chair, his hands on his chest, his fingers drumming. Will felt sick. His mind was muddled. He glanced at Farrow who glared daggers at him.

Will heard Drysdale's voice demanding the truth. The truth he wanted.

Will knew what he should do. He should tell Luke's truth. He should stand up for his friend, for what was right. But in Will's world standing up for the truth never did any good. When he told the truth bad things happened. *Life isn't fair, William,* he heard his father's voice in his head. *Life is ugly.*

'Crawford is lying,' Will said. 'I was there. Farrow was mucking around and Luke cut him with my penknife. That was all that happened. He's lying.'

'No, Will! Tell him the truth. Please! Blood brothers, remember? I'll watch your back, you watch mine. You said—'

'Shut up, Luke!' Will screamed, clamping his hands over his ears. 'I hate you, don't you understand? I hate you. I wish I'd never met you. I hate you!'

Then he'd pushed up from the chair, so hard it fell over, and with burning tears running down his cheeks, he ran from the room, ignoring Luke's cries and Drysdale's shouts for him to get back that instant. And that was the last time he saw Luke Crawford until that Sunday lunch at Emma and Ian's when he walked back into his life and turned it upside down.

CHAPTER TWENTY-NINE

It was Frank's message on the landline voicemail that galvanised her. Will had been in custody now for approaching forty-eight hours. She felt desolate, worn out from trying to face the very real possibility that her husband was going to prison for murder.

'Harmony, dear, it's Frank. I've called a couple of times but must have missed you. I hope you're bearing up. I've made a cottage pie. It's a bit large. Enough for eight, really, but maybe you could eat portions of it over a couple of nights. A lunch or two as well, if you fancy. Though maybe that would get boring. Anyway, I'll bring it over on my way to work in the morning. If you're not in I'll leave it on the doorstep wrapped in a few carrier bags, with a packet of custard creams as well. I just know he didn't do it. Keep strong, my dear. Bye for now.'

'You're right, Frank,' she said out loud as she put the phone down. 'He didn't do it and at the moment the man who did is walking free.'

She picked up the phone, grabbed the Post-it that was stuck to her computer screen and dialled the number. The lawyer Will had appointed answered the phone with an efficient brusqueness.

'I want to know why they haven't arrested Luke Crawford?' she asked her.

'He has an alibi. He was with people from eight until four in the morning. The police have questioned him, but there was nothing to hold him for, I assume.'

'But he did it,' Harmony said, shaking her head and gripping the phone. 'I know he did it, so why isn't he a suspect?'

'As I said already, he has an alibi.'

'What has he told them he was doing?' she demanded.

'He was entertaining a client. They were in London, drinking, and then they went back to his place with a couple of prostitutes, apparently. Which is nice,' she said with obvious distaste.

'He's lying.'

'That's beside the point. He has an alibi and there's no evidence whatsoever pointing to Mr Crawford. Worryingly for us, however, there's an awful lot of evidence pointing to your husband, including,' she said, with a loaded pause, 'the fact he has no alibi whatsoever. This wandering around the countryside for twelve hours with no witnesses apart from a dead and buried father does not look good at all. Luke Crawford and this client … ' She paused and Harmony heard the rustling of papers from the other end of the phone line, '… a Mr Barratt-Jones were—'

'Who did you say?' Harmony barked. Her heart started pounding.

'Mr Barratt-Jones.'

'Ian?' she asked. 'Is the man called Ian?'

'Yes,' said the lawyer. 'Do you know him?'

'Yes, I bloody do,' said Harmony, suddenly incensed. 'And he's bloody lying too.'

As soon as she put the phone down, Harmony grabbed her keys from the hook and ran out of the flat to the car. As she drove she drummed her fingers against the steering wheel. Ian was Luke's alibi? Why? Why would he lie to protect Luke?

She turned off the M40 and took the road that led to the village where Emma and Ian lived, her mind seething.

'Answer the door!' Harmony shouted, banging on the door of Oak Dene Hall with the flat of her hand.

She knew they were in; she'd seen Emma cross in front of the kitchen window when she pulled up. Harmony banged again on the door. 'Emma! Let me in. I need to talk to you!'

Emma hadn't returned any of her phone calls since the police arrested Will and now she knew why. Harmony kicked at the gravel in frustration, then marched up to the kitchen window and peered in. She saw a flash of one of the children and swore under her breath. She went back to the front door and began to hammer on it again. 'Emma! I'm not bloody leaving!' Harmony paused but still her friend didn't come to the door. 'I just want to talk to you,' Harmony said, no longer shouting. She rested her head against the door, suddenly feeling alone and desolate. Then she turned and sat down on the step, her head in her hands. She heard the door open and jumped to her feet.

'Harmony,' said Emma. 'What are you doing here?'

She was dressed in tracksuit bottoms and an old sweatshirt, and wearing no make-up, the skin around her eyes pink and puffy. Harmony couldn't remember seeing Emma without make-up. Even when they were younger, make-up was always done first thing in the morning. Her face looked old, wrinkles she hadn't been aware of lined her eyes and lips. Her hair was clean and brushed neatly.

The two women stood either side of the door frame, neither of them moving. 'Is Ian here?' Harmony said. 'I need to speak to him.'

Emma shook her head. 'No, he's not.'

'Can I come in?'

Emma glanced at her quickly and Harmony saw the hesitation on her face.

'Please?'

She saw Emma wavering.

'I promise I won't stay long.'

Emma stepped to one side and allowed Harmony in. The house smelt of Pledge and floor cleaner. In the kitchen, the surfaces shone, not a speck of dust or an out-of-place paper anywhere to be seen. The sound of children's television from the den broke the silence.

'Would you like a drink?' Emma asked, without making eye contact.

'Will didn't do it.'

Emma turned away from her to fill the kettle from the tap. She turned the tap off, but kept her back to Harmony and put her hands on the edge of the sink and gripped it.

'Will didn't kill that man,' Harmony said again.

Emma turned around and crossed her arms. 'I don't know what to say, Harmony.'

Harmony felt the sting of tears and her stomach knotted. 'Just say you believe me.'

'The court will have to—'

'Fuck the court!'

Emma turned slowly round to put the kettle back on its base and flick its switch.

'It was Luke Crawford.'

Emma shook her head, there was a stoop to her shoulders that aged her.

'Luke killed him.'

Emma turned to face her. 'He didn't.'

'Because he was with Ian the night that man was killed? Why didn't you tell me Ian was Luke's alibi?'

'I don't know. I didn't really know how to. I didn't think it was relevant.'

'Not relevant?' Harmony cried. 'Of course it's relevant! My husband is in custody facing trial for a murder he didn't commit and the man that did it is going to get off because he was supposedly with your husband?'

Emma visibly winced and her eyes shot to the floor.

'And we both know he's lying. We spoke that night. You told me you were with Ian. You remember?'

'No, you're mistaken,' she said, her eyes giving her away, darting from one side to the other. The kettle reached its boil noisily and clicked off. 'I was here alone.'

'No, you told me you were both here, watching a film. One he'd picked up at the supermarket.'

'No, you're wrong. I—'

'Stop it!' cried Harmony, slamming her hand on the work surface. 'Do you know what you're doing? My husband could go to prison for murder.'

Emma crossed her arms around her body, her hands pulling at the sides of her sweatshirt. She shook her head. 'He won't. If he didn't kill him he'll get off. They won't send someone to prison without evidence. If he's innocent he'll get off.'

Harmony laughed bitterly and looked at the ceiling. 'Don't be so naive! People go to prison all the time for crimes they didn't commit. Why are you lying about where Ian was?'

'I'm not. Ian was with Luke that night. He was being … entertained.' She said the word 'entertained' as if it caused her physical pain.

Emma lifted her head and locked eyes with Harmony. Harmony didn't understand. Why was she lying? Why would Ian protect a work colleague – his lawyer, for God's sake – over one of his oldest friends?

Then suddenly it was if a mist had cleared. 'Oh my God,' she breathed. 'Luke has something on Ian, doesn't he?'

Emma's face fell in panic and Harmony knew she was right. Emma glanced through the kitchen door to the hallway, then squared her shoulders. 'Ian and Luke were out in London. Ian was entertaining Luke. They stayed out late.'

'You're lying,' Harmony said. 'I know you are; I've known you all my life. I can tell.' Harmony took a step towards her but Emma stepped backwards. 'Do you know what Luke did to that man, Emma? He tortured him to death. He beat him and cut him and kicked him in the stomach and head and genitals until he broke almost every bone in his body.'

Emma threw her hands up to cover her ears and squeezed her eyes shut like a child.

'Do you really think Will could do that? You've known him for twenty years. He can't even kill a bloody wasp. It was Luke, Emma.' Harmony couldn't help her voice rising. Frustration and contempt began to boil over inside her. 'Why are you covering for him? My husband's sitting in a cell, right this minute, while yours is out gallivanting on some golf course and that cold-blooded murderer is free.'

Emma tightened her arms around her quivering body. 'Please, Harmony,' she whispered. 'You need to leave now, or I'll … or I'll … call the police.'

'And what?' Harmony shouted. 'Tell them more lies? Try and get me locked up as well? You could try breaking and entering. Maybe tell them I stole some jewellery. Say I hit you.'

'Don't—'

'You know … ' Harmony had to stop speaking to allow the lump of emotion to subside in her throat. 'You know he's stalking me.'

Emma's face contorted in confusion. 'Stalking you? Who is?'

'Luke. He's been following me, and Will. I went to his apartment and saw photos he'd taken.' She paused. 'We had an affair, Emma.'

Emma stared at her in confusion.

'That's right. An affair. Christ,' she said then, still unable to believe what was happening. 'I can't even call it that. We had sex.'

'But how—'

'How did we have sex? Will and I had an argument, then Luke and I met up and we fucked.' Harmony saw Emma flinch at her words. 'We fucked and then I realised I loved my husband. I told Luke it was over and told Will I loved him and we started getting our marriage back on track.' Harmony took a deep breath, laughed bitterly. 'We're actually going to try for a baby. Can you believe that?' She rubbed her face. 'But no, Luke didn't like that. He blames Will for something that happened when they were children. He texts and calls all the time. He turned up at my sister's. Emma, I'm scared. I'm scared because I know Will didn't kill that man. And I know Ian was here with you that night, which means I'm pretty sure Luke is a murderer and I am scared for my own damn life, scared he's going to appear one night and do something to me. He's a murderer, Emma, and you're protecting him.'

Emma dropped her eyes to the floor.

'So that's it? You're happy to risk my life, to let Will go to prison?'

'You don't understand.' Emma spoke so quietly Harmony could barely hear her.

'No, you're right,' Harmony said with angry frustration. 'I don't understand. Please, please, Emma, explain it to me.'

'There is nothing at all to understand.'

Both women jumped at the sound of Ian's voice and turned to see him looming in the doorway. Harmony was shocked by how exhausted and dishevelled he was.

'I thought you weren't here.' Harmony stared pointedly at Emma.

'I wasn't. Now I am.' Ian walked over to the large American fridge-freezer, opened it and got out a bottle of beer. 'So did I hear you right just then? You and the handsome lawyer have been having a bit of fun?' He said the word in a way that made Harmony's skin crawl.

'Why are you lying? Why are you protecting him? And don't say you're not because I know you are.'

'You know?' He retrieved a bottle opener from the cutlery drawer and opened the beer. He drank straight from the bottle, chucking the bottle top onto the kitchen worktop. 'How do you know? Were you there?'

'I rang Emma the night it happened, when you were supposedly out with him. You were here, watching a film together. You'd bought it from Tesco or Waitrose or wherever. It was a war film and Emma wasn't enjoying it.'

'You're mistaken. She was watching the film on her own because I was out.' He sat down heavily at the table, his beer clasped in his hand, his gaze seeming to lose its focus. 'I was with Luke, drinking champagne, enjoying some whores.'

Harmony looked at Emma but she'd turned her back on them and was looking out of the window that overlooked the driveway.

'Luke and I were together all night. And there's bugger all you can do about it.' He lifted his head and looked at her. 'Do you understand now?'

Harmony knew then that she was wasting her time. It was there, clear fom the stoop of Emma's head and shoulders, the way she gripped the side of the worktop, and the monotonous conviction in Ian's dishonest words.

'You disgust me,' she spat. 'You both disgust me.'

Then she turned and walked out of the kitchen and into the hallway, hoping she'd make it to the car without collapsing. She fumbled with the latch on the front door, then pushed it open and stumbled down the steps. She stopped before she reached the car and stood still in the middle of the enormous expanse of new, clean gravel, and realised she had never been so alone in her life.

CHAPTER THIRTY

Harmony drove straight to her sister's, and when Sophie opened the door she fell into her arms and held her tightly.

When they finally pulled apart, she followed Sophie into the kitchen. It was quiet and tidy, with Ella Fitzgerald playing softly in the background. Harmony saw her mother then, just as she used to be, before the illness had ravaged her beyond recognition. She remembered how the soothing tones of Ella would float through her bedroom wall. How she'd climb out of bed to creep along to the sitting room and peer around the doorframe in the hope of catching her mother dancing around the room, totally lost in the music she loved.

'Where are the boys?' Harmony asked.

'George is at football, Matt's at a friend's and Cal's at his girlfriend's house.'

'His girlfriend? Really? Is she nice?'

Sophie nodded. 'She's lovely, actually. Bright, pretty, good strong opinions, and seems to really like him. God knows why. She even laughs at his jokes, including the dreadful ones.'

'He's a great kid, he deserves someone lovely.'

Sophie put her arms around her and gave her another hug. 'You know what we should do?' she said with a soft smile.

Harmony shook her head.

'Come with me,' Sophie said, as she opened the back door and took Harmony's hand. They wove their way through the assorted sports paraphernalia that littered the terrace and onto the lawn. Sophie sat down and patted the ground beside her. 'How about a bit of cloud staring?'

Harmony burst into tears and laughed at the same time. She and Sophie lay back, their legs out straight, holding hands. Harmony searched the sky for animals. They used to do this with their mum if they'd had a bad day, if someone had been mean to them or they'd been upset by a teacher or embarrassed themselves somehow or – towards the end of her illness – when one of them was feeling particularly sad or scared. She'd kiss them and give them a chocolate biscuit then whisper: *How about a bit of cloud staring?* Then they'd lie on the grass holding hands, like a paper chain of people, and silently scan the sky until they found a creature lurking in the clouds, maybe a running fox or a jumping hare, and then they'd point and cry out with such excitement that soon the bad thing was forgotten.

'Luke Crawford reminded me of our dad,' Harmony said.

'How?'

Harmony searched the clouds above her but there were only large amorphous shapes that offered her nothing. 'The mystery, maybe. The excitement I felt reminded me of what Mum described, how she said she felt when she was with him. That shortness of breath, the thumping heart. And he had the same hands.'

'The same hands? You can't possibly remember Dad's hands.'

'No, I don't, but Mum said he had long, elegant fingers, like a concert pianist.'

Sophie snorted. 'He was a waste of space, not a bloody concert pianist.'

Harmony turned her head so she could see Sophie. Her sister looked beautiful in profile, her nose small and neat, her skin clear, with fine, even creases around her eyes and long eyelashes that were tipped with blonde.

'Why do you hate him so much?'

The sisters had never discussed this. It was as if they'd come to an unspoken mutual agreement whereby Sophie was allowed to loathe him and Harmony was allowed to love him. Harmony had no reason to love him other than her desperate desire to do so. As a child she had idolised him, had chosen to adopt her mother's rose-tinted memories in place of her sister's hateful ones.

Sophie stayed staring at the clouds. 'We shouldn't talk about it; you love him and it's not fair for me to bad-mouth him.'

Harmony smiled. 'You've done nothing but bad-mouth him

since she died.' She rolled back to stare at the clouds again. 'Please tell me.'

Sophie didn't answer immediately. 'He broke my heart, that's all,' she said at last. 'Mine and Mum's. I loved him so much. He was my world.' She hesitated. 'He left the day she found out about the breast cancer.'

'No, surely you've remembered that wrong,' Harmony said. 'The same day?'

'I was with her. She was crying. There was a typed letter in her hand. It must have been from the hospital. She sat me on her lap and I cuddled her and told her it would be okay. When he came home she handed him the letter and I watched his face. Everything went dark, like he was cross with her.' Sophie paused. 'That night I heard him shouting. I sat in the corridor outside their room and I heard him say we were suffocating him, which I didn't understand then, I thought he meant actually suffocating. And then I heard him tell her he didn't want to spend the rest of his days looking after her. That he was a free spirit, not a nursemaid. Then he started screaming at her, telling her to stop crying, to stop laying on the guilt. It scared me, and when I heard him coming out of their room I ran back to bed and hid beneath the covers. He was gone in the morning.'

'Poor Mum,' said Harmony. 'I can't imagine how desperate she must have felt.'

'He took his toothbrush, his passport and all the money in the joint account, and just left us. I used to sit there sometimes, watching her sleep, her face pale from vomiting, those drugs attacking her body along with the cancer, and think about how he'd broken her heart. How he'd left me to look after her, left me to try and be both a mother and father to you. I gave everything up when she died: my exams, my friends, my life. I wanted to be an architect. Did you know that?' She turned her head to look at Harmony.

'I had no idea. I thought you weren't interested in exams. I thought that's why you left school.'

'No, I left school to look after you.'

'I'm sorry you had to do that.'

'Don't be sorry.' Sophie looked back at the sky. 'It's not your fault. And it was worth it; you did so well. I'm very, very proud of you. As proud of you as I am of my sons.'

Harmony squeezed her hand and felt Sophie squeeze her back.

'I called him the day after she died. Dad, I mean.' Sophie's voice was soft and distant. 'I found an old number for him and talked to a woman who knew where he lived. He was living just north of Birmingham. I was terrified before I phoned. I remember shaking so hard I could hardly dial the number. The first time he answered I put the phone down as if it had bitten me. Then I plucked up the courage and rang him back and told him that she was gone and that Nan didn't really want us to move in with her and could we come and stay with him.'

'What did he say?'

Sophie didn't answer.

'Tell me.'

'He said he wasn't interested in us. That as far as he was concerned he wasn't our father.'

Harmony was quiet for a moment or two. 'Why didn't you tell me?'

Sophie looked at Harmony. 'I didn't want to hurt you. I knew how important it was for you to love him. It gave you strength, and I didn't want to take that away from you.'

A large white cloud crept across the sky, changing shape imperceptibly as it went, from one nothing to a different nothing.

'What do you think Mum would say to me now?'

'She'd tell you Will didn't do it. She'd say you were a daft idiot for sleeping with that nutter and then she'd tell you she loved you more than all the grains of sand in the world.'

Harmony smiled. 'I'd forgotten she used to say that.' She thought of her mum sitting on the edge of her bed and stroking her forehead just before she turned the bedside light off.

I love you.

How much?

So much.

How much is so much?

Oh, goodness, more than all the grains of sand in the world.

Is that lots?

Gazillions. It's the biggest number you can think of plus a million.

And then she'd kiss the very tip of her nose and tuck the sheets snugly around her.

'I miss you, Mum,' Harmony whispered at the clouds.

They lay there until the grass grew damp and the sun set below the houses at the end of the garden.

'Do you want to stay here tonight?' her sister asked as they walked into the house.

'No, I'm okay. I want to get up early in the morning and do some gardening. I want it to look nice in case Will comes home.'

'He *will* come home, Harmony. I know he will.'

When Harmony finally fell into bed, after staring at rubbish on the television until her eyes grew sore, she shuffled over to Will's side and pulled his pillow into her. She loved the way it smelled so strongly of him, a musty manliness mixed with his deodorant and shampoo.

She woke in the middle of the night with a start, thinking her phone had rung, that it was Will calling. But the phone registered no missed call; she'd imagined it, the ringing only a dream.

'Please come back to me, Will,' Harmony said, her voice loud against the dark silence. 'I miss you so much it hurts.'

She slept heavily and when she woke it took a few moments for her to work out where she was. The bedroom seemed alien and it was only as the fug of sleep lifted that things began to appear familiar. She put her dressing gown on and went into the kitchen to make some tea.

The doorbell rang, making her jump. She glanced at the clock on the wall; it was half past seven. It rang again. And then again.

'Oh my God,' she whispered under her breath, as a sudden fear gripped her. 'Luke.'

Her stomach knotted. She pulled her dressing gown tighter around her body. She wouldn't answer it, she'd pretend she wasn't here. But the ringing became incessant. She crept through the living room and peered carefully through the window.

But it wasn't Luke. It was Emma. Her heartbeat slowed as the panic left her. She went to the front door and buzzed her in, then opened the door to the flat. The two of them stood and stared at each other. Emma looked tired, as if she hadn't slept since she'd last seen her, and was dressed in the same tracksuit and sweatshirt.

'I'm sorry it's so early,' she said. 'I wasn't sure what time you left for work.'

'I'm working at home today. I can't face the office at the moment.'

'Oh. Right.' Emma's fingers pulled at one of her sleeves and her foot tapped nervously.

'Do you want to come in?'

Emma hesitated then stepped into the flat.

They sat at the table in the living room. Harmony didn't speak. She had nothing to say. She sat as if made of stone and stared at Emma.

'I told the police Ian was lying,' Emma finally said, her voice weak, almost a whisper. 'I told them he was at home with me that night. I told them to talk to the supermarket where he bought the film. He was there around eight. They've probably got him on their camera things.' She took a deep breath. 'He wasn't with Luke Crawford.'

Harmony covered her face with her palms and let the words sink in. Relief crept over her so that she found she was shaking uncontrollably. Just like that, she was going to get her husband home. She became aware of Emma on the other side of the table. As she looked at her, relief was replaced by anger.

'Why did he lie?' she demanded. 'How could you do this to us? I can't even begin to understand what you did. You're supposed to be my best friend.'

'Ian was involved in something at work. He … ' She broke off and sniffed loudly. 'He was stealing from the company, and not just petty cash. He was stealing hundreds of thousands of pounds. I had no idea. That was why he was being secretive and drinking. It wasn't another woman at all. It was because he was about to be found out.

All I know is we would have … ' She stopped herself. 'He told me we would lose everything and he would go to prison unless I lied about him being home that night.'

'And you were willing to send Will to prison instead? For murder?'

'I had no idea Will was involved,' she said quickly. 'Neither Ian or I knew anything. I didn't even know there'd been a … ' Emma paused for a moment. 'A murder,' she said in a hushed tone. 'All I knew was Ian telling me we were up shit creek and if he didn't tell everyone he was in London all night with Luke we'd lose the house, our savings, the children would have to leave their school, and he'd go to prison.' She looked at Harmony. 'Ian had been stealing money from the bank. Siphoning it off. Luke was involved. He'd told Ian about this scheme, said everyone was doing it, that all Ian needed was a good lawyer to cover his tracks. He was paying Luke a lot of money in fees, but of course,' she paused, 'Luke made sure nothing could be connected to him. That's why Ian was in such a state. The idiot wanted to get out but was in too deep, and when Luke threatened to expose him unless he helped, well, he panicked. Ian had no idea why Luke asked him. It was only when I heard your message on the answer phone, when you told me Will had been arrested for something that happened that night, that I realised it might be linked.'

'But even then, when you knew Will was involved, you knew he was sitting in some shitty cell awaiting a murder trial, you didn't say anything.'

'We didn't know what to do. We kept going over it, we had such vicious rows, and we sort of convinced ourselves it was fine, that the two things were unrelated. Ian told me Will would get off if he was innocent.'

'What do you mean *if*?'

'I knew he was. I never doubted him. We should have told the police, I know that, but Ian was in such a state. I—'

'Don't even go there!' shouted Harmony, shaking her head at Emma's audacity. 'I can't talk about this anymore. It's too upsetting. Luke killed a man and then tried to frame my husband and it nearly worked because my best friend lied.' Emma's face crumpled and she tried to reach out for Harmony. 'No, Emma.'

Emma didn't move. 'I'm so sorry, Harmony. I … didn't … I know you must hate me.'

Harmony looked at her friend and felt her hardness towards her recede a little. 'I don't know how I feel about you,' Harmony said. 'To be honest, I'm just relieved you told the bloody truth.'

'Will he be okay now?' Emma asked. 'They'll arrest Luke? You'll be safe and they'll let Will come home?'

'I hope so,' Harmony said. 'I hope to God they will.'

CHAPTER THIRTY-ONE

Luke set the alarm for five in the morning. It was his favourite time of day. The air was fresh and London was only just beginning to wake properly. He put his dressing gown on and made himself a strong coffee, so strong it was almost as thick as soup. He drank it down in one and then turned the tap on and rinsed the cup. He dried it carefully and then opened the cupboard and placed the cup neatly beside the others.

He went into his bedroom and opened his wardrobe. He unwrapped a suit from its dry-cleaning bag and took out a brand new shirt. Then he opened a drawer, took the wooden box out and opened the lid. He stared at the Swiss Army knife and stroked his finger over its polished red handle. He took it out of the box, opened the blade of the knife and stared at the cold message Will's father had had etched into the shining metal.

He remembered the first time Will had shown him the knife. They'd gone to the woods and made spears out of ash branches chatting happily while one of them carved a point on one end of his stick and the other smoothed his with a stone. Then they swapped. They'd pretended they were pirates, marooned on an island, surrounded by cannibals.

'Don't let them see you,' Luke whispered to Will as they hid in the bushes and watched the cannibals walking across the field to play rugby. 'If they catch us, they'll eat us.'

And the two of them had run in the opposite direction, leaping over fallen tree trunks, scrabbling up slopes, and finally scaling the branches of the huge oak tree and whooping from the leafy canopy like Red Indians as they brandished their sharpened spears.

Luke reached for the photograph and slipped it into his inside jacket pocket with the penknife. Then he looked around his bedroom. He'd taken the rest of the photos to the dump in West Norwood. It felt odd to see them lying on the piles of household waste in that big stinking hanger, cars reversing in and out, people depositing all manner of things, things that had once meant something, that had once had purpose but were now disposable. He saw the satisfaction on their faces as they dusted off their hands and climbed back into their emptied cars, feeling freer, feeling cleansed.

He drove out of London and headed onto the M25. His head was strangely clear. Alastair Farrow was there, of course, but not at the forefront. He wasn't sure at what point he'd decided to kill him. He thought back to the night his wife died, to the row they'd had, his temper flaring uncontrollably, the look of hurt on her face as he'd screamed at her to leave him alone. Her begging him to stop shouting. Telling him she couldn't take it anymore. That she couldn't help him. Tears had scorched her face. Her beautiful rounded belly stretching the fabric of her dress. Then later answering the door to the sombre-faced policemen. His world ceasing to turn. He had sat on the floor of their kitchen, destroyed, memories of what happened at school battering him.

He remembered a few months later, sitting alone in silence on the sofa in his new apartment, tears falling unchecked down his cheeks, struggling to draw breath. He needed to know where they were and what they were doing. Farrow and Will. Those two boys responsible for this. Farrow, the monster who violated him, damaged him, defiled him, then left him in the woods alone, and Will, his friend, the boy who'd untied him from the cross, the boy who pledged his loyalty in blood, who then betrayed him like Judas Iscariot.

Both men had been easy to track down. Will English had a photography business in south-west London. Luke had pored over its website until he'd memorised every word, every image, on it. Trading had recently ceased. There was an apologetic voicemail message from Will, pathetic in its plaintive humour, making light of the economic downturn with a second-rate quip about the recession. Then there was a wine shop. A little-used Facebook account with no privacy settings. A beautiful wife, pictures of whom filled the gallery on the photography website. There were other people in the photos too. And a wedding.

Ian and Emma Barratt-Jones, July 2001.

There was a picture of Will's wife in the line-up, beaming, arms linked with the bride. They were good friends. A quick Google search and he discovered that Ian Barratt-Jones, a City banker, had come fourth in a tournament at his golf club in Oxfordshire. From there it was easy. The man was arrogant and stupid and sucked up the attention of the glamorous, wealthy lawyer he met at the golf club bar. Luke had learned long ago that it was good to be prepared. Ian was ideal, greedy as well as stupid, and more than willing to risk his family, their security, everything he should have protected, for a quick, illegal buck. Luke knew from the off he'd do anything to stay out of prison. People like that were useful. Getting to Will, destroying Will's happiness, had been in his mind from the start. Why should Will be happy after the devastation he caused? It should have been Will who Farrow raped. Luke had stood up to him. Faced him. And then Will had buckled. Stepped back. Watched as Farrow meted out his punishment on Luke. And then, in Drysdale's office, when he could have saved him, he delivered his final crushing blow. He had turned his back. Abandoned him.

He hadn't expected to feel anything for Harmony, but he'd been touched by her honesty and passion, the way she'd battled with herself as she betrayed her husband. There was a naivety about her that was intoxicating, and for a while he was convinced he might be happy with her, that perhaps she was his last chance at something resembling a life. But in the end her loyalty to Will was too strong. The irony in that was bitter; her rejection, the cold look in her eye when she turned her back on him, mirroring the expression on Will's face all those years before.

Everything fell into his lap like gifts from the gods. In a way it was too easy, discovering that Will had met up with Farrow and caused a scene in front of witnesses; being with Harmony as she put the code into the padlock; then her calling to say Will had disappeared. Will and his stupid night walks – rambles, didn't he call them? – that lasted for hours. He didn't know how long he'd be gone but it was worth the risk. That idiot Ian agreed to lie without batting an eyelid. And what poetic justice that was, Will sent to prison for the murder of Farrow because a friend betrayed him; it was perfect.

Luke checked in his rear-view mirror and moved across into the slow lane in preparation for coming off the slip road. He drove carefully along the country roads. He slowed when he saw the signpost, then put his indicator on.

Farringdon Hall.

Just seeing the name made his skin crawl. He remembered being driven away by his aunt, a lady inaptly named Grace, of which she had none. His parents sent her with a message for him from the outpost in Kenya. She was to pass on their deep displeasure at his expulsion. He had humiliated and disappointed them. He was to stay with Grace and attend the local comprehensive. He would continue to see them once a year when they returned to England for Easter, but as far as they were concerned he was on his own. His aunt had apologised to Drysdale for any inconvenience caused.

'My brother is terribly embarrassed by all of this,' she said shrilly, her thin lips barely moving. 'This child is the black sheep of our family flock.'

Luke pulled up in the car park behind the main school. It was early, the boys and staff were still getting up, making beds, eating breakfast. He passed a couple of caretakers, who nodded their heads in respectful greeting. He nodded back and continued to walk. The school hadn't changed. Everything was the same, even the smell coming out of the kitchens, that greasy, institutional smell that spewed from the ventilation pipes at the back of the building.

He squeezed between the gap in the bent railings that used to be his and Will's route out and walked into the woods. It was peaceful, with just the sounds of songbirds in the beech trees above his head, their branches thick with brilliant green leaves, last year's brown ones fallen at his feet, a carpet of softness slowly breaking down, throwing up that mulchy smell that brought memories so vividly back to him.

When Luke reached the oak tree he stood still. He looked up at it. Studied it. Every bit of bark, every twist in every branch, each leaf, each twig. The perfect tree to climb. Their favourite tree, where they would come to play in its huge, comforting boughs, hidden from the rest of the world, a mean world they didn't need when they had each other. He listened to the breeze blowing through the leaves, rustling above him, as if the tree were speaking to him. Apologising, understanding, waiting for him.

There was nothing left for him. It was time for him to take control. His life never really got going; cut down in childhood, it was never allowed to grow freely. He was tired but he didn't feel sorry for himself. Self-pity was something he'd never succumbed to, and this gave him great satisfaction. Self-pity would have been easy. Perhaps, he thought, as he stared up at the tree, self-pity might have been his salvation. Perhaps it was his continuous quest to beat them all, to come out on top, to show them they hadn't broken him, that now left him with no other option.

He took his shoes off one by one, placing them in a neat pair, before taking his jacket off and folding it beside them. He wasn't scared. He was calm. There was a tranquillity about him that was unfamiliar. He imagined he was floating in the middle of huge ocean, the waves lapping at his face and body as he bobbed in the water, the sun warming his face. He bent down and opened the bag he'd bought. He took out the rope and the knife. Then he pulled himself up onto the first branch and climbed the tree with ease, just as he'd done years earlier, following Will up into the branches, excited and happy.

He tied the rope then opened the knife and admired its shining blade one last time. He held open his palm and drew the blade along the line of the scar that crossed it. Blood flowed like cherry juice and he watched it, transfixed for a moment or two as it fell in drops to the earth at the base of the oak. Then he threw the knife into the undergrowth below as the bell for morning lessons rang out across the courtyard, resounding in the branches and leaves of the great tree that held him.

EPILOGUE

The late November rain was falling heavily from the charcoal-coloured sky. Cars drove along the New King's Road with their wipers working overtime. Headlights lit the four-thirty dusk and the pavements were covered in a sheen of wet with water flowing in rapids along the side of the road and into the drains.

Will and Harmony walked carefully, avoiding the deeper puddles, and trying not to snag anyone with the umbrella they shared. They kept their heads low to fend off the bite of the cold. As they reached the covered area outside the Chelsea and Westminster hospital Will stopped to shake the rain off the umbrella and close it before they pushed through the revolving doors into the heady warmth of the hospital's foyer.

'That's better,' he said, as they walked through the airy reception area towards the lifts. 'I've never seen so much rain.'

She smiled up at him. 'You look terrified,' she said, and reached up to kiss his cheek.

He forced a smile back in an attempt to mask the nerves he was battling.

'Don't worry,' she said. 'It's going to be fine.'

The truth was, he *was* terrified; so much so, he could barely walk straight.

He pressed the button to go up and glanced at Harmony. Her hand was on her stomach, resting lightly on its roundness. A picture of Luke, dressed in his suit, shaking hands with him in Emma and Ian's garden, flashed into his head. These unwanted images would always be there, however much he fought to keep them at bay.

It was two older boys, sixth-formers, who'd found his body. The boys had been bunking off prep for a cigarette and stumbled upon him. Will had heard enough detail for him to picture the scene: Luke hanging from the oak tree, bare-footed, his hand cut across the palm. It was an image he knew would haunt him forever.

The story had made the national news and triggered a police investigation into abuse at the school when Luke and Will had been pupils. Will had found no satisfaction or release while raking over those days with the police, but there was an element of uneasy relief when Drysdale and a handful of ex-members of staff found themselves facing prosecution. He'd followed the trials closely. He hadn't wanted to appear in court so sent a statement to be read on his behalf. His was circumstantial evidence, more linked to the atmosphere and culture of the school than specific events. It was hard reliving those unpleasant days. In the end he was left feeling empty as the full extent of the rot was revealed and Will discovered there were numerous men whose lives had been torn apart as children. He knew he'd got off lightly. The policewoman who'd talked to him had shown him a photograph that was found inside Luke's jacket at the scene of his death. It was the Polaroid of the two of them taken in the summer before it all went wrong. Luke had wanted to send it to his parents to show them who Will was. They'd asked one of the other boys to take it, then hooked arms around each other's shoulders and grinned. Luke had loved the photo so much he'd decided to keep it. Seeing it in the police file, knowing he'd had it on him when he took his life, was heartbreaking.

The receptionist called Harmony's name and he followed his wife into the small windowless room off the main waiting area. She took her coat off and a nurse asked her to climb onto the bed and lift her sweater over her bump and unzip her trousers.

The sonographer smiled and introduced herself and then pulled the top of Harmony's knickers well below the swell of her stomach and tucked green paper towel into them.

'This will feel cold to start with,' she said. 'Sorry.'

'That's fine.' Harmony smiled at her.

She squeezed a large dollop of gel onto Harmony's tummy. Then she took hold of the ultrasound scanner and pushed it hard against her, moving it around in the gel, while staring at the screen.

Will noticed Harmony wince. 'Does it hurt?' he asked.

'No,' she whispered back. 'Just a bit uncomfortable. I drank a pint of water before I came out and haven't peed.' She looked at the woman, who stared intently at the screen. 'Apparently, it makes the picture easier to see.'

'That's right,' the woman said with a nod, her eyes still fixed ahead.

Will looked at the screen too but found it hard to see anything that resembled a baby, just a mass of shapes in black and white. Then there was a deep, fast, beating sound and the sonographer centred on that part of Harmony's stomach, pushing the scanner deeper into her, making her wince for a second time.

'Are you sure it doesn't—' Will began.

'This is the baby's heartbeat,' the woman said.

Will looked at the screen again and saw a tiny black mass pulsing in time with the sound they could hear.

Harmony reached for his hand.

'And there's baby's head.' She paused and moved the scanner. 'There's the spine.'

'I can't see it,' he said, leaning towards the screen and squinting.

'Don't worry, most people can't,' she said. She pointed at the screen with her fingers. 'This is the face. The nose, lips.'

Just then the baby opened its mouth and seemed to yawn.

'Oh my God,' said Harmony, a small laugh escaping her lips. 'That's amazing.'

It was a peculiar feeling. One of dread and excitement. This is it, he thought, as he stared at the indistinct face of the child on the screen. There was his second chance.

Luke's child.

He thought back to when she'd told him. She'd been devastated. He sat on the sofa and stayed quiet as she dropped to her knees at his feet, took his hands in hers, and apologised over and over.

'If you want me to … ' She couldn't finish the sentence. 'I will though … I will understand. If you want me to do that … I'm sorry, Will. I'm so, so sorry.'

He'd sat in the garden, at the wrought iron table, tracing his fingers over the filigree patterns in the rusting metal. Harmony was pregnant. He faced a huge decision. This wasn't what he wanted. If he was to have a baby, it had to be his. The pain inside him was intense. He wanted her to be carrying his child. Could he ask her to get rid of it? He heard his mother's words in his head: *You selfish, selfish boy.* She was right, he knew that. He'd learned a lot about himself in the last seven months. He thought back to Drysdale's office, of how he'd watched the light seep out of Luke's eyes when he'd failed to stand beside him.

He was responsible, not alone but in part, for the jigsaw puzzle of Luke's tragic life. He knew that if ever there was a chance for atonement this was it. This was his opportunity to make amends for those things he'd done wrong, the selfish decisions he'd made again and again over the years. He could be a father to Luke's child and give it all the love and support that had been denied Luke himself. He finally had the chance to prove his own father wrong, that life isn't always ugly, and that, sometimes, it is fair.

'Is the baby healthy?' Harmony asked. 'There's nothing we should be worried about?'

'Everything looks fine,' she replied with a reassuring smile. 'I've got a few measurements to take but otherwise all good.' She turned to them both. 'Do you want a picture of the baby?'

Will smiled at Harmony, who gripped his hand as if her life depended on it, then leant forward and kissed her forehead.

'Yes,' he said then. 'We'd like a picture of our baby.'

NOTES FROM THE AUTHOR

An idea for a book can come from anywhere. From an overheard snippet of conversation. From a newspaper article. From an exchange you witness between two strangers in a supermarket quite by chance. Sometimes, of course, an idea will spring from personal experience, from something close to home, something that affects you directly.

A few years ago my husband got a telephone call from the police whilst he was at work. It was a call that threw him completely off balance for a period. As the woman took a moment to explain who she was he experienced a familiar and unwelcome wave of nausea that he had not felt since childhood. Beyond the fact that it was a female police detective asking him to confirm his identity he had no clues as to what the call might be about. An odd thirty seconds ensued. He described to me how the world seemed to close in around him, his conscious awareness of the situation diminished and he became an almost third party observer of the call. His subconscious took over and released waves of long and very deliberately buried memories and emotions from many years before. As the detective finished introducing herself he experienced a strange conviction that he knew what the call was about. "Does this relate to what went on at my school 25 years ago?" When she asked how he'd guessed he replied that he'd been expecting the call for years, but until that moment hadn't realized it.

My husband was sent to a tiny boarding choir school when he was eight years old and left at thirteen to go to the local grammar school. His parents wanted what they believed to be the best for him, and his musical abilities afforded them the opportunity to give him this privileged start to his education. Little did they know that the very fabric of their chosen school was infected by child abuse.

Thankfully my husband wasn't one of those physically abused, but the violent and oppressive atmosphere of the school stayed with him for many years. He didn't know, nor could he have understood, what was happening to his less fortunate classmates, but he had an uneasy awareness of the further hidden malevolence. Nearly three decades later, two members of staff were being investigated following allegations made by men who'd been victim of their abuse, and the police were seeking other victims and witnesses from the time.

What both upset and fascinated me was the Pandora's box of emotions that was opened by that phone call. My husband began to look up the names of boys he'd been at school with. He became obsessed with discovering what they'd gone on to do, whether they'd married, had children, whether, essentially, they'd survived their ordeals and managed to find happiness. Tragically, some had never recovered and this hit him hard. It was sobering to talk to him about these boys, these innocents, damaged for good. I became preoccupied with the idea of damaged childhood, not necessarily damaged by physical abuse, but by an array of incidents: the death of a parent, a father withholding affection from his only son, a child witnessing cruelty, bullying – from both the bullied child and the bully's point of view. I didn't want to write about sexual abuse – principally because I'd touched on it in my first novel – but the subject of bullying came back to me repeatedly. I started toying with the idea of two boys, one who actively denies his past, papering over his painful memories, focussing instead on his adult relationship as his salvation. Then another more ruined boy, unable to find peace, a desire for revenge that consumed him. It was then that the characters of Will and Luke began to take shape. I saw them clearly even before I knew what route my story would take, these two boys, their troubled childhoods indelibly marked by a single, brutal event, both affected differently, both using alternative ways to cope. I imagined them growing up, one carrying guilt into his adult life, the other anger. And how, if I pushed them together years later, their pasts might wreak havoc on their lives. As the story began to take shape, I started to think about what each of them had to lose, what was at risk. For Will it was his wife, Harmony, his 'anchor in the storm'; his salvation. To threaten his marriage was to threaten to destroy his survival of the past. And there began the third leg to the story; Harmony and the dangerous love triangle she finds herself trapped in.

At the beginning Harmony was a fairly neutral character, stable, calm, balanced, but as the themes became clearer, I gave Harmony her own demons from childhood to battle. Though loved by her mother and sister, Harmony had experienced grief as a child and also abandonment. On the surface she seems fine, well-adjusted, rational, but the fallout from her past – the fault lines – were there. Childhood is the most precious and fleeting of times, as is the innocence that goes hand in hand with it, so fragile, so breakable. Any emotional trauma to a child will leave scars, some deep, some less so. Trauma in childhood can have a considerable impact on adulthood. It can influence the decisions people make, tamper with their ability to cope in certain situations, affect how they interact with others, how they deal with the things life throws at them. The inescapable truth is we are all a unique and individual tapestry of our past experiences. Everything that happens to us becomes inextricably woven into what makes us who we are.

What struck me as I began to research the book was the number of times people said things like 'that's just what went on' or 'it was different back then' or 'oh, yes, adults knew it was happening'. Blind eyes turned again and again. Children betrayed. Very quickly betrayal as a theme pushed to the front of the book. The exploration of betrayal. What broken trust means to different people. How easily one person can forgive a betrayal and how violently another might want revenge. Or redemption. The concept of betrayal worked its way into the veins of *The Judas Scar*. With it came love. Love and betrayal are inextricably linked. Betrayal is the antithesis of love, and the stronger the love, the harder the bite of betrayal and the deeper the scar left behind. Love and betrayal link all the stories in the book in different ways: between lovers and spouses, between children and parents, between friends. And where betrayal takes place there are only two options; forgiveness or the absence of it. And where there's absence of forgiveness comes anger, comes blame, comes guilt, and sometimes, revenge...

Amanda Jennings, March 2014

ACKNOWLEDGEMENTS

My heartfelt thanks and appreciation go to my agent, the incomparable Broo Doherty, who from day one has taken care of me, and always makes me laugh, even when I don't feel like it. To Paul Swallow for his belief in this book, his incredible passion, and his generosity when it comes to cupcakes. To those friends and family who read various versions of this book, but especially Charlie Jolly for his encouragement, Tiina Verran for her early suggestions, Cosima Wagner and Lou Botham for their expert proof-reading skills, and Sian Johnson who read far too many drafts of this book and offered insightful advice throughout. To Sean Costello for editing with a sensitive and skillful touch and being such a pleasure to work with. To those people I love on Twitter – authors, readers, book bloggers and like-minded souls – who offered support, distraction and laughter whenever I needed it. I have been blown away by the generosity of so many of you. I owe you much. Special mention to Tamar Cohen and Elizabeth Forbes for always being on the end of a phone. I am privileged to have amazing friends, both old and newer, you are my life-blood. Thank you. And then to my family, my three inspiring daughters who make me proud every day, my wonderful parents and sister, and of course, my husband, whose strength and integrity know no bounds and without whom I'd be lacking my very best friend. I love you all.

If you enjoyed Amanda's book,
you may also enjoy the following from
Cutting Edge Press:

Twin Truths – *Shelan Rodger*

Jenny and Pippa are twins. Like many twins they often know what the other is thinking. They complete each other. When one of the twins disappears the other woman is left to face the world alone as she tries to find out what happened to her "other half". Vividly set in Argentina, Brazil, Greece and the UK, Shelan Rodger's stunning debut is a beautiful examination of identity and how much this is moulded by our relationships with others.

Nearest Thing to Crazy – *Elizabeth Forbes*

Dan and a group of his friends enjoy a Sunday lunch together on a perfect summer's day. They're pleased to welcome their glamorous new neighbour and novelist, Ellie, who has rented a house in the village to work on her book. She likes to place herself in the centre of her plots, she says, although it's hard to see what she'll find to write about in this quiet country backwater. As Ellie slots effortlessly into the village social scene, Dan's wife begins to feel increasingly alienated from her friends and isolated from her family, but, for the life of her, she can't fathom why.

Who Are You – *Elizabeth Forbes*

Alex, a career officer in an elite regiment, returns from Afghanistan a changed man. The mental scars he has brought home disrupt his relationship and drive his wife Juliet to seek comfort by chatting in online forums. As Juliet relies more heavily on her life online, she is confronted by her weakest vulnerabilities and her worst fears.